DIARY OF ANNA THE GIRL WITCH 2

WANDERING WITCH

VIC CONNOR

ILLUSTRATED BY

RAQUEL BARROS

HELVETIC HOUSE

ISBN-13: 978-1520271217

Contents

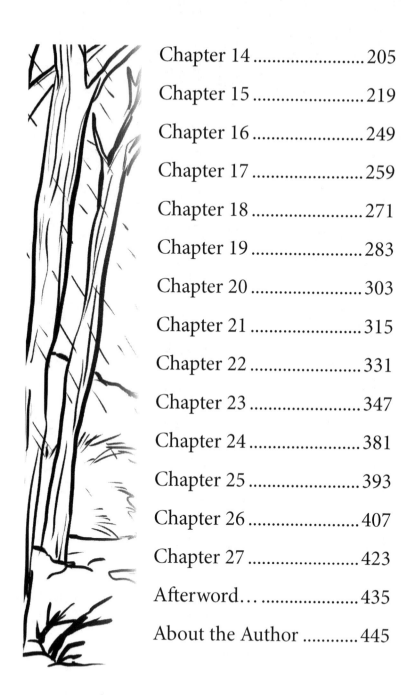

Chapter 1

Dear Diary,

The only thing keeping me in this chair in this beautiful Italian villa is that I have two whole hours to wait before we leave for the airport, and it's jangling my nerves. That's right; I'm off on another adventure before my visit to Tuscany even gets started.

All because yesterday, I got a letter from Uncle Misha via a black crow. (Isn't that crazy? Who sends mail by crow? My Uncle Misha, that's who.) Here's what the letter said:

My dear Anna Sophia,

I don't know if you have received my recent letters. I fear not. Forces have been working to keep us apart. Our enemies may have intercepted my mail. But I trust dear Bartholomew, my faithful crow, to find you with this letter.

I'm afraid he brings terrible news, though. Your father is missing and I fear he may have been taken by the Red Horseman — the Horseman of War. Unsettled spirits watch my every move and I cannot go to his aid.

I know you have never met your father, and you may feel that he abandoned you. Nothing could be further from the truth. I promise, Malyshka, as soon as I see you, I'll explain everything. You must hurry. Meet me at Mama Bear's den by the new moon, or I fear that it will be too late to save your father.

Trust Monsieur Nolan, but speak of this to no one else. I cannot wait to hold my little Malyshka again.

Your loving Uncle Misha.

Things moved really fast after that. Almost panicking, I called Monsieur Nolan, the solicitor in Geneva who takes care of my mother's estate, and asked him to book me a ticket to Moscow. The conversation went something like this:

"Hi, Monsieur Nolan, I made it safe to Tuscany, but now I need to go to Siberia. Fast."

"Siberia?" he gasped. "I can't let a child fly to Siberia alone."

"Well, I thought we'd fly to Moscow and take a train the rest of the way, or maybe a car with a chauffeur. I really have to go. Uncle Misha found my father and he needs my help. And besides, I'm not a child anymore."

"Humph." Monsieur Nolan has great respect for Uncle Misha, not only for his honesty but also for having found me only a few days after I was born, nestled in a bear den. Mama Bear had adopted me as one of her own and kept me warm. But Uncle Misha knew babies couldn't live with bears for long, so he took me home to his cabin tucked beside a lake in the woods. Many years later, when I needed to go to school, he took me to Geneva, where Monsieur Nolan set me up in an orphanage and later, at the Collège du Parc Cézanne.

But you know all that. I'm sorry. It's just that I've got to keep writing to fill up the time till we leave, or I think I might go mad.

"I still can't let a young woman fly to Russia alone," grumbled Monsieur Nolan.

"I'll go with her," said Lauraleigh, who had her ear pressed to the phone, listening in with interest. Lauraleigh is the kind of person I want to grow up to be. She's beautiful, graceful, and funny. She does everything well, but she's especially good *at friendship. She graduated from the Collège this spring and plans to backpack around Europe before starting university.*

"Lauraleigh!" Monsieur Nolan protested. "This is a private conversation between a solicitor and his client. You should not be listening in!"

Lauraleigh laughed. "Don't worry, Monsieur Nolan. Anna doesn't mind. And anyway, it makes sense. I can fly with Anna to Moscow, then start my backpacking adventure from there. It'll be great. And I promise to keep her out of trouble."

We all know I'm a magnet for trouble, but Monsieur Nolan couldn't argue with those ideas. Lauraleigh is eighteen, after all. That makes her a full-fledged adult. So I let him grumble, and I grinned as wide as the ocean when he said, "Okay. Your tickets are booked. I'm making special arrangements for Lauraleigh's entry visa to Russia; you, Anna Sophia, don't need one, of course. You need a special letter for minors unaccompanied by parents. Check your email. And be sure to arrive at the airport in plenty of time."

"Thank you! Thank you!" I shouted. If Monsieur Nolan had been standing in front of me instead of sitting in his office five hundred kilometers away, I'd have kissed him on his silly mustache.

And now I wait (not so) patiently for our ride to the airport.

I'm going to see my father! I can hardly believe it.

That is, if I can find him — before something happens to him.

Not that I'm a world traveler, but I feel sure our flight to Moscow was the worst trip in the history of trips. First, we were late getting to the airport because of traffic. The line at security snaked halfway around the airport. Right after we'd dumped our bags and jackets on the x-ray belt and gotten scanned by security, we had to grab our things and run for our gate just as they were about to close the doors.

Even Lauraleigh looked frazzled as we dropped into our seats. Her normally straight hair clung in damp curls to her face. The collar of her jacket stuck out at an odd angle. I'm sure I looked even worse. We smiled at each other, with only a moment to relax before the plane zoomed forward for takeoff.

My muscles were jelly from our long run through the terminal, and the force of momentum pressed me into my seat. Usually, I love that feeling, but today I was too anxious to enjoy it. My father was in danger and we were still so far away. I had no idea what awaited us in Moscow or later in the wilds of Siberia.

For the first time in over six years, I'd see my beloved uncle. I could only hope that he'd be proud of the young teen I'd become.

All these thoughts swirled in my head. It was enough to make me restless.

Just before the plane took off, a flight attendant asked me to take another seat — it had something to do with me being too young to sit near an emergency exit. The screaming baby behind me didn't help me relax, nor did the old man with bad breath, snoring beside me. Somewhere in the back of the plane, a troupe of kids started singing "The Wheels on the Bus." By the time the wheels went "round and round" for the twelfth spin, I had become a very cranky witch.

Magic churned in my stomach, aching to be released. I wanted to zap Mr. Stinky-Breath beside me, put a sleeping spell on the screaming baby, and maybe make the plane fly faster so I wouldn't have to listen to another round of sing-along.

I took a deep breath and squashed the magic back into my gut. Angry magic wasn't the good kind. And I had vowed to myself that I would never again let the bad magic out. Already part of my soul was shadowed by the evil that came along with dark magic. I wouldn't let the shadows have one bit more of me.

That was easier vowed than done.

By the time we finally arrived and exited the plane, tripping along behind the hordes of people looking for luggage and family, my frustration had grown until my magic was ready to boil over. And it did. Someone grabbed my shoulder roughly from behind. I spun around, eyes flashing, fingers sizzling with blue energy — and I zapped the man who had dared to attack me.

My charge stung him like an electric shock. A spasm convulsed him and he jumped back, his single eye bulging, teeth clanging together.

"What did you do that for?" the man whined in Russian, rubbing his arm. "I only meant to introduce myself. I'm Gavril. You must be Miss Anna Sophia Medvedeva. Monsieur Nolan hired me as your guide."

I heard the shadows laughing. It was so easy for them to win another little part of me.

"I'm so sorry," I said. "I thought you were a thief or something."

In fact, Gavril looked very much like a thief from a storybook. He was small and wiry with a big nose and one shifty eye. The other eye was covered with a black patch. His lips were already wet, but he licked them repeatedly with each sentence he spoke.

I'm ashamed to say that I took an immediate dislike to him.

"You should've announced yourself before grabbing me like that," I said angrily.

Before I could insult our guide further, Lauraleigh stuck out her hand and introduced herself. Gavril licked his lips and held out his calloused left hand. His right sleeve was empty and tucked into his jacket pocket.

I wondered what terrible disaster had caused the loss of his eye and arm.

"My name is Lauraleigh. I'll be traveling with you to Siberia," she said in English.

Gavril shook her hand reluctantly. "Monsieur Nolan didn't say anything about two girls." His English was perfect although heavily accented. "I bought only two train tickets."

"Well, we've had a change in plans," Lauraleigh said brightly. "I was supposed to leave Anna here in Moscow, but I have a taste for adventure and I'd like to see Siberia. Those are our bags over there. Would you find us a baggage cart, Mr. Gavril?"

"Just Gavril," the grumpy man said as he turned away to find the cart. "Fine, I'll buy another ticket. You understand dollars, yes? That'll be five hundred dollars if you want to go first class. A hundred if you want to smell stinky feet and bed farts in a communal *wagon*."

"First class, please," I said quickly, trying not to show my disgust with Gavril's speaking manners. "Lauraleigh and I will take a coupé, thank you very much." I had no intention of spending three nights in the same train compartment as Gavril.

Lauraleigh steered us toward the baggage conveyor belt.

"What are you doing?" I whispered.

"No way I'm leaving you alone with that creep," she said. "Looks like we're on this adventure together."

And suddenly, all the anxiety of the day faded. There was no one I'd rather share this journey with than Lauraleigh.

The train ride east was more relaxing than the plane trip had been. We were traveling first class, after all, and the car was clean and well kept. As soon as we left the city behind, I pressed my nose against the window, fascinated by the unending countryside. The groves and entire forests turned into villages and towns, which gave way to more forests. Although it was rather basic, the scenery was pleasing to look at. Comforting. It was where I'd come from.

My mind wandered.

Setting out, I'd been overjoyed at the idea of seeing Uncle Misha again. Even though we hadn't seen each other in six years, we'd kept in touch through letters, and he was still the father of my heart. But now, as we got closer to him, I began to doubt. My real father overshadowed our reunion. The only thing I knew about him was what my mother had said in that one precious letter I had received from her: He had brown eyes. What would he look like? Did he even know I existed? Would he be happy to see me?

I didn't even know his name.

There was a light knock on the door, and Gavril walked in. He sat down on the edge of my bunk and asked, "Want anything? Food, drink?"

I shook my head. Lauraleigh caught my sigh and tried to make conversation to pass the time.

"Mr. Gavril, do you know the trails of Siberia well?"

The man grunted. "Just Gavril. Told you already."

"Okay. Gavril, do you know Siberia well?"

"Well enough."

"Were you born there?" she asked.

"Dunno. Maybe." That seemed like an odd answer. Lauraleigh raised an eyebrow, and the grumpy guide fidgeted under her stare. Sister Constance, our housemother at the orphanage, would have been proud. "I been hunting there since I was a wee sprite," he said. "At least until a bear got ahold of me." He pointed to his eye patch and missing arm.

"A bear did that?" I asked. "What did you do?"

"I shot it." Dangerous fire flashed in his eye. "Dead."

I winced. I hadn't meant, *What did you do to get away?* I had meant, *What did you do to antagonize the bear in the first place?*

"You're a bear hunter," I said hollowly. I'm not against hunting in general. People in deep Siberia use what their harsh environment gives them to survive. Uncle Misha trapped small animals like ermine and mink. We ate the meat and sold the furs to traders who came around in spring. But to me, hunting bears is like hunting angels.

"I was," said Gavril. "Now I'm a guide for foolish tourists who want to hike in the Sayan Mountains."

"What makes you think that we're foolish?" Lauraleigh asked in a perfectly polite voice.

Gavril nodded at our bags in the overhead bins. "How many fancy pairs of shoes you got in those bags?" he asked.

Lauraleigh glared at him but didn't answer.

"I bet you've got at least three pairs and not one of them will stand up to the mountains." He sat up straighter in his chair, warming to his tirade. "And what about sleeping bags? Did you bring at least one? Nights around Lake Baikal are cold even in summer. You got anything to keep you warm at night?"

Lauraleigh pursed her lips and considered the ugly little man. "We may be unprepared, Mr. Gavril, but we are not foolish. That's why we hired a guide. It's your job to get us to the mountains safely. So why don't you stop complaining and start educating us about the tools we'll need?"

Go Lauraleigh, I thought.

Gavril licked his fat lips and squinted his one good eye. "We'll be able to gear up at our next stop," he said grudgingly. "But don't expect me to carry your fancy bags full of fancy, useless shoes. You'll be leaving those behind."

"Fine," said Lauraleigh. She flipped open a glossy magazine and ignored Gavril, who continued to glare at us both.

I turned to look at the pretty landscape whizzing by.

It was going to be a long trip.

Chapter 2

ear Diary,

I'd forgotten how harsh the landscape of my home is. Harsh and beautiful. Siberia clings to the earth with stubborn determination. The sky is blue and sharp. The terrain is rough and bumpy. We've passed through forests with trees older than memory, tiny clusters of houses that pass for villages, long stretches of dense lowlands, endless steppes and swamps, and broad, powerful rivers.

We've passed big cities and small: Kazan with its ancient Kremlin, Christian churches, and Muslim mosques; Yekaterinburg with its modern skyline neighboring Byzantine-style churches; Novosibirsk; Tomsk... All these cities I feel I should know, and Lauraleigh was itching to jump out and explore them. I feel a little sorry that she couldn't. But then she chose to come, and I'm so glad she did.

The environment here feels sturdier, cleaner, and healthier than back in Europe. I don't know why. Maybe because it renews itself so completely every winter.

I've had a lot of chances to practice my Russian. The train attendant was a chatty young woman who kept *bringing us tea and snacks, and personally escorted us to the dining car for lunch and dinner. The food she recommended was surprisingly good for a train. It was like she'd taken us under her wing — and she visibly disliked Gavril.*

It was three days before the train left us at a large and busy train station in Irkutsk. Irkutsk is a picturesque city, only a couple of hours from Lake Baikal. I was surprised to see that the green-and-yellow train depot deep in Siberia was almost as large and busy as the one back in Moscow. I don't know why; I guess I'm just used to thinking of Siberia as nothing but emptiness, inhabited only by people like Uncle Misha in his lonely cabin and the bears in their dens. I find myself shocked every time I'm forced to remember that there are actual cities here.

As much as I hate to admit it, Gavril was right about our thoughtless packing. Nothing in our bags would have been useful on the rugged journey we are about to begin. We left most everything in a locker in the train station. I took only my dream stone, my mother's letter, and Squire.

Monsieur Nolan had sent an emergency credit card along with our travel tickets. We used it to buy the rest of what we'd need at a small camping supply shop on the edge of town: sturdy backpacks, a tent, sleeping bags, cooking supplies, and dried packs of food that don't look very edible. I hope to find more nourishing fare along the way. Many years may have passed since I left this place, but I'm sure I haven't forgotten the few skills Uncle Misha taught me. As the days move toward July warmth, I'll be able to find us some berries and greens to eat along the way.

My stomach worries about the distance to the bear den. The new moon is only three days away. I hope we aren't too late.

We used Monsieur Nolan's credit card to book ourselves into a nice hotel to take much-needed showers and change. After we were done, Gavril met us outside.

He waited in a rusty yellow Niva car, the Russian off-roader. The engine sounded almost as cranky as he did, and he gunned it as soon as we hopped in. The city was jammed with morning traffic of all kinds: cars, pedestrians, and mopeds scooting in and out between the vehicles. Lauraleigh looked a bit shocked. Though she was getting better, she was still used to the new and expensive cars we drove in Geneva, not to mention Switzerland's more restrained road habits.

We arrived at the wharf on the Angara River, whose wide waters were covered with huge barges loaded with shipping containers. They were gigantic beasts of rusted metal and cables, with men crawling over them like ants. For a moment, I wondered if Gavril planned for us to travel on one of those. But the traffic finally moved and we drove past the docks without stopping.

We left town, going southeast toward a range of mountains, and the road immediately became pitted with holes and rocks. It was clearly not very well traveled. We bumped around the back of the Niva without seatbelts as Gavril navigated the barren stretch of road like a race car driver. At first, we followed the bank of a relatively narrow river; then we turned onto a forest road that cut straight through the old, tall Siberian woodlands.

After two or three hours of nothing but trees, the ground began to rise.

"Where are we?" Lauraleigh asked.

"Mount Burghed," Gavril grunted. "Means 'Eagle' in the Buryat language. That's what they speak around here."

Even though we were now climbing a mountain, Gavril didn't slow down. The Niva careened around twists and turns, some of them hairpin curves that bent the road back on itself. Gavril didn't pay any attention even as we lurched way too close to the edge of the road on the side of his blind eye. Lauraleigh and I fought to brace ourselves.

After an hour of this, Lauraleigh finally lost her cool. "Slow down!" she shouted. "You're going to kill us. You only…" She cut herself off in mid-sentence, but I thought what she wanted to say was, "You only have one eye and one arm, Gavril!"

"Lots of things in these mountains can kill you," said Gavril over his shoulder. "My driving isn't one of them."

"How can he even drive?" Lauraleigh whispered to me in French. "Isn't it illegal to drive with one hand? And a manual car too!"

"I have no idea," I whispered back.

"If we roll over, can you save us with your magic?"

"I'll try," I said. But I didn't feel very sure.

The road evened out eventually, and Gavril went even faster. In my mind, I started calling him "Gunner." Maybe it was the speed. Maybe it was the thought of him shooting my beloved bears. In any case, Gunner's driving made it impossible for Lauraleigh and me to relax on the remaining hour-long drive to Babagai, a village at the base of Mount Burghed.

We stepped out of the car, and I shook my legs and arms, trying to get feeling back into my limbs. My muscles were cramped from straining to keep still in the jostling Niva. Gavril gave us no chance to recover but simply tossed our packs at us.

"Wait here," he said gruffly, and went inside a shack beside the road.

Babagai was a village in name only. In reality, it was no more than a crossroads with a small store and a single gas pump. Behind the store, a rundown barn leaned against a fenced pasture where six shaggy ponies grazed. Three more ponies were tacked up and tied to a rail in front of the store.

"Our noble steeds," Lauraleigh whispered with a giggle. I didn't know how she had the energy for humor right now, but I was glad for it.

I smiled and felt better. Amazing how something as simple as a smile can turn a painful situation around.

The day was warm, with cloudless blue skies that brought back vivid memories of my days in the mountains with Uncle Misha. The air was clearer here as if nothing stood between me and the huge blueness above. Uncle Misha had always said that in the mountains, we were closer to the moon than anywhere else in the world. I believed him too. And when I looked around, there it was: the moon hanging like a sickle in the sunny sky. With my old friend at my back, I suddenly felt energized. I could take on anything, even a grumpy, one-eyed and one-armed guide. I studied the moon through my dream stone, and I felt much calmer.

Gavril came out of the store with a grizzled old man.

"This is Anton," said Gavril.

Anton spoke to us in Russian. It had been over six years since Uncle Misha had left me in Geneva, and Anton's accent was different — he sounded more Ukrainian than Russian. Despite my chatting with the train attendant, my Russian was still rusty. But I understood him well enough.

"He wants to know if we can ride horses," I said to Lauraleigh.

"A little bit," she answered.

I translated for Anton. The Russian words still felt clumsy on my tongue. Clumsy but good, like finding a treasured storybook you haven't read since childhood.

"I haven't ridden in many years," I added. The last time I'd been on a horse had been during one of the many birthday parties that Sister Daphne put on for the orphans.

Anton grunted and tightened the girths around the horses' bellies. While he did this, Gavril filled the saddlebags with our extra gear and tied our sleeping bags behind the saddles. He was using his one hand and teeth, and I had to admit that he moved with rough, efficient grace.

Anton laced his fingers and mumbled something to Lauraleigh. I strained but didn't understand a word at first. He repeated himself for me.

"He wants you to put your foot in his hands," I said. "He'll give you a leg up on the horse."

After one failed attempt, Lauraleigh swung her free leg over the horse and found her seat.

"What's her name?" she asked, running her fingers through the dark brown mane.

"Dushá," said Anton, and I translated the rest. "She's a gentle mare and will carry you far." He patted her neck. Anton might be a crotchety old man, but he loved his horses.

"Your horse is Kísa," he said to me. "She's fat and lazy. So if you fall off, she won't run far."

Great. I didn't know whether to be insulted or thankful.

"Come," Gavril said. "We have a full day's ride. I don't want to be caught in the mountains after dark."

I found that remark odd. We would spend at least two nights in the forest before reaching Mama Bear's den or Uncle Misha's cabin, which were much farther up in the Sayan Mountains. Perhaps I'd misunderstood.

But before I could question him, Gavril kicked his pony into a walk and headed up the dirt road. Dushá followed automatically, but Kísa seemed to be dozing.

"Give her a kick," said Anton. I did, hoping I didn't hurt the poor beast.

Anton grunted. It might have been a laugh. "Flies sting harder than that kick."

I kicked harder, and Anton made a kissing noise. The horse lumbered forward — and I nearly pitched off the saddle.

After I had stabilized myself, I turned to Anton. The old man stood on the roadside, looking at our horses and beaming.

"What a strange name for a village," I said. "Babagai. It's not even a Russian word." I wondered if Anton had named the place in his native Ukrainian.

"It means *bear* in the Buryat language," Anton said. "Many bears around here."

Bears, huh. Well, that sounds encouraging, I thought.

By the time I caught up with the others, my butt was already sore from pounding against the leather.

I'd said it before. This was going to be a long trip.

As we rode through the mountains, I was excited to see this land again, to feel the magical, comforting presence of the trees and rocks around us. But for some reason, it felt strange to be here in such a small group. A little unsafe, even. We were small dots lost in the harsh Siberian wilderness, and my chest tightened at that thought. There was hardly a person between us and the North Pole thousands of kilometers away. Only the forests, hills, rivers, and lakes.

I guess living in Geneva had spoiled me a little. When I had lived here, though I had known no one but Uncle Misha and the bears, I'd never thought of my home as empty. But after being in a big city for so long, I'd gotten used to people always being around, even if I wasn't paying any attention to them. Being this alone was making me light-headed. On this brilliant summer day, why was I even thinking of the North Pole, where it's always winter?

I tried to calm myself by thinking of the fairy tale Uncle Misha used to tell me. I started to imagine that the various cliffs and rock faces looked like Volots, mountain giants who are too heavy for the Earth to hold, which is why they always stay in the mountains. As I started seeing craggy eyebrows and straggly beards and great, gaping mouths in the gray stone surrounding us, I began to giggle a little. My anxiety waned.

Lauraleigh's voice jolted me out of my dream world. She sounded thrilled. "Wow. What is it? I've never seen anything like that."

Ahead of us, on the left-hand side of the little path we were following, was a small hollow that seemed to radiate violet light. I jumped off Kísa and walked over to look closer. I didn't know what I had expected to find, but it certainly wasn't a beautiful gemstone the size of a chicken egg, with sunrays playing on its many sides. It was a stunning sight. I no longer had to imagine visions in the rocks to be astounded or reminded of fairy tales. I had never encountered anything like it before, and I was sure Lauraleigh hadn't either.

Gavril glanced at us with a fierce grin. "You've never seen that before? How come? I thought Swiss jewelers had every kind of stone at their disposal."

Lauraleigh clambered off her horse and moved closer. "What is it?" she asked, examining the stone carefully. She leaned over it and stretched out her hand to touch the scintillating stone.

Gavril said, "It's a charoite. You won't find this stone anywhere else—"

He didn't have time to finish his explanation. He froze and put a finger to his lips.

A sound of tinkling bells was fast approaching, accompanied by a gust of wind. Gentle female laughter floated through the air.

Who was here? I'd just been thinking that there wasn't a person around… But now there was someone else out here too. An invisible young woman with a melodic voice and tinkling bells.

The sound of laughter came closer and closer until it seemed right next to us, as if someone were laughing in my ear. But I could see no one.

I glanced around desperately and tried to stay silent, just as Gavril had instructed. I wanted to take out my dream stone and see if it would let me find the visitor, but when I tried to move, Gavril made a gesture at me that clearly meant "No."

The sounds slowly moved away until they faded completely.

Gavril didn't seem surprised in the least. Lauraleigh and I stared at him, dumbfounded and questioning.

"Charoites are our unique stone," he said with a sigh. "They're millions of years old, they say. You'll find them only here, in a few square kilometers around this spot. Some of it gets mined and taken away to your Swiss jewelers. But others — well, they say there are those stones you're not allowed to take. Those the Mountain Mistress visits when people come close. As long as you don't take them, she's going to be calm. You can look at them and even touch them, just so long as they remain in their place. If you try to move them, then…"

He shook his head grimly.

"Get back on your horses," he said. "We've wasted enough time with your female foolishness and fondness for pretty things."

Luckily Kísa hid my face from him because it gave me a moment to wipe the anger from it. If we hadn't needed him, I would have told him a thing or two. I could see the same thought in Lauraleigh's eyes. But we didn't dare snap at him.

Seeing us struggling to return to our saddles, Gavril dismounted and helped us. He was probably cursing at us inside and thinking we weren't just foolish but also weak and useless — but at least he was doing his job.

The forest became denser as we rode steadily uphill. These trees were not the kind you saw around cities. They were ancient pines and firs, their trunks barren of branches near the ground. When I looked up — way up — I saw the branches tangled together in a vast canopy of green that let in only flickers of sunlight.

Our trek was eerily quiet through this dark world. The ponies' hooves were silent on the crush of pine needles underfoot. We rode in single file, which made conversation difficult. I didn't want to speak anyway. It seemed wrong somehow to fill this place with human sounds. Instead, I tried to ignore the sore spots on my body where the saddle rubbed and enjoy the peaceful ride.

I'd been hearing the hushed sounds of water for nearly an hour before we passed a low waterfall. Gavril stopped upstream and let the horses drink. My legs jiggled like rubber bands when I tumbled off Kísa's back. The pony gave me a backward glance and a whiffle before joining the others at the stream. From his backpack, Gavril handed out sandwiches, and we all drank from our canteens.

"When you said there were lots of things in the forest that could kill us," Lauraleigh said, "what exactly did you mean? Things like that Mountain Mistress?"

Gavril chuckled. "No. Wolves. And bears."

"I'm not afraid of bears," I said automatically.

"Then you're a fool," Gavril mumbled around a mouthful of sandwich.

"We don't use words like *fool*," said Lauraleigh in such a perfect imitation of Sister Daphne that I almost laughed.

"Then you're a fool too." Gavril shoved the rest of his sandwich in his mouth as if our stupidity meant nothing to him. And it probably didn't.

Lauraleigh glared at him. I wondered if Monsieur Nolan had paid our guide ahead of time, or if he was withholding payment until he had gotten proof that we had been delivered to Uncle Misha safely.

The shadows of the forest suddenly seemed more sinister — and it wasn't because I imagined wolves hiding behind every tree.

"Why did you say that you didn't want to be caught in the woods after dark?" I asked.

Gavril aimed his one squinty eye at me and took a long sip from his canteen. "I meant that we had better be camped before dark, with a nice fire burning to scare off the wolves."

"Oh." That seemed right.

We packed up our garbage and lured the ponies away from the sweet grass growing along the creek's edge. Gavril swung into his saddle and his horse walked off down the forest path. Lauraleigh and I looked at each other.

"I guess he expects us to mount on our own this time," she said. "Come on, we can do it. These ponies can't be more than thirteen hands high."

I knew that horses were measured in hands, but I had no idea how long a hand is. All I knew was that Kísa's head topped mine by at least ten centimeters. To me, she was big. Lauraleigh helped me get my left foot in the stirrup and swing my right leg over the saddle; then she hopped up on Dushá. Having had twenty minutes off the saddle, my rear throbbed with pain as soon as I sat again.

"I don't know how people do this for days on end," I grumbled.

"I think it's like learning to play the guitar." Lauraleigh giggled. "You eventually get calluses or something, and it doesn't hurt so much."

Great. Just what I need, I thought. *Calluses on my butt.*

We stopped three hours later, when everything below my waist was numb. I slid off my pony and clung to her bronze mane until my feet had remembered what they were made for.

"Why are we stopping?" Lauraleigh asked. "We have hours before dark."

"You know how to put one of these up?" Gavril tossed a small tent bag at her.

Lauraleigh, who looked as tired as I felt, dropped it. "I don't."

"You'll figure it out before dark," said Gavril. "Probably want to collect some wood for a fire before then. Fire starters are in the saddle bags, and you have food for another two days."

"Wait! You mean 'we,' right?" I said. "*We* have enough food for two days."

Gavril scratched his head just under the elastic that held the patch over his eye.

"From here on, the trees start to thin," he said. "When you get to the point where the horses can't go any farther, just loosen their girths and let them go. They know the way home."

"Now listen here!" Lauraleigh rose to her full height, which was several centimeters taller than our shrimp of a guide. "You can't just leave us here. Monsieur Nolan paid you to take us to Anna's uncle."

"No one goes into the Reaches." He nodded toward the upper mountain. "The Great Trapper holds court up there. He don't take to strangers in his woods. Not my fault if your Monsieur Nolan doesn't know that."

"That's ridiculous," I said. "There's no such person as the Great Trapper."

"No? You are what, ten years old? You know all the secrets of the universe?" Gavril sneered. "You go on then and trespass on the Great Trapper's lands. But I know better. He sees all. He's like a vengeful ghost that can hide behind every tree at once. Last time I went up there, only a few kilometers into his lands, he set his bears on me." He flicked his eye patch with his good hand. "They gave me a beating to remember. No one goes into the Reaches."

"Well, I'm not afraid." I really wasn't. "I was born on that mountain, and my Uncle Misha still lives there."

Gavril's one eye widened. "Misha — meaning *Medved?* The Bear?"

I nodded. Misha was a usual name for bears in Russian fairytales, but Gavril said the name like a title. Without saying another word, he turned his pony and kicked it into a gallop. After a minute, even the hoofbeats were lost in the dark silence of the forest.

"And I'm thirteen!" I called after him.

Lauraleigh and I were alone.

Chapter 3

ear Diary,

An orphan learns to enjoy being alone. Even when we're surrounded by other orphans and our caretakers, we are somehow alone. The fact that we have no families makes us little islands in the sea of ordinary people.

Other kids gripe about their brothers or sisters. They complain when their parents ground them for staying out too late. They moan about spending the holidays with boring cousins again. Orphans watch all this from our islands, mystified that anyone could take the treasure of family for granted.

Every step I take through this forest brings me closer to my unknown family and to my beloved Uncle Misha. Nothing will stop me from finding them, not bears or wolves or even our cranky one-eyed guide — who betrayed us.

I don't know what I'll find when I get there. My father may not even welcome me. But I have to try. Who knows, maybe while I'm here, I'll even find my grandmother, the witch: the Iron Queen.

We stood alone in an ancient forest with night creeping up on us like a thief. Gavril was long gone. My tired muscles chilled and grew stiff.

"Should we turn back?" I asked.

Lauraleigh chewed on her lip. "I don't know. How far are we from your Uncle Misha's cabin? Does anything look familiar to you?"

I gazed around at the enormous trees. One looked much like the next. I clasped my fingers around my dream stone, hoping for inspiration. The stone was warm and vibrated in my hand, but as usual, I didn't know what it was telling me. Sometimes, I wished for an instruction manual to understand at least some of this stuff.

"I think we're close," I said. "But you're the adult and in charge. If you think we should turn back, we will." That was the deal I had made with Monsieur Nolan: Lauraleigh was in command. I hoped she would decide to stay. My father was in trouble, somewhere up the mountain. My father, who I didn't even know existed a few weeks ago.

Besides, I didn't think I could drag my sore butt back into that saddle again.

"We'll stay," Lauraleigh said. "But let's get this tent set up and some wood collected before dark."

First, we took care of our horses. Dushá and Kísa deserved our attention after that long ride. We took off their saddles and bridles and rubbed them down with a cloth before tying them to a tree near a stream.

For the next hour, we kept busy with chores, setting up the tent (somewhat crookedly) and building a fire. Recent rain had dampened the wood; our fire smoked and fizzled but refused to light. Night came quickly under the trees. We needed that fire for warmth and protection from predators who would come out after dark.

"I could … uh, zap it," I suggested. "You know, with magic."

I didn't usually flaunt my magic. The mystery of it still made me nervous. I had all this power but very little control. And if I used magic with bad intentions, a bit of darkness would creep inside me. It was a horrible feeling to know such evil could lurk inside me. After the last time, when the shadow had almost made me kill André and Marie Montmorency, I had sworn I would never use magic for the wrong reasons again.

The problem was that the wrong reasons sometimes disguised themselves as right reasons.

"Magic is part of you," Lauraleigh said, "isn't it? You shouldn't be ashamed to use it."

I nodded. Lauraleigh had seen me struggle with the decision to let the Montmorencys live, even after they'd hurt our friends. She had never doubted I'd make the right decision. I hoped I could live up to her faith in me.

Shadows filled in the spaces between the trees. Soon it would be pitch-dark, and we'd be easy prey for any of the animals who roamed in the darkness. If I wanted to act, now was the time.

I gathered my will and centered myself in my stomach. That's where I imagined the magic started, where it felt like it resided. It was a pool of energy that I drew from. I held out my hands and concentrated. The pool gurgled and tingled inside me. I felt the humming energy flow up my chest, around my shoulders and down into the tips of my fingers. A hot, white light burst from my hands, blasting the damp sticks and setting them on fire.

I listened to myself. Had I become just a little darker? It didn't seem so.

"Much better," Lauraleigh said with a smile.

With no cooking pots, we ate more sandwiches from our packs and drank from the stream. It was an incredible feeling, drinking from the stream and knowing the water was cleaner than what we had back in our very civilized Geneva.

After dinner, we sat beside the fire to keep warm. Even in summer, nights grew cool this high in the mountains. We were exhausted, but neither of us wanted to sleep yet.

The fire was so bright it hurt my tired eyes. I looked into the cool shadows of the forest and froze. Something white and ghostly was flitting from tree to tree.

"Did you see that?" I asked Lauraleigh, pointing into the forest. But the vision was already gone.

"See what?" She strained to look into the shadows.

"Nothing. I just thought … for a moment … something was watching us."

Lauraleigh shivered.

"Do you really think there are bears and wolves in the forest?" she asked.

"Bears, for sure," I said. "But we don't have to be afraid of them." I wasn't so sure about the wolves.

"Maybe we should sleep in shifts. You know, to keep a lookout."

"I've got a better idea." My backpack, with my mother's precious letter, was never far from my side. I pulled out a small carved statue of a hand, smaller than my own fist. I held it over the fire, letting the flames tickle the smooth stone.

The hand jerked. It exploded in size and came to life, zipping around the fire like a comet; then it dove and tickled my ribs.

"Squire! Stop it." I laughed, and pushed him aside.

Squire floated in the air before me. If he'd had a mouth, he would have been grinning. I scratched him on his hairy knuckles and he leaned into my touch.

"I missed you," I said.

He made a fist and bobbed up and down — Squire's version of a nod.

Lauraleigh watched us with wide eyes. She had seen Squire the night we stopped the Montmorencys, when we were all shocked and tired. But never before had she seen him up close or animated from stone.

"Squire, meet my friend, Lauraleigh."

Squire tilted to the side and held his fingers straight. Without flinching, Lauraleigh reached out and grasped him in a handshake. Did I mention that Lauraleigh is amazing?

"Nice to meet you, Squire," she said. "We're on a big adventure. Will you help us?"

Squire bobbed up and down, nodding.

"Do you recognize this place?" I asked.

Squire bobbed up and down; then he twisted from side to side. I guessed that meant he wasn't sure. "Will you keep a lookout for us tonight? There may be wolves in the forest."

Squire saluted with two fingers and zoomed off into the woods.

I felt better knowing that Squire was watching over us.

I looked at Lauraleigh to make sure she was still okay and not just pretending. Magic still had to be pretty weird to her, after all. But she didn't look weirded out. She looked thoughtful.

"You know," she said after a moment, "there's an old Russian myth about a witch who has pairs of animated hands as servants."

That made sense. Squire had told me about his friend Knight. They were a pair. I wondered if Knight lived somewhere in this forest.

"Her name is Baba Yaga. And she has three henchmen: the Black Horseman, the Red Horseman, and the White Horseman." Lauraleigh eyed me carefully, waiting for my reaction. We'd both met a man called the Black Horseman back in Geneva. He had tried to kidnap me and other children from the orphanage. And Uncle Misha's letter had mentioned the Red Horseman.

"You don't think she's real, do you?" I asked. I vaguely recognized the name Baba Yaga, but she was just a fairy tale creature.

"Didn't Squire say that you're a witch?"

"Yes," I said, still doubtful. "And he said my grandmother is a witch too. He called her the Iron Queen."

The fire flickered over Lauraleigh's face. "Did you know Baba Yaga's teeth are made of iron? Apparently, she likes to eat people, and the teeth help her chomp through the bones."

"Oh, great." I tried to hide the chill that had just gone through me. "You're telling me my grandmother is some kind of cannibal witch with a bad dental plan."

Lauraleigh held up her hands. "I'm just telling you what I remember from my classes in Russian literature. But ... the animated hand. The Horsemen. Iron. The details kind of fit. And you can't tell me you don't believe in such things. Not anymore."

She was right. In the past month, since my thirteenth birthday, I'd learned that anything was possible. The possibilities, however, left me with little but questions.

If Lauraleigh was right, and Baba Yaga existed, and we were dealing with her, and even if she was my grandmother, why did she send her Black Horseman to find me? And what connected him to my father? Who *was* my father? Uncle Misha might know the answers, but he was still at least a day and a night away.

"Tell me what else you remember about this Baba Yaga character," I said.

"Well, let's see. She's not really considered good or bad, just powerful. Like an avalanche that doesn't care who it buries. She likes to trick people. And she's very private. She lives alone in a very peculiar house."

I swallowed. "Let me guess. It's a house on chicken legs."

"Exactly!" She looked surprised; then she smiled. "But of course you know. You're Russian."

I didn't answer. From my backpack, I took out my mother's letter and the carefully folded picture inside. I glanced up, worried that the moonlight would bring the image to life, but the moon was hiding behind the thick canopy of trees. The picture stayed lifeless as I handed it to Lauraleigh.

"Be sure to keep it out of the moonlight."

Holding it so she could see it in the fire's glow, Lauraleigh examined the old drawing. It showed a cabin perched on spindly chicken legs, surrounded by a fence topped with skulls. In the background, an old woman with a big nose and vicious teeth rode in a mortar. She carried the pestle and a broom.

"That's her. Look at those teeth! I wouldn't want to floss those."

"Why do you think she carries a broom?" I asked, although I knew the answer from my own experience.

"If I remember correctly, she uses the pestle like a paddle in the air, and the broom to sweep away all traces of her passing. Weird, if you ask me. I always thought witches flew *on* their brooms."

"Not as easy as it looks. Trust me." The one time I had tried to fly on a broom had been an epic fail. Like my grandmother — and I was becoming pretty sure that Lauraleigh's guess was right — I was better at flying in a vessel. In my case, I'd used a bucket. Not the most glamorous vehicle, but it worked for me. I said, "To be honest, I'm not even sure we need something to fly on. Or in. But it feels kind of safer to do so."

Lauraleigh smiled, shaking her head. This conversation probably sounded too out there for her.

"Isn't it crazy?" I asked. "I should be able to fly without toting that extra weight. But I can't. I need a bucket to stand in."

Lauraleigh looked like she was struggling between laughing and admitting that this was all too weird. In the end, she just shook her head and didn't say anything.

She looked at the photo again.

"What's so interesting about it?" I asked.

"Well, come on. I've studied her. There are all sorts of paintings and drawings of her. And now I can compare with the real thing. What's not interesting about that?" She suddenly brought the picture much closer to her face. "Huh," she said, "so that detail's true."

"What?"

"Well…" She handed the photo back to me and pointed at the fence. "You see there? If you look closely, you'll notice something weird with the fence."

"I don't see anything weird. I mean, aside from the skulls."

"No, not that. Right at the end of the fence, there's one fence post that doesn't have a skull on it."

I peered. She was right.

"It's another part of the myth," said Lauraleigh. "There's always one empty fence post, just in case you show up and don't mind your manners, or it's the wrong time to bother

her, or whatever. So she always has a place to put your skull when she's done with you."

"Let me get this straight," I said, putting the photo back into my back. I didn't feel like looking at it any longer. "You're telling me that Baba Yaga eats humans, tricks people, kills you just because she's feeling cranky and then uses your skull to improve her home decor — and *people don't necessarily think she's evil?*"

Lauraleigh grinned. "If you're polite and it's the right time of day, she may let you go or even help you," she said. "It takes a lot to get called evil, you know."

It was a weird thought that you could get away with doing truly horrible things if you balanced them with some good ones, but in a way, I supposed it was also somewhat comforting. After all, I'd come pretty close to doing some horrible things myself. Maybe I didn't have to worry quite so much that I might turn evil if I wasn't careful.

By now, we really were tired. The fire had faded a little, so we built it up again until our little clearing had brightened. Hopefully, the light would keep away the wolves. Our snug tent had just enough room for the two of us. We slipped into our sleeping bags, and I lay awake listening to the crackle of the fire.

"Lauraleigh?" I hoped she was still awake, even if we had a long ride tomorrow.

"Yeah?"

"What do you think my father will be like?"

Lauraleigh didn't answer right away. She was an orphan too. Maybe she was thinking about the few memories she had of her own father.

"I guess he'll just be your dad, you know? There won't be anyone else like him."

I fell asleep with that thought in my mind. I dreamed of ice cream. Strange, I know. But I'd always thought that if I'd had parents, they'd have taken me for ice cream. Sister Constance never let us have ice cream. She didn't approve.

I awoke to Squire tugging urgently at my shoulder and the sound of wolf howls echoing through the forest.

Chapter 4

ear Diary,

Suppose you see someone about to get hurt. Say a bully is about to throw a rock at another kid. If the only way you can stop the bully is to use magic, is that good magic or bad magic? Your intentions are good, right? So that's good magic. But what if you hurt the bully while saving the kid? That's bad magic, isn't it?

I just don't know. Does the dark shadow come only when my intentions are bad? The first time it happened, I set André's handkerchief on fire. It wasn't a terribly bad thing to do; he only got a burn, and anyway he deserved it for what he'd done to me and the other children. But my life wasn't in immediate danger when I did it. I set his handkerchief on fire out of spite — and it could have been worse if he hadn't managed to put it out so soon. Is that why the shadows seeped into my heart? What if the rest of his clothes had caught fire too?

Sometimes, when the night is really quiet and I can't sleep, I can feel the darkness shifting around inside me. It feels like heartburn — only oilier.

Let's get back to the kid about to be hit by a rock. What if the bully didn't throw it? What if a toddler, who didn't know any better, threw the rock? What if I hurt the toddler while trying to save the other child? What if I didn't mean to hurt anyone? What if I just tried to move the rock, but I didn't notice that others were in the way and it hit them? Does that still leave the door of my heart open to the shadows?

I just don't know. And not knowing might be my most dangerous weakness.

The fire had gone out during the night. Glancing at the small patch of open sky above us, I guessed dawn was near, but the forest was still dark. A wolf howled and another answered the call. Dushá and Kísa stomped their hooves. Their eyes glowed white all around.

"It's okay," said Lauraleigh. "We won't let those big bad wolves hurt you." She patted Dushá's neck and soothed the ponies with her singsong voice. I wasn't so sure we could protect the horses — or ourselves — from a pack of wolves.

The howls echoed through the trees again, sending shivers up and down my spine. They seemed to come from all around us now, and there was a deeply disturbing edge to their voices: sour, unsettled. I remembered a line from Uncle Misha's letter: *Unsettled spirits watch my every move.*

Then a scraggly black wolf stepped out of the shadows.

"Quickly, move to the fire!" Lauraleigh shouted, and ran into the small circle of light from the glowing embers.

Squire and I joined her. Another wolf stepped into our camp right beside Dushá. The mare screamed and reared, tugging the rope that tied her to the tree.

More wolves poured out of the dark. Sleek and savage, they ran through our camp, two of them tearing up our tent with their powerful teeth. Lauraleigh screamed as a wolf knocked her over. I tried to gather my magic to strike them but there were too many of them, and trying to keep them all in sight made it impossible to concentrate enough to summon anything. They dashed madly from shadow to shadow so that even if I could have used my powers, I would have been afraid to hurt either Lauraleigh or the ponies.

At that moment, as if in response to my thoughts, the ponies panicked, broke their leads, and galloped off.

"Let them go," Lauraleigh said, picking herself up from the dirt. "They know the way home."

I nodded. The wolves didn't seem interested in the horses. There were eight of them now. They circled us, with lips curled back to show gleaming fangs. Their eyes shone with unnatural intelligence.

These weren't ordinary wolves.

Unsettled spirits, I remembered again.

Squire bobbed at my shoulder and Lauraleigh had my back. We circled the crackling fire, trying to keep all the wolves in sight. Magic was seething inside me now, wanting to lash out, but I held it back, not knowing what would happen if I used it. I looked around for any kind of weapon. I spied the thick branch that we had used to stir the fire, but when I stepped forward to grab it, one of the wolves snapped at my hand. I jerked it back.

"They're keeping us here," said Lauraleigh. "Like prisoners."

She was right. The wolves continued to circle us, but as long as we didn't try to escape, they let us be. They were waiting for someone.

A few minutes later, a pure white wolf, taller than the others by a head, stepped out of the darkness. He appeared so suddenly, it was like a visit from an angel — if it weren't for his raging red eyes and snarling muzzle bristling with finger-length fangs. *Maybe a really angry angel*, I thought.

The other wolves stopped in their tracks and lowered their heads.

The white wolf leaned back on his haunches and rose up on two legs with a growl of pain. His body trembled, and then — I couldn't believe my eyes — his shape started to change. His teeth snapped, first heavily, then lightly, while his face shortened and became rounder. As his limbs straightened themselves, the skin on the back of one of his hands split open, and a few drops of hot blood fell on my face. Fur wafted off him like mist in the morning sun, and a man stood before us.

His hair was long and white, and his eyes were red with hate. His face was creased with deep lines. He wore dirty white furs and leathers tied around legs as thick as tree trunks.

I gasped. "You're the White Horseman!"

He narrowed his eyes and pinched his bloodless lips together. Another growl, low and threatening, escaped his throat.

"My brother said not to underestimate you." His voice was surprisingly light. "He said you wield powerful magics."

"I do!" I jutted my chin forward and tried to stand as tall as I could. *Maybe I can bluff our way out of this*, I thought, *as unlikely as it seems*.

"You look like nothing more than a scared, scrawny girl." He curled a lip back in a wolfish grin. "Your friend is just about to faint too."

I glanced to my side. Lauraleigh was frozen, her eyes staring. Nothing of her moved, just the pulse at her throat, which was beating much, much faster than it should have been.

I'd never seen her so discomposed; that frightened me almost more than the wolves.

"What do you want with us?" I said.

"There's no 'us,' just you," said the Horseman. "Your grandmother wants you. The other girl is not invited. I'll leave her here for my pups. They had a long run last night to track you down, and I expect they're hungry."

Lauraleigh pressed closer to my side. No way would I leave her to the wolves. I didn't want to meet my grandmother anyway. Not now. Not knowing who she was. And not with her sending wolves after me.

"You can tell old Iron Teeth that I respectfully decline the invitation," I said.

The Horseman shot out a hand to grab my throat. I ducked and rolled to the side. Just as the Horseman's fingers grazed the top of my head, I dropped to the ground and kicked at his knee. He growled and stumbled. Lauraleigh screamed, finally breaking from her trance, and turned to run, but the wolves kept us inside their ring with snapping teeth and growls.

Anger burned inside me. I felt power boiling in my gut again. Fear did that; I was never stronger than when I was faced with a horrifying death. I could send a bolt of pure fire into the Horseman and stop his heart. I knew I could. The power was building up fast inside me, begging for release. It was almost impossible to keep holding that energy inside me.

But releasing it to hurt the wolves or the Horseman would lead to darkness entering my soul again. I didn't want to hurt anyone at that price, not even one of my grandmother's henchmen, not even his wolves.

Instead, I summoned the hot energy from my stomach and drew it up into my fingers. Then, with a cry of relief, I let it go. The magic surged from me, but at the last minute, I turned and blasted the pile of extra kindling beside our fire pit. Blue and red flames shot into the air. Instant bonfire, scorching hot!

The wolves leaped back, growling. The Horseman jerked away, his furs smoldering, his red eyes open wide in shock, maybe even in fear.

I used his brief moment of distraction to search for an escape. I needed a bucket or some kind of vessel to fly in. Something big enough to carry both Lauraleigh and me. The wolves had destroyed our tent. Our sleeping bags and clothes were scattered across the dirt. Could a sleeping bag be a vessel?

While the Horseman swatted at his burning clothes, I leaped toward a sleeping bag. Out of the corner of my eye, I saw Lauraleigh swing a burning stick at a wolf. The wolf growled and snapped its teeth at her, but it stayed out of her reach. Squire was more effective. He zipped around the camp, punching wolves in their ribs, hitting them on their heads, making them jump, snort and growl.

I grabbed the sleeping bag and tried to pull it toward me. It didn't move. The Horseman had reverted to his wolf shape and was standing on the other end of the bag. He didn't look amused. The fur around his neck was singed and sooty. His hunched shoulders made him look even bigger. He was pulling his lips back, and a rumbling growl escaped his throat.

"Nice doggie," I said, leaning toward the bag.

He growled with rage and sprang forward, jutting his huge black nose in my face and baring his enormous teeth. His foul breath made me gag.

I was out of options… I had to blast him with magic. I had to save Lauraleigh. The magic began to coil in my stomach again, building up for release. The shadows that were already living in my heart danced with glee. Every bit of my magic that hurt someone else made them stronger. I took a deep breath…

And the white wolf was flung to the ground, far from me.

But … but I hadn't touched him!

A roar shook the trees. I looked up, and up some more to the brown, furry face of rage towering above me. "Mama Bear!" I yelled. Mama Bear had come to my rescue!

The bear pounced on the white wolf. She was even more massive than I remembered, and the sheer weight of her body flattened him. Other bears were lumbering into the camp, swinging their heads back and forth like giant pendulums. The wolves fought back for a full minute. Chunks of fur and bloodied flesh flew all around us, and the air filled with wild screams of fury and pain. Lauraleigh and I stood huddled together in the middle of the animals, all of them clawing and biting, clearly trying to kill.

Three wolves cornered a smaller bear near a small grove. One of them leaped and locked its jaws on the bear's paw. A yelp of triumph — or gloating — rose over the wolves, echoed by a cry of hurt from the bear. Unable to hold back, I released a massive bolt of energy at the attacking animal. It screamed and let go.

The wolves cowered. They yipped and ran off into the trees as if on command. Only the White Horseman remained, flattened on the ground under Mama Bear's bulk. Deep, sticky darkness filled my heart. After a second or two, most of it seeped away into the air — but some remained.

Five giant brown bears surrounded us. They were moving about, rolling on the earth, jumping, even playfully batting at each other with their paws. Apparently, they were taking their time cooling off after the battle.

When they'd calmed down a little, I ran into Mama Bear's embrace. She folded me in her massive arms, and I felt safe for the first time since I'd opened Uncle Misha's letter. Mama Bear smelled of cold caves and autumn leaves, just as I remembered. She smelled of my childhood, of the time when the world was a beautiful, friendly place.

"I missed you," I murmured into her thick pelt, which I noticed was speckled with gray.

An answer rumbled through her chest: She was glad to see me too.

"Uh, Anna?" Lauraleigh whispered somewhere behind me. "Are these friends of yours?"

"Yes!" I said. "Lauraleigh, meet Mama Bear, and I guess these are her latest cubs."

"You mean ... you really were raised by bears?" Lauraleigh's face was white. In the dusk, she looked like a ghost. "I thought that was just some silly rumor the other kids made up about you."

I found the strength to smile, although my chest and stomach were still heaving with all the excitement of the battle. And with the fear of the new darkness that had entered my heart.

"Nope. It's true," I said, stepping away from Mama Bear's embrace. "She found me in the wild and kept me until Uncle Misha came. I'd go visit her and the new cubs whenever I finished my chores." For six years, I had lived and played with the bears. They were the only friends I'd had while growing up on the mountain.

Lauraleigh continued to stare. Then she collected herself and bowed her head a little to Mama Bear. "It's nice to meet you," she said.

Mama Bear rumbled a greeting in return.

"She's pleased to meet you too," I said with a little laugh. I'd never been more amazed at Lauraleigh's ability to take things in stride. I could see that she was already getting used to the idea, weird though it was — and she was able to keep her manners in the middle of it all. Sister Constance would have been so proud.

Dawn was starting to break. Mama Bear stood and poked the White Horseman with her snout. He was slowly returning to his human form, and it wasn't a pretty sight. Fur was falling off his face in bloody white patches and teeth were retracting and bleeding in his mouth. His arm was bent at a painful angle. He was breathing in short, rough gasps, but he seemed to be out cold. Mama Bear sneezed as if his smell offended her.

"What should we do with him?" Lauraleigh asked.

"Looks like he'll survive. So let's leave him," I said firmly.

"If the other Horsemen are nearby… Well, we need to find Uncle Misha as soon as possible."

Lauraleigh sighed. I felt a wave of fear coming from her, fear that she was doing her best to conceal. "Without the horses, it'll be a long hike up the mountain," she said.

Mama Bear must have noticed Lauraleigh's fear, too; she grumbled encouragement and gave Lauraleigh a reassuring lick across her face. For a split second, I was afraid my friend would react with disgust at this wet sign of support, but she smiled and patted Mama Bear on her giant paw. *Oh, Lauraleigh.* I was so proud of her at that moment, as if I were her elder.

"We might not have horsepower." I grinned. "But we've got bear-power."

Lauraleigh's mouth dropped open. Honestly, you would have thought that by now, she'd be expecting the unexpected around me.

I let Lauraleigh ride on Mama Bear's sturdy shoulders. She was bigger than I and, even though the cubs were all yearlings, they still didn't have Mama Bear's massive strength. I rode on the shoulders of a young cub. Bears only stay with their mothers for two years, so he was a stranger to me. Even so, it only took one growl from Mama Bear for him to lower his shoulder to the ground so I could hop on his back.

Bears don't have smooth trotting gaits like horses. They amble from side to side. I'd ridden bears all my young life and the swaying motion didn't bother me, but I could see Laura-leigh hanging on to Mama Bear's ruff for dear life.

"It's no wonder I can't handle a horse," I said, my voice resonant with excitement. "This is the way to travel! Isn't it amazing?"

Lauraleigh lifted her head and smiled weakly. "I feel a bit seasick, to be honest."

I laughed. I felt incredible! The summer sun dappled the ground as it shone through the leaves. Trees thinned as we climbed, and the mountain peak became visible, a shining beacon calling me home. I'd never felt less like an orphan in my life. I was back with the family I'd had as a child, with Mama Bear and soon with Uncle Misha. I was with Laura-leigh, who was practically a sister by now. And I was finally going to learn about my other family, the family I'd waited thirteen years to meet. I didn't know if that family would welcome me or if I'd even want to know them. So far, I wasn't impressed with Granny Iron Teeth. But I was ready to find out more.

I could feel the bear's strength under me as we moved through the forest, and it gave me courage.

The bears' ambling gait ate up the kilometers. Twice I caught glimpses of ghostly apparitions running along beside us. Wolves? Ghosts? Forest spirits, akin to the laughing Mountain Mistress?

But the bears paid them no mind, so I ignored them, too. At noon, we stopped by a small stream to refill our water bottles. We'd left most of our stock at the camp, and each of us carried only one small backpack. Mine held my precious gifts from my mother, including Squire, who had returned to stone after his exhausting morning of terrorizing wolves. We had no food left, though. If we didn't find Uncle Misha before dark, we'd have a long, hungry night ahead of us.

By mid-afternoon, the bears had begun to tire. The slope steepened. Lauraleigh and I dismounted and walked beside them. My hand was buried in Mama Bear's thick fur, and she tugged me up the steeper parts of the trail. My heart beat faster as I recognized bits of the landscape: the curve of a river that I had often fished in, a flat rock face with an eagle's nest perched on top, a grove of cedars where the bear cubs and I had played hide-and-seek.

I was puffing hard by the time we reached a ridge and the trail finally evened out. Lauraleigh looked about ready to collapse. Sweat was streaming off both of us like water from standing under the Jet d'Eau fountain near the orphanage in Geneva.

As we caught our breath, the bears ambled up to a crack in the mountainside that led into a deep cavern system. Mama Bear snuffled at me with her big wet nose. We weren't going inside the caves with the bears. This was where we'd say goodbye.

"Thank you for saving us," I said, curling my arms around her massive neck. "I have to go see Uncle Misha now, but I'll be back to see you soon."

She pushed me with her grizzled snout, nudging me away from the cave. She was getting old, Mama Bear was. I knew that if I wanted to see my friend again, I'd better not stay away for another six years.

"Thank you for everything," said Lauraleigh. Mama Bear dipped her head in acknowledgment.

One by one, the bears disappeared into the cave. We were alone again.

"Now what?" Lauraleigh asked.

"Now we go home," I said. "This way."

We climbed around the boulders that hid the opening to the caves, and we stood at the head of a beautiful valley. Below us, the ground rose and fell in gentle green hills to the base of a small lake with the purest blue water. The mountain rose up again on the other side of the lake, where a single log cabin was nestled among the trees. The afternoon had turned to evening while we'd hiked, and a single candle burned in the cabin's window.

It was the most beautiful site I'd ever seen, and I was suddenly filled with such warmth I thought I might burn up inside.

I was home.

"How do we get there?" asked Lauraleigh.

There was no way around the lake. Thick bushes crowded the shore on each side with no visible path through. On our side of the water, a weathered dock jutted from a small rock beach.

I looked up at the sky. The new moon floated there like a trusty companion that was always with me. We had made it in time.

"Like this," I said, and ran for the dock.

Lauraleigh stumbled along behind me. I knew she was tired, but now I was too excited to feel my own fatigue. I ran to the end of the dock, where a cold torch rested in an iron holder. Usually, there were matches nearby, hidden in a weatherproof pack, but I didn't waste time looking for them. My magic was ready. I zapped the torch and it flared to life. I waved it from side to side like a flag; then I placed it back in the holder.

And I waited.

The sun sank below the tree line. A door opened across the lake. An old man emerged from the cabin and walked down a dock, twin to the one we were standing on. He hopped into a small boat and started to row toward us.

Schloop, schloop, schloop. I could hear his oars splashing in the water long before he was close enough to be seen clearly. He rowed with his back to us. His shaggy hair was more gray than black. Like Mama Bear, the years had aged him. The first stars had peeked from the sky when he finally docked the boat and jumped out.

"*Malyshka!*" he said. "You came."

Uncle Misha gripped me in a hug that rivaled Mama Bear's, and I knew I was well and truly home.

Chapter 5

ear Diary,

There once was a little girl raised by bears, so the story goes. Mama Bear found her alone in the forest and brought her back to the cave with her own cubs. The nights are cold in the mountains even in June, but the baby snuggled next to her furry brothers and sisters for warmth. Until a kind trapper, following a plea from a spirit, found her and took her home to his little cabin on the lake, where he kept her safe for six years.

The only identification on the baby was a locket with instructions to take her to an orphanage in Geneva. Every summer he'd tell himself that the girl needed to go to Geneva, but when the fall came, he couldn't bear the thought of a long, lonely winter without her.

"Next summer," he'd say. "I'll take her next summer."

And so it continued for six years until the little girl was big enough to go to school. Then the trapper knew he could no longer keep her tucked away in the Sayan Mountains, and they undertook the long journey to Geneva.

At least that was the story Uncle Misha had told me time and time again, whenever I had asked him about my family.

After our long, sweaty hike up the mountain, the wind on the lake was refreshing. The rocking of the rowboat lulled Lauraleigh into near sleep, but I was far too excited to rest now. I asked Uncle Misha dozens of questions, firing one after another, not even giving him time to answer.

"Where's my father? Did you know my grandmother is Baba Yaga? Why does she want me? Has she taken my father? Can I see him?"

He chuckled softly. "All in good time, little Anna Sophia. Let us get out of the damp night and put some food in your bellies. Then we will talk."

Another question rushed to my lips, but I held it back. Uncle Misha strained under the weight of the oars. He had no breath to answer my questions now.

I studied him. He looked almost exactly as I remembered him: long, wild hair, bushy eyebrows, kind eyes. But his hair was more white than black now, and his face was lined with wrinkles that hadn't been there before. They made him seem softer than I remembered, like a chalk drawing that's been partly rubbed out.

"Would you like me to row?" I asked, worried that the task might be too much for him now.

"No, child. You've had a longer journey than me."

A few minutes later, the boat bumped up against the dock. Lauraleigh, who had started to doze, jerked awake. I jumped onto the dock and tied the boat to the dock just as

I'd done a hundred times as a child. Then I helped Lauraleigh onto the dock.

She shivered.

"I've got a fire inside and some dinner," Uncle Misha said. "Come, let's warm you up."

Inside, the cabin was almost exactly as I remembered it, with a few new touches. The floor, walls, and ceiling were all made of rough-hewn logs. Rugs hooked from old rags warmed the floors. I remembered when Uncle Misha had taught me the art of rug hooking. I looked around... Yes, there it was. My first attempt at a rug was still in its place of honor by the stove.

The furniture was old and worn, but comfortable. The great room was divided into a kitchen and a living room only by a wooden table. There I had spent many enjoyable afternoons, sipping hot apple cider and reading a new picture book whenever Uncle Misha had been to town.

I was surprised to notice a few modern additions. A coffee maker sat on the counter beside the stove. A radio played classical music beside the hearth, and the old icebox had been replaced by a new refrigerator-freezer. How was he getting electricity here? Was it all solar-powered? I didn't hear any generator outside.

We had each eaten two bowls of stew before Uncle Misha was satisfied that we wouldn't perish from hunger.

"You are a good friend to have come all this way with Anna," Uncle Misha said to Lauraleigh.

"She doesn't understand," I said. "Let me translate."

Uncle Misha's bushy eyebrows crawled up. "A foreigner, huh? And what tongue does she speak?"

"French," I said. "Also English and some German."

He smiled. "You are a good friend to have come all this way with Anna," he repeated in perfect French. Not only that but he spoke with a clearly articulated Swiss accent. How was that possible?

I gasped. "Uncle Misha!"

He chortled and patted me on the head.

"Anna collects good friends," Lauraleigh said. She smiled as if Uncle Misha speaking French were the most natural thing in the world. "She's the bravest, kindest person I know," she added.

I tried not to blush under their gazes. I hadn't gotten over Uncle Misha's language ability. I decided to ask about that later since he didn't seem open to talking about it now.

"Anna was raised well by the bears," Uncle Misha said, but I knew he was pleased. "I am glad to meet Anna's friend. As glad as I am to have my little *Malyshka* back with me again." His eyes turned somber. "I just wish it were under happier circumstances."

"Please, Uncle Misha," I said in French. "Tell me about my father! Your letter mentioned only that he's in trouble, possibly taken by the Red Horseman. But why? Why would Baba Yaga want to hurt my father?"

"Ah, so you know about your grandmother," said Uncle Misha. "I should have guessed that a smart child like you would figure some things out."

"Actually, it was Lauraleigh who realized that's who she is. I don't really know much about her. I read some stories when I was younger, but I don't remember much. All I really know is what Lauraleigh told me. And I got a letter from my mother when I turned thirteen. But it didn't explain much."

"Well then," said Uncle Misha with a sigh, "we would better start at the beginning."

This is what he told us.

It was not the story I was used to.

"First, you need to know about Koschey," Uncle Misha said.

I didn't know the name, but Lauraleigh tensed beside me.

"Koschey goes by many names," Uncle Misha continued. "The Eater of Death, the Immortal One, the Deathless are but a few of them. He is the spirit of death, the dark angel who helps souls after they find their way into the afterlife."

"Like the grim reaper?" I asked, confused.

"Grim, yes, but nothing like that hooded creature with a scythe. Koschey has always been a bit of a stern, forbidding character, though he can be quite handsome and charming when he wants to be. He is immortal, which is why he is grim. Eternal loneliness will do that to a fellow. You see, when everyone around you dies eventually, it is difficult to give your heart away or even strike up friendships. If you know you will have to face the grief of a friend's death — if it is absolutely guaranteed they will leave you and you will remain behind — well, you can see how it would be easier to try and cut yourself off from all that, can't you?"

"So he's an orphan too," Lauraleigh said softly.

Uncle Misha's bushy eyebrows rose.

"Yes, Miss Lauraleigh," he said thoughtfully, "I suppose he is, in a way. I had not thought of it that way before."

His respect for Lauraleigh had definitely grown. So had mine. I wouldn't have made that connection either, but she was right; to be cut off from everyone was to be orphaned. But at least orphans like Lauraleigh and me did have some family: the other orphans, her grandparents, my uncle. Did Koschey have no one at all?

Already I was starting to feel sorry for him.

"Well," Uncle Misha went on. "In his early years, before he had become quite so gloomy, Koschey often fell in love with mortal women — usually ones with flashy tempers and high spirits, as I recall! The relationships did not always end well; when two strong spirits clash, it often does not. But he would be happy enough for a time. Still, even if things lasted, eventually his women would grow old. Eventually, they would die. And as the centuries passed, the less he interacted with people, the fewer his romances became, the more he merely attended to his duties, the more he refused to risk leaving his castle to walk the world, the less he dared speak with those he did not know, for fear he would grow too fond of them. That is when he began to be feared, I suppose — when he retreated and became a mystery to people instead of someone they were familiar with."

We were silent for a moment. Then Lauraleigh said, "You mentioned he deals with souls after they reach the afterlife. Does he also help them on the way?"

"Ah! Aren't you the clever one?" Uncle Misha said with a smile that seemed sad, even rueful. "Certainly, the people who are afraid of him think that. Nobody wants to die, after all. But as I said, Koschey is not a reaper." He gave his rueful smile again and looked at me. "Who do you think stands with one leg in the world of the dead and the other in the world of the living?"

I noticed he didn't quite answer Lauraleigh's question, but his own question distracted me. An old childish rhyme came out of my mouth before I could even think about what Uncle Misha had said. "Baba Yaga — *kostyanaya noga*." Of course! Baba Yaga with a bone leg. How could I have forgotten all those stories? It felt like a veil was being lifted from my memories. "We read all those stories together in this very cabin," I said. "Why did I only just remember that?"

Uncle Misha shrugged. "I do not know, *Malyshka*. Maybe you were simply too young to remember. Or maybe someone has played with your memory. If you do not mind, tell me: What was in the letter that you received from your mother?"

"I don't mind at all," I said. I pulled Mother's letter, Squire and the drawing of the house on chicken legs and gave them to Uncle Misha. "The drawing comes alive in the moonlight. And Squire in a flame."

"I know," he said. "I will not read your letter. Words are private." Instead, he looked at Squire and the drawing. He tapped the old woman in the drawing and sighed. "Yes. This is how she looks now.

"But she was not always ugly. Once, she was young and beautiful and full of fiery passion, just the sort of woman Koschey had always admired. And they were colleagues of a sort, both working with the souls of the dead: she at the moment of their death, he after.

"Now I do not know the entire story," he said. "Neither Koschey or Baba Yaga ever revealed it. There are many versions as to why they became enemies. The rumor I have heard most often — though I have never had the courage to ask Koschey about its truth — says that she attempted to make him fall in love with her. Those who tell that story disagree as to whether it was because she was in love with him or because she wished to trick him in some way. But what they all agree on is that for whatever reason, he spurned her."

Uncle Misha stopped to fill his pipe. For a long moment, we sat in silence, thinking about his words. Uncle Misha lit the pipe and settled back in his chair to continue.

"Well, Baba Yaga has never taken well to being rejected. Some say this was when she lost her teeth, from gnashing them together in her rage. I do not know if that is true, but certainly, at some point, she lost her youth and beauty fast, like a dandelion tossing seeds to the wind. And as her beauty faded, her power increased. Again, some say it happens to all witches; their lost youth is the price they pay for their power. But I do not know that. I stay away from witches."

I felt hot blood rush to my face. "*I'm* a witch, Uncle."

He reached out and ran the back of his hand along my cheek. "Do not get upset, *Malyshka*. You just need to stay human. Do not use that power that tries to settle inside you. Ignore it."

"Ignore it?" I didn't even try to hide my disappointment.

"*Monsieur Michel*," Lauraleigh said before I could protest any further, "do you mean Anna Sophia will lose a bit of her youth every time she uses magic?"

Uncle Misha nodded.

"That is how I understand it," he said, "but I may well be wrong, for I am no expert in magic and have no wish to be one. My own affairs are with the living world, where there is no more magic than the turning of the seasons, the blooming of the flowers, and the growing of the trees. I deal not with spirits, for the lives I am concerned with are those of the animals: the beasts, be they predator or prey, and the birds, whose power to fly comes from the strength of their wings and not from some spell. Their lives have been set in their pattern for generations, the pattern that things must germinate and be born and ripen, and one day die. Then from their bones may grow that which their children and their children's children may feast upon so that they too may flourish and be fruitful — and have no need of witchery."

Uncle Misha's voice seemed to grow deeper and stronger as he spoke, as if thunder were rumbling beneath his words. He suddenly seemed impressive in the dim light as though the years had fallen from him. A sense of power enveloped him that I had never felt from him before. Even Lauraleigh seemed to feel it.

Again, we sat in silence for a long while, each lost in our private thoughts. I found that silence unbearable. What did he mean, I should ignore my power? No matter what he said, how could I give up that wonderful feeling of freedom that came from using it? The ability to fly? To protect those I cared about?

"No, no, that can't be right," I said. "It's only when I use my magic to hurt someone—"

"That darkness enters your heart," Uncle Misha said, interrupting me. "Yes, I know. But Anna, can you risk its use? The bears do not need magic, Anna. Assuredly, you do not either."

I didn't know what to say.

Uncle Misha continued his story. "In any case, there grew a feud between Koschey and Baba Yaga, whatever its cause. It became dangerous to be friends with either of them, for then the other inevitably became your enemy. But it was just as impossible to stay neutral. Nobody knew how it would end, because nobody understood what victory would be for either of them. Some rumors said that Baba Yaga was seeking to bind Koschey to her will, while others claimed that Koschey had started it all by refusing to let Baba Yaga continue escorting the dead to the gates of his realm. How could such a war ever end?

"But then, one day, something entirely unexpected happened. I do not know how. One does not learn these secrets. You must understand, this was not open warfare, at least not often. Koschey and Baba Yaga are not the types one sees often. So there will always be gaps in the tale.

"But this much is certain: At some point, Koschey met and fell in love with Baba Yaga's daughter, Sereda."

"My mother?" I asked in a squeaky voice, forgetting my disappointment at what Uncle Misha had said about my power and the price I was paying for using it. Those thoughts were of no importance. Uncle Misha was talking about my parents, and that was all that mattered now. My mother. Sereda. With whom Koschey had fallen in love.

And now I knew why Uncle Misha had started talking about Koschey.

He nodded. "Your mother." His eyes gazed at a point far away as if for him, the little cabin had melted away and my parents stood before him. My parents. My mother, whose name I now knew, and my father, whose name I had just learned as well.

I wished I could see them in my imagination too, but for me, they were still fuzzy inkblots in a story that seemed too fantastic to be true. Except that I'd seen a wolf turn into a man. I'd seen a statue of a hand come to life. I'd flown in a bucket, and I'd felt cold darkness creep into my chest. I knew that even the most fantastic story could be true. And despite the horrors in this tale, I wanted it to be true. I wanted to believe that my parents had fallen in love and were being kept apart — kept away from me — only by an evil witch.

"This part of the story I do know," Uncle Misha went on. "For I played my part in it. I knew your father, Anna Sophia. He used to visit me quite often. He liked the peacefulness of this little lake. Koschey would sit on the dock with fishing poles, not really expecting to catch anything, and he would tell me stories of his youth. Oh, those stories. Even then, I knew I was privileged to be the recipient of such tales. Though he would never tell me everything.

"But one day he showed up without my expecting him at all. I had never seen him like that. Bedraggled, exhausted, with a look in his eyes I would have called fear, had he been anyone else. His clothes were as ragged as his breathing. And he had a young woman with him. Sereda.

"That was the first time I met your mother," said Uncle Misha, nodding at me. "She was not well. So very pale, and circles under her eyes, as much from sorrow as from tiredness. She would not speak. I took both of them into my cabin and fed them. For three days, Sereda scarcely moved. She just lay there on that bed, sipping the soup I spooned into her mouth but nothing else, staring up at the ceiling. Koschey never left her side. He sat right here on the hard floor, his gaze fixed on her, his hands clutching hers. I had never seen such devotion and never have since."

Uncle Misha took a deep draw on his pipe and let the smoke out slowly. His eyes were distant as if he saw in the smoke what he was telling us.

"After three days, she finally fell asleep, and I was able to take Koschey aside. I walked him out to the shore. He was as malleable as a child. It was frightening; he seemed utterly defeated, and worse — uncertain. I told him he had to let me know what was going on. If nothing else, by the laws of hospitality, he owed me the truth.

"That was when I discovered who your mother was, Anna Sophia. I will not say it was not a shock, because it was.

I knew, vaguely, that Baba Yaga had a daughter, of course. But I had no idea she was anything other than a child. And for her to be here with Koschey, and for him to be so clearly in love with her — well. There were always stories in the old days that Koschey was in the habit of kidnapping the women he loved. But this was clearly different.

"I had to shake his shoulders more than once to get the story from him. I cannot begin to explain to you what that was like. Your father is not the sort of man one touches, let alone roughly. But it seemed the only way to make him react. Still, eventually he told me. For some reason, he had been in Baba Yaga's house. He would never tell me why or for how long, but he had been.

"He met Sereda, and they fell in love behind her mother's back. But at some point, she found out, and her anger was terrible. They had to run, to flee from her. So he took her to the only safe place he could think of, the only peaceful haven he knew. Where his friend, the Great Trapper, could keep watch over them and Baba Yaga would never look for them."

"Did she?" Lauraleigh asked. She was clearly as caught up in the story as I was.

"Perhaps," said Uncle Misha, "but if so, she did not find us. The lives of beasts are of no concern to her, and the bears gave us good protection. It is not good," he said with a growl, "to disturb the bears. I have no doubt that she could defeat them all, but she would have to try hard, and the price she would pay would be bitter. She knows better than to attempt it. Perhaps she guessed where your parents were, but she was wise enough not to test her guess."

"What happened then?" I asked. I didn't want us to

waste our time playing guessing games; I wanted to know everything I could be told.

Uncle Misha sighed. "Well, your parents stayed here for some time. Sereda was … in shock, I suppose you could say. She had never known any other life than living with her mother, and she had never faced anybody's anger before. You must understand that your mother was the kindest person I have ever met. But sometimes kindness is paid for with trust, and Sereda had too much of that. When that trust was broken … she did not know how to react. She did not know what to think, what to feel.

"I told you she lay motionless for three days. She did. Then she slept for three more. When she awoke, she wept. Quietly, without a sound, but constantly. I almost wondered if she was mute. And when she did start to speak again, all she said were questions that almost broke my heart. 'Where is my mother?' she asked. 'She must still love me. What did I *do*?' She was utterly lost."

Lauraleigh and I didn't have to look at each other to know what we were each thinking, but we did anyway. We'd heard those questions before; even asked them ourselves. Every time a new orphan came to the orphanage, we heard those questions. The feeling that it must have been your fault you had been abandoned or your parents had died. Yet with the insistence that you'd be found, that your parents were searching for you and would find you eventually, if only you were good. Those feelings never quite left you.

"We did what we could to help," Uncle Misha said, breaking into our thoughts. "Well, me especially. Koschey was almost useless; he had never been very good at comforting people, and besides, he had hardly gotten his strength back either. It was a long recovery. The animals helped, though. Your mother loved animals, Anna Sophia. They would come right up to her hands without fear. She would let ermines run up her arms and tickle her nose with their tails, and birds would settle on her shoulders and chatter at her as if telling her secrets. Then she would laugh, and I would catch a glimpse of the happy girl she must have been. She liked the bears, too. Especially the bears. Sometimes she would even spend the night with them. I think they made her feel safe. Indeed she felt comforted, wrapped in their arms, in the warmth and softness of their fur.

"Slowly she stopped being quite so distraught. She did not become glad, but her tears dried and she stopped asking the questions she knew couldn't be answered. And when she looked at Koschey, there was an expression on her face that said it had all been worth it.

"I kept my ear to the ground, of course. All those I talked to concurred; Baba Yaga had withdrawn even further into the woods. No one knew why, but she had almost disappeared from view. Naturally, this disturbed people who wanted to know what she was plotting. But eventually, it became the new way of things. So much so that your father and mother felt it was safe to leave my cabin and go to Koschey's home."

Uncle Misha heaved a great sigh.

"I will not deny I was somewhat glad. I like my solitude well enough. And perhaps I was more worried than I had let on. I would never have refused Koschey, of course, particularly not after seeing him in the state he had been in when he had arrived here. But even for me, it was better not to get on the bad side of the Boney-Legged One."

"So what happened then?" asked Lauraleigh. "It sounds like the moment when you're supposed to say 'They lived happily ever after,' but it isn't, is it?"

"No," said Uncle Misha gravely, "it is not. Though then again, perhaps for you, it is. For if the story had ended there, you and Anna would never have met."

Lauraleigh looked shocked. "That doesn't mean I wish that — well, that whatever happened next had happened! How can you suggest that?"

"No," Uncle Misha said, and I thought I caught a glint of a smile behind his beard. "Of course not, and I apologize if it seemed I was suggesting you would be glad. But … do you think you would be happier or even as happy as you are, if you did not know our Anna? No, you do not have to answer that. I am merely trying to show you… When a tree falls, it is a great pity, of course. Yet it will become a home for badgers and squirrels and food for insects that will become the food of birds. Do you see? However great the misfortune, there is something good, however small, that will come of it."

Lauraleigh looked as though she wanted to protest, but she could find no argument.

"So what did happen?" I said timidly. I wasn't sure I wanted to know, but it was too late to stop now.

Uncle Misha tapped his pipe against his heel. As he continued, he began to clean and refill it.

"Humans are curious creatures," he said. "Humans and those of us who are like them. Look at the animals. True, they love one another. But at some stage, the parents will chase the younglings away. Look at Mama Bear. Before today, you had never met any of the cubs who are with her now. When they reach the right age, she pushes them out of the den, and then they must find their own way. And it is well; they survive on their own, and if they meet their mother in the wild, they will not fight, but they will never seek her out. Birds will push their fledglings out of the nest, only weeks after they were carefully bringing them food. It would seem an unalterable law of nature. And yet for us, it is not so. We cling to our families. Even after we leave because it is our time to leave, we keep in touch, and when that link is broken, we suffer for it. But I do not need to tell you that, you who grew up in an orphanage."

I don't know if Lauraleigh had grabbed my hand or I had grabbed hers, but we were squeezing each other's hands for comfort.

"It was the same with Sereda," said Uncle Misha. "However happy she was with Koschey, no matter how much time passed, the loss of her mother had wounded her deeply. So how could we expect her to react, the day Baba Yaga sent her a letter, promising that all was well between them and begging her to visit?"

I gasped.

Uncle Misha nodded gravely.

"Yes, indeed," he said. "You came swiftly enough when your old Uncle Misha sent you a letter asking you to visit. What would you have done, had it come from your mother?"

"So Sereda went?" said Lauraleigh.

"Yes. Much to Koschey's fear. But he would not stop her, for he loved her too much to command her to do or not do anything. But he had two good reasons to fear. Not least *because* of how much he loved her. You see, sometime before — maybe not long after they had escaped from Baba Yaga, I'm not sure — he had given her the greatest proof of his love and trust in her that he could. He had given Sereda his heart."

There was a long silence.

"I don't understand," I said at last.

"Neither do I," said Lauraleigh. "That's just a phrase people use, isn't it? It just means you're really in love with someone, if you give them your heart."

Uncle Misha chuckled. "Miss Lauraleigh, you must forgive me if I laugh. I had forgotten that you are human," he said. "And you, *Malyshka*, I had forgotten that you had lived so long among humans.

"No, when I say that Koschey had given Sereda his heart, I mean it quite literally. I cannot really explain it to you; it is not an area in which I am an expert. But certain beings — certain persons with enough power, like Koschey or perhaps Baba Yaga — can actually extract their hearts from their chests.

"Your heart holds your life and much of your power. Anyone who got ahold of it would be able to do anything to you: kill you, take your strength, or… I do not even know. So it is a grave matter to remove your own heart.

"But Koschey did it. I think he was worried in case he ever found himself in Baba Yaga's power again. You see, without his heart, even if she did capture him, there was a limit to how much she could do to him. Certainly she would not be able to take over the Kingdom of the Dead, if that was her intent."

"So even if she has him, he's safe?" I interrupted.

"Perhaps," said Uncle Misha. "Perhaps. We must hope so. But this was not the main reason Koschey removed his own heart. I think he did so mostly to prove to Sereda how much he loved her, how much he had faith in her. To let her know she was that cherished, that trusted. After having been abandoned by her mother, it must have meant the world to her.

"Koschey told her to hide it somewhere no one else would think to look, and to tell no one — not even him — where it was. That way, if Baba Yaga captured him, even he could not tell her where his heart was. However, if Sereda ever turned against him, he would be entirely in her power. That was how much he trusted her.

"Yet he was still worried when she received that letter from her mother. However much he trusted her, he still worried that Baba Yaga might manage to trick Sereda into telling. He felt certain that Baba Yaga had discovered that he had removed his heart and Sereda knew where it was hidden. Well. He need not have worried. As it turned out, Sereda loved him more than she did her mother. Much to her misfortune."

Silence fell over us once again. Uncle Misha seemed reluctant to go on.

"What was the other reason?" Lauraleigh suddenly asked.

"I beg your pardon?"

"The second reason. You said Koschey had two good reasons to fear if Sereda went to visit her mother."

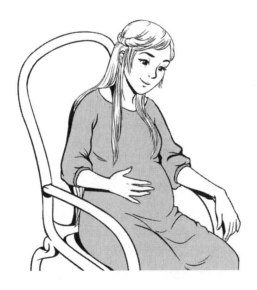

"Ah, yes, so I did," said Uncle Misha. He knocked his pipe on his boot again, added more tobacco, and lit it again. He puffed on it, closing his eyes as though he wanted to avoid what was coming next. Then he opened them and fixed his gaze directly on me.

"Sereda was with child," he said.

Somehow, the room had grown colder. Despite the wood stove in the corner that was well lit against the evening cold, despite the coziness I had felt only moments before, the snug little room now felt like a vast, gloomy stone hall. Uncle Misha and Lauraleigh were no longer there, just fuzzy visions out of the corners of my eyes, as unreal as the patterns of the rugs hanging on the walls.

Uncle Misha was still talking, and I heard him as if I were at the bottom of a well, his voice distant and echoing, unreachable but inescapable.

"It soon became all too obvious that Sereda was a prisoner in Baba Yaga's hut," that deep voice went on. "Koschey was frantic, all ready to gather an army to fall on her but terrified that doing so would put Sereda — and the baby — in danger. He was paralyzed with indecision, not wishing to risk his beloved but terrified that soon Baba Yaga would break her resistance to revealing her secret and enable her to conquer him once and for all.

"But Sereda was no longer the helpless girl she had been all those years before. She had realized soon enough that she was her mother's prisoner. She managed not to reveal her secret, to trick Baba Yaga into thinking that she was docile, she did not know. Then she escaped. No one knows how, but she did. She fled to the one place of safety she knew: the cave of the bears where she had once felt herself protected. She told no one as she nestled up against a whelping mother bear, who put her arms around her in comfort as they both

86

groaned in childbirth. And Sereda's daughter was born along with the mother bear's litter of cubs. But she had been weakened by her flight, Sereda had, and by the ordeal of pregnancy and giving birth. Soon after, she died."

I covered my mouth with my hands, but Uncle Misha went on relentlessly.

"But the mother bear took the child into her arms like one of her very own cubs and kept her warm and fed, and Sereda's spirit appeared to the one friend she knew could help. And so the Great Trapper came to the bear cave and found there a small human child. He gathered her up and wrapped her in furs and took her to his home. And desperately though he might have wished to have his daughter with him, Koschey knew that he could not risk it. If Baba Yaga learned of her existence, she would seek to use the child just as she had used her own.

"So little Anna Sophia stayed with the Great Trapper, and she listened to fairy tales and learned how to hook a rug and catch a fish, and Koschey pretended not to know she existed. But Baba Yaga found out about you, Anna. And she has been looking for you. She has never given up on finding Koschey's heart, and I think she believes you know where it is or you can find it.

"And now, though I do not know how they caught him, she had her Horsemen kidnap Koschey. In hopes of luring you home, I think."

I could see the thought in Lauraleigh's eyes: *And it worked.*

"I know this is not the story I told you, Anna Sophia," Uncle Misha said. "But you were bound for Geneva one day, as per your mother's wish, and I felt your best protection against the dark forces who would seek you out was your innocence. I would never have risked bringing you back here if the need were not great. If Baba Yaga does not release your father soon, we will all be in grave danger. Without him, souls can no longer stay in the afterlife. They cannot reach their rightful place. We are being overrun with angry, unsettled ghosts. And Baba Yaga will not release him until she has his heart, which will only make things worse. With it, she will be able to control those ghosts. Every single one of them."

I shivered at the thought of so many ghosts haunting my beautiful home. And if Baba Yaga could control them, what kind of horrors could she unleash?

"But what can I do?" I asked in a weak voice.

"We shall see, *Malyshka*," said Uncle Misha. "We shall see. But it is safer for you here with me than in Geneva, where Baba Yaga's henchmen found you. It is safer for all of us."

He puffed deeply on his pipe again. It seemed his tale was over.

Uncle Misha's story swirled in my head. So many pieces of a puzzle. So many questions still unanswered.

"So you're the Great Trapper?" I asked, remembering Gavril's fear at the mere mention of the name.

"I am," said Uncle Misha gravely. "Koschey would not have given himself in friendship to an ordinary man. To him, mortal men live and die in a heartbeat."

"You're immortal?" Lauraleigh asked with wide eyes.

He laughed. "No. Not immortal. But enduring. I have lived as long as a score or more of men, even those liars in the Caucasus who insist they all live till they're a hundred and twenty. But the winters seem harsher to me now. Even in the summers, my bones ache in the mornings. One day, I will enter the land of the dead just like everyone else, and there will be another Great Trapper, somewhere, who will take my place. But you, my darling *Malyshka*, may not be so lucky."

"Me?"

Uncle Misha put down his pipe. The fire had burned low, leaving only a red glow to light our faces.

"You, Anna Sophia, are Koschey's heir. It is said he cannot die. But should something happen to him, should he no longer be able to fulfill his duties, you will inherit his kingdom. With all the power and responsibilities that come with it. You will become the Deathless One."

Chapter 6

ear Diary,

My mother's name is Sereda. My father is Koschey, and I'm the heir to the kingdom of the dead.

I write these words down to make them feel real. It still seems so impossible, like a fairy tale that Uncle Misha spun around a campfire. Maybe, when I meet my father, he'll seem real. For now … he's nothing more than a shadow.

Lauraleigh refuses to go home. I know I must continue on my journey. I must find my father, as much for his safety and the world's as for my sanity. But it will be dangerous, and I don't want Lauraleigh caught up in this strange family feud. From what Uncle Misha says, my granny can pack a mean punch.

But Lauraleigh says she will see this through. "I was looking for adventure, after all," she said.

Adventure. Right. This isn't the same as backpacking across Europe and staying in youth hostels while visiting museums and attending concerts. That's the kind of adventure I wish for her. Instead, I've invited her along to storm a witch's home and possibly visit the kingdom of the dead. What teenage girl wouldn't beg for such a trip?

We had no time to waste. Every day my father was held captive, more souls were entering death without being able to find their rightful place in the afterlife. I thought of the ghostly figures I'd seen in the forest and wondered if those were lost souls.

"Could be," Uncle Misha said. "Though I have not seen any this far up the mountain. I expect villages and towns see a lot more."

I shuddered, thinking that the cities could soon be smothered in a fog of the dead. We had to find my father fast.

After some discussion, we decided that the best course of action was to go to the source.

"You understand that we cannot just walk up to Baba Yaga's house and demand to see Koschey," Uncle Misha said. "She has wards — powerful magic, like booby traps — set up all around her place."

"But we need to know if she's keeping him there, Monsieur Michel," said Lauraleigh. "We don't have to ring her doorbell, but we should at least scout the house and the surrounding area."

I nodded in agreement. "Even if Koschey isn't there, we need to learn as much about our enemy as possible."

Uncle Misha sighed and gave me another of his sad smiles. "Your enemy, huh? It pains me to hear you speak of your grandmother in such a way."

"You mean old Iron Teeth?" I asked. "How else should I think of her? She kidnapped my father and made my mother die in a bear's den. And she tried to kidnap me too! Her Black

Horseman stole children from our town. Who knows how many they had taken before I stopped them? And what did she do with those children?"

Uncle Misha's face looked bleak. I suspected he knew exactly what Baba Yaga did with children but he wasn't about to tell me. I remembered what Lauraleigh had told me about the myths, and my mind conjured up the story of Hansel and Gretel. *Ugh.*

"Just remember," he said. "She is your blood almost as much as Koschey is. Maybe we can find some advantage in that."

I decided not to remind Uncle Misha about the shadow that grew inside me every time I used my magic for evil. How many people had Baba Yaga hurt with her magic? How black were the shadows in her heart? I'd never let the shadows take over as she likely had.

We packed for a long journey.

"Can't the bears take us again?" Lauraleigh asked.

"Best to let them rest," Uncle Misha said. "This is berry season. Bears need to pack on the weight now to get through the long winter. Another journey now will set them back in their feeding. But I have just the solution. Mama Bear and her cubs cannot help us, but the grizzlies can."

Now I knew Uncle Misha was being silly. There were no grizzly bears in Siberia. But when I told him that, he only smiled knowingly and threw his pack over his shoulder. Lauraleigh and I followed him around the back of the cabin. For the first time, I noticed a new shed built of rough timbers. Uncle Misha pulled open the door, which rolled up like in a garage. Inside were two green, mud-spattered ATVs.

Uncle Misha beamed proudly. "Grizzlies!"

"You mean the Great Trapper rides an ATV?" Lauraleigh said with a grin. "Wouldn't that shock our friend Gavril!"

"Uncle Misha!" I protested. "You hate technology! You always told me it makes people lazy. And now you don't just have a radio and a fridge, but ATVs?" I was actually more shocked than I sounded.

Uncle Misha grinned.

"It does make you lazy," he said. "It leaves you with no actual connection to the land. You cannot feel the slow growth of the seeds beneath the snow and the soil when you ride such machines. But sometimes..." and he waggled his thick eyebrows, "they are useful. Besides, I am old. I am allowed some comfort and a little music. Not to mention some inconsistencies. It is the best thing about getting old."

"Monsieur Michel!" Lauraleigh exclaimed in a sharp tone that sounded so much like Sister Constance that I gaped. Then she grinned. "I do believe, sir, that you are a terrible rogue."

Uncle Misha grinned back again and did not deny the charge.

After a quick driving lesson for Lauraleigh, I hopped on the ATV behind Uncle Misha and wrapped my arms around his waist. Starting right from the back of the shed, Uncle Misha had already carved a path through the thick trees. The four-wheelers plowed steadily up the steep hill.

"We can't go over the mountain!" he yelled over the noise of the engine. "The path gets too rocky. We'll have to skirt around the side!"

Soon our path leveled off. The ATVs were faster than bears, faster than horses too — I felt a sudden pang, thinking about Dushá and Kísa. I hoped they had returned safely to Anton's barn.

Before the sun hit high noon, we had already made it to the other side of the mountain. We stopped to drink from our canteens. After the constant roar of the engines, the silence of the forest was unsettling.

"Unless she has moved — and I have no reason to think she has — your grandmother lives in a ravine just over that ridge," said Uncle Misha.

I nodded as if he were just talking about the weather, but my stomach was a jumble of knots.

I jumped when a man stepped out from behind a tree and walked right through one of the ATVs. He looked shimmery, like from an old movie, and pale. The apparition didn't stop to notice us but just kept walking. He had a confused, angry expression on his face — an *unsettled* one. Not a twig moved as he melted into the shadows between the trees.

I gasped. "A ghost!"

Lauraleigh grabbed my arm. Though apparently she couldn't see the ghost, my alarm at its sudden appearance terrified her.

"This one got far. I fear we will be seeing more of these before the end of this journey," said Uncle Misha. "We must hurry!"

We jumped back on the ATVs and drove in the same direction as the ghost had gone. We didn't see him again. Neither did we see any sign of wildlife. I expected the loud engines to scare off everything but the wolves, but even the White Horseman and his pack were strangely absent. I started to hope that we'd reach my grandmother's house without any fuss.

I should have known better.

We raced along a riverbank. A field of wildflowers rolled down to the river on our right. The forest still crowded the far side of the bank, and the river headed toward the opening of a steep ravine.

Uncle Misha stopped his ATV, and Lauraleigh pulled in beside us.

"Her house is in that ravine." He pointed to where the river disappeared between two massive outcroppings of stone. "We cannot take the ATVs in there. She will hear them. And we will have to move slowly, checking for traps along the way."

But Uncle Misha made no move to get off the ATV.

"What are we waiting for?" I asked. I wanted to get this over with. Now that we were so close, I wanted to meet my grandmother, for good or ill.

"Ah, *Malyshka*, have you forgotten everything I taught you?" asked Uncle Misha. "We are always both the hunter and the hunted. Never forget that. Even when your prey is within sight, stop and test the wind. Make sure that some other bigger predator isn't waiting in the shadows."

So we waited. Uncle Misha's eyes were focused on the ravine. And just when I thought he'd have to give up, I heard the sound of hooves clattering over stone.

"This way!" Uncle Misha fired up the ATV and pointed to the open field. The ATVs strained up the steep bank; then they burst onto the field. I chanced a glance behind us and saw the three Horsemen riding out of the ravine. One was all in black, with a long ponytail flying behind him. One was dressed only in red, with a bushy beard like a lion's mane.

And the other was the White Horseman, the white wolf. Their nimble horses had no trouble with the steep bank, and they were soon galloping across the field in our wake.

Birds scattered before us. We bounced over hillocks and into crevices until I thought my teeth would be jarred loose from my head. We nearly tipped over on one bump, and Uncle Misha slowed down. With her knuckles white on the handlebars and her expression bleak, Lauraleigh kept her grizzly close. But the horses could leap over all the obstacles that were impeding us. They were gaining on us.

Though the jarring of the ATV was painful, I couldn't help but turn in my seat and watch our doom speed toward us. The three Horsemen were only a couple of hundred meters away. Their horses — black, red, and white — foamed at the mouths. Then they were fifty meters away. I could see the ferocious grimace on the Black Horseman's face. Probably he still hadn't forgiven me for breaking up his little business of selling children into slavery. Then twenty meters away.

They were going to catch us!

The ATV leaped out of the field and onto a solid dirt road. Uncle Misha hollered with glee. He revved his engine and we sped off, leaving the Horsemen in the dust.

After quite a ride, we rounded a corner and stopped.

"You all right, Lauraleigh?" I asked.

She nodded. Her entire body was visibly shaking. "I thought they had us for sure!"

"They might have three horsepower altogether," said Uncle Misha with a grin, "but my grizzlies have forty-five horsepower apiece. They will not catch us now. Come on.

Blackwood Castle is not too far. We can stop there for the night."

To call Blackwood a castle was generous of Uncle Misha. Once it might have been a beautiful and forbidding structure, but now it mostly resembled a pile of rubble with turrets. Sometime in the last century, most of the great arched windows and doors had been bricked up. We parked the ATVs in a space that had probably been the keep but which was now crowded with brambles. An ambitious sapling had grown through the gate into the watchtower above. Crumbled stones littered the ground.

Something in the air made me nervous. Not the obvious aura of death and ruin that surrounded the site. Something else. I … felt the hum of magic here. Old magic. It made my fingers tingle and the hairs on the back of my neck stand at attention.

Uncle Misha tried the main door, a massive oaken plank bound in iron. It moved only a few inches when he shoved. Stones and leaves showered him from above and he jumped back. The lintel above the door was crumbling to dust.

"We'd better find another way in," he said.

I wasn't convinced that we should stay among these ruins at all, but around the back of the manor, we found a cellar door in surprisingly good shape. It didn't even squeak when Uncle Misha pulled it open.

"Come on," he said. "I expect we have been heard by now."

We followed him into the dark cellar.

"Heard? By whom?" I asked. "The vultures who'll pick our bones when we die in this place?"

Lauraleigh snorted back a laugh.

"Do not be dramatic," Uncle Misha said. "I have stayed here many times. We will be most welcome."

A huge black beast jumped from the shadows and flattened Uncle Misha onto the dirt floor. I saw a flashing of sharp white teeth and a spray of drool. Magic flared in me; it had become instinctive. But before I could zap the creature, Uncle Misha laughed.

"Koshmarik! Get off, you great oaf!"

The beast — called Little Nightmare, no less — had Uncle Misha pinned under two massive paws and was licking his face with a tongue as big and slimy as an eel.

"What is that?" Lauraleigh asked, her voice squeaking with tension.

My hands shook with unreleased magic. How close had I come to killing a friendly beast out of fear? Had I forgotten Uncle Misha's talent with animals, forgotten that he was the Great Trapper and did not have to fear them? I was trembling; I'd have to control myself better.

"It's a hellhound," said a sharp voice from the darkness. "Given to me as a pup from the Eater of Death himself. Let the poor man up, Koshmarik."

The hellhound stepped off Uncle Misha and he stood up, wiping the creature's drool from his face and shirt. The beast was as tall as my shoulder, with patchy black hair and a grotesque face, like a cross between a monkey and a bulldog. His tongue lolled happily from his black lips, and drool puddled at his feet.

"Your breath has aged like fine cheese," Uncle Misha said, patting the hound on his head. "And how have you fared this past winter, Egor?"

A small man dressed in rags came out of the darkness to shake Uncle Misha's hand heartily.

"As well as ever, old friend. Glad to see you still alive and kicking, Misha. So many of the old gang are gone now … so many gone." Egor's eyes glistened a bit, but his smile showed several crooked yellow teeth. He was bald on top, but long wispy white hair hung down from his chin and the back of his head.

"It is still good to be alive," Uncle Misha replied. His words were strangely formal, and I wondered if this was a traditional greeting between the two men.

"So who have you brought us for a visit?"

"This is my niece, Anna Sophia. And her friend, Lauraleigh."

Egor looked way up to take in Lauraleigh's height and grinned. She was at least a head taller than he was. He took her hand and bowed as low as he could over it, which wasn't much, and gave it a dramatic kiss. She gave him a nice smile, although I could tell she understood very little of what was going on. Uncle Misha and his friend were speaking Russian.

Egor took my hand and a spark of magic shot between us. I jerked my hand back, shaking away the sting.

"Oho!" he said. "You brought a witch to visit me! How delightful. We'll have to put out the good china for certain." He hurried away down a long tunnel that I had only just noticed as my eyes grew accustomed to the dark cellar. Koshmarik bounded after his master, and we followed.

After a few steps, the tunnel changed from a dirt passageway to a stone-lined corridor. Every ten paces, strange blue torches burned without smoke in iron holders along the wall. The floor sloped upward at a steady angle.

"He lives in here?" I whispered in French. "Is it safe?"

"The ruins keep all but the most determined tourists away," Uncle Misha said. "Egor likes his privacy. I assure you the inner keep is quite safe. Old magic holds up these walls."

We emerged from the dark tunnel into a courtyard. Egor had made an effort to keep this one clear of weeds and brambles, but the small stone huts that had once been the smithy, the stable and other essentials of castle life had fallen into rubble. Egor walked past these ruins without a glance and led us into a tower and up its unending spiral staircase. I was nearly winded by the time we reached the top. He swung open another huge oaken door and closed it behind us with a chilling thud, after which he dropped a heavy plank into place across the door.

I looked nervously at Uncle Misha, but he seemed unconcerned that we were essentially prisoners of this strange little man. The room was round and cluttered with shelves of books and trinkets. On a table in the center sat a large scale, a telescope, and several other pieces of equipment that would have looked at home in an alchemist's lab.

"Well, let me just clear this mess, and we'll have some dinner, yes?" Egor waved his hand, and all the junk on the table disappeared. After an initial surge of panic, my mind settled down. *Of course, Egor just cleaned the place up*, I thought; *I must have simply glanced away.*

Another jiggle of his fingers, and platters of food appeared along with jugs of beer and water, plates, and cups. With a final twitch, he set a roaring fire in the hearth.

I blinked. "You're a wizard!" I exclaimed. My memory was desperately trying to serve up images of Egor cooking in the hearth, although I knew the new memories weren't real. But my mind seemed in urgent need of logical explanations.

"Of course I am," Egor said. He paused, looking at me with a smirk before adding, "Although it doesn't take much to master such things. It's all here." He patted his stomach. "The timeless intent."

I didn't understand what he meant, although I did recognize that magic came out of the pit of the stomach. Mine did too.

"You don't understand, huh?" he asked with a smile.

I shook my head. "I'm confused. It's like my brain is trying to explain things. Things I know didn't happen."

He clicked his fingers as though looking for words. "How can I say it simply? See, time is that illusion people have. Mirage. Hocus-pocus."

I rolled my eyes — not to annoy him but to play along. I was starting to like this strange little man. "Right."

He composed an exaggerated frown on his face, teasing me. "Time doesn't exist," he said slowly. "It's just a marker of sorts, separating one event from another. So when I would like hot food on my table, the power of my intent travels back in time. It's like an arm of pure energy, reaching out from my belly button. *Et voilà!* It turns out I had already cooked all this food just before you came. On that fire." He nodded toward the roaring hearth.

"You did?" I asked with some relief. "You cooked all this?"

Egor gave me a happy wink and smiled. "I love cooking." He bowed and performed a series of gestures welcoming us to the table. His moves were decidedly medieval in their complexity. "Now let's eat before you tell me why those three Horsemen have parked themselves outside my keep."

I translated for Lauraleigh, and we ran to the window and peered through the shutters. Sure enough, three horses — black, red, and white — and their riders were in the yard where we had left the grizzlies. The Horsemen sat in their saddles, unmoving, watching the keep.

"How did they find us?" I asked.

"Those metal beasts you rode in on are hard to miss," Egor said. "They leave a stink a kilometer long and tracks that are easier to follow than a railway."

105

"I hoped they would not find us so soon," said Uncle Misha grimly. "I wanted to be away from here before they tracked us."

"That's always your problem, Misha," said Egor. "You forget that others can track as well as you." His words sounded harsh, but his eyes sparkled as if he'd told a great joke. "Remember that time I stole a beard hair from that old wizard? What was his name?"

"Bogumil," Uncle Misha said with a shy grin.

"Right! And you said he'd never find us in the forest? Ha! That old codger tracked us within half a day. Gave us such a hiding with his magic cane, even my father felt sorry for us — and he was never one to go lightly with the cane!"

"I remember." Uncle Misha rubbed his backside as if it still pained him.

"What did you need the beard hair for?" I asked.

"For a spell, of course," Egor said, and stuffed a whole pickled egg in his mouth.

"Young wizards think they can boost their magic by adding the hair of a more potent witch or wizard," said Uncle Misha. "But if you ask me … it is all show. The real power comes from inside you, not from some old grump's hair."

Egor nodded along in agreement, but his mouth was too full to speak. He looked well satisfied with my uncle's explanation.

"Didn't you say using magic makes you grow old?" I asked Uncle Misha as I tried to study his friend without being too obvious.

Egor swallowed his egg, winked at me, stopped my uncle with a gesture and said, "Well, it can, if you're foolish enough to use too much of it. See, there are many ways to build up your strength, but you can only keep so much energy at once. Or you'll explode like a balloon! So you have to use it at some point. But if you try to use more than you have — well, the magic must find the energy somewhere, and so it takes it from your life and youth. And oops, suddenly you look like old Boney Leg! And there's no going back from that." He chortled.

"And if you're not that foolish?" I asked.

Egor licked his fingers with gusto and said, "Then you use other ways to build the energy. Like I do. But let's leave this topic for now. Enjoy your food."

Uncle Misha sipped his ale. The drink smelled of honey. "Well, I am sorry to bring trouble to your doorstep again, Egor," he said.

"It's no matter. A little excitement is good for my blood." Egor tossed a large shank of meat and bone on the floor. Koshmarik pounced on it and started gnawing with great snuffles and snorts.

I was doing my best to translate into French for Lauraleigh, but there was no way I could replicate Uncle Misha's and Egor's amusing intonations. It felt like those intonations combined with their words to form communication; they were creating an odd feeling of distance from my daily reality, of soaring above the castle, of not taking anything too seriously. Even Baba Yaga seemed rather unimportant ... and even the search for my father.

Egor listened to my translation with a raised eyebrow and a distracted expression. He approached Lauraleigh and sniffed the air in front of her. "Ah! You don't have the Russian spirit at all, foreign girl," he said in smooth French that sounded nicely old-fashioned. His words were odd although his intonation, again, was spellbinding. "You shouldn't be here. No, no. You must go away soon."

Lauraleigh looked as startled as I was. "What do you mean?" she asked.

"Lands … territories … they have certain energies, you see. They make some people stronger and others weaker. It all depends on, well, your frequency."

"My *frequency*?" Lauraleigh seemed ready to laugh at this nonsense.

Egor looked unaffected by her change of mood. "Yes. This particular spot, my castle, gives off a mixture of Buryat and Russian energy. You…" He sniffed Lauraleigh again, making her take a step back in mock alarm. "You're tuned to a foreign wave."

"I still don't understand what this means, monsieur," Lauraleigh said.

"You'll suffer here, that's all," Egor informed her with a dismissive wave of his hand. "Ah, to come so far into a foreign land! What were you thinking?"

Uncle Misha picked a sliver of meat from a platter on the table. "Do not listen to him, young ladies," he said. "And you, Lauraleigh. You are among friends here. That is the only wave that matters."

A stubborn wrinkle appeared on Egor's bare forehead. "She'll suffer," he insisted. "May die too."

"So what should we do?" I asked. I didn't like where the strange old man's words seemed to be going. I had already exposed Lauraleigh to a lot of dangers; I did not intend to make things even worse for her.

"At least have her drink lots of local water," Egor said. "That'll help adjust her energy. Well … a little."

Lauraleigh and I filled our plates and cups. Although alarmed, I was suddenly starving. Breakfast had been hours ago, and I'd been running on adrenaline for the last while. There were freshly cooked meats, piles of fruit, and bread still warm from the oven. All of which Egor had conjured with the wave of a hand. (My mind was reluctantly starting to accept that.) As I gobbled down my dinner, I resolved to learn how to master magic too — without using the power of my life, if possible. No matter what Uncle Misha had said, one day it might mean the difference between starvation and survival.

"So did this witch just show up at your cabin like the last one?" Egor asked. He wiped a greasy hand on his beard and grinned. "Seems all the pretty witches find their way to your cabin, don't they? Especially the ones with red hair."

"I guess they do," Uncle Misha said. "In fact, this pretty witch is the daughter of the last one."

Egor choked, and Uncle Misha pounded him on the back.

"You mean…" Egor coughed, looking at me. "You mean you're Sereda's daughter?"

"That's what Uncle Misha tells me," I said.

Egor's happy demeanor seemed to dim a little.

"I should have known," he said quietly. "You look like her. Well, little witch, I'm glad to know you. I just wish it were under happier circumstances. You know, do you not, that your father is a captive? And of whom?"

"I know," I said. "I'm going to get him back."

Egor shook his head, but the look in his eyes was not displeased.

After dinner, we saw that the Horsemen were gone, but we all knew they'd return, possibly with my grandmother in tow. We planned to be gone before then, but Egor refused to let us travel by night.

"There are darker things than the old Queen's henchmen in those woods," he said. "You know that, Misha. Rest here tonight and travel by day when the monsters sleep."

Sounds like a good plan to me, I thought.

"I'm going to move the grizzlies around back," said Uncle Misha.

"I'll come help," Lauraleigh offered.

"Take Koshmarik with you," Egor said. "He'll warn you if those blasted Horsemen show up again."

I watched them leave, and once again, I wished I had not gotten Lauraleigh tangled up in this mess.

"Come," Egor said. "I have something to show you." Instead of opening the big oaken door we had arrived through, he waved his hand, and a small door appeared in the wall beside the hearth — and suddenly I remembered it always being there. He pulled the iron handle. The door opened, and out fell a clutter of brooms, cooking pots, buckets, and other household items.

"Sorry," said Egor. "Wrong door." He kicked the debris back inside the small closet, shut the door, and waggled his fingers again. This time, when he opened the door, it led to a steep stone staircase.

"This way," he said, and started to climb. For an old guy, Egor was pretty nimble, and by the time I crawled up the last stair, he was standing on the far side of the tower roof, looking out over the valley below. The wind shrieked through the ramparts that stuck up around the edge of the roof like broken teeth. Egor's wispy hair and beard flew around his head and face.

"Look. Look!" He pointed eagerly to the thick forest that surrounded the castle. I saw only black clumps of trees, stretching for miles, unbroken by fields or roads. From up here, the trees looked no bigger than shrubs, but I knew they were enormous pines and oaks, untouched for centuries by the ax of a man. The bitter wind whipped tears from my eyes. I squinted through them and saw a faint light glowing in the trees far to the north.

The roar of an engine made me jump, but it was only Uncle Misha and Lauraleigh moving the grizzlies. I turned back to study the odd light glowing in the trees. It flickered like firelight but had a sickly greenish cast rather than the happy orange glow of fire.

"What is it?" I asked.

"That, littlest witch, is your destination. That is the stronghold of the Iron Queen."

"My grandmother!" I gasped. We seemed so close, and yet I knew that distances were deceiving in the forest.

"Your grandmother," agreed Egor, "though I don't think she'll be glad to be reminded that she has a granddaughter."

"She's been looking for me," I said. "But I don't know that she'll be pleased with who I am and that I know who she is and what she's done. She'll have to answer for those things."

"Well, yes, won't we all someday. But the question is, will she answer to you?"

I chewed my lip, thinking this over. Egor was right. I couldn't just walk up to Baba Yaga's door and demand to know why she'd kidnapped my father. I needed a plan. I needed magic.

"Could you teach me about magic?" I asked.

Egor's beard blew into his mouth and he sputtered on it before answering. "What do you mean? Haven't you been taught? Every parent knows that the first years are the most important for any child. Especially one like you. Didn't you have proper tutoring?"

I felt my face grow hot. It wasn't my fault — or Uncle Misha's — that I had grown up in an orphanage surrounded by people who knew nothing of magic. I didn't even know there were magic tutors!

Egor's face softened as if he were listening to my thoughts.

"No, I didn't," I said. "My mother wasn't around long enough to enroll me in preschool, let alone magic school. My father has never so much as sent me a birthday card. And Uncle Misha never told me who I was. So how was I supposed to know that I had magic?" I felt the power heaving in my stomach again. My fists clenched and tingled with the urge to zap something.

"Stand down, girl!" Egor said. "Before you blast a hole in my tower. I meant no offense."

But I couldn't just shut off the magic. It had been simmering in me all day, with all the anxiety about finding my father, meeting my grandmother, and being chased by her Horsemen. It was all too much — and the magic spilled out of my hands. A blue light zapped the parapet, sending bits of rock flying over our heads.

"Now see here!" Egor shouted. "I'll have none of that rough stuff in my castle." His hands made a swooping motion, and a heavy weight, like a wet blanket, fell on me.

"Oomph!" I fell to the floor, the air flattened out of me, and my magic fizzled out as if I were a torch that had just been dunked in cold water. When I could finally take a breath, I found Egor staring down at me with his crazy hair fluttering around him like a white nimbus.

"Can you teach me?" I croaked.

Egor held out his bony hand and pulled me to my feet.

"Only if you promise to keep your temper," he said. "This tower is held together mostly by luck. I don't need you undoing all my hard work."

He humphed a bit and paced the roof as though trying to come to terms with how magically stupid I really was. "Well, tell me. What can you do besides blast things?" he asked finally.

"Not much," I admitted. "I can fly, but only if I have something to fly in, like a bucket. Not so great on a broom."

"Just like your granny," he mumbled.

"Oh, and once I made a vine grow really fast, but that was to trap an evil man who was kidnapping my friends. But blasting is my best trick."

Egor glared at me.

"And that's it? Do you not realize that magic has wonderful uses besides blasting and trapping? You can make crops grow for the hungry or find lost travelers. And all without losing your own energy and growing old too fast."

"I guess." I stared at my shoes and rubbed my chest. Should I tell him about the shadow inside me? I hadn't hurt anyone with that last zap of magic, so it hadn't grown any bigger. But every time I lashed out in anger, the shadow seemed to dance with glee inside me, fiery like an intense heartburn.

Egor saw me holding my chest, and his eyes softened. "You've got a little bit of darkness inside you, haven't you, little witch?"

I nodded, too upset to speak.

"It's no worry." He patted my shoulder with his narrow hand. "We've all got a bit of darkness. It's what makes us strong."

I glanced up at him in surprise. "Strong?" The shadow made me feel weak as if it wanted to take over all of me.

"Yes, that bit of dark chaos inside makes us strong. All emotions are assets to us, even anger. Would you believe it? It's what you choose to do with those emotions that makes you a dark witch or a white wizard." His voice rose and fell, spellbinding me, commanding all my attention.

"I never knew I had a choice," I said.

"Choice is the greatest power, little witch. Use it wisely."

"But Uncle Misha said—"

"Bah," said Egor, "Misha is just a grumpy old bear. I mean no disrespect; he is a fine man and my friend. But who are you going to trust about magic: the man who knows how to hook a rug or the fellow who can make one appear out of thin air?"

His bony fingers squeezed my shoulder and, for the first time in a long while, I felt some hope that the shadow inside me could be defeated.

"By the way," I said, "what's with your voice?"

Egor laughed — and despite his odd looks, it was the most beautiful laughter I'd ever heard. "It's just the wizard's voice. The most basic of all things."

"Is it magic, too?"

"No, not at all. It's a skill you develop. See, magic is all about how you use your energy." He stared at me as though he were wondering whether I'd be able to comprehend what he was telling me. Apparently, he saw something that gave him hope because he added, "That, and how much you're attuned to the world."

"How interesting," I said, not really understanding him. "Attuned to the world, you say?"

Egor gave me a patient smile. "See, the world is but a Sound. It's a Word." He stressed those words with his voice, making them seem capitalized. "Have you read the Bible, little witch?"

"Ah, yeah. Kind of."

"Kind of," he mimicked, pulling on his beard. "Ha-ha-ha! You either read or you don't read. There's nothing in between. Anyway, let me remind you." He puffed his chest out, filling it with air, and intoned in a deep, melodic voice, "In the beginning was the Word, and the Word was with God, and the Word *was* God." His laughing eyes studied me. "That's all there is to it. You need to know nothing else about magic, see. I've just saved you years of study, ha-ha!"

"Um," I said, "well, thank you … I guess."

"Ah, little witch. Think about it when you have a moment of leisure. You're just … a wave. A frequency. A sound." His voice did a strange thing, becoming louder and then softer, reminding me of the gentle waves of Lake Geneva rolling onto our school's private beach. That made me feel better and even put a gentle smile on my face.

"You're tricking me," I said. "You've been playing with my mind all along."

Egor threw his head back, making his beard look at the sky, and laughed. "I've been teaching you. Imagine yourself as a wave on the surface of a vast sea. What can it do? How can it reach the shore one day? Huh?"

I wrinkled my forehead, thinking. The odd little man seemed intent on passing some thought on to me, so I decided to play along. I shrugged. "By moving along with the sea."

"You got it!" Egor clapped and bowed like I had just made a major discovery. "By being in harmony with it." He winked. "But enough for today. What are your plans for tomorrow, little witch?"

"Tomorrow, I have to go see my grandmother," I said. "My father needs me. But maybe…" I didn't know how to ask without sounding rude. "Maybe when I come back, you can teach me some more?"

"I think that's a splendid idea," Egor said with a smile.

But I didn't get to visit my grandmother the next day. We woke to dark skies. The clouds were heavy and purple with rain.

"I think you need to see this," Egor said as soon as Uncle Misha, Lauraleigh and I had stirred. We followed him back up the steep steps to the tower roof. Lightning shimmered in the north.

The three Horsemen again stood at the castle gate, but this time they had brought an army of ghosts.

We were surrounded.

Chapter 7

ear Diary,

Today I realized that I have much to learn about magic. Or as Egor puts it, about the use of energy. It's a dizzying thought. It was only a few weeks ago that I first discovered that I had magic within me. I sat at the river's edge with Squire, trying to stop the flow of the water. How silly I was! How naive! Since then, I've done some amazing things with magic. And some pretty scary things too.

But never have I sat down and imagined all the wonderful things I could do. Up until now, I've had a live-and-learn attitude about magic. Not anymore. Now I want to learn it all. In a few short hours, Egor has shown me more of the universe than I had ever thought possible. I will no longer be happy with studying simple algebra, grammar, and history. I must learn how to do this!

One day, I'll be a great witch. One day, I'll have magic to rival my grandmother's. Then nobody will be able to hurt the people I love again. This I swear to you, Diary.

Today, I, the witch, was born.

"What is it?" Lauraleigh asked. Her face was pinched tight with worry. "I can sense something, like the pressure of a storm, but all I see are those three Horsemen."

"Ghosts," I whispered. "Dozens of them." I wasn't sure whether it was better to see them or, like Lauraleigh, to live without that terrifying sight but still know we were surrounded.

"Anna, do you have that dream stone I sent you?" Uncle Misha asked.

I nodded.

"Let Lauraleigh look through it."

The stone hung from a leather cord around my neck. Its solid weight against my chest was a comfort, but I gladly handed it over to my friend. She held the stone to her eye and gasped.

"So many!" she said.

The ghosts flickered in the morning light like twinkling stars. They shifted around, passing through the hills and trees surrounding the castle ruins.

"Why don't they come onto the castle grounds?" I asked.

"I've got it warded against all but the most powerful magic," said Egor. "It's quite simple when you know how — like a wall of special sound. The Horsemen will eventually break through, but it will take time. The question is why are they here? Has Baba Yaga finally found a way to control the dead?"

My heart sank at the thought. Uncle Misha had suggested that was my grandmother's dearest wish. Maybe even the reason she'd kidnapped my father. With his power, she'd finally control the kingdom of the dead. But if the ghosts were here under her command, did that mean that my father had already given up resisting her? Could he even be dead, even though that was supposed to be impossible? Was my father one of those ghosts?

"I do not think so," Uncle Misha said, reading the emotions on my face as if I were yelling my feelings out loud. "Look at the way those ghosts move. They are passing right through the Horsemen."

Uncle Misha was right. The Horsemen looked annoyed as the ghosts flitted around and through them. The horses were trained for war, but even they stamped their hooves and tossed their heads. They didn't like being mistreated by the ghosts either. I remembered the feeling of the ghost passing through me: cold, like a hand of ice squeezing my heart.

"So if the Horsemen didn't bring the ghosts, why are they here?" Lauraleigh asked.

"It's me they want," I said. "Isn't that right?"

I hoped Uncle Misha would deny it, but he nodded. His eyes were filled with deep sadness. "We do not know where your father is," he said. "With no one to help the ghosts in their afterlives, they are restless. Perhaps they sense your father's strength in you. Maybe they have been drawn here, hoping that you can give them the peace they deserve."

"Can I do that?" I asked. "Can I really help them?" There were so many! How could I be the one responsible for those souls?

Uncle Misha shook his head. "I do not know. Our best chance is still to find your father."

I turned back to the army of specters camped on our doorstep. The three Horsemen sat on their mounts like statues. Black's fierce gaze pinned me even though he was hundreds of meters away. He knew I was here. He hadn't forgiven me for messing up his plans. The other two might be here on Baba Yaga's orders, but for the Black Horseman, it was personal.

"What will the Horsemen do with me when … if they catch me?" I asked.

"They'll follow their orders," said Egor. "They must. Your granny compels the very blood that courses through their veins."

"So they'll kill me," I said. "That's what she wants, isn't it?"

Egor shrugged. "Who knows the twisted mind of that witch? Maybe it's your blood she wants, a few drops a day. They may simply take you to her."

"But that's what I want! Forget the blood. I need to find my father, and if she has him—" I almost ran down the tower stairs, ready to throw myself at the Horsemen.

Uncle Misha stopped me with a firm hand on my shoulder. "Do not be so impulsive," he said. "Even if they do not kill you here, you need to face your grandmother on your own terms. Not hers. That will make all the difference."

Before I could ask what he meant, the Red Horseman shouted something to his brothers. His yell was so sudden and loud that a flock of blackbirds erupted from a nearby tree. They swirled in the air, a great mass of black shadows, banked left and headed for the deeper forest. Uncle Misha let out a sharp whistle. One of the birds changed course and flew straight at us. His hand shot up and he caught the bird in his fist. He opened his hand and the bird flopped sideways, plainly stunned. Uncle Misha whispered soothing noises and petted its head. After a few seconds, the little bird chirped and stood on steady feet.

"Go quickly now, my little friend." Uncle Misha released the bird. It flew high above the tower and swung past the Horsemen. Red swiped a bow from his back and let loose an arrow. It whizzed past the bird, which flew higher and disappeared over the mountain.

"Good," Uncle Misha said, still beaming after handling the bird. "Hopefully, she'll bring help."

"Help?" I asked. "From who?"

"The bears, for one. But other beasts may take up the call. They know that the Great Trapper wouldn't ask for help lightly."

"So now we wait?" asked Lauraleigh.

"Now we fortify our defenses!" Egor said. He pulled himself up to his full height. "Now we get ready to fight. The Horsemen will attack at dawn, methinks."

"Then we must hurry," Uncle Misha said. "Tell us what to do."

Misha, Lauraleigh, and Koshmarik left to check the gates. The hellhound was strong enough to move boulders and wood beams to reinforce those that were in danger of falling down.

I worried about my friends as soon as they had left my sight. Egor saw my tense look. "They'll be safe enough while the wards hold," he said kindly.

"So what will we do?"

"We'll make sure the wards hold." His grin couldn't hide the grimness of his tone. "Come. It's time you learned some useful magic, not the junk that fills you now."

At the base of the crumbling tower, Egor dug in the dirt until he found a small bundle of tiny grayish-white sticks tied with a rag. No — those weren't sticks.

"Are those what I think they are?" I asked, feeling a little light-headed. "Bones?"

"Hmm, yes. Bones. The best wards are made from the bones of someone who lived and died in the space you want to protect. Luckily, the tower is infested with rats. Their bones can be turned into potent charms." He examined the little bundle. "This one is nearly spent. The magic needs to be renewed every few months." He plucked a hair from his long beard; then he reached and yanked a hair from my head.

"Ow!" I rubbed my scalp. "What was that for?"

"Blood is best, but we've got a lot of wards to refresh.

Hair will have to do. And two wizard hairs are always better than one." Egor twined the two hairs into the mess of bone and rag. He spoke into the bones, "Protect!"

My head tingled where he'd plucked the hair. The bones pulsed with light bright enough to be seen in the morning sun. Suddenly I ceased to be worried or to question. Seeing the process, feeling it work, caught my attention. I wanted to see, to know more.

"Ah, good, good," said Egor. He reburied the ward and patted down the earth. "This tower is our last line of defense. We'd best check the other wards."

So we circled the tower, digging up bundles of rat bones, plucking hairs, and refreshing the wards. After the tower, we did the same around the crumbling walls of the keep. Every time Egor whispered, "Protect," my scalp itched until I felt like my hair must be standing on end. It was long, tiring work, and when we were done, I wanted nothing more than to get some lunch and take a rest.

"Shall we take a break?" I suggested.

"Not yet!" Egor said. "We have one more important task, and it's best done on an empty stomach."

That didn't sound good.

Back inside the tower, Egor led me down into the tunnels. The distance between the odd blue torches grew and grew until I could barely see Egor in front of me. We were headed deep into the earth. The tunnel bent at a sharp angle, and suddenly there was no more torchlight in front of us. The last torch was hidden behind the bend.

Egor stopped and fiddled in the pockets of his robes. "Aha! Here it is. Misha isn't the only one who has a way with beasts." A green light lit his hand to reveal a large bug jittering on his palm. The bug's butt glowed bright enough to light our way.

"What's that?" I'd seen fireflies before, but this one was the size of a hummingbird and seemed tame.

"Luster beetle," said Egor. "Handy little critter. But he'll only have enough light for an hour. We must hurry now."

We jogged down the tunnel. Every few meters, I tripped over stones or stumbled over cracks — but Egor ran with effortless grace. When I fell over a discarded torch and slammed into the wall, he stopped and gazed at me with a stern "Harrumph."

"Not the stealthiest child, are you?" He held out a hand and pulled me to my feet. "You must learn to make your feet work for you, not against you. This is one of those times that the shadow inside can help."

"What do you mean?" All the magic we'd been doing had agitated the shadow in my chest. It could sense the anticipation in me — as if it, whatever it was, wanted to take part in the coming fight. Take part, and possibly grow stronger as I fought. I had been firmly ignoring it all morning — and now Egor wanted me to use it?

"Stand still," he said. "You young ones are always fidgeting."

I tried to stand as still as possible. My heart was beating impossibly loud.

"Now, close your eyes and take hold of the shadow. Where is it?" Egor demanded.

I placed a hand over my heart.

"Yes, shadows like the heart. But you can control it. Push

it out. Use the strength of your blood to drive that shadow all the way down to your feet."

I opened my eyes, hesitating. Most of his magic was odd, as though it weren't magic at all, but instead some complex manipulations with voice, attention, and now blood flow. I opened my mouth to ask him for an explanation.

"Do it now!" Egor boomed.

I slammed my eyes shut again and imagined the shadow. To me, it was like a big dark moth fluttering in my chest. I tried to grab its wings, but they slipped through my imagination.

"Use your blood!" Egor repeated.

My heart still beat loudly. I concentrated on it. Then I felt it. My blood, my energy, my magic; they were one and the same. My heart pumped it through my body, touching every bit of me. All I had to do was give the shadow a little push. So I concentrated even more and sent it coursing through my veins, where it soon split in two and pooled it my feet.

I took a deep breath. For the first time in weeks, my heart was filled with light!

"Good," said Egor. "Now put those shadows to work. They will make your feet fly on silent wings. As for that light in your heart, pull it up into your head. Maybe you'll begin to think faster." He chuckled as if he'd made a clever joke.

And his trick worked! Egor ran ahead, holding the luster beetle above his head to light the way. I ran after him. This time, no rocks tripped me; I moved as swiftly and nimbly as a deer.

"This is amazing," I said, leaping over a pile of crumbled stone.

"Nimble Feet," said Egor over his shoulder. "Basic spell, if you want to use that traditional word. But not for the faint of heart. A witch has to have lived a little — faced a foe or two — before she has the power to use it."

"Oh, I've lived," I mumbled as we hurried on. I'd faced a few enemies too. And one of them was waiting for me outside the castle walls and had brought friends. I hoped that Egor would stop this mad dash through the darkness soon.

He did. He stopped so suddenly, only my Nimble Feet kept me from crashing into him. I peered over his shoulder.

We stood at the edge of a pool set in a small cavern with a high ceiling. The water was perfectly still, with only a jagged rock breaking the surface like an arm reaching up from the deep. Water dripped faintly all around us.

"Know what a golem is?" Egor's sharp voice bounced around the stone cavern.

"Isn't that some sort of monster?" I asked.

"Are bears monsters?"

"Bears? No, of course not." I couldn't follow his train of thought. My eyes were fixed on the luster beetle reflected from the inky water. This place was creepy, and I wanted the magic lesson to be over.

"Not to you, who were raised with them. But to the unwary hiker, a bear can be a ferocious monster. It's all in how you look at the thing. A golem is just a servant. Only you can make it a monster. Anyway, it's an idea I've borrowed from the Jews of Prague. It's a robot of sorts, powered by the energy of human thought. A creature of the mind." He chortled as if the description made no sense even to him.

I really want to leave now, I thought.

He sucked on his lip for a moment and added, "See, I told you this world is a Word. Think: Electricity is a wave. And sound is a wave. They're all just a type of energy. So a golem isn't that dissimilar to a—"

"Oh, could you get on with it already?" I pleaded, shivering in the damp cavern. "I appreciate your lessons as much as ever, but—"

"Hold this!" Egor impatiently dumped the luster beetle in my hand. The little creature seemed to have wilted and its light had dimmed. "The trick with golems is that you have to know their names. Names are powerful things in this world... Hmm... Now where's that pen?" He patted himself all over and finally pulled out an old-fashioned quill pen, a bottle of ink, and a small scroll of paper. I wondered how he managed to keep all of that in the pockets of his cloak of tattered rags.

"Here we go." Egor flopped to the ground and opened the ink bottle. "Hold that light closer," he said urgently. "This is ancient Jewish magic. Primeval. Magic of the Word. And in this case, the golem's name is the word that'll bring him to life." He dipped the quill in the ink, unrolled the scroll and wrote with a flourish: *Aazhaei.*

"Aazh—" I started to say.

Egor shushed me. "Never say a golem's name aloud unless you are prepared to control him. And you are not, my girl."

I clamped my mouth shut. Egor blew on the ink, rolled the scroll and tossed it into the water. For a moment, the paper floated on the surface; then something jerked it below.

"Aazhaei," Egor said in such a commanding voice that even I had an urge to snap to attention. "I call on you to serve me and protect these walls!"

Nothing happened. The silence in the cave pressed in on me.

"Aazhaei! Rise and attend to me!" A faint wind stirred Egor's beard.

A hand lurched from the water and grasped the stone in the middle of the pool. It hauled a slimy gray body behind it. The golem's face was smooth and wet as if someone had just formed it from clay. Its eyes were small indentations and the bump between them only hinted at a nose. It had no mouth. With sloshing steps, it lurched toward us, enormous clay hands spread wide, ready to grab anything within reach.

I jumped back.

"I command you, Aazhaei! Stop!" Egor said. His voice was calm yet powerful — and I felt a new urge to obey.

I guessed the golem didn't hear too well without ears. But it must have sensed something — what Egor had described as "frequency," perhaps — because it jerked to a stop at the edge of the pool. Its hands opened and closed as if it wanted to strangle something with its fists.

"I command you, Aazhaei!" Egor said again, his voice echoing through the cavern even though he was not shouting.

The golem's arms dropped to its side. It stood still, not breathing, not twitching, just waiting.

"Amazing!" I whispered. "Has it been here all the time, waiting in the pool?"

"No," said Egor. He wiped a trembling hand through his long beard. "The golem only comes into being when you call it. Before that, it's just a thought. Your energy takes that thought and forms it into a being of clay. You could call this same golem from any suitable pool anywhere in the world. If you were strong enough, that is."

I saw that he was nervous. "Why are you shaking?" I asked.

Egor shook his head. Sweat had popped out on his forehead even though the underground tunnel was cool. The whole experience didn't seem like the magic I'd imagined; it was real, messy, and tiring, with none of the dashing spells they show in the movies. It seemed Egor used part of himself every time, and he was getting quite tired. I gasped, thinking about how much of my own energy I had wasted: stopping time back in Geneva, burning things up with rays of pure energy, flying around in a bucket... I groaned.

The luster beetle winked off, leaving us in total darkness; then it burst back into light.

"We must get out of here before we lose our light," Egor said. "Come, Aazhaei. Follow!"

We ran as fast as our tired bodies would allow. I concentrated on keeping the shadows in my feet so I could flit over any obstacles in our way. The steady clomping of the golem's feet beat like war drums behind me. The luster beetle dimmed for good just as the blue torches began to light our way again. When I smelled fresh air and saw the brittle white light ahead, I found a last burst of speed and fell into the sunlight with a gasp of relief.

The golem lumbered by me and headed for the outer wall.

"He was fighting me for control," Egor said. His breath rasped, and he bent over to catch his breath. He fell to the ground next to me. "But I think he'll be fine now."

The golem slowly circled the inner wall, passing by the gates that Uncle Misha and Lauraleigh had barricaded.

"Let's see those Horsemen try to get past that!" Egor said.

I wasn't so confident. The golem certainly looked like a formidable enemy, but what if Egor lost control of him at the wrong time?

"Your magic is strange," I said after I could breathe normally again. "It looks like hard work."

Egor smiled. "Maybe you misunderstand magic, little witch."

Chapter 8

Dear Diary,

The ghosts are restless, but I suppose that's the thing about ghosts. They can't rest. That's why they knock on the walls of the castle, trying to break through our wards. They don't have anything better to do. Or maybe they can sense the magic in my blood. It's strange to think that I might have the power to command the dead.

Why do they even need to be commanded? Why can't they just go away and find peace on their own? These are questions that no one here can answer for me. My father is probably the only one in the world who can.

I wonder where he is.

I slid with my back down the stone wall of Egor's room until my knees hit my chin. To me, the wailing of the ghosts was unbearable. I'd tried to block my ears against it, but that didn't help. The wailing was *inside* my head. Lauraleigh couldn't hear that horrible, incessant, piercing noise, which sounded like the universe was tearing itself into two halves.

I couldn't sit still, so I paced around and around Egor's tower. Koshmarik was guarding the door, and Egor was tinkering with some device at the table. Uncle Misha was reading by the fire. Only Lauraleigh slept peacefully, safe in the silence of her lack of magic.

"Maybe I should just go to them," I suggested for the hundredth time.

Uncle Misha didn't even bother to answer. We had already gone over all the reasons why that was a bad idea. I didn't know how to control the ghosts. But why should I want to control them? I just wanted to help them. Maybe Baba Yaga had found a way to control them, or maybe they had been acting on their own, and all they wanted was help finding their way into the afterlife...

Wherever that was.

Just thinking about it made me realize how little I knew about my powers. I couldn't help the ghosts at all! I couldn't help my father either. What had I been thinking, racing across the world to save him? Why had Uncle Misha thought it was so important for me to come here, when I had been safe and hidden from Baba Yaga in Tuscany?

I jumped up and started pacing again.

If my grandmother controlled the ghosts, then as soon as they broke through the wards, they'd tear us apart. That thought kept me pacing until Egor growled at me to sit down. I slumped against the stone wall and watched the fire flickering. The flames were like the ghosts, angry phantoms of pure energy. When I finally slept, both the flames and the ghosts filled my dreams.

I awoke before dawn, tired and sore from sleeping on stone. The tower was silent. The ghosts had finally stopped wailing, as unexpectedly as when they had begun. Sometime in the night, Koshmarik had curled up at my side. The fire had burned low, so I was glad for his warmth. No one else was awake. Koshmarik snorted when I got up to stoke the fire, but he was soon snuffling away in doggie dreams again. I warmed myself in front of the hearth, wishing that Egor had taught me how to conjure some food. Golems and wards were all good, but they didn't fill an empty belly. I poured a cup of water and drank it down. I decided to head up to the roof and see if we were still under siege.

I scrambled up the stairs and took a gulp of fresh air. I hadn't realized how stuffy the tower was. I peered over the stone parapet, squinting into the east where I had last seen the three Horsemen standing guard. The hills had just started to glow with the dawn, but there still wasn't enough light to see anything but the vague outline of the trees against the sky.

Everything was perfectly still, except for the faint, lurching footsteps of the golem as he made his rounds. In the quiet, I finally understood the meaning of the phrase "the calm before the storm." I felt like a stretched-out arrow, taut as the bowstring got ready to send me flying toward my fate, without any idea where the journey would take me. Then the sun sparked over the trees, and I gasped. The Horsemen were still sitting on their mounts before the crumbling gates. The field behind them was filled with ghosts.

"Are they still there?" Lauraleigh asked behind me. I jumped, startled; I hadn't heard her come up the stairs. Her hair was messy from sleep and her eyes were red.

"More than before," I said. "Many more. But they're not moving much. I wonder what they're waiting for. Hey, where's my dream stone?"

"Egor asked for it," she said. "He's trying to make some kind of gadget for me so I can see them better." She paused and gazed at the Horsemen. "It seems unbelievable that we're really going to fight. I mean, how *do* you fight ghosts?"

"I don't know. I just hope that Misha and Egor do."

"Yeah. Come downstairs now. Breakfast is ready."

We ate in silence, each of us busy with our own thoughts.

Finally, as we cleared the table, I said, "Egor, can you teach me to conjure food? I think it would be a useful trick to know."

"Ah, yes. A most elemental job. It's easier if you only try to multiply food the first time. Here, take this." He handed me a heel of bread. "Take a crumb between your fingers and rub it. Feel the ingredients that go into bread: flour, water, salt, yeast. Bring them each to your mind, and hold them there."

I did as he asked. The crumbs were gritty in my fingers.

"Now summon your energy, not the shadows but your normal energy. Don't lose the image of the bread, and imagine how you'd just mixed the ingredients together and baked them in an oven."

"Are there any words to say?" I asked.

Egor smiled. "You can say anything you wish; the sillier, the better. Surprise yourself. It also helps to make a gesture like snapping your fingers or jumping over a chair."

I looked into his eyes, trying to see if he was mocking me, but he seemed sincere. "Why?" I asked.

"To distract your own mind. See, what we think of as our mind isn't really ours. It belongs to... Ah, never mind that now. We'll discuss that some other time. But remember this: A snap of your fingers or a jump over a chair moves you to another world where the bread already exists. Where you've just finished baking it."

I pulled from my source, that strange boiling spot in my stomach where my magic lay. I felt it rumble and gurgle. "Uh... Levor manna!" I called, and clapped three times. I even imagined jumping to another world, whatever that meant.

Nothing happened. Egor smiled.

"It takes practice. Go watch the gate and study the bread. Visualize how you *already* baked a nice warm loaf of it. Smell it and taste it in your mind. You'll get it eventually."

So I spent the morning studying a loaf of bread. I tried several times to make new bread with my magic. "Manna from the sky! Yellow rhino!" I yelled again and again. I jumped over chairs, pinched myself, and even stood on my head. But the crumbs stayed crumbs, and my frustration grew.

Lauraleigh watched the Horsemen. They hadn't moved. Neither had the ghosts, except to shuffle around a bit. The golem's constant clockwise trek around the tower was the only sign of time passing.

At midmorning, I gave up on bread making. Maybe I was too tense. Unused magic sat in my gut like heartburn. I stuffed the lump of bread in my backpack and joined Lauraleigh at the wall.

"They haven't moved all morning," she said.

The Horsemen stared up at the tower. Even from this distance, I could see the scorn in their eyes.

"I wonder what they're waiting for," I said.

The golem lumbered by beneath us. His face was now a maze of fine cracks; he was drying out in the sun. I didn't know how much longer he could keep up his watch.

Then, as if by some prearranged signal, the ghosts attacked.

Dozens of them ran at full speed and slammed into the gate. You'd think that something as transparent as a ghost wouldn't do much damage, but they did. When they hit, a blast like cannon fire rang out across the mountain. The gate shook but held. Dust blew up around it like a cloud. More ghosts rammed the gate, and the second blast shook the morning.

"What's the matter?" Lauraleigh asked, watching my face. Apparently she hadn't seen or heard anything unusual.

"They're ramming the gate," I said.

The golem stopped. He stood by the gate, waiting. I wondered how he would fight the ghosts. How would *we* fight the ghosts? They were incorporeal, after all. It wasn't like we could hit them with anything.

Uncle Misha came up to the roof and spoke to Laura-leigh. "Egor almost has your new eyeglass ready. He wants you to go down for a fitting."

She nodded and left.

Uncle Misha and I watched the ghosts in their mad frenzy. They seemed mindless and hysterical, throwing themselves against wood and stone without any fear of pain.

"I thought the waiting was the worst part," I said. "But I was wrong. This is much worse."

"They are lost and desperate, easily controlled. And it will get nastier still, when they finally break down the walls," Uncle Misha said.

"But how is it that they don't pass right through? I've seen ghosts walk right through things before. One even walked through our grizzly. How can they slam against the wall?"

"Ghosts... They are attuned to a certain wavelength. It is like radio, you know? Many channels exist in the same space, and you tune your radio to listen to this one or that one. And you can build screens that do not let radio waves pass through."

"That sounds like basic physics," I said, watching the chaos below. "You and Egor make magic seem so ... natural."

"There is nothing unnatural about magic. Ghosts and people simply exist on different radio channels, if you wish," Uncle Misha said. "Egor's wards act as a screen against their channel. Do you understand?"

I nodded.

"So our friends down there must break that screen down. By doing so, they will let the Horsemen in."

I thought about that. Now it seemed like a lot of work for nothing. "Maybe warding the walls wasn't such a good idea," I said. "Wouldn't it have been better to let in the ghosts if we could keep out the Horsemen?"

"Perhaps," said Uncle Misha. "Right now, we don't know which of the two is the greater evil. But I suspect we will soon find out."

"You and Egor said that the ghosts probably want me to do my father's work. Maybe I should ... I don't know ... go and calm them down? Somehow?"

"My brave girl." He smiled. "But do you know what to do when a ghost approaches you?"

"No ... not at all."

"Now listen to me, *Malyshka*. I am going to ask something very difficult of you." Uncle Misha's bushy eyebrows were pulled down, shadowing his eyes. The last time I had seen him so serious was the day he had left me in Geneva.

I nodded slowly. I'd do anything for my uncle, but a lump of fear settled in my throat as I waited for him to speak.

"If the ghosts break through the wall, I need you to leave here. Leave all of us and run as far and as fast as you can."

"What?" I burst out. "No! I can't leave you ... and Lauraleigh... I got her into this mess and I won't leave her to die here."

Uncle Misha wrapped his arms around me. His hug was like a bear's embrace, and it brought back memories of my childhood before I had ever gone away. Before I had learned about magic.

"I promise you, *Malyshka*, I will try to protect your friend. The ghosts cannot touch her; she holds no interest for them. And I will keep her safe from the Horsemen. But you must find your father. Without the King of the Dead, the world will soon be overrun with ghosts. You can stop this madness. You must promise me you will find him — you will stop at nothing to get him away from your grandmother." He paused and stared me right in the eye. I felt as if he could see into my soul.

"Why can't we all go ... together?" I tried to hold back the tears that prickled my eyes.

Uncle Misha sighed and kissed my forehead. "I should not ask such a tremendous job of one so young," he said. "But life and death do not care about young and old. And I truly believe that no one but you can save your father now. Egor and I will be the distraction. While the Horsemen are fighting us, they cannot follow you. Hopefully, you will be long gone by the time they realize their prize has escaped."

"Okay," I said. "I'll go, but you must keep Lauraleigh safe."

The ghosts continued to blast at the gates, the walls, and any other part of the crumbling castle they could reach. The Horsemen sat in their silent vigil.

"Don't those guys ever eat?" Lauraleigh asked. "They don't even seem human." She now wore a strange headgear with a metal loop over one eye. The loop held the dream stone so she could look through it and see our enemy.

"Speaking of eating," I said, "I'm hungry." I'd been trying the bread spell at times all morning but without success. Once I had thought I felt the crumbs vibrating between my fingers, but that was all. Magic was much easier when I used it to blast things. Actually creating something from nothing — or imagining I had already baked the bread I was trying to make appear — was hard. Maybe that's why witches turned evil and grew old fast: The violent magic was way easier.

I had no time to ask Egor about my theories. He came up the tower stairs, carrying a basket of food for lunch and three daggers. He handed one to each of us.

"Use them to defend yourselves against the ghosts," he said.

"Won't they just go right through them?" asked Lauraleigh.

"I've charged them with the right kind of vibration," Egor said. "See?"

I touched the tip of one blade. It actually did vibrate — with high, searing frequency. "Wow," I said. "You're using sound again."

Egor chuckled. "One touch of this blade and the ghosts will be no more. Poof! They dissolve to the great Void from which we have all come. Most of them are simple lost souls to whom all this seems part of a lasting nightmare. Don't kill them unless it's to protect yourself. And Lauraleigh, the ghosts can't touch you, so use it only if you must protect Anna. But Anna, you ... you... Just don't let the ghosts touch you."

"Why?" I asked. "What will happen?"

144

"Just don't let them touch you," he repeated. He'd never looked so grim.

That did not make me feel any better. Suddenly, my stomach was too jittery for food. I fed half my sandwich to Koshmarik, who seemed only too happy to take my leftovers.

An ear-splitting crack rang out. We all jumped up and peered over the tower wall.

The ghosts had finally torn down the gate.

Shards of wood and stone hailed down in the yard. A gossamer figure jumped through the gap. The golem snagged a ghost by its throat and … ate it. At least, I thought he ate it. One moment, the ghost was there; the next, it was being pulled into the golem's smooth face like a great puff of smoke.

Another ghost popped through the gap.

"We must fight now!" Egor shouted. He ran down the stairs with Koshmarik at his heels. Lauraleigh stared at me with huge eyes. Then she found her determination and followed Egor. Uncle Misha and I brought up the rear.

I had only a moment to watch Lauraleigh piling stones and beams against the broken gate while Egor chanted new wards. Ghosts swirled all around them, but Lauraleigh worked as though she didn't know they were there — which, of course, she didn't. The golem plodded through the mass of spirits, gobbling them as fast as they could push through the gate. He looked like a bizarre vacuum cleaner from some madman's nightmare.

"Come," Uncle Misha called. "It's this way."

We hurried away from the battle to the west end of the castle, past the parked grizzlies and toward a shorter tower. This one was a crumbled ruin, but Uncle Misha ducked inside. The air was heavy and damp. Only the light from the open door lit the tower, but I could see that it had once been a bunkhouse of some kind. Bunk beds lined the round walls. The roof had caved in on a table in the center. Uncle Misha moved quickly and with confidence. He pushed aside a moldy carpet to reveal a wooden trapdoor. With a great heave, he yanked it open. A rickety ladder led down into darkness.

Uncle Misha noticed my hesitation. "It's a short tunnel," he said. "Straight out under the west wall. You'll come up in the forest and no one should see you. This is from Egor." He handed me a small bundle.

I had no time to look at it now. I just shoved it in my backpack before slinging that over my shoulders.

"I have nothing to give you, *Malyshka*, but my love and my confidence. I know you will succeed. Now go!" He gave me a quick hug.

I stepped onto the ladder. I didn't think about it; I just did it. I knew that if I stopped to think, I wouldn't go. The last rung broke under my weight and I staggered into the damp tunnel. Uncle Misha left the door open above, but after a few steps, it didn't matter. I was plunged into complete darkness.

Above me, I could hear the wailing of the ghosts and the blasts of magic as they tried to break through more of Egor's wards.

I ran. Feeling sick about leaving my friends behind, I ran — because this way, I was probably saving them. And my father.

I hoped.

Chapter 9

 *Dear Diary,*

Uncle Misha has a theory that the ghosts are looking for me, the heir to the Deathless One. I don't know which I fear most — that he's right or not. If the ghosts want me, then my friends will be safe. I'll run and the ghosts will follow, leaving Lauraleigh, Uncle Misha and Egor safe behind the wards. But if the ghosts come for me, what will I do? I'm ashamed to say that as I ran through that horrible forest, a tiny part of me was hoping that Uncle Misha was wrong and the ghosts weren't following.

Maybe this selfishness is the weakness that lets in the shadow.

But Egor had said that weakness could be turned into strength. I hope he's right, because I'll need all the strength my thirteen years have amassed to fight an army of ghosts by myself. And what if I win? What's my prize then?

And the thing is I don't want to kill them either. These ghosts are just someone else's pawns, confused and terrified.

Oh, right. Then I get to face the Iron Queen, the witch that other witches fear. My granny.

The setting sun flickered through the trees. It did less to light my way than to confuse me with odd reflections from the leaves. I ran without caring where the forest took me, so long as it was far away from Blackwood Castle.

I pulled the shadow into my feet as Egor had taught me, and I ran on Nimble Feet. No roots or stones tripped me. But as the light faded, I couldn't see the branches that slapped me in the face and tugged at my hair. Still, I didn't stop. I ran until my sides ached and my chest felt tight. I ran until I had no breath left.

Finally, I stopped at the edge of a small creek and forced my breathing to slow before I took a drink from it. The water burned an icy path down my throat. I waded the ankle-deep water, heading downstream. I hoped that would erase my trail in case someone was following me. And if my grandmother lived in a ravine, wouldn't the river flow into it at some point? I hoped so, because otherwise I had no idea how to find her.

When my feet had grown numb with cold, I left the river. The trees opened up, and a clearing spread before me. The moon broke through the clouds, and the dew-covered grass lit up like glittering jewels. It was such a beautiful sight, I stopped to catch my breath and take it in.

And that's when I saw the ghosts. Two of them, floating through the trees on the opposite side of the clearing. I dropped to the ground. The grass was nearly knee-high and hid me well. Or at least, it would've hidden me from a normal, living enemy. A spirit drawn to me was a different matter. I peered through the grass, hoping that the ghosts would just keep flittering through the trees without sensing me.

They stopped.

As one, they turned and stared in my direction. I ducked low in the tall grass and held my breath.

The forest was as quiet as death. With shaking hands, I spread the grasses and peered into the gloom. The two ghosts stood about twenty meters away. They wore casual clothes: jeans and work shirts. One was tall and thin, the other short and stout, but they didn't stand the way normal humans do. They didn't slouch or lean against a tree. They stood ramrod straight and stared at the grass where I was lying.

They stared at *me*.

Had I made a sound to alert them? Could they smell me? No, Uncle Misha had been right. They simply sensed me. No hiding spot would keep me safe.

One of the ghosts took a step closer. Then another step. Except he didn't actually step. His legs didn't move; he *floated*. In the faint light, they both glowed as if lit with some inner light. Another floating step closer. The second ghost followed.

I had to do something. Something other than pressing my face into the dirt and shaking with fear. I thought over all the tricks that Egor had taught me. Would any of them help me now? I had no bones with which to make a ward. I didn't dare call the golem, even if I had a proper pool to call him from. Using Egor's dagger meant killing them — dissolving them, whatever — and that seemed way too cruel. And what good would Nimble Feet be against ghosts who could float?

But wait! Maybe Nimble Feet was the answer. What was it if not stealth? Maybe I could use the shadow to hide myself…

I checked the ghosts again. They were closer still. But they seemed uncertain. I closed my eyes, trying to push back the panic that was constricting my throat. I was exhausted. But this wasn't the time to give in, and I wouldn't give in. Egor had warned me not to let the ghosts touch me. I had to hide in a place they wouldn't be able to reach.

I summoned my magic. It boiled in my stomach, heated my chest, and was ready to burst out of every pore. No, that wasn't good. I had to control it or I'd start blasting rays of energy all over the forest. The shadow in my heart chittered happily. It loved it when I lost control. That gave it power. The more people I harmed, the stronger it became.

The ghosts floated closer. Their arms were stretched out, hands reaching for me. Bottomless black eyes mesmerized me.

Hide! I had to hide! Dark fluttering wings tickled my insides. I suddenly knew what to do. I wrapped my energy around the shadow … that is, I infused the shadow with my own magic. In my mind's eye, I could see the sparkly blue energy spreading through the darkness that lived in my heart, clinging to it like a sticky cobweb. Then I forced the magic into every cell in my body. The shadow went with it. My skin tingled. The hair on my arms and neck stood on end. A dark haze covered my eyes, and my hearing became muffled as if I'd just plunged underwater.

The shadow now covered me from head to toe. I dared to peek at the ghosts again. They'd stopped no more than an

arm's length away. The first one cocked his head as if confused. I shivered. The ghost stuck his transparent face into
the air above my hiding spot. His fingers made fists in the
empty air above my head. The grasses blew right threw him.
Behind him, the second ghost opened his mouth and let out
a long, sad wail. They were looking for me. I held on tightly
to the shadow that hid me, wondering how much magic I
was using, if I was growing older with each passing moment.

Then the ghosts floated away. Evidently, they thought I
had vanished. And maybe I had. Maybe vanishing or invisibility wasn't anything more than hiding under a shadow. I
didn't know, but now wasn't the time to ponder things like
that.

I tucked the magic and shadow around me like a cloak
and ran. I ignored the thirst that stuck my tongue to the roof
of my mouth. I ran up hills and down ravines. I tore through

brambles and sloshed through streams. The moon crested the treetops, and still I ran, safe in my invisibility.

Then, exhausted, I fell to the ground, paralyzed by gulping gasps. I felt as if I'd never have enough air. I had dropped my magic cover some time ago, and my shadow had retreated back inside me. I had no strength to keep them up. Every ghost in Siberia could find me now.

And I didn't care. I had to rest. I had to…

Sleep overcame me.

Chapter 10

Dear Diary,

I'm only just learning that family is a tricky thing. I never really had a family before. I have Uncle Misha, but I always knew he isn't my real uncle. And then there are Sisters Daphne and Constance in Geneva. But they aren't really sisters either.

I wonder why we give family titles like "Uncle" and "Sister" to people who aren't related to us. Is it because, somewhere deep inside, we have a burning need to build a family around us even when there is none?

The night was so black under the trees that when I awoke, I thought I was blind. I passed my hand in front of my eyes and could barely see the outline of my fingers. My throat ached for water. I had only a little left in my pack and I drank it all down. I'd need to find a stream soon.

For several long minutes, I sat in the darkness, listening to the night shift and chirp around me. I was afraid to move. What if the ghosts were still nearby? But the only way I could save my friends and find my father was to get to Baba Yaga — and I wouldn't do that by sitting around.

But I had no idea how to get to Baba Yaga's house. Uncle Misha had pointed me in the general direction, and I had hoped that the slope of the mountain would take me there. Now I might as well have been blindfolded and spun around a hundred times. Even in the daylight, I'd have no idea which way to go.

Then I remembered Squire. I fumbled in my pack and found him still wrapped in the soft cloth. With little effort — my magic came easier now — I summoned a flame and blew it on him.

Squire exploded to life. He doubled in size and long black hairs popped out of his knuckles. He stretched his fingers, bobbed around for a bit, and dove for the tickle. The flame went off, leaving us in the darkness.

"Stop that!" I giggled, and batted him away from my ribs. My voice was too loud in the quiet forest. "Stop it!" I said again, this time in a harsh whisper.

Squire backed up and floated before me, a faint shade in the black forest. He seemed a bit droopy, sad maybe. I hadn't taken the time to be with him lately.

"I'm sorry," I whispered. "It's just that there are dangers around here and we need to be quiet."

Squire bobbed in understanding.

"You once said that you had a mate, the left hand to your right."

Squire nodded again.

"Did you both live with Baba Yaga?"

Another bob, this one more hesitant.

"Does she live near here? Can you show me the way?"

Squire dove into my backpack. I couldn't believe it. Was he hiding? Squire had faced the Montmorencys and their wicked partners with me. He'd fought the Horseman's wolves. I'd never seen him afraid of anything.

"Come out," I whispered. "I know you're scared, but this is important."

Squire peeked out of the bag.

"I need you, Squire. No one else can help me now. Will you show me the way to my grandmother's house?"

If Squire had shoulders to straighten, he'd have straightened them then. If he had lungs, he'd have taken a deep breath. Since he had neither of those, he just bobbed once and took off into the darkness.

"Wait," I called. "I can't see you." Quickly, I searched the bundle that Uncle Misha had given me. It was full of odd bits and pieces, including stones, bones and yarn — tools with which to make a ward. (If only I had thought to look in the bundle when I'd been confronted by the two ghosts.) Also in the package was — yes! A luster beetle. I gave it a shake. It jittered in my hand; then its rear lit up, filling the night with its soft green light.

Squire bounced in the air a few paces ahead. He beckoned with one finger, and I followed.

I didn't know how Squire could find his way in the darkness, but he did. We walked for what seemed like hours, but the sky was still dark when we came upon a fence.

A fence in the middle of a wild Siberian forest was odd enough. A fence with skulls atop each post was downright scary.

Squire bobbed up and down. I couldn't tell whether he was excited to go on or trembling and wanting to run away. But I wasn't ready to do either.

I held the luster beetle up to examine one of the skulls.

Its black eyeholes suddenly blazed to life. I jumped back and fell against a tree. Blue fire burned from the skull's eyes, reminding me of a jack-o-lantern. Then one by one, the skulls lit up along the fence, like the guiding lights on a runway. They wound through the trees to a rickety old gate.

"I think we found it," I said.

Squire hid in the crook of my arm.

I didn't know what we'd find inside the house, and I decided that Squire would be safer in my pack for now. "Go to sleep, Squire," I said, and he fell into my hand, once again becoming nothing more than a small stone sculpture. I tucked him in my bag and followed the line of glowing skulls to the gate. The fiery eyes seemed to track my movements, and a shiver ran up my spine. I tried not to look at the one fence post, right next to the gate, that didn't have a skull.

At the gate, I got the first glimpse of the house. It was tall and bent, like a witch's hat. *Appropriate*, I supposed. A large porch wrapped around the front and side. On the porch jostled an old rocking chair. It swayed back and forth, back and forth, with a faint creaking of boards. But no one was sitting in it. Beside the chair, a big black-and-white cat washed a paw and watched me. The gardens around the porch were full of dead bushes and headless stalks. The windows were dark and dirty. In the faint glow of the skull torches, they shone like large eyes.

Then I noticed something weird: There was a path leading right up to the house, but there were no steps up to the porch and no door. How were you supposed to get in? I remembered Lauraleigh telling me how Baba Yaga was known to be very private. Apparently, she really did dislike visitors, since she didn't leave a door for them.

Well, that was just too bad for her. Now that I'd made it this far, I wasn't going to chicken out at the last minute. But I hesitated. Lauraleigh had also said that Baba Yaga didn't like impolite people. Surely it was impolite to just walk up to a house with no door. I couldn't forget that empty fencepost. It felt like it was burning a hole in the back of my head, as if even without a skull, it were glaring at me the hardest.

As I looked closer, I saw that the house was definitely standing on two stilt-like things: chicken legs! Why did Baba Yaga have them? And then I remembered Uncle Misha mentioning the possibility that my grandmother had moved.

Well, it's not as if there were a lot of houses around here. She couldn't have just gone to a real estate agent to find a new place to live. And why would she, when she had everything she needed here and a house on feet? Surely she had enough power to make it walk around if she wanted?

I looked more closely at the feet. In the blue light of the skulls, I thought I saw one of them shiver as if from the night chill.

I bit my lip, glancing back up at the porch. What I was thinking of doing might be dangerous. But Baba Yaga would find out I was here soon enough, and I might as well get it over with. The black-and-white hare on the porch looked back at me.

Wait. Hadn't it been a cat a moment ago?

It was my turn to shiver. There was a lot of magic in this place. I could feel its low hum. Who knew what might happen next? It was time to try something.

I stared at the house's legs and whispered the formula that floated up from my memory. "Little house, turn your front to me and your back to the forest." It sounded like something I'd picked up from one of Uncle Misha's picture books when I was small.

At first, nothing happened, and I thought I'd have to try something else — or risk walking up to the house after all. But then there was a great creak, and slowly the house began to rise up into the air. The two chicken legs were unbending. They seemed to stretch out. Then with what looked like tiny little dance steps, they started to move, slowly turning the house around.

It was one of the weirdest things I had ever seen, and the last couple of months had set the bar for that pretty high.

Another wall of the house came into view, looking just like the one I'd seen, except without a rocking chair. And then the front turned toward me, and the chicken legs set themselves down with a heavy *whomp*. A set of stairs lined up perfectly with the path and led right up to a door.

The cat — wait, hadn't it just been a hare? — slunk around the corner and looked at me mockingly. From inside the house, I heard muffled cheering and applause.

Swallowing hard, I walked up the path, hoping I looked more confident than I felt. When I reached the stairs, there was another burst of applause. What was going on? Was this one of Baba Yaga's jokes or something? I hadn't heard that she had much of a sense of humor, but maybe she'd put an enchantment on the house to congratulate people who had made it this far before she killed them. That sounded like what I imagined about her.

The front door was open a crack. I knocked and pushed it wide, just as the sky lightened. Dawn comes quickly in the forest. The skulls winked out, leaving the porch lit by the pink glow of sunrise. The light barely filtered inside, though, and the room I walked into was dark, until another skull sputtered to life in the corner. I studied the cluttered room.

It was furnished with pieces of dark wood, a table, a chair by the fire, and several chests, some open and spilling out blankets and clothes. Large bunches of herbs hung from nails on the beams overhead. Every available space was covered with trinkets, potion bottles, jars of herbs, and other oddities. I saw skulls of large and small animals, dolls fashioned from sticks and yarn, a statue of a fat man and another of two thin women back to back.

But what really shocked me were the hands. They were everywhere! Just like Squire, they were animated and they floated in the air, doing all kinds of chores. One hand was grinding dried herbs in a mortar. Another was dusting a shelf of trinkets. A third was stoking the fire, and two others were working together to knit a long scarf.

None of them paid me any attention, so I followed the sounds of voices into another room. This one was a kitchen, with a large hearth along one wall and a worn butcher block in the center. The block seemed dark with old blood. In here, more hands were washing dishes, stirring a pot of stew that was hanging on a hook over the fire, and chopping vegetables.

I tiptoed through the kitchen; as before, none of the hands bothered me. I went through another door. This one opened into a dark bedroom that smelled musty and sweet as if someone had been burning herbs in the fireplace.

I'd found the source of the voices. On a dresser sat an enormous flat-screen TV — one of those new, curved types. Its flickering lit the room. At that moment, a contestant on a game show won the grand prize and the audience burst into applause. I blinked in the bright light and tried to see the rest of the room. Other than the TV, it was occupied by the biggest bed I'd ever seen, piled high with mismatched blankets. Perched in the middle of the bed was a wizened old woman with her hair in curlers. She had sunken, wrinkled cheeks and a huge cone of a nose. Her teeth seemed too big for her mouth and oddly gray.

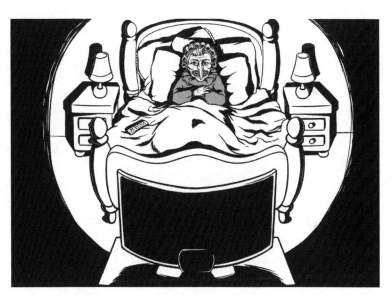

"It's about time you got here, girl," Baba Yaga said. "Don't just stand there gaping like a ninny. Make yourself useful. Fetch us some tea."

Chapter 11

ear Diary,

My grandmother is one of the most powerful witches in the world. She's also undoubtedly the weirdest person I've ever met. I don't think she has a heart. She let her own flesh and blood die in childbirth in a bear's den. She may have killed many girls abducted by the Montmorencys and the Black Horseman around the world. And she kidnapped my father. On top of all that, her house is very strange. The main furnishing is a massive TV that's bigger than anything I ever saw back in Geneva. I certainly didn't expect to find that in a little forest cabin on chicken legs. My grandmother is from another world. So how is she connected to the world I used to know? Nothing about her makes any sense to me.

Then again, she is my grandmother, and I have to deal with her to learn about my family secrets and save my father.

Maybe she can even teach me some magic. Just so long as that doesn't make me as weird as she is!

I stood frozen in place in front of my grandmother. I had often tried to imagine our meeting, but not in my wildest dreams had I ever pictured such a casual greeting from her. Fetch us some tea? Who greeted a granddaughter she'd never seen before like that?

On the other hand, at least she was coming across as somewhat friendly and almost bordering on *normal*. For a woman who'd chased her only daughter off to have a baby in the wilderness, surrounded by bears, she was being … unexpectedly nice. Well, not nice exactly, but I had suspected, based on movies and books, that it would be something like this — kids making tea for the older people in the family. It was as though she had accepted me as her granddaughter so quickly that she expected us to take on our normal roles at once.

She looked as if she were centuries old, and she didn't seem very healthy at all. Her face was drawn and sunken; her body was thin and spindly. She did seem in need of a granddaughter to look after her and help out. Maybe even the most powerful magic in the world wasn't enough in the end? Maybe she was regretting her treatment of my mother and father?

After a second of contemplation, I decided to play along.

"Hello, Granny!" I chirped. Since I'd never been here before, though, it was impossible to play house with Baba Yaga without getting some clarification. "Where's your kettle?"

She puffed her lips, clearly annoyed. "Go into the kitchen and ask the hands. There should be a pair in there that isn't busy."

I headed for the kitchen and looked at the disembodied hands scuttling around the place. A pair was washing dishes in the sink. Another pair was dusting. The final pair was tidying the counter, not doing anything serious, it seemed.

"Hello," I said to them, not sure where to look. I had never seen more than one disembodied hand at a time before, and I didn't know if they'd take to me as quickly as Squire had. "I'm Anna Sophia." One hand reached out and I shook it. This was very odd. "Would you mind making some tea for my grandmother and me?"

The hands scuttled off. They brewed tea in an ornate samovar and arranged beautiful cherry pies on an elaborate silver tray. I settled on a little stool and observed them. I wasn't sure if you were supposed to speak to disembodied hands as they worked. But surely my grandmother spoke to them? Whom else *would* she have spoken to, holed up in this place all by herself? The hands placed two glasses in intricate metal holders on the tray and scuttled off to help the other pair dust.

"Thank you, er, hands," I said, acutely aware of how strange this interaction was. I was in Siberia in a cabin on chicken legs, talking to a pair of disembodied hands. Ghosts flew about, and my friends fought multicolored Horsemen with the help of a Jewish monster made of clay. My life had morphed into some fantastic dream.

I went back to the main room.

"You took your time," my grandmother grumbled. She was still in her bed, watching the TV.

I placed the tray down gently next to her and took a seat in a big armchair nearby.

After fiddling with the remote and lowering the TV's racket to a low mumble, she slowly poured the tea, her arthritic fingers cracking as the dark brown liquid filled the clear glasses. She didn't ask how I took my tea. Wordlessly, she spooned sugar into it before stretching her hand out to me. "Here, Anna Sophia."

I took the glass from her and took a sip. The tea was very nice. It was when I tasted its sweetness that I really started to feel I was at my grandmother's house. Even though my grandmother was an evil old witch and there was a chance that the tea was poisoned… It wasn't a big chance, but there were certain risks when dealing with Baba Yaga.

Still, she was drinking tea from the same samovar, so unless the poison was already in the glass… I remembered the orphan girls that the Black Horseman had been hoarding for her in the Montmorency castle dungeons back in Geneva. But Geneva seemed a long time ago and far away. Did it even exist? Surely the quiet, orderly Geneva couldn't exist in the same world as floating hands and ghosts and children being raised by bears? Obviously, this was the real world I was in, the one where houses had chicken feet and walked about and cats changed into hares. It had to be the real world because I was there. So was Geneva a dream, then?

I sipped more tea. Yes, this is what families were supposed to be like, wasn't it? Grandmothers and granddaughters sitting together, having tea. Granny giving me a treat, a bit more sugar in the tea than Mother — I mean Sister Constance — would have allowed.

"Eat up, Anna," said Granny, passing a plate to me. "You've had a long trip. Let me fatten you up."

"Thank you so much, though I don't know if I want to get very fat," I replied with a smile, and bit into one of the pastries. It was quite delicious.

I leaned back in the chair, happy to let my feet rest. *It was a long trip*, I thought, *with all that running*. I was actually feeling a bit sleepy. I drank more tea. Tea was good for staying awake, wasn't it? That's why Sister Daphne always had a pot of it ready at night to be sure she'd stay awake until curfew. I smiled a little. What a silly thing to do, make tea in a pot. Why would you do that when you could use a coal-powered samovar?

Silly, those dreamlike people in dreamlike Geneva, I thought. *Why would I ever dream of such a dull little place, where hands couldn't fly and you almost never got treats?* I picked up another cherry pie and began to eat it.

"Everything is absolutely delicious," I said.

"Only the finest for my granddaughter," she croaked, and gave me a tentative smile as if she weren't used to smiling and had nearly forgotten how. "I've been waiting for you for a very long time."

"You have?"

"Almost since your birth. I've always known you were my kindred spirit, Anna Sophia. Not like your parents." I thought I saw an expression of intense anger flash across her face. But I must have been wrong; she was smiling again.

I finished my pastry and tea and curled up in the chair, tucking my legs under me and watching the screen. This was *so* normal. I was full and tired, and I fell into a light sleep. I dreamed that Baba Yaga was a normal grandmother, who lived somewhere in dream-Geneva. I lived with my parents a few blocks away from her but loved to drop by for tea in the afternoon. We ate pies and watched TV on her fancy flat screen. She gave me advice about life, cooking, and sometimes, with a little giggle, about boys, even though she knew it embarrassed me.

I was awakened by loud yelling. It was confusing; in my dream, I had thought the noise had been coming from rowdy children throwing a ball around outside Granny's apartment, and she'd yelled at them to be more careful.

But when I opened my eyes, I was definitely in the cabin in the woods and Granny was yelling. She wasn't facing the window, as in my dream. I didn't immediately understand what I was seeing. My dream had been a lot more realistic, after all. My grandmother, the unstable old witch who lived in a house full of disembodied hands, was screaming at the television on her wall. She had gotten out of bed and was pacing up and down, a torrent of vitriolic abuse pouring out of her mouth.

The man inside the television was smiling widely, holding a small device in his hands. "As you can clearly see, the latest phone model has an array of new features that justify the price increase. The screen is bigger, the handset thinner, and the battery lasts two hours longer than in the previous models. And look here. Under the hood…"

"Well, as long as the battery lasts longer," Baba Yaga yelled over him.

"The camera is also much better," the man said, as if responding to her. "We're going to talk to one of Instagram's most-followed users, who will tell us about why he has chosen to upgrade to this model. Let's welcome him to the studio, ladies and gentlemen."

"He's one of the most followed people on Instagram. Of course he is! Thank goodness we have an expert in being followed on the Internet! Thank goodness there's someone who can tell us about why it's better to have a bigger screen because of the *idiots who follow him on a website!*"

Baba Yaga was pacing up and down, gesticulating. From the way she was carrying on, I wondered whether the men in the studio could hear her. Surely nobody would get this upset without being able to impact events? And besides, why was she so angry at a man on the technology segment of a program? It seemed ridiculous. It was surreal. Baba Yaga, the world's most powerful witch, was having a one-sided shouting match with a man on TV.

"Granny?" I asked, my voice squeaking.

She spun round, her eyes wild. "Oh! I forgot about you."

171

"Are you all right?"

"No, of course I'm not all right, you silly girl! How can I possibly be all right? Look. Look right there!" She pointed at the man being interviewed.

I frowned, even more confused now. "Why are you so upset? I don't understand. They're just talking about phones, aren't they?"

She seemed to deflate, the anger leaving her body. She moved over to the bed, appearing to age by the second. When she spoke again, her voice was older, crankier.

"I am angry at our world, Anna Sophia. When I was your age, people cared about real things. Real issues. Determination and change were in the air. People *cared*."

"They still—"

She stopped me with a raised hand. "Then as I got older, they stopped caring. They started focusing on other things. At first, I thought it was just the people around me. But this TV shows me people all over the globe, and all of them are busy with absolute nonsense. They don't care about each other or real problems. They're playing with toys and shooting their guns at each other and buying new cell phones to get more followers from places to which they will never go."

I felt the need to defend the world I had come from. "It's just—"

"A follower should be able to follow you, Anna Sophia. Not be a virtual set of pixels on a screen. Why does this man need a new cell phone if the one he has works well? So that he funds the company, and the company sends money to the government who runs the army, and they go shoot people so that they can earn even more money and buy more toys!" She leaned back, apparently tired from her endless rant.

"And this all worries you ... why?" I asked.

When she looked at me, the sorrow of the entire world seemed to show in her ice-gray eyes. "People used to believe in me. And so I was ... strong. Now, even the dead ones ... they don't even know my name. Just a nameless old hag taking their souls over into the Great Beyond." She spat on the floor. "Pathetic."

I felt a twinge of fear at the base of my spine. I wasn't sure why I was scared, but suddenly I remembered the look in the Black Horseman's eyes as he stared at me back in Geneva. And I remembered how the Montmorencys had hoarded children in their dungeon of a basement so they could be sent to this woman — my grandmother — who was so deeply angry at what the world had become. I doubted this great witch would be defeated by some cell phones.

She had a plan. She had to.

And however good her cherry pies were, I was worried it was a wicked plan.

Chapter 12

ear Diary,

I've been at my grandmother's house for a full day now. We're getting along fine, but I haven't gotten any closer to figuring out where my father is. Granny just doesn't want to talk about him. Instead, she watches TV and rants about consumerism! I don't know much about cell phones. To be honest, I don't really care. But I do care a lot about where she's got my dad hidden.

At least I've been able to make her call off the Horsemen from Blackwood Castle. She wasn't very happy about doing that. There seems to be bad blood between her and Uncle Misha, and she wanted him taken captive. But she did as I asked. She said someone called the Great Trapper had called up many forest animals and they had pushed the Horsemen back anyway. One Horseman had been maimed by a bear, she also said.

Today, I've decided to go exploring. I'm going to try to forage for information. Granny is too busy yelling at the men on the television to pay much attention to me...

Another thing. I wish I had my dream stone with me. I truly do. It could have shown me the way to my father ... but I guess I left it back at the orphanage. Didn't I?

"Go on, show me another clip of her Tiffany diamonds!" Granny shouted at the screen. I'd learned that she particularly hated TV ads. They seemed to set her off big-time.

I'd never really spent too much time thinking about everyday things before I got to Baba Yaga's cabin. Although my trust fund had allowed me to go to one of the best schools in Switzerland, Monsieur Nolan had never approved of luxuries. I always had nice clothes, stationery, and books. Perhaps some of my things were nicer than what the other kids in the orphanage had, but I never paid too much attention to that. The only time I was offered *nicer* things was when the Montmorencys tried to woo me. But I wasn't easy to bribe with possessions. I always thought there was something suspicious about people who had too many things, like Marie with all her jewelry. Now I wondered if that was Baba Yaga's spirit playing inside me the whole time! Granny and I do have a lot in common, after all.

Watching the ads, I remembered that a lot of children I had grown up with *had* thought about material things a lot. Kids used to talk to each other about trading cards and new cell phones and fancy gadgets. Girls chatted about clothes and jewelry while boys discussed all the different cars they wanted to own when they grew up. Jean-Sébastien even saved up enough to get that scooter of his. I remembered that I had ridden on it once, which had been fun.

But many of the children in the orphanage were poor, so while they sometimes dreamed of being rich, such conversations rarely went on too long. We tended to be realistic, focusing on what we knew, what was within the four walls of our house and school and what the Sisters discussed. I had been shielded from the world, I suppose. Sister Constance didn't seem to approve of the world. And now I was being exposed to it from Baba Yaga's cabin, of all places.

Baba Yaga leaned against a pile of pillows on her bed. Picking her long nose, she grumbled, "You see, Anna Sophia, people have lost all good sense these days. All they do is stare at screens scattered around them. They forget about real things, like life and death."

"Hmm?" I said, wondering if I could steer this conversation to the topic of where she was holding my father.

My grandmother blew her nose into a paper napkin (how did she manage to get that in this isolated place?), crumpled it, and tossed it into a corner of the living room. A pair of hands whizzed in from the kitchen and cleaned it up.

"They forget about love. About hate," she continued. "And they care about money because they need it to buy what the TV tells them they need. Not want, you see? *Need*. And what happens then? When they get that, they're told they *need* another something. These screens have turned people into drones. They're no better than my flying hands! Just like them, they don't have any brains of their own."

"But why do *you* watch that thing, Granny?" I asked, curling up in my chair. I had been wondering about that ever since the first time I'd seen her shout at the television. Living in this secluded cabin in the woods, wouldn't it have been better for her to ignore the rest of the world and be happy?

"Only cowards hide away from things they don't like. Brave people confront them."

"But it makes you unhappy!" I exclaimed. "Turn that thing off. Let's go outside for a walk—"

Baba Yaga narrowed her eyes at me. "Don't be silly. If you want to go outside, you can. But I won't be coming with you. The next program is on in ten minutes. I don't hide from the problems of this world. I never have."

"Why do you live in the forest, then?" I asked, drawing my knees up and wrapping my arms around them. "Why not live in a city, where you can deal with these problems head-on all the time?"

"You're too young to understand, *vnuchechka*," she said, waving a dismissive arthritic hand. That's what she called me, that or my full name. It was either Anna Sophia or *vnuchechka*, little granddaughter. It was odd, but I liked it.

Little granddaughter. Family. Mine.

"Oh, sure," I said.

She coughed. "Bring me some water from the kitchen."

I nodded and scuttled off, much like one of my grandmother's hands, except with feet. She often told me what to do, giving me silly chores around the house. Perhaps it made her feel a little less lonely. What was weird (aside from the hands everywhere and Baba Yaga's odd views) was that she never acknowledged I'd only just arrived in her life. She didn't ask about my past, and she never told me anything about my parents or what had happened before I got here. She just complained about the people on TV and in the world at large, and bossed me around. There was another weird thing … a memory … no, a hint of a memory. Like there was something or someone I had forgotten after entering this house.

I took the glass of water into the living room and stood studying Granny. She was watching a game show. "Here you are," I said.

"Look at this, Anna Sophia. These girls in their skimpy clothes! How much do you think they're being paid to open a briefcase? This game's just a matter of chance. It's clouding up people's minds, don't you think?"

"I guess you're right," I replied, giving her a tiny shrug. It wasn't that I thought she was wrong as such; I just didn't care about people on TV. I wanted to find my dad. I wanted to know about my mom. I even wanted to know more about my grandmother. But she never talked about any of that, and I hadn't found a way to get her to tell me.

Instead, she rambled on. "Why do they need more money? Do you think this man knows what to do with a million dollars? It's not like he's going to use it for anything important. No, people who do important things don't go on TV. It's—"

"Were you being serious about me going outside for a walk?" I interrupted. If Baba Yaga wouldn't talk to me about my parents, I'd have to find things out by myself.

She looked at me carefully. "I was. If that's what you want to do, of course."

"Thank you, Granny. I'll just take a look around."

I opened the door and walked out onto the porch, smelling the air outside. I patted the black-and-white cat, who immediately morphed into a hare. The house was standing upright on its chicken legs, and I had to clamber down the stairs to get to the ground. I looked around. I'd had to leave my backpack inside so Baba Yaga wouldn't suspect I was up to mischief. But for the sake of my father and for the sake of—

Of what? What *was* it? Friends, maybe? Or something.

But I had a family now. My very own granny. What did friends matter?

Blackwood Castle. That name kept popping up in my mind like it meant something.

I had to stop sitting around watching that silly TV. One full day doing that was already one day too many.

The skulls on the fence seemed to scrutinize me. I hadn't noticed that when I'd first arrived here, but then again I'd been on the other side of the fence. I scowled at them. They didn't move. Obviously, Baba Yaga had put them there just to scare people off. I shrugged at them and made a face. I was being silly. They were just skulls; they weren't alive. After all, if they were, I'd be able to tell, wouldn't I? I'd feel the magic.

That was strange.

Now that I thought about it, I wasn't feeling that familiar churn of dark energy inside me. In fact, I didn't feel any magic inside me at all. It was as if I'd somehow walked into a place where my special powers just didn't exist. In fact, I could barely even feel any magic around the house. Hadn't I found it almost overwhelming when I'd arrived?

I shuddered and headed for the little gate. At every step, it felt like the skulls' eyes were following me. Which was impossible.

I ran the last few steps to the gate and was about to open the latch when the skulls began to whirl about. The two nearest ones flew off their posts and pounced on me. I screamed and batted them off, and I dashed back toward the house. The two skulls were chasing me, biting at my heels like little demon dogs.

"Leave me alone!" I shouted, kicking at them, unable to call up the familiar energy to scare them off with a good blast. "Leave me alone! Shoo!"

I didn't know if they could actually do anything to me. They were just making a racket, and I was terrified that my grandmother would come out onto the porch and figure out that I had been trying to escape.

"Shh!" I said to the skulls, putting a finger to my lips. "Stop it. I won't go anywhere; I promise."

The skulls continued to clatter around me as I reached

the steps, but as I began to climb them, the chicken feet gave a sudden lurch and I was thrown to the ground. Faint applause from inside the house accompanied my fall.

I winced, realizing I'd be bruised from this escapade.

The skulls returned to their posts, their eye sockets still fixed firmly on me. I stood up, rubbed my arms, and went inside, struggling for breath.

The game show host was instructing a new contestant, making the audience laugh and applaud. Baba Yaga sat in bed, watching the screen as if nothing had happened. Did she know what had gone on outside?

I flopped into my armchair.

"Had enough fun?" she asked.

"Yeah," I said softly. "It was pretty boring."

"Being alone can get boring," she admitted, turning to look at me with her icicle eyes. "I think that's why I started watching TV so much."

This is my chance, I thought. *Maybe she'll talk about Mom.* "Why were you alone, Granny?" I asked quickly.

She waved at me dismissively and turned back to the screen. "Everyone's alone, Anna Sophia. We're all just watching each other on a screen in the end. You never really know anyone."

That's it, I thought. *She is the strangest person I've ever met.* How could she claim to be alone when I was right here with her? How could I get anywhere with her?

"By the way," I said. "I couldn't feel any of my magic powers out there. And I don't feel them now. Isn't that strange?"

Baba Yaga chewed on her lower lip, blew her nose into

a fresh napkin, and smiled. "Nothing strange. I took it all."

I stared at her, speechless. "You did what?"

With a groan, my grandmother climbed down off her massive bed and stood facing me. The translucent gray skin on her old face hung around deep worry lines, and her gray eyes had a weary, sunken appearance. "I took your energy," she said. "You don't mind, do you?"

I felt my eyes widen as my heart accelerated. "Why would you do that?"

"It's all your fault, anyway," she said, still staring into my eyes. "You released those orphan girls selected for me. I'd have eaten well for a while. But now I only have you until the Black Horseman finds someone else for me."

"Wait, wait," I protested, raising my hands.

"Well, I'm not literally going to eat you," she continued. "I hardly eat any meat, anyway. Nasty things, those animals, with their illnesses and worries and pains. But young girls, once in a while, for a feast..." She licked her lips and gave me a sinister wink. "Not you, though. You're far too useful."

"Oh, Granny," was all I could say. The room felt smaller around me, as if the walls had pressed together a little.

Suddenly the TV switched to a music channel, and a young woman began to sing "All about That Bass." Baba Yaga leaped into the air with a wild yelp. Her bulky clothes swung about her, filling the air with her old person's smell.

I stepped back. "I... I ... need to go outside." I needed air. I was about to faint or panic and run — and hang the consequences.

"Yes!" she yodeled. "Let's go out!"

"Oh please," I whispered, though I didn't know whom I was pleading to. "Please, please, please..." I had never been so frightened.

Baba Yaga grabbed my hand and dragged me to the porch outside. The house, probably responding to some unheard command, lowered itself to the ground. The rocking chair began to rock madly. The black-and-white cat meowed sharply again and again — but at least it wasn't changing into a hare. The skulls rattled on the fence, and the music from the TV grew unnaturally loud.

"Let's dance, Anna Sophia!" Baba Yaga bellowed, dragging me around with rough, jerky motions. "Dance!" She pushed me into her garden of dead plants.

I didn't want to dance with this dangerous witch, but her gray eyes, hypnotic and irresistible, were locked on mine. I tried to pull my hands out of her grasp, but she only laughed and held me stronger. Shaking her derriere in rhythm with the music from the TV, she pulled me left and then dragged me right, twisting my body from side to side, twirling me around. I could barely stay on my feet, unable to grasp any method to her mad outburst of movement, her scornful laughter, her vitriolic screams, but knowing it was there.

"Feel it!" she yelled. "Feel it rise through the soles of your feet!"

"Feel what?" I asked, desperately trying to free myself.

"Stop fighting me, you young fool," she said. "Your grandmother won't do anything to hurt you. Feel it! Feel it float up from the earth!"

"Feel what?"

"Everything! Life! Power! The world!"

She forced me to spin, sidestep, lean backward and forward. She made me jump, and because she was holding my hands, we were jumping unnaturally high. Maybe as high at the golden peacock whirling in the wind on top of the roof, maybe even higher. I couldn't tell because the world was becoming unreal around me, the colors more intense, the air lighter and sweeter. A powerful wind arose, making the trees around us dance as well.

Warmth began to spread from the soles of my shoes up along my skin, a jittery sort of warmth like hundreds of hot ants crawling.

I yelled in alarm, but Baba Yaga only laughed. "Do you feel the energy, Anna Sophia?" she screeched. "Do you feel the power of this land?"

Yes — I did feel that energy. And I wished for this grotesque ballet to stop. She let me go, and immediately, a bolt of lava rose from the earth and traveled up my spine, making me cry in surprise and fear. The heat spread itself to all my limbs and into my head, filling each cell of my body with tingling and a sort of electric buzz.

"Draw in as much as you can and hold it in your heart!" my grandmother screamed right into my face.

My limbs began to vibrate as if I'd plugged myself into a wall socket. The energy — I knew what it was now, an infusion of my stolen power — was so potent and fresh that my spine arched, throwing my head backward. I felt like a fishing line, stiff and frozen, pulled taut by the jaws of some mighty monster.

Opening my mouth wide, I screamed with all the power I had in me and fell flat on the soft earth. But I could not rest. The energy was still flooding into me as if that earth were a giant battery charger, making me jump around like a like a ball suspended in the air by the jet of a fountain.

Then it all became quiet — and only the shadow inside my heart laughed gleefully.

"What was that, Granny?" I asked, looking at the sky above. My magic was back; I felt its familiar hum.

"Some energy practice. A witch should know how to draw power from the land." She paused and asked, "Do you have a magic wish, Anna Sophia? Something you tried before but couldn't do?"

"Yes. To find my father."

She snickered. "Apart from that."

I sat up and then stood, swaying slightly from side to side. "That bread loaf," I said. "I couldn't make it appear before." I rummaged in my pockets, but I couldn't find the crumbs Egor had given me. I shrugged. Did it really matter whether I had those crumbs or not? I mean, they were just crumbs I'd picked up. It's not as if they were a precious gift from a friend or anything. After all, I didn't have any friends. What on earth did I even mean by the name "Egor"?

Anyway, it was about time Granny taught me to use my magic properly, after all those years of promising to. Filling my lungs with air, I prepared to say my magic phrase.

Baba Yaga raised a hand. "Wait. For the bread loaf to appear, did you jump in place thrice, pulling yourself by your nose?"

I shook my head. "What? Of course not. Are you crazy?"

"And besides, did you chase a cockroach while running on your hands and feet and singing 'Jingle Bells?'"

"Granny!" I rolled my eyes.

Baba Yaga put her hands on her hips. "Ha! I knew it. Of course your spells didn't work. Now do as I say."

I gave her a sidelong glance.

"Go on. Jump thrice, pulling yourself by the nose. Then find a cockroach — the king, mind you. Chase him while you sing 'Jingle Bells.'" The appalling thing was she seemed perfectly serious.

The energy tingled inside me, urging me to act. The mad dance of a few minutes ago had left me warm and shocked, and maybe it had made me a little more open to experimentation than usual. With a sigh, I jumped up three times, pulling myself by the nose.

"Hey!" she yelled. "Do it again. Now with feeling!"

I repeated the silly jumps.

"You won't get anywhere like that. What kind of witch are you?" She laughed and mimicked my half-hearted jumps.

"This is how you do it. Look!" Grabbing the tip of her nose with both hands, she pulled on it — making it at least twice as long — and jumped a whole meter in the air three times. "Now you!"

I shook my head. What was I doing here in this Siberian forest, outside this mad woman's house on its daft chicken legs? A faint memory stirred and disappeared before I could register it.

But there was nothing to be done. I decided to just enjoy the silly practice. Closing my eyes to visualize the bread loaf, I repeated Baba Yaga's actions as best I could.

"Good!" she cried out. "Now find the cockroach king. There are plenty where the house likes to sit."

What did a king cockroach look like, anyway? I approached the house. *Might as well go through with it*, I thought as I yelled in my best commanding voice, "Get up, you slovenly chicken!"

The house, visibly shocked at my rudeness, shuddered and got up.

I pushed away the thought that it could get back at me by dropping down on top of my head when I was beneath it. I walked ahead until I found a whole nest of fat red cock-roaches. They scurried away. Not losing a moment, I fol-lowed the largest of them, singing "Jingle Bells" as loudly as I could. When the song was over, I yelled, "Manna from the skies!" I had to keep from rolling my eyes again. The whole experience was nothing but idiocy.

"Done," I said.

"And there you are," Baba Yaga said behind me.

A hard, maybe mocking edge to her voice made me

pay attention. Feeling all my blood rush to my face, I turned around. On the central flagstone sat the black-and-white hare, and on a plate before him rested a large, round, steaming loaf of rye bread. Walking toward it, I seemed to remember that I had just finished baking it — right before we came out for the insane dance.

"But I baked it myself," I said, scowling. "What's so magical about it?"

My grandmother smiled. "Did you now? Did you actually bake it, or is your mind suggesting an explanation so you don't go barking mad?"

I stopped, shocked by the idea. What she had said was surprisingly similar to how Egor had explained the instant conjuring of things from thin air. *Wait*, I thought. *Who's Egor?* Still, I wasn't about to give up.

"Those floating hands of yours baked it and brought

it here," I said, but the sarcastic look on Granny's face had told me the answer before I even finished the sentence. "No, huh?"

I broke off a small piece of bread and chewed it. It was delicious.

That night, after we'd eaten more of my bread with some borsch and had tea with pastries, Granny fell asleep watching her TV.

I decided to take another risk. I was going to wake up Squire. Strangely, I'd almost forgotten about him, but there were so many hands floating about that another one didn't seem special. But earlier that day, I'd found him when I was getting a clean shirt out of my pack. I smiled when I found him. It had been so kind of Granny to let me have one of her hands.

I found some old yellowed paper in the back of the kitchen cupboard and fished a pen out of my backpack. I didn't want to talk to Squire in the kitchen in front of the other hands. Instead, I crept out onto the porch and woke him up there.

Squire seemed excited when he came to life. He was bobbing up and down far more than usual, but at least this time he didn't try to tickle me.

"Hi there," I said, happy to have a friend. Granny was right; being alone was hard — but at least I had Squire.

He wrote on the paper, *Hello Anna Sophia! I missed you!*

I smiled and asked, "So is this where you're from?"

Yes, I know this place well. He paused and then wrote

carefully, *Have you seen Knight, Anna Sophia?*

I shook my head; I hadn't seen any pairless hand in Baba Yaga's house.

Squire seemed to lose his excitement a little.

"I promise I'll keep a lookout, Squire. But in the meantime, I need your help."

He bobbed and then wrote, *Anything for you.*

"I need you to find out where Baba Yaga keeps my dad."

I'll do my best, he wrote.

I smiled. "I'm going to miss you while you're gone. I've already missed you. It's hard to be alone."

Squire nodded slowly in understanding.

That made me feel bad. If anyone knew about loneliness, it was a pairless hand. "I'm sorry. I promise I will look for Knight."

Then I watched as Squire scuttled off.

I sighed, crumpled up the paper, and stuffed it into my backpack. I didn't want to lose this conversation with one of my few friends.

I went back inside and fell into a troubled sleep.

Chapter 13

Dear Diary,

I had been waiting to meet my father for a long time, but I guess I never knew quite what to expect until I actually saw him. Especially since meeting my grandmother has taught me to expect absolutely anything from my family!

Luckily, I found out that my dad is the best in the whole world. Now I just have to figure out a way to set him free. It's good that I'm his daughter and Baba Yaga's granddaughter — I think their spirits are playing inside me. I'm sure I have a few tricks up my sleeve, and it's quite likely that soon my dad and I will be a proper family.

I woke up later that night feeling thirsty. It was dark, either the middle of the night or early morning. I decided to go to the kitchen to fetch some water. I stood up, crept down the corridor, and … walked right into my grandmother.

"What are you doing?" she asked, seemingly as startled as I was. Her voice was harsher and more suspicious than usual. She took a quick step back, and her eyes darted around. She appeared unusually defensive.

This was odd. Odder than I'd come to expect from her, and that was really saying something. If she couldn't sleep, why wasn't she watching late-night TV reruns? That seemed more her style. What was she doing walking around the house in the middle of the night? She rarely moved about, even in the daytime.

"I just wanted to get some water, Granny," I said.

"Then get on with it!" She seemed irritated, and she muttered something incoherent as she shuffled back to bed.

I watched her retreat down the hall; then I walked into the kitchen, which I surveyed carefully. Everything there seemed the same as before.

Why had she been up at this time of night? I wondered if one of the hands would be able to tell me. But none of them seemed to be around; she must have put them all to sleep too.

How fortunate they were. I didn't manage to fall asleep again, even after I had curled up under the blanket once more. Maybe Baba Yaga had also been fetching some water or grabbing a snack in the middle of the night.

But there was also the possibility that she had been visiting my father. The thought thrilled me. Maybe I could follow her and find him!

I took care not to get too excited, though. I had to be vigilant and make sure that I didn't do anything too rushed.

In the morning, I started the day exactly as I had the one before. I went to the kitchen and fetched tea and bagels for our breakfast. Granny turned the TV on as she always did. Then she started her usual rant about the clothes of the breakfast show presenter being different from those the day before.

"Who needs that many outfits, Anna Sophia? What do you think she does with the ones she wore before? Does she just chuck them out into the street?"

I alternated between nodding and shrugging. I wasn't listening to her at all. I was formulating a plan.

I knew that Squire wouldn't be able to come during the day; as the only pairless hand, he'd be way too conspicuous. It was worth waiting to see if he'd come at night — but at the same time, it was better to work out something I could do if he didn't. I didn't know when Squire would return, after all. It might not be for a few nights, and I wasn't willing to wait that long. Not when her previous night's wanderings suggested that Granny was up to something.

The day dragged by. Not having slept well, I was tired. I was careful to stay awake the whole time, though, because I was worried that if I fell asleep, I'd miss my chance. I drank a lot of tea, hoping it would keep me up — or at least, I'd awaken to go to the bathroom in the middle of the night. Even when Baba Yaga went to bed and finally turned off the TV, I lay with my eyes open. To stay awake, I sang songs in my head and told myself the most exciting stories I could still remember from my childhood. Still, it was a challenge; I was seriously sleepy.

All the while, I listened for any unusual sounds. Eventually, I was rewarded for my careful vigil. Granny's bed squeaked. I heard muttering, similar to what I'd heard the night before as she had gone back to bed. It was the exact opposite of her loud, rambling rants toward the TV: soft, indistinct, scarcely more than a few muttered words.

"Insomnia … insomnia … I can't sleep at all," she murmured, shuffling into the corridor.

I silently got out of bed and crept after her. I was barefoot and tried to step gently so as not to make any noise at all. I pressed myself against the wall, desperate to stay in the shadows.

She was heading for the end of the corridor. There was nothing there, just the wall. I wondered if I'd been wrong to suspect her of anything. Maybe Granny was just walking around at night because she couldn't sleep. I was disappointed and prepared my excuses for when she turned around and headed back my way. I opened my mouth to say that I was up for water again, but … suddenly she spoke.

"Open, open, magic door!" she said in a steady, confident voice completely different from her earlier mutterings. Then she sat down and stood up three times, danced the hula, and burped.

And all of a sudden, a door sprang open in the wall at the end of that corridor. My eyes widened in surprise (and relief). I hadn't been paranoid after all. Baba Yaga *had* been up to something!

Behind the door was a massive, ornate, gilded cage, suspended in midair even though it wasn't attached to anything. A man was sitting behind the bars, his feet bound by thin gold chains linked to the cage's floor.

"Good evening, *Koscheyushka*!" Baba Yaga exclaimed. "Missed me?" She made a kissing noise and giggled. "We have to quit meeting like this, you all chained up in a cage."

"Greetings, old woman," the man replied in a collected tone of voice. "How is my daughter doing? And when shall I see her?"

"She is doing very well." Baba Yaga paused. "I'm taking much better care of her than you or Sereda would ever have managed to. That much is certain."

Koschey didn't take the bait. "And what is she like? Tell me."

Baba Yaga puffed up with a measure of pride as she responded. "Well behaved. Helpful. Nice. Clever. Not at all like my daughter, and nothing like you. I don't know where she gets it from — she must've taken after my spirit."

My father laughed. "She's nice, you say? That doesn't sound like you at all. The cleverness I'll grant you. But while you're very many things, *nice* is not one of them."

Granny stood silently for a moment. "I think I might love her."

"You can't *think* you love someone, you silly old bat.

That's not how it works. When you love someone, you *know*, deep in your heart. Not that you have one."

"Stop it," she snapped. "I forgot that you consider yourself some kind of philosopher. I'm tired of it. I don't know why I still put up with you after all these years. I don't know why I didn't just hex you to smithereens when I'd first set eyes on you and heard your particular brand of madness."

"What exactly do you want me to stop? You're the one who came to visit me. I never invited you anywhere. I didn't ask you to come to my cage tonight. I never asked you to visit the kingdom of the dead. But that never worried you much. You rather like showing up uninvited."

"Yes, yes, now stop. Let's return to our discussion. Your daughter's lovely."

"How long are you going to have her stay with you?"

"I rather thought I might keep her here with me forever, actually."

Koschey stared. "Ah, but you are one twisted creature! You never cease to amaze me, even after all these years. What if she wants to leave? Why would you force somebody you claim to love to stay with you forever?"

"To keep me company. I get lonely here, all by myself."

"Ha!" He snorted. Then he smiled sardonically. "You have me."

"You're so stupidly stubborn that I can't even let you out of your cage. And you're boring. We've known each other too long. I know your best stories and your worst jokes. We're as bad as an old married couple now."

"I think you fail to understand how feelings work and how marriage works," Koschey said. "For starters, in a marriage, it's generally considered bad manners for one spouse to lock the other up. If you've decided to replace me with my progeny, are you planning on releasing me?"

"I'd release you in a heartbeat." Baba Yaga gave one of her little chuckles. "But only if you agree to join my work."

My father was silent for a while. He didn't sound nearly as snarky when he said, "What are you talking about now, old woman?"

"I've come up with a plan, but I need your assistance for it to work, Koschey. If you agree to help me, I'll let you and your daughter go free. On the condition that you come regularly for Sunday teas, of course. We'll eat my pies and—"

"Focus, you old bat! This isn't the time for your domestic fantasies." He was no longer laughing. "I was married to your own daughter, for goodness sake. She's the one I'll always love; not you."

I pressed myself closer to the wall and inched forward so I could see them better. Baba Yaga stood with her back to me, and she blocked my line of sight to my father. A strange thing was happening. From where I stood, she now seemed a young woman with a vigorous body and a thick head of long, flame-red hair. For the first time, I saw the powerful witch I'd heard about rather than the frail old woman with her crazy mutterings and ranting at the television. For the first time, too, I could see some resemblance between her and me.

"Fine, I'll tell you," said Baba Yaga. "Even though you're interrupting me like an annoying mosquito."

"Go on then."

"You remember the old days, eh, Koschey?" she asked, walking to the cage and stroking its thick metal bars. "Fewer people lived in this world, yet you and I were so much stronger. A paradox."

"Nothing paradoxical about it," said Koschey. "They loved us. Or hated us… No matter; they felt something about us."

"Not only felt. They *feared* us. Every night, they told stories about us to their children, who then spent hours being afraid. They sang songs about us. They drew pictures of us. Some even prayed to us. There was a town…" Baba Yaga signed.

"Ivanovo," Koschey said. "I remember that town where they venerated you."

"That was before the Christians expelled the witches of Ivanovo." My grandmother's voice trembled with deep, potent pain. "All that remains is a song about that town having too many women without husbands. And no one remembers why … no one remembers me."

Sadness permeated Dad's voice when he replied. "In those days, these chains of yours would be nothing to me. This cage would be nothing. I understand what you're saying, old woman. And?"

She reached inside the cage and caressed Dad's hands. "And I'm proposing to you that we bring that time back. The time of our power. That we show *them* what really matters."

"Show whom, and how?"

"There are some powerful leeches out there in the world. They consume people's emotions as we do — but instead of fear, they control with greed. You know, I have that magic screen in my bedroom. I've been watching it for a year now;

it shows me true pictures from the world outside. And …
and sometimes I even catch myself wanting a cell phone."

"Leeches, then," Koschey said.

"Yes. Leeches. People's emotions used to feed religion, so
we paid the scientists and misbelievers to ridicule it. People
used to worship their empires, so we stirred wars and rev-
olutions to bring those down. People used to adore powerful leaders, so we bankrolled dissidents and faked history
records to make those leaders seem monsters. And we had
some good times, eh, *Koscheyushka*? You remember?"

"I remember. The times of Chaos. The good times."

"Oh, the Chaos! The superstitions, the fear and the pain,
the search for magic solutions to people's woes. You could
bewitch anyone! And now we have the leeches of greed in
control." She sighed. "The strongest of all. How do you fight
them off to bring back Chaos?"

"I don't know, Yoga," Dad said.

My ears perked. *Did he just call her* Yoga? *I must have
misheard.*

"But I know — and I need your help." She lowered her
voice almost to a whisper. Try as I might, I could only hear
bits of what she said next: "Ghosts … and cities… All the
people … their cars and diamonds … life and death!" She
cried out the last two words, making them ring in the silence
of the sleeping house. Then she whispered, "Only then …
and your daughter … and you."

Oh, what was she talking about? She sounded mad. The
time I'd spent at her place had lured me into thinking she was
almost normal — a lonely old granny who filled the silence
around her by playing the television too loudly and yelling at

it. I had almost forgotten about girls having been kidnapped and held in the Montmorency Castle dungeons for her, Mom having died because of her, Dad having been held captive. Was I that naïve, that desperate to find some semblance of a family that I'd accept everything? Or had she bewitched me?

My father echoed my thoughts. "You're insane," he said with quiet, terrifying anger. Suddenly it didn't seem so unreasonable for Granny to keep him locked up in a cage. "There's no way it would work. Love, life, death... Leave these ideas alone."

After a pause, Granny responded — and to my surprise, her voice was full of sadness. "You're not listening to me, Koschey. It's not only about our feeding. I can make people understand. Think about saving the very foundation of this world, the link between the people, us, and *them*."

She pointed a finger upward, and her hand was the smooth-skinned, slender hand of a young person. "I can do it with or without your help."

"You assume too much," Koschey said. "You assume you know how it all works."

"Don't *you* know?" she asked in an intonation so soft and vulnerable that a wave of sympathy for her washed over me.

"Oh, drop your tricks," my father grumbled. "They no longer work on me."

"They don't?" Baba Yaga said in a soft, alluring voice. I didn't know how my father would be able to resist.

He sighed. "You're a survivor, I'll give you that. You're also an angry old witch. There, behind this beautiful illusion, is saggy flesh, rotten breath, and thinning hair."

Baba Yaga laughed. "That's very true. And you're a silly old man who can't keep his temper."

Koschey said nothing. It seemed they were replaying an old argument for which he had run out of words.

"I like to see you angry," she said. "Watching you turn into a tornado — oh, what fun! Now I have my TV for entertainment, though. So really — what need do I have of you? I've seen your tornado act a thousand times before. And you never say anything interesting. Just that same old pretend philosophy. But the TV... Do you know, the people on it even change their clothes from time to time. A lot, actually. Not like you, still wearing that silly robe you'd had on back when I'd first met you. You're getting outdated. What use are you, anyway? I haven't gotten a single new idea out of talking to you, all this time you've been here. But the TV... Oh, the two of them give me interesting ideas. That TV. And your little daughter."

"Get out of my sight," said my father in a tired, colorless voice. A blast of cold wind burst from his cage, making it sway madly. It pushed Baba Yaga out of his small room and slammed the door behind her. The wind blew with such force that it threw me down the corridor. Panicking, I remembered the Nimble Feet spell and was able to run through the shadows almost noiselessly before my grandmother could see me.

I had seen and heard enough. Without a glance back, I crept into my room and slid into my bed. Tomorrow I had to find a way to visit my father.

My grandmother was insane — and she had way too much power bubbling inside her. That combination couldn't possibly lead to anything good.

Chapter 14

ear Diary,

I need to find a way to talk to Dad. Now that I know where he is, I just have to find a way to distract my grandmother.

I can't believe I'm going to be able to talk to someone from my family — really from my family, I mean. He'll be able to tell me more about Mom. Though I don't know how much time we'll have for catching up, because there's a far more pressing issue on my mind: What is Baba Yaga up to?

So many things to do! I'm trying to sort them out in my mind. Figure out a way to set Dad free. Make sure Lauraleigh and Uncle Misha are safe. And Egor. I think I remember them now. How could I not think of them for so long? How could I forget what we'd done, where I'd left them? That old woman is bewitching me, and I'm so gullible. But not anymore.

I must stop whatever it is my grandmother's planning to do...

Then maybe, one day... Oh, but I'm scared to even think about it. Maybe one day, I'll be part of a real family.

Because a father is already a family, even if he's alone.
It's wonderful, just thinking about it.

In the morning, I found a note from Squire on my pillow: *I found out a lot. I'll visit you right after sunset. Wait for me out on the porch.*

That was encouraging although a little late; I already knew where my father was. But I wanted Squire to come back to me. At least he'd keep me company when I went to help Dad.

I had a plan — and although it was a complicated plan, I felt positive about it. As we ate breakfast in the kitchen that morning, I was smiling, imagining how I'd soon be able to get time alone with my father.

Baba Yaga noticed that my mood had improved. She looked at me over her cup of tea and grunted, "What are you so cheerful about?" So much for encouraging her granddaughter's good spirits.

"I'm not particularly cheerful, Granny. I just had a good night's sleep."

"Really? Well, that's good then." With a sigh, she launched into a new set of complaints. "I wish I was that lucky. I suffer from terrible insomnia; must be old age."

Now there was a possibility I hadn't thought of before. What if I could sedate her for a few hours? "I know some herbal teas that can help people fall asleep," I said. "Why don't we find out which herbs we need, and I'll make some for you this evening."

"Find out?" Baba Yaga looked at me with her mouth open. "I know more about herbs than anyone else. Who'd we find out from, if not from me?"

"Oh," I said, defeated.

She smiled. "Some chamomile tea could help."

Grandmother stood and opened her cupboard. I got up and peeked over her shoulder. The shelves brimmed with faded cartons, jars of herbs, and stranger things. Every item seemed meticulously marked, but some of the markings were so old and washed out that I couldn't even guess what they said. I did make out the words Dragon Blood on a glass jar of black liquid, Dried Mice Tail Powder on another, and Hare's Heart on an old box. I wasn't sure if it was an actual heart, because the box was sealed.

Somehow, I imagined that it was.

Eventually, Granny found and pulled out a cotton bag that read Chamomile and handed it to me.

"Since you had this bright idea, why don't you make your old grandmother a glass or two of tea before bedtime tonight?" Her intonation was a little sharp, like she was annoyed with me.

"Um... Granny," I said slowly, "I've also heard that too much TV isn't very good for sleeping. Maybe you should get some fresh air today. Take a walk in the forest. So you'll sleep better."

She cocked her head and looked at me with narrowed eyes. Then she shrugged and said, "You might be right. I've been cooped up here for ages. Maybe I ought to go pay a visit to my neighbor."

I felt my eyes widen. "You have a neighbor?"

"I sure do. Old Leshiy."

She must have seen that my surprise was genuine. I hadn't expected her to have any neighbors dotted about the forest, especially since she'd kept complaining about how lonely it was here. I wasn't sure who this Leshiy was, and I certainly couldn't picture my weird grandmother paying a social call — or having friends in the first place.

With a bemused chuckle, Granny clarified the situation for me. "You don't know who Leshiy is?"

"Not at all."

"And how could you," she said, rolling her eyes extravagantly, "with those parents of yours sending you away to some far-off place… When, instead of a talented witch, they've turned you into a clueless little girl. Into an empty shell."

This was the first time I'd heard her mention my parents. I wondered if it was a good time to ask her about them. She said they had sent me away, but from what I'd heard, she'd chased *them* away.

"Well, *vnuchechka*, Leshiy is a sylvan. I hope you know what a sylvan is, at least."

"I'm sorry, but I don't." I pulled my feet up and hugged my knees. I looked around the living room, at the massive bed with colorful blankets, the huge TV, the cobwebbed, wooden walls. What was I doing here? There was something about my father … or was it a search for my mother? I wasn't really sure. "You're right. I'm an empty shell. Aren't I?"

Granny gave me a crooked smile. "It's not your fault, Anna Sophia. You're a clever girl, and if you listen to me carefully, you'll be fine."

"Thank you, Granny." I grinned back at her. "I've never had a grandmother before, have I? It feels great having you." It did — didn't it? I wasn't sure if I was being honest. I vaguely remembered that I had to make her feel I was trustworthy enough for her to leave me alone for a while. At the same time, part of me was growing to love this nice old woman. *She does love me*, I thought.

"No need to get sentimental, Anna Sophia," Granny snapped, although I could tell she was pleased with my show of affection. "Pay attention and learn. A sylvan is a forest creature. He is a tree, actually."

"A tree?"

"Yes, and half the time that's all too obvious." Granny giggled. "He can be as dense as wood. But all things considered, he's a decent man, and he lives close enough for me to pay him a visit."

"Do you go to see him often?"

"Certainly not. One can't visit Leshiy too often or for too long. He's intolerable in large doses." She smiled at me. "You want to come meet him?"

Taking a walk with my grandmother did sound like a lot of fun. But for some reason, it didn't feel like what I was here for. I was trying to accomplish something more than that — wasn't I? "I don't know," I said sincerely. "Maybe next time? If you haven't seen him for a while, maybe it's best you catch up, just the two of you?"

"Perhaps you're right," Granny said. She went into the bedroom and returned with a flowery kerchief on her head and a broom in her hand. She wagged her finger at me and said, "Don't get into any mischief while I'm out."

I scratched my head. "What mischief could I get into, Granny, all by myself? I think I'll take a nap."

She looked at me suspiciously, and I wondered if I had made a mistake. But which one? Something funny was happening to my memory. My life had been a little too sheltered and simple, maybe. For years, I'd awaken in the morning in my room, do the chores around the house, play with Cat the Hare, take a nap in the afternoon. Then cook for my grandmother. My mind seemed to focus on the idea of a nice nap; I could hardly think about anything else. I yawned.

"The hands will look after you while you nap," Baba Yaga said. Her calm, melodic voice was the most important thing in the entire world. I had to do exactly what that voice said. "And the skulls."

"They always do," I said, heading for my bed. "Oh yes. I'm so happy here in your house, Granny."

Just before falling asleep, I glanced out the window. Granny was pulling an intricate wooden bowl out of a small lean-to near the fence. She danced around it, kicking her feet up, climbed inside, swept her footsteps with a broom, and cried out, "Ready, steady, go!"

The mortar flew up into the sky and Granny waved down at me, just as she always did every day. It was such a happy sight. For a moment, I wondered if I had seen a photo of that somewhere; it would be nice to have one. But then I shook my head. Why would I need a photo of something I see every day?

I grinned and waved back at Granny from the porch. Then I dropped into the bed.

A splash of shocking coldness jerked me out of my slumber. I screamed in instant all-consuming rage, rolling out of the bed. My heart sank into the swirling shadows of dark magic, and I had to restrain myself from zapping everything around me with blue flames. What was going on?

The first shock passed and I gasped for air. Still screaming, I wiped freezing water from my eyes and looked around. One of Baba Yaga's domesticated hands was floating just above me, holding a dripping bucket. It looked smug.

"Go away," I cried out, fighting to calm down. My belly was heaving in spasms, all my clothes were wet, and my teeth began to chatter with cold.

The hand dropped the bucket and dove in to attack me. No — it actually dove in to tickle me.

"Squire!" I yelled. "How come I didn't recognize you? And what are you doing?"

My old friend bobbed left and right like he was shrugging. He dropped a note into my lap.

I stood up, pulling wet hair out of my face. Why did he have to wake me up, and so dramatically? "Let's see," I said.

The note said: *Let's go see your father.*

I frowned. "What father?" I asked. "I came to find my Granny. I found her."

Squire froze for a moment as though in surprise and then scurried away. He returned with a pencil and wrote, *Are you losing your memory?*

"Of course not."

Do you remember that you came here to see your father, Koschey?

What is he talking about? I'm an orphan, I thought. *I don't have a father.* Feeling rather confused, I smiled. "You're scaring me. Koschey is a character from old fairy tales."

Squire flew a frustrated circle around me and struck my forehead with a knuckle. Painfully. Then he scribbled a few sentences on the paper.

She's making you forget, his note said. *She hypnotized you to sleep while she visits her friend. Now is the time to see your father. Follow me.*

Squire didn't let me ask any more questions. He crumpled the paper and flew off to toss it into the smoldering fireplace in Granny's room. He returned and pulled me by the hand.

He seemed so purposeful that I could not resist. Clearly, Squire was trying to tell me something. As ludicrous as it sounded, he seemed to believe he'd found my father. I almost laughed out loud. But I walked after him.

The other hands were everywhere. Still a little unsteady on my feet, I sat in Baba Yaga's armchair and observed them going about their daily tasks. They seemed busier than usual. I suspected they knew I was up to something — even if I didn't quite know what it was — and they were extra careful to spy on me. There had to be something I could do.

I wondered whether I could put them to sleep like I did with Squire. After all, surely all hands worked in the same way? It was worth a try. I slowly rose to my full height and shouted, "Go to sleep, hands!"

The hands froze in their places and then fell to the floor with dull thumps, like so many ripe fruits from a tree.

I dashed into the kitchen and yelled there too, "Sleep, hands! Go to sleep!"

All the hands stopped whatever they'd been doing. They rested on the table and countertop and in the sink, like strange sculptures.

Squire punched my shoulder gently. He pointed toward the corridor, urging me on.

I hurried down the corridor, trying to stay quiet so as not to awaken the hands in the process. I stopped at the end of the corridor. I felt as though very recently, maybe just yesterday, something important had happened in this very place.

"Why did you bring me here, Squire?" I asked. "It's just a corridor."

He dropped a new note into my hands. *Remember you saw the Iron Queen open this door to speak with your father? Open it now!*

"Ugh," I said, straining my memory. Yes … there was something in what Squire wrote … something familiar, important and emotional. "A door, huh?"

I stared at the blank wall before me, wondering if I had finally gone mad. There was no door. And why was I standing here, talking with this creepy floating hand? I yawned and removed a lock of wet, cold hair from my forehead. *I've been sleepwalking*, I thought. *I need to go back to bed.* I stretched, cringing at the touch of my soaked clothes, and turned to go back to my room.

Squire charged at me and slapped me across my face. The sound exploded like a gunshot in the quiet house. My cheeks burned.

"What—" I began.

Squire dove at me again and smacked me again. He punched the empty wall as if insisting I had to go there.

"Ah, is that what you want?" I cried out. "You want to fight? Well, then—"

The hand stuck a finger out and began to tickle me. He was doing it with an air of desperation that I didn't like in the least.

"Leave me alone, you stupid piece of stone!" I yelled, trying to bat him off.

Squire whizzed back to the kitchen and returned with some paper and a pencil. He dropped to the floor and scribbled furiously.

"I'm tired of you," I said, stifling a yawn. "Sleep, Squire."
He shrank and became still.

The shadows in my heart told me to kick him into the farthest corner of the house and burn his paper. That seemed excessive, however, so I just pushed him aside and picked up his unfinished note.

Uncle Misha has sacrificed… the note said.

I chortled. Why did I have to care about some Uncle Misha who had sacrificed something? It was absurd.

I poured myself a glass of water in the kitchen and gulped it down. All these disembodied hands were starting to get on my nerves, and especially that thug Squire. I had to get rid of that guy. Maybe I should even burn *him*, along with his silly note.

But as I dragged my feet into my bedroom, a faded image slowly appeared in my mind's eye. An old man with a thick beard was carrying me through the forest. We were surrounded by bear cubs. A giant figure — both terrifying and kind, both dangerous and full of love — stood among the boulders behind us. Mama Bear.

I froze just before my bed, my mouth hanging open. "Uncle Misha?" I whispered. "How could I have forgotten you?" Slowly, I turned around and looked into the corridor. "Squire?"

I grabbed a splinter of wood from the pile of tinder in the corner and set one of its ends aflame in the hearth. I ran to where Squire lay lifeless and placed him into the thin flame. In the very next second, he burst into life and hovered a safe distance away from me, waiting.

"I'm sorry, Squire," I said, blowing out the splinter. "Something bad is happening to me. I had forgotten…" I snapped my fingers, trying to remember the name of the man with the beard who had carried me through the forest in my memories. "Who was that man?"

Squire picked up the pencil and paper and wrote, *Stay focused. You have to open this door.*

"All this is creeping me out," I grumbled. I turned to the empty wall and said with all the confidence I could muster, "Open, magic door."

Nothing happened.

I felt disheartened. Then I carefully sifted through my recent memories. And I realized that those hadn't been the exact words Granny had uttered the night before. I closed my eyes and thought back to that night. What had happened in this corridor? It seemed to have been about some cage ... and an embittered man ... and my beloved grandmother.

But now I remembered it, the code phrase that Baba Yaga had used to open that accursed door. In my deepest voice, trying to mimic Granny's hoarseness, I said, "Open, open, magic door!" I sat down and stood up three times, danced the hula, and did my best to burp.

A few seconds of silence followed, and I thought my lack of knowledge had failed me once again.

Suddenly the door trembled and swung open. And there, right in front of my eyes ... was my very own father.

Chapter 15

Dear Diary,

It's very difficult to describe what it was like to meet a father that, for the longest time, I hadn't even known I had — and about whom I'd all but forgotten.

And even when I knew I had a father, I certainly had no idea what it would be like to finally meet him. I realize that meeting long-lost relatives is going to be weird for anyone, but even in that context, our chat was seriously, seriously bizarre. We couldn't hug or do anything else that normal people would do, because Dad was locked in a cage. But we managed to have a good talk, and I'm grateful for that. I have endless questions for him, but I feel like things will start to make sense soon — as much as they can when your father is Koschey the Deathless and your grandmother is Baba Yaga the Boney Leg!

What I saw when the door opened was a man slouching in the back of the cage that hung in the middle of that room. He glanced up and froze with a puzzled frown on his thin, nervous face.

Slowly, my father stood up — the cage rocked back and forth, and he had to grab its bars to steady himself — and moved to the front of his bizarre aviary. He was gaunt; I hadn't noticed that the other night. He studied me warily, almost as if he were expecting some kind of trick. His eyes glinted with angry suspicion as they looked at my hair.

"So," he said. "What sort of spirit are you?"

Mobilizing all my confidence so as not to seem like a whiny child, I swallowed and said, "Hello. I'm your daughter."

Dad didn't look entirely convinced. "Anna Sophia?" He reached out of the cage with a slim hand and beckoned. "Come."

Feeling odd under his mistrustful stare, I approached and took his hand into both of mine. "It took me a while to find you," I said. "But I'm here."

He closed his eyes, caressing my hand with his lank, dry fingers. I didn't quite know what to feel. My memory still wasn't working that well, and I had a strange feeling of both remembering my search for him and my life as an orphan in Switzerland and wondering what I was doing here. I wanted to feel more ... more what? More emotional, closer to tears, more grateful that I'd finally found Dad? But all I felt was confusion.

Koschey opened his eyes. Now he held my hands in both of his, giving me the slightest squeeze. "Anna Sophia," he whispered. "*Malyshka*."

"I... I'm so happy to see you," I said. An unusual kind of warmth was spreading from Koschey's touch up my hands and arms. It was a relaxing, light warmness, and it felt ... friendly, as if affection itself had materialized and was seeping into my body. I shuddered. Was this what a parent's touch was supposed to feel like? Or was it just some sort of magic?

"*Malyshka*," he repeated, rolling the word off his tongue syllable by slow syllable. He looked right into my eyes — and in his eyes, I saw the everlasting darkness of a night sky, wisdom beyond even Uncle Misha's, and Lauraleigh's gentle tenderness. "It's so good of you to have come. More than good, in fact. But you shouldn't be here."

"I don't mind the risk," I said. That warm feeling was spreading through my chest and stomach now, making me want to curl up on the floor before the cage and ... talk. Talk to my father until I had told him all about me and learned all about him.

"Squire," I said, "can you go keep a lookout please? Just in case?" I wasn't actually worried that we might be caught, but I wanted to be alone for this. I didn't even look to see if Squire had obeyed.

Koschey smiled. "You shouldn't risk spending your life in a cage. It gets boring." He pressed my hands to his heart (though did he even *have* a heart?) and closed his eyes once more.

"She won't know I'm here," I said. "She went off to visit her friend Leshiy. And I put all the hands to sleep. So it's just you and me ... Dad." It felt so strange to use that word, to really use it and really mean it — even as I wondered whether it was the right one to use. "We have time to talk."

Dad chuckled and looked into my eyes again. It seemed like he was trying to see something only he could see. I felt like a book being pored over by an exceptionally interested reader. Well, if a book had feelings, that is.

"Anyway," I said, "let's figure out a way to free you." Although I didn't mean it that way, the words came out sounding a little too self-important, and I cringed.

My father smiled. "This cage was built to keep me locked up forever," he said. "I'm feeble inside it. At times, I even forget who I am and what I was born to do."

I caressed his shoulder, watching him lean into my touch. My heart felt like it was filling with something — something gentle, warm, and incredibly powerful.

With love?

So, I thought, *that's what children with families grow up feeling... That's how love feels.*

"Dad, I'm not in a cage," I said a bit roughly, not wanting to reveal what I was feeling. "Let's think together. Let's make a plan. What do you need to restore your power?"

He gave me a sad smile. "Look. This cage was built to

siphon almost all my energy from me. Do you see what I mean?"

Confused, I shook my head.

He nodded patiently. "Each person," he said, "or rather each soul creates immense amounts of energy when alive. So much, in fact, that if people didn't waste it on feeling miserable and getting distracted, they'd all live till they were nine hundred. Like in your Bible."

I bit my lip, not believing him but still trying to understand what he was saying. "And?"

"And this energy runs the world around us. But not in the way most people think. With their energy, the people feed ... well, they feed creatures like me and Baba Yoga and your Uncle Misha. And even you." There was that *Yoga* again. My ears perked up, but I decided to let that pass for now.

But I didn't like what he was saying. I frowned. "What do you mean? Are we some kind of vampires?"

"Yes, I suppose you could say that." He raised a finger to my lips, stopping my objections. "And it's normal. Souls create that energy, and the universe consumes it. The entire universe is a vampire, really. But it's a vampire that also makes its energy, its life force, available to anyone who knows how to take it. The universe both takes and gives."

I withdrew my hands from his and stroked the rough bars of his cage. "And this cage? What does it do?"

"It permits my life force to escape into the world outside, which always happens anyway. But it blocks the incoming flow. I can get no *prana* to restore my power."

"*Prana*?" I asked.

"Yes. *Prana*. The force that comes from the sun and the stars. The basic power from which all life arises."

Prana sounded like an Indian word to me, not something Koschey would say. But then again, so did *Yoga*. I should have ceased being surprised by now. How could I have imagined that I'd understand even a fraction of what he was telling me? That I'd be qualified to judge?

I brought my mind back to the problem at hand. That, at least, I could deal with.

"So we've got to break this cage," I said, tapping its cold bars.

"Yes. Either break it or have your grandmother switch it off so I can build my strength again."

"Would she ever do it?"

He glanced at me and smiled. "Do you think she's capable of such grace?"

I caressed his shoulder again, feeling that new, warm emotion spreading through me. My heart felt like it was becoming bigger than my chest, and my eyes were welling with tears. It was fascinating. "I don't know her nearly as well as you do," I said. "All I know is… I know she has some sort of plan … I think … something involving ghosts?"

"Ah," he said. His thin shoulder shuddered against the palm of my hand. "The ghosts. The rootless souls, looking for the way home — the way they forget while living as men. I used to help them find that way, guiding each to the afterlife of their choice … or of their beliefs. But now I'm here, and they're drawn to this place, but they can find no relief. Confused, scared, anxious, they're easily manipulated. And they may do anything for a remedy."

"Why can't they find the way on their own?" I asked, puzzled.

"As I said, they forget; that's just how it works. Your grandmother is the only person in the world who belongs to both worlds. She is both alive and dead. Have you noticed her bone leg? That's the leg with which she stands in the kingdom of death." He sighed. "And I've been locked up here long, haven't I? There must be scores of restless souls in the world of the living…"

"Has she always been this mad?" I asked.

"It's very complicated, *Malyshka*."

"Can you try to explain it to me?"

"Explain?" He grinned. "No. But I think I can show you."

He took my hand with his slim, dry fingers — his skin was cracking, showing white bone underneath — and pressed it to his forehead. "Close your eyes," he said, his voice deepening and growing in strength. "I'm not strong enough to escape, but I can still do a few things. Listen now. Listen to my thoughts."

Koschey's voice filled my mind, mixing with the warm feeling in my heart, demanding my full attention. And then this new wave of sound seemed to open a new dimension in my mind. It was as though my thoughts were melding with his. Not completely, but I could hear what he was thinking. I could even see some things — like a thirteen-year-old girl with red hair standing with one hand on the bars of a cage.

Is that me? I thought. *Is that what I look like to you?*

Yes, he thought. *But that is not important now. Listen to me. Listen to my tale. Listen to your tale.*

I did.

And suddenly, I could hear his thoughts as if they were mine.

The girl is waiting for me to speak. To explain. But how can one explain these things to such a fragile creature, young, untaught, and still so very, very mortal? Still, just as she said, I have to try.

"I've known your grandmother for a long time," I begin, framing the words in my mind, knowing that they will fill hers. "Longer than you can imagine. Eons. Millions of years. When I first knew her, she didn't look as she does now. She was young, beautiful. Can you imagine how long ago that must have been?"

The girl looks blank, trying to absorb this. I feel the confusion in her mind as she hears both my thoughts and hers, tries to balance the two, to pick them apart — and grasp just what I'm saying.

"Beautiful?" she says, dazed.

"Oh, yes. Very. Even frighteningly so. Pale cheeks just blushed with sunrise. Eyes the violet of a sunset. And hair that fell to her ankles, shimmering copper and bronze and gold in the sunlight. Oh, she was fair; she was fair."

I can see the question in the girl's eyes: Is her own hair that same color? It will be interesting to see whether she asks or prefers not to know.

She says nothing, and the silence may be too long. I forget how silence unnerves the mortals, who have so little time that they must rush everything they say, rush their every thought. Best to carry on.

"Yes. Beautiful; she was beautiful. On the outside. But inside… I don't know how best to explain this. Not only am I ancient, Anna Sophia. I do not see the world the way you do. Just as your days are limited, so are your senses. There are so many colors in the world you cannot see…"

No, this isn't helping. She is only growing more confused.

"Open your thoughts," I whisper. Just for a moment, I push my mind further into hers so that, for an instant, she catches a glimpse of how I see the universe, the limitless space teeming with color and life. Her eyes begin to sparkle with an excited glow — the glow of remembering something she long since forgot.

I pull my mind back. She is far too fragile to risk letting her share my thoughts that completely for too long.

And besides, this way there are things I can keep secret.

"See what I mean?" I say. "And other things you cannot see either, like the color of a person's soul."

"What do you mean?"

"I can see a person's soul, Anna Sophia. I can see what they are, what they hide in themselves, the good or the evil they carry, whether they are aware of it themselves or not. And Yoga ... she was aware of it; she knew perfectly well what she was. And so did I. When she first appeared, I couldn't take my eyes off her. She must have been used to that; most beautiful women are. But I also saw the contrast between her face and her body. Within her was utter darkness, a blackness so profound I could hardly believe it possible. I had never seen anything like that before. People's souls ... they aren't like that."

"What are souls like, usually? What's mine like?"

They always ask that. But I never tell.

"Most souls are ... mixtures. How could they not be, humans being what they are? Some lighter, some darker. Some that from afar look gray, but get closer and it's like..." How to put this in terms her human mind can understand? I think of a moth's wing and let her mind see it as well. "You see?" I say. "From afar, it seems dull and brown or gray. But as you get closer, you see that there's a rainbow of shades there, that its scales overlap and change depending on how that moth spreads its wings or how the light strikes them. Just like humans, whose souls alter in response to events, in proportion to the choices they make. But Baba Yoga's..."

My mind goes blank, traveling back in time, remembering that first sight of her. The few moments of contemplating her beauty, and then the hammer blow of seeing her soul, threatening to knock all air out of my lungs. I let Anna Sophia see the briefest echo of that image, and she gasps, trying to push away from me, trembling, but I hold her hand tightly pressed to my forehead. Even if I do not let her suffer the full strength of what I'd seen, she must know, must understand…

"See? Blackness, darkness redefining the notion of black. It was like staring into an abyss. But it wasn't some empty darkness. No, it was something worse: not the absence of white but the distinct presence of black. It was overwhelming and tarry, and I knew that if I let her soul touch me, it would stick to me like pitch, that her soul could corrupt anything it chose to. Even me."

"Why was she like that?" the girl asks as I let the image fade. She seems so lost, trying and failing to ground herself between our two minds.

I let the image of Yoga fill that space where our thoughts are one. Yoga, her grandmother's original name, corrupted to Yaga by the inhabitants of this land. Yoga is the constant search for knowledge, for enlightenment. And Baba Yoga, who wasn't at all a Baba — an old woman — at that time, reached that knowledge after years of meditation, energy practice and quests. Enlightenment stemming from a pure heart usually makes a person's soul clean and bright and full of love for the Creation. But her heart hadn't been pure.

"I had seen her soul, and she must have known," I say. "But she poured green wine into cups and we drank. It would have been rude to refuse." I hesitate, not sure how much to tell.

"What did you do? Why was she there?"

I remember how Yoga whispered to me and how there was such temptation in her voice, warm as honey to offset the snow-chilled wine. The things she said made so much sense. She poured more wine, and I grew as thirsty for it as I was for her to speak again. I drank her words and let the light shine on her hair, her skin, the jewels of her dress — anything that might glitter and let me forget the void underneath.

But I cannot tell my child this. Although … although I probably just did.

"Dad?"

How long have I been lost in my reminiscences? I must pull myself together. I cannot let this prison cloud my mind.

"She proposed that … with our powers, the two of us could take over the worlds of the living and of the dead. And that we ought to."

"Are we not made for each other?" she said, a finger trailing over the hem of her dress. "And are not the worlds made for us too?" The wine shone on her lips, and I found myself thinking that I could kiss it from them, that she was offering me the universe for the price of a kiss. It seemed a bargain, a bargain I so longed to make. Yet beneath the shining crown of her hair, there was blackness, blackness, blackness…

I cannot let my daughter see that memory.

"I won't deny that I was tempted," I say. "To rule not just one world, but both of them! But … no, not with her. I told her so. I told her to leave, to let me be, that I didn't wish to make a deal with a woman who had turned herself into a devil."

It took so much strength to say those words, to pull back from the brink of her lips.

"So that's why she has a grudge against you?" Anna Sophia asks.

Oh, to be so innocent. I even laugh. There's something about the guilelessness of the young, their ignorance. How little they can grasp how the spider's web is made, how every strand depends on another, how much more complex everything is than it seems.

"It is not that simple," I tell her. "Nothing ever is. At that time, she simply ... left."

Yoga didn't rage as I had feared, or attempt to attack me. No, she merely nodded and stood to leave. And just as she was about to — she turned, and she smiled a sweet smile, a delicate one. That smile pierced my heart like a shard of ice and stayed there.

Then she left.

"She left," I repeat. "And then, sometime later ... I don't know how long it would seem to you, whether it was a length of time or not. One gets confused. But ... well, whether it was a lifetime of yours or ten of them later, she sent me a letter. A raven flew to me to deliver it. 'Immortality is lonely,' she had written. 'Though we cannot be partners, can we not at least sit down and talk as friends?'"

There was more than that in the letter, but I cannot tell the child this. I cannot. Already she sees me trapped by my weakness. How much more can I let myself be debased in her eyes, this child who has come so far to find me...

My daughter.

"Immortality *is* lonely," I say. "The lives of mortals are so brief they pass away like butterflies on a summer's day. You are born, you grow so quickly, and then you die. How can you build a real friendship with someone who will be gone in the blink of an eye? How can a human ever be much more than a pet, a close companion? One day you'll have to sit next to one as he or she dies.

"And so I was glad to receive Yoga's letter. And I was glad to agree to see her. Loneliness grows on you so slowly, sometimes you don't even realize how solitary you've become. But her letter brought mine to the fore. And I realized it could be painful to be alone. The very word, loneliness… It became like ice in my heart."

I still wonder whether Yoga had enchanted that letter or whether it was my own mind that turned her smile into that wound in my heart.

"And so I allowed Yoga to come to me. She too knew the burdens of immortality, so who better to speak with? And she was good company, clever and magical, knowing so many things. And still beautiful, of course. We talked about so many things, about the deepest reaches of magic and about the funny things we had seen mortals do in our time. She made me smile; she even made me laugh. Her sense of humor was not quite so vicious then. Or at least she hid her bitterness better. I enjoyed her company immensely."

And all the time within her was churning that tarry maelstrom of blackness, and I closed my eyes and pretended not to see. Especially not when she leaned close to me and I could smell her honeysuckle and blackberry scent, feel the warmth of her pulse beating in her throat and her lips golden with mead, and hear her voice whisper those three words, those three deadly little words…

"She told me that she was in love with me, Anna Sophia. That no one else could truly understand her, that no one else was worthy of her or me, and I... I..."

I couldn't turn away; I didn't want to turn away. I let her press close to me. Her lips were sweet with mead, her breath fragrant as apples. And she was so warm in my arms, so soft and warm in my arms ... and her hair was thick and copper and shone bright as the rising sun as it drowned my hands... I closed my eyes and tried to forget everything but the taste of apples and mead and the smell of blackberry and honeysuckle. I closed my eyes and refused to see — pretended not to see — the cascading darkness. I only saw the bronze waterfall into which my hands were plunged, nothing else, nothing else, nothing else...

"I was weak," I rasp aloud, pulling Anna Sophia's hand away from my forehead so she can't see what I'm remembering. "Weak and foolish." They are among the hardest words I have ever spoken.

I wait for disappointment to blossom in Anna Sophia's eyes. It does not come.

Softly, she puts her hand back on my forehead.

"Well," I say. "I was younger then. And foolish, as I told you. That's no excuse, of course, but it's a fact. I could still see all that evil inside her. Her soul had not grown even a little bit lighter. If anything, her darkness seemed to have become thicker. But ... what she said made sense. We were the only ones who could understand each other. So... I decided I was in love with her. And I told her so."

"But you weren't?"

I wonder if this child has ever been in love. Even if she has, at her age, how could she know all the subtleties of desire, all the little tricks we play on ourselves, everything we mask by using that word "love?" Yoga was in my arms, and my loneliness was abated. It was spring; the air was drunk with blossom. To admit that something was wrong would have broken that spell. Not that she had enchanted me. Not in the proper sense of the term; at least I don't think so. It was a spell I had cast on myself or at least collaborated on. And how could I let myself bring that dream to an end?

Weak, weak.

"Perhaps I was in love; perhaps I merely said I was because I didn't want to lose her company. I don't know. We all lie to ourselves at least as much as we do to others. Probably more. I don't know if I was lying whenever I said 'I love you' to her, but I lied to myself every time I told myself I couldn't see the darkness pouring out of her. But ignoring it proved a terrible mistake. I should have known, I should have guessed, I should at least have *suspected* what she was up to. Your grandmother never does anything without a reason, without some profit for her. You must remember that. All the time I was with her, she was siphoning off my life power — my *prana*. Adding its strength to her own, draining me dry, as if I were an orange she'd sunk her teeth into to suck out its juices and leave its flesh and rind parched and arid."

Yoga was subtle about it at first; I have to give her that. She didn't start immediately. And when she did, she took barely a drop, the faintest lick of my life force gone with every kiss, so little it might have happened accidentally. And then the theft of my breath as I slept, the extra flavor in our wine I couldn't place, the lullabies she sang me as she kneaded my shoulders, the little charms she spun, the net she wove so finely that I didn't even notice it trawling my being and catching my strength in it. How patient she was, so that even now, I'm not sure how long it was before I noticed I was weakening, and even then I did not suspect...

"I grew ill," I say. "I dried out. And still I spent time with her, let her visit me, went to visit her. I ignored all the warnings. I ignored that I was losing *prana* and she was there, as powerful as she'd ever been and still overflowing with her evil. I even let her become my nurse because who else could understand what I was going through? I grew weaker and weaker until not only my strength but my body was affected. I'd never realized before how much my health depended on the strength of my magic.

I fell bedridden in her home, and still she sat by my side, seeming to do all she could to cure me, stroking my forehead while whispering kind words — and still sapping my strength away. Replacing it with her darkness. I should have known; I should have noticed. I had touched her pitch and it was flowing into me, a cancerous, devouring flood.

"Eventually she must have grown bored with playing nurse by the fire, and she left me to wallow in the sweat of my sheets on my own. From time to time, she would come by to take more from me. She had dropped all pretense, but I was too weak to notice. I could hardly even think. I remember I was so feeble I wondered whether this might be what it's like to die. If I was about to discover that I was, in fact, mortal."

I can't help but shudder and see that the girl is entirely captivated by my tale. Caught in my memories, she's almost forgotten that I'm still here, alive.

"Yoga must have worried about that too, but by now she couldn't be bothered with me. There was little enough to drain. But letting me die might be a waste. If I built up my strength, maybe my magic would return. And then before I had grown too strong, she could come back and leech it from me again. Can you imagine? To have a permanent source of powerful life force to enable her to build up her own strength. To leave me trapped in that bed, like a tree you plant and then torture to make it produce more fruit. It was all she had ever wanted from me… And now that she didn't have to pretend, she didn't have to waste time curing me. She could leave that distasteful task to someone else.

"So she sent her daughter. Sereda."

"Mom," the girl says softly.

"Yes," I say. "Seredushka. She came in, carrying some jars and herbs to make a sort of healing potion. At first I thought it was Yoga herself, and I turned to look at her and—"

How to explain?

"Can you imagine if you'd lived all your life in the darkness, in some night without stars or moon, and the only light you'd ever seen was a candle flame? Then one day you awoke and found that the sun had risen? Seeing your mother for the first time was like that. She was beautiful, yes — almost as beautiful as her mother, though in a softer way. But it wasn't that. It was her soul. Her soul was blindingly white. I don't know who her father is. But he must be a very good man."

Unable to put my feelings into words, I let Anna Sophia see another memory, just a hint of her mother's soul. It was whiter than a fresh snowfall at noon, achingly, entirely white. Looking at it almost hurt my eyes, but I couldn't turn away. It was as if the sun had risen and I could hardly remember what the candle flame looked like. I couldn't believe she was Yoga's daughter. How could anything so perfectly pure be linked to that hag's soul? How could anything so dark have molded this blazing whiteness? It was as if Yoga had set out to build a snow maiden and somehow the pitch of her hands had not stuck to the snow.

"All the cobwebs of my mind were blown away," I say. "I was still sick, but I knew what Yoga had done. And I knew that I could trust Seredushka. There was no guile, no deceit in her soul. I doubt she could even have understood the concept. She nursed me with all the skill she had. She talked as she did so, and as my strength returned, I replied. We talked about everything and nothing. She made me smile. This was what Yoga had wanted me to believe she was. This was the mask she had worn to gain my trust. But with Sereda, it was real. I was smitten in an instant. After all that time enmeshed in Yoga's web, I saw clearly. I didn't have to lie to myself. There was nothing to pretend not to see. I didn't have to be guarded in any way. Realizing that was such a relief … a weight lifted from my mind that I hadn't known was there.

"The surprising thing is that Sereda grew fond of me as well. I wouldn't have expected that."

Thoughts crowd in on me, and I let my daughter see them.

Sereda spooning broth into my mouth. Sereda telling me of the songbirds in her bower whom she refused to cage. Sereda taking snow to chill the drink she would offer me in a few moments while chattering about her childhood. Sereda humming. Sereda laughing at something I'd said.

Sereda leaning over me and pressing a soft kiss on my dry and burning forehead.

The shard of ice in my heart beginning to melt.

Of course, it couldn't last.

I've wandered off again. The child — my daughter, Sereda's daughter, who doesn't know how much of her mother is in her, whom I dare not tell how much she looks like her grandmother once did — is looking at me, waiting for me to go on. Her eyes are shining, but I am not sure if it is happiness or tears provoked by that sight of her mother.

"Sereda — Seredushka — would sneak into my room far more often than she was supposed to. We talked for hours, day after day. Just seeing her, just hearing her laugh, made my strength return. I was growing much stronger than Yoga had planned on. Seredushka and I falling in love was an extra ingredient in the healing potion that no one could have counted on. It's not an ingredient you can add to a recipe. You can't plan on it. You can't trap love in a bottle and dole it out drop by drop. But when it happens, when it truly happens, when neither partner has any second thoughts and their love is as pure as your mother's soul, it intensifies the power of a good spell or potion.

"So I was growing stronger. Not necessarily wiser, though. I couldn't think of leaving Sereda, and I didn't think to ask her to come with me. I wasn't sure she cared for me quite that much, and I couldn't bear the thought of hearing her refuse.

"And then one day, Yoga found us together."

Suddenly she was there, standing in the doorway. My arm was around Sereda's shoulder and her head was resting on my chest. There was no way to hide, no explanation for our posture. Yoga knew.

I had never truly understood the meaning of fear before.

Yoga's eyes darkened. They crackled with blue sparks of energy, and I saw the black tar of her soul flooding them. Her beauty was as terrifying as flames on the edge of a blade. Fattened on my own *prana*, she was as powerful as she had ever been or would ever be, more powerful than any witch had ever been, more powerful by far than I was. She didn't speak; she didn't need to. Rage was etched in every line of her body.

I had seen all this before Sereda had time to turn and see her mother. So it was I who saw our death written in Yoga's now-dark eyes. Or, since I cannot die, our pain.

My one thought was to shield Sereda from this knowledge. To keep her heart from breaking.

I interrupt this flood of memories before the child can see them. There is no need to frighten her.

"Your grandmother was … displeased," I say.

"She got angry?"

"Yes. You could say that."

Memories fill my mind again.

The first blow came almost immediately, an instinctive lashing out on Yoga's part with no thought behind it, a curse whistling through the air like a whip and smashing me across the face. Sereda tumbled from me and fell to the ground, her head striking the table. She slumped to the floor, knocked unconscious before she could realize what was happening. *Good*, I thought. *I can concentrate better if she can't distract me … protect her better.*

I ignored the pain and looked at Yoga's face to see if lashing out had been enough, if she was likely to calm down.

But no. She was gathering her strength, her knowledge. Gathering up her power and letting her soul flood it so that her next blow would be more effective than the first.

"Furious might be a better way to describe it," I tell the child. "She shattered the air with her curses. Threw everything that she could think of at us. I was stronger than I had been, but I wasn't strong enough to fight back. All I could do was shield us, protect us, try to deflect Yoga's curses. It wasn't easy. She showed no sign of faltering, of calming down. No, her rage grew the longer she couldn't hurt us. I remember her pausing at one point, having to take a breath, spittle dripping from her open mouth, even the rasp of her breathing filled with hate. Then she gathered up her power and struck again."

I remember much more than that, but there is already enough fear in my daughter's eyes. She doesn't need to know how Yoga was like a cobra spitting venom, like a blood-hungry boar sharpening its tusks, like a lioness bristling with claws. How she feinted, light on her feet as a fencer, trying to get past my guard, yet her every blow as heavy as an ax swung overhead, as a hammer smashing against rock. She doesn't need to hear the echoes of Yoga's spells streaming from her mouth, pure vocalizations of her fury transformed into deadly vibrations. The attack was constant and unending, and I felt the floor shaking. I was unable to do anything but crouch over Sereda, hold her to my heart, and hope that love could work on shielding spells as well as it did on healing potions.

There was a moment's pause. I dared to look. Yoga was half-crouched over, her eyes narrowed, thinking. The next attack would be worse.

But that was when I saw our one hope of escape: the color of Yoga's hair.

It had begun to turn gray.

"I thought her screaming was going to bring down her house and crush us," I say to Anna Sophia. "She must have built it solidly. But she used so much power... That was the day she aged and became an old woman — a Baba. You remember how, as she drained my magic, I grew weaker? The same thing happened to her. She had amassed so much power, but she threw it all at us. So much of it in so short a time... She aged. Her hair started to turn gray, her perfect skin grew liver spots, and the flesh began to hang off her bones. She must have noticed me realizing this because she paused in her attack to look at her hands and some strands of her hair. I don't know if she figured out what was happening. I took the chance, grabbed your mother, and leaped from the room. And we ran."

"Did Baba Yaga follow you?"

"No. But she continued to curse us. She stood on the roof of her house and watched and threw even more spells at us. I couldn't believe it. She must have realized what was happening to her, but she didn't care. She called down lightning to try to strike us; she made the earth shake beneath our feet. I'd never seen such a display. She ground down her own teeth to call the thunder, causing a hailstorm that raged all day around us as we escaped. I'm still not sure how we did. It was … terrifying."

The details Anna Sophia doesn't need to know crowded behind my eyes.

Fissures gaped in the earth around us, and we could hear Yoga's screams borne to us on the wind. The lightning flashed around us, strangely colored, clearly attempting to find us. Hailstones thicker than cherries struck around us, blinding us. The thunder rumbled so loudly, it was as if it were inside us, shuddering in our bones and veins. We wrapped our arms around each another, Sereda's warmth the only thing I was certain of, the only proof she was still there, still alive.

I could hear Seredushka crying. She was probably in shock, suddenly cast out from everything she had known. But her soul still shone.

There was another crack of lightning. And then a more terrifying sound: as if from only meters away, the sound of an enraged tiger in the taiga. One of those roars that turns your very guts to water, that leaves you paralyzed for the moments it takes the beast to reach you.

It was not a real tiger, though. I recognized Baba Yoga's voice. I looked up and froze.

The sky was ablaze.

She had called fire itself down from the heavens, and it was gathering in a whirlpool to strike us like a fist.

"Terrifying…" I repeat. My mind is wandering again. "All we could do was huddle together and hope it would end, hope she would exhaust herself, and in the end, she must have…"

The fire fell. Huddled on our knees together, we looked at each another, not knowing what would happen. Sereda's soul, white though it was, was burning less brightly, tarnished by fear and pain.

I looked at her. "I love you," I said.

"I love you," she said. And suddenly, desperately, we were kissing, and I raised a fist against the heavens as they showered fire on us and the flames broke around us like water on a rock.

Anna Sophia's voice jolts me out of my memories.

"Was that when you went to Uncle Misha together?"

I start.

"Yes. Of course, you'd know some of this already, wouldn't you?" I should have thought of that, instead of losing myself in recollections I spend all my days going over anyway. "Did the Great Trapper tell you about that?"

"Yes," she says. Quickly, as though she is worried I might think I was boring her, she adds, "But I don't know very much more than that, not all these details. Just that you'd been there and that … and that, at some point, you gave Mom your heart."

"Yes…" I say. "My heart. It's a silly phrase, you know, you hear people say that their beloved has stolen their heart. But I suppose I felt that Sereda had. And I actually am able to make that saying real. So yes, I gave Seredushka my heart as a sign of love, a sign of trust. And she hid it. I didn't ask where.

"There's not much else to tell. After we had left the Great Trapper, time passed. We were happy although there was a blight on Sereda's soul: the sorrow left by the break with her mother, the thought that her mother hated her. Then one day a raven came bearing a letter. It was from Baba Yoga, of course. She told us she'd repented, she'd forgiven us. She asked us to forgive her rage and said that she wanted to make amends. She wanted us to be a family. She wrote that immortality was lonely and we who were afflicted with it — that was her word, 'afflicted' — should be friends.

"I didn't trust her. Not a word. Not just because I remembered what had happened the last time she had talked about loneliness. I knew that this woman, this being I'd known for millions of years, this walking cloud of utter darkness, had never been up to any good. Even the slightest action she'd taken that might have seemed in her favor had been done for her own purposes. There wasn't a redeeming spot on the entire sulfuric, stinking surface of her soul. So I told Seredushka we had to ignore the letter."

"What happened? Why didn't you?"

I shake my head regretfully. I don't know how the child will take what I'm about to say. Am I about to praise her mother — or condemn her? I have never been able to decide.

"I told you, most people's souls are mingled shades. It's how they can deal with an imperfect world where there are no absolutes — and it's because they mindlessly waste all their precious energy. It's how they can bend when they have to, how they can convince themselves to ignore their feelings when their reason tells them to. But your mother's soul was untainted. White as fresh snow, though muted now by her sorrow. The moment she read the letter, before I could express my doubts, that shadow lifted. Her soul burned as bright as ever, just at the thought of reconciliation.

"When I told her we couldn't go, the shadow returned. She fretted for days. Then she told me that she needed to visit her mother, she trusted her plea for forgiveness, she couldn't believe otherwise, and she couldn't bear to keep living with all this hatred.

"I tried to prevent her. Not by force; how could I? I loved her... But I tried to stop her. I failed. She was determined and stubborn — as I suspect you are."

She is, I can tell, and her sudden shy grin confirms it. She couldn't have made it here otherwise. She gets it from her mother ... and her grandmother. Not all of Baba Yoga's traits are inherently bad.

"And when she came here, Baba Yaga took her hostage?" she asked.

"Of course. She didn't make it obvious at first; she played the happy mother. And the happy grandmother-to-be since Sereda was pregnant with you. A little later, she began to ask about my heart. I'd warned Sereda about this, but she was so happy, so trusting that she didn't see the trap until after she'd already admitted that she'd hidden my heart somewhere. She was smart enough not to reveal anything about where, though. And realizing she had learned all she could, Baba Yoga locked her up."

"But she got away. I know this part of the story. She got away and escaped to Mama Bear's den."

"Yes," I say. "If you know that, then you know all there is to the story, really."

"But how are you here? That's the part I don't understand. How did she catch you?"

I close my eyes. I am about to hurt her, to lay a burden on her she does not expect.

"The same way she does everything: tricks and lies. She sent me a message saying that she'd captured *you*."

I look. Her eyes are wide in shock, her mouth half-open, and I can see guilt gathering over her like a cloud. But I must tell her all, tell her the truth.

"She sent me a *morok*, an evil dream that showed you sitting here in this cage, trembling and afraid. Alone. I believed that dream and I panicked… So I came here to look for you. She drew me in and trapped me like a bird in this magical cage."

Anna Sophia's eyes have filled with tears. And I feel my own weakness. I have used too much of what little energy I have left to speak with my daughter.

Koschey gently took my hand off his forehead, severing that magic pathway into his very mind. I looked around me, disoriented, unable to focus my eyes on anything in the room.

Now that our direct connection was broken, I felt lonely — even abandoned. For a moment, I felt like I was back in the orphanage, with no one truly caring about my existence.

But that was wrong, of course. My father was right here before me, and I knew that he cared.

He was seated again, his eyes closed, breathing deeply as if he'd just run a race.

I stood in silence, wondering what to do, finding no obvious solutions, trying to ignore the heaviness in my heart.

Eventually, Dad opened his eyes and said, "You should go now. I doubt your grandmother will be able to tolerate Leshiy for too much longer."

"I'll see you soon, Dad," I said, my voice trembling. And then, impulsively, I added, "I love you."

He smiled and patted my hand through the bars of his cage. "I love you too, *Malyshka*." He pressed my hand in his a little longer.

"And listen," he said. "Listen to my words and believe them, for they are true: It is not your fault that I am here."

It was all I could do to gulp and nod. And then I couldn't bear it any longer. I pulled my hand away, closed the door on him, and ran into my bedroom and cried.

Chapter 16

Dear Diary,

It doesn't matter what my father says. Even if he's right that it's not my fault he's a prisoner, I still feel responsible. And I'm the only person who can help him. Though despite what he probably thinks, I'm not alone; I've got Squire.

I've just got to be sure not to let Baba Yaga trick my memory anymore. I'll have to be careful and act like I still think I've lived here all my life. I have no idea if I know how to act, but I guess I'm going to find out.

I've also got to practice getting and keeping energy. I don't know if my grandmother is going to keep siphoning it from me, but I know I'll need as much magic as I can get to rescue Dad.

I am going to rescue him, however difficult it looks. I mustn't forget that that's why I'm here.

I need a plan and an opportunity...

When I stopped crying and came out of my bedroom, the sleeping hands were dotted around everywhere, lying about like so many statuettes of white bone. I took a deep breath and lit a candle. One by one, I woke the hands with a small flame, and they resumed their tasks once again as if nothing had happened.

Satisfied that I'd done my best to erase all traces of my adventure, I went to switch on the TV in the bedroom. I wanted Granny to think that I'd slept for most of the time and watched TV during the rest. I wasn't sure if I'd be able to conceal the return of my memories, though, so I had to be very careful.

I had my eyes trained on the screen when my grandmother's mortar landed with a loud crash in the yard. I decided not to meet her at the door; I would pretend to be sleepy instead. The less I saw of her, the better.

The door swung open and Granny waltzed in, draped in necklaces of dried forest berries and mushrooms. Her mood seemed vastly improved. There was even a smile playing on her lips. For a moment or two, I saw the image of the beautiful young woman my father had shown me earlier and which I'd also seen when she had talked to him the other night. She seemed airy, light, and joyful. I gave her a surprised, involuntary smile. Her happiness was infectious.

"Anna Sophia, my darling girl," she said, and blew me a kiss. "How are you doing this afternoon?"

"Not nearly as good as you," I replied, yawning. "What happened?"

"Oh, that Leshiy is a charmer and a half," Granny said with a little giggle, sounding a bit like some of the teenage girls at the orphanage. "I had the nicest visit. I really should go and visit him more often."

"What're all those things on your neck?"

"These?" Granny fiddled with the strings of forest flora. "Leshiy insisted on giving me presents for paying him a visit. The silly beggar's so lonely, just like me. He couldn't stop giving me little treats. They're all freshly picked and wonderful."

"I'm happy you had a nice time," I said, my eyes turning back to the screen.

Surprisingly, Granny switched off the TV and came over to me. "Oh, Anna Sophia, stop wasting your life on the people on the screen!" she said in what could have been the most hypocritical statement in history. She took a strand of mushrooms off her neck and gracefully threw it over my head. "Smell these, *vnuchechka*. They're picked fresh off the forest floor."

I held the mushrooms to my nose and breathed in the scent. She was right; it *was* a delicious aroma. I gave her a smile.

"I'm going to teach you how to make a wonderful soup with them," Granny said. "And I'll teach you how to make jam with the berries. We're going to start stocking up for the winter."

"Am I going to stay with you over the winter?" I asked before I could stop myself.

Granny's big smile faded a little. "Where else would you go?" she said, a bit sharply. "We're a family, and a family is supposed to stay together."

"I didn't mean anything bad," I said quickly. "I just don't know what your plans are."

"And you don't need to," she said, raising her voice some more. "You're still a child, after all, and children should trust their elders." She gave me a sidelong glance that lasted longer than it needed to. "You do remember why you're here, don't you?"

So that was it. Within the first minutes of her return, she had already suspected that something was wrong.

I frowned, pretending to be puzzled, hoping that my face didn't show the cold fear starting to spread from the pit of my stomach. "What do you mean, Granny?" I asked. "I've always been here." I paused for a moment; then I added hesitantly, "Haven't I?"

I waited, wondering if I'd overdone it. The bizarre thing was, the hesitation wasn't entirely fake. My memory was playing tricks on me again. I remembered Dad locked up in the hidden room, and I had a vague memory of a bearded man called Uncle Misha, and I had a friend called Squire who was a floating hand. But how had I gotten to Baba Yaga's cabin? When? And where had I spent my childhood?

In fact, hadn't I always been here? Where else would I have met Squire, who was one of my granny's hands?

Granny took off the remaining strands of forest produce and tossed them down on the bed next to her. "Take these through to the kitchen, Anna Sophia. I'm tired. We won't do any cooking today. It's getting late, anyway." She turned on the TV and took off her headscarf, hurling it onto the floor. I had clearly overstepped her boundaries by reminding her that I might want to leave her one day.

"Would you like some of that chamomile tea, Granny?" I offered, trying to placate her.

"If it wouldn't be too much trouble for you, ask the hands to make some," she grumbled, her eyes glued to the screen.

I picked up her berries and mushrooms and headed for the kitchen. I could hear her start to mumble about "materialism" and "immorality."

"Can you make some strong chamomile tea?" I asked a pair of hands that didn't seem particularly busy. They did as I asked, and I returned to Granny's bedroom with the huge samovar. I poured her a cup, stirred in some honey, and offered it to her with a light bow.

"Don't you also want some?" she asked, taking a sip. She'd started calming down, having spent some of her irritation on the people on TV instead of on me.

"No, thank you," I said. "I sleep very well most of the time. In fact, it seems like I slept through the whole afternoon. I don't suffer from any insomnia."

"The other night you woke up," she replied. "And after sleeping that much during the day, you might not at night. You could do with a nice cup yourself."

"Maybe not just now," I said. I couldn't afford to get too sleepy; I was meeting with Squire at sunset.

Granny shrugged and seemed to give up. She grumbled a bit more about the state of society and had another big cup of tea. After that, she got quiet. I slid off my chair and peered at her closely. She was fast asleep. A part of me wanted to take this opportunity to visit Dad again. I was greedy; I wanted to spend as much time with him as possible, now that I knew where he was. But it was late, and the sun would soon be creeping below the horizon.

I went out onto the porch and sat cross-legged in the rocking chair, watching the clouds, the slowly sinking sun, and the rustling of the breeze. I liked the forest, I decided.

I could see what kept my grandmother here. No city could provide the same peaceful state of mind, not even the lakeshore back in Geneva. If Granny weren't crazy and keeping Dad caged, I could possibly be happy here.

I was thinking about that, about my weird, magical family when suddenly I felt a tap on my shoulder. I almost jumped out of my skin. I'd thought Granny was asleep and we were the only ones there.

"Who's—" I started to say in an intimidating tone, gathering power in my hands in case I needed to fight. Then I realized it was just Squire. I let out a big sigh of relief. "Boy, am I glad it's you!" I grinned, happy to see him. It was good to remember I had a friend in this place. Granny had Leshiy and Cat the Hare. I had Squire.

I had forgotten a pen and paper, so I had to sneak back into the house to get the items Squire and I needed to talk.

"I managed to speak to Dad," I whispered to Squire as he bobbed up and down excitedly. I was a little worried that Granny would wake up, but I hoped the chamomile and fresh air had knocked her out for the night. "Thank you so much for keeping watch."

Of course, Squire scribbled on the paper. His handwriting was messier than usual as though he were impatient and writing too fast. *I have good news as well.*

"What is it?" I asked.

I found Knight!

"Well done! Where is he?"

Up in the attic. Baba Yaga caught him and locked him up there. He's in a deep sleep. I can't rouse him. Can you help me?

"Sure." I smiled. "Let's go right now."

I put Squire in my pocket, and the two of us carefully snuck back into the house and up the rickety stairs. I tiptoed, scared of getting Squire and Knight caught, aware of how irritated Granny had been with me earlier. I was worried that she might be getting suspicious, so I had to be very careful.

Some of the stairs creaked under my feet, and I kept stopping to listen for any unusual noises from the bedroom. At last, we managed to make it up the stairs to the trapdoor to the attic. It was locked.

"How do you know Knight's up there?" I whispered.

He floated out of my pocket and carefully lifted a loose plank. He sneaked in through the gap. But while the gap was big enough for a hand, a girl couldn't possibly push herself through.

I decided to try the trick I'd learned before. In a quiet yet commanding voice, I ordered, "Open, open, magic door!"

Nothing happened. I glowered. Maybe there was another phrase.

Or — I sighed — maybe I had to do another silly dance.

Rolling my eyes, I turned around three times on one heel, skipped once as I tried to land lightly, and wiggled my hand in front of my nose.

"Open, open, magic door!" I said again.

The trapdoor swung up and I hauled myself through. Clouds of dust billowed up around me in the darkness. The dust tickled my throat, and I had to try hard not to sneeze or cough. My nose wrinkled. Evidently, Granny hadn't ordered the hands to clean up here.

"Where's your other half?" I asked Squire.

He took my hand and led me around the clutter to an ornate wooden box.

I opened it, and inside was a hand. It looked just like a mirror image of Squire: exactly the same size, every finger just as long, even — as I just noticed — an unusual tiny little twist on the knuckle of each thumb. I smiled at Squire. "I always knew you'd find him."

Squire bobbed out of my view.

"Where'd you go?" I asked, puzzled.

He returned in a few minutes, holding a candle.

As Squire held it just under Knight, I channeled what was left of my inner magic to light it. Knight woke up almost instantly and bobbed out of the box. He seemed scared. That wasn't exactly unreasonable; the last thing he'd probably seen before being locked up was my grandmother about to curse him.

"Calm down," I said. "Look who's here with us."

It took him another moment or two to orient himself and realize whom I was talking about. Then he jumped on Squire. The two of them started shaking each other passionately. It was hard to stop myself from giggling. Even after everything I'd been through in the past year, I'd never seen anything quite as surreal as two disembodied hands happily shaking each other in midair.

After they'd had a few minutes for their reunion, I said, "I'm sorry to interrupt, but ... do you think you two will be able to help me rescue Dad now?"

The two hands bobbed up and down in agreement.

Now the trick was to establish our four-handed rescue plan.

Chapter 17

Dear Diary,

Now that we've found Knight, I have two allies with me who ought to be able to sneak around when I can't — so long as Baba Yaga's other hands don't tell. But that doesn't help me find a way to rescue Dad. Squire and Knight can't open his cage. Only magic can do that.

But even if I manage to use a little bit of magic from time to time, there's a limit to what I can do. My grandmother knows so much more, and she is so much more powerful. Partly because she's still taking some of my power away from me.

So before I can set Dad free, I have to find a way to get Granny to give me my power back.

Granny was still snoring when we crept back down. For safety's sake, I put the two hands to sleep after telling them I'd wake them up once I had a concrete plan in place. Then I dropped them into my backpack.

I sat around thinking. Even if I got back as much power as I'd had when I'd first gotten here, it might not be enough to break Dad free. Baba Yaga hadn't just been sucking power away from me; she'd been taking Dad's away too, all this time. She'd taken his strength and used it to trap him. The more I thought about it, the worse it seemed. It was his own power that was keeping him prisoner! It was like Baba Yaga had stolen all his money and then melted down the coins to make chains for him.

How could somebody so wicked be my grandmother? How could her daughter have been as good as Koschey said she'd been?

I fell asleep, still with no plan, just questions about human nature.

When I woke up in the morning, Granny wasn't in the bedroom. This was unusual. Typically she started the day with a good rant at the TV. Sometimes she'd even awakened me by suddenly turning on some loud game show with terrible music. Had I overslept? No, the sunlight was falling just where it usually did. Had she gone out without telling me? Was she visiting Leshiy again or some other forest friend?

As it turned out, she was puttering around in the kitchen, looking more active than I'd seen her in a while. She was bustling with activity, ordering this hand to do that and that one to do something else. There were several pots on the stove and a tray of pies going into the oven. After a full night's sleep, Granny was looking as fresh as a daisy. Well, maybe not quite. But she certainly looked as fresh as an old witch with iron teeth, a bone leg, and an almost perpetually bad mood could look.

"Morning, *vnuchechka*," she said over her shoulder. Though she sounded cheerful, there was something in her tone I didn't like.

She pulled out a jug of fresh milk and poured me a tall glass, setting it in front of me with a smile. Now I was getting suspicious. She'd never gotten me anything before, not without being asked first. What was she up to?

Trying to act casual, I carefully glanced around the room as I sipped my milk. I couldn't spot anything unusual, other than all the cooking that was going on. Why had Granny started cooking so early, anyway? And why so much food?

"Are we having company, Granny?" I risked asking.

"Hmm? No, why do you ask?"

"It's just so much food," I said.

Baba Yaga grinned.

"Well, as I said, we've got to get ready for winter, girl. Time to stock the larder." She glanced out the window. "Ah, and here's the main course now."

Her eyes snapped back to me, and she looked at me with a crafty expression on her face. I had begun to understand that look — she was judging me, waiting to see how I'd react to something. Those were the moments when I had to be most careful not to reveal what I was thinking so she couldn't tell I could break through whichever spell she had cast on my memory. But what on earth was so special about this morning? I looked out the window and—

No.

No-no-no-no-no-no-no.

The rage exploded inside me like a small bomb, and I could feel its flames licking at my ribcage as I turned back to my grandmother with a snarl like a bear's. I felt what little magic I had left welling inside me, that knot of darkness

261

awakening. My every instinct was to pounce and attack, to hurt that evil hag standing in front of me.

"You can't!" I screamed. "How dare you, you can't!"

How could I have forgotten who she was? How could I have forgotten that Granny was the Iron Queen? I'd known that the orphans in Geneva were being sent to her; I'd been told! I'd also heard what she did to them. How could I have let her trick me into thinking she was just my doddery old grandmother who liked to yell at the TV?

"I can't? Can't what, *vnuchechka*?" She was still looking me right in the eye.

"*I won't let you!*" I yelled, magic flickering at my fingers, threatening to erupt from me as I struggled to take control. I could hear my voice echoing as I recalled how I'd treated all the child traffickers back in Geneva, recalled Mama Bear's roar as she came rushing to rescue me from the wolves. To rescue me and Lauraleigh.

Lauraleigh, who was now kneeling in my grandmother's courtyard where the three Horsemen had thrown her. Her arms were tied behind her back and there was a gag in her mouth. Her beautiful hair was disheveled and dusty, and there were tear marks on her dirty face. She was trying not to show how scared she was, but she was unable to hide it as she looked at the fence of skulls and saw the empty fencepost.

Baba Yaga grinned at me and zipped my mouth with two fingers, and suddenly I couldn't speak. Then I started to feel weak. However angry I was, my power was falling away.

No — being drained away. Baba Yaga was taking it from me.

"Delicious," she said. "Thank you, Anna Sophia, dear. Strong emotions always make energy so much tastier. Not to mention easier to siphon off."

"You can't," I managed to grumble. "She's my friend, you can't. I won't let you."

"Friend?" she said with a strange look. "What on earth are you talking about, Anna Sophia? It's just some wretched human. Come, let's go have a look and see what my Horsemen have brought us."

I felt my mind growing foggy.

But no. It didn't matter what Baba Yaga said, I wasn't going to forget that Lauraleigh was my friend. I wasn't going to forget that she'd helped me, that she'd come all this way just to support me. I fought back with everything I had against the spell the Iron Queen was trying to cloud my brain with as we stepped out of the hut and went into the yard.

The Black Horseman looked at me and sneered; then he nodded at my grandmother. The White one gave me a look of pure hatred. His arm was on a sling — so the bears did maim one of them after all.

The three Horsemen rode off as we drew close to Lauraleigh, who seemed torn between staring pleadingly at me and looking at Baba Yaga in terror.

"Ah, yes, this will do nicely," said my grandmother as she looked over Lauraleigh and started to poke at her. "Bit lean, of course, but then they all are these days, starving themselves all the time to try and look like those supermodels that are just bones with a bit of skin on them. Still, beggars can't be choosers, and there's enough here to stock the larder. We'll pickle some and smoke most of the rest. Some nice flank steaks, and there can be chops, too. Maybe enough to get some bacon. And sausages, of course — mustn't forget the sausages; waste not, want not. You'll find them nasty to make, I suppose, but you have to learn to get your hands dirty sometimes, and they're so tasty… The bones we can grind up to fertilize the vegetable garden after we make some stock from them. Most of it will go straight into storage, of course, but we'll have us a nice roast for dinner tonight. It's about time I taught you to cook properly."

"You can't eat her!" I shouted, but my voice sounded weak, like I was just a little girl again.

"Why on earth not? It's been a while since I've had a proper feast. And you need some protein, girl."

"No! She's my friend. She's good, she's nice, she's kind! And she's got nothing to do with your stupid war with my father!"

Baba Yaga hissed, pleased. I'd just revealed that I knew about her feud with Koschey.

"It's just a human, *vnuchechka*," she said. "Completely irrelevant to beings like us. You're quite right, it's got nothing to do with me or your father. Its fate is of no interest whatsoever. But that doesn't mean it can't serve a purpose. And I'm hungry."

"But she's got something to do with *me*," I protested. "She's my friend!"

Baba Yaga sighed.

"I'm sorry I had to leave you with those humans for so long that you started to think of them as pets," she said. "But you must know that however much he likes a cow, a farmer will still turn her into hamburgers someday."

"I won't let you!"

"Oh? And how are you going to stop me?"

I struggled to find something to say. Baba Yaga sneered, and then suddenly, without warning, she grabbed one of my wrists and swung me around until I fell to my knees on one side of Lauraleigh.

Baba Yaga knelt too, her long nose only inches from mine. I hardly even had time to yelp at the pain before she was snarling at me, not a trace of kindliness on her face, both my wrists held tight in her grip.

"You think you can hide from who you are?" she spat. "You think you can run from *what* you are? You think you're too good to do what you have to, to survive? You think you're better than me? Eh? Do you? Just because you like this pathetic, weeping creature? Just because of who your father is?" She shook me, hard, and I was too scared even to be angry anymore. "Come on! Show me just how *good* and *decent* you are!" She yanked one of my hands high and pressed it on Lauraleigh's forehead, just above her terrified, pleading eyes.

"You feel that?" my grandmother hissed. "You taste that? Terrified, isn't it? Can you taste its fear? All that lovely fear spicing its energy? And it's sad, and it's worried, and it's looking at you and trying to work out who you really are and what you're doing here. And it's all delicious, isn't it? *Isn't it?* Can you really stop yourself from feasting on that?"

She cackled — because it was true, I could feel Lauraleigh's energy, it was so clear and present, and almost without thinking, I was drawing it off. I could feel my own strength growing, and I closed my eyes. I'd never felt anything like that before. It was better than a glass of water after a hot day in the sun. Better than walking out of the snow into a warm room. Better than plunging into a bath after days tramping through the forest. Better than turning around when you were feeling lonely in the orphanage and realizing that Lauraleigh has come to see how you were...

I pulled my hand away. *What was I doing?*

I opened my eyes. Granny was standing a couple of meters away, a satisfied look on her face. Lauraleigh had crumpled to the ground. I could just see a pulse at her throat.

"So," said my grandmother. "You are a witch after all."

I wanted to blast her with all the magic I had, all the power I'd just gained from Lauraleigh, and hit her, hurt her, make her suffer for what she'd done. The shadow in me laughed at the thought. But I didn't. Somehow I didn't. I had to keep control. I had to save Lauraleigh — and somehow my father.

Granny looked … smug.

She thinks she's won, I thought. *Maybe I can use that against her.*

Lauraleigh wasn't important to her. She'd just been a test for me. That didn't mean Baba Yaga didn't intend to eat her; it just meant that the meal was only a side benefit.

"What do you want for her?" I asked.

She raised an eyebrow. "What's that?" she asked.

"What can I do for you to let her go?"

"Are you attempting to bargain with me, *vnuchechka*?" she said quietly.

"No," I answered, my voice steady. "To trade."

She tapped the side of her mouth with a finger.

"What on earth could you do that my Horsemen and my hands can't, though?" she said. "Or I can't?"

"I don't know, Granny," I said. "You tell me."

Unexpectedly, she burst into peals of laughter. "You're cleverer than I thought, Anna Sophia," she said. "I was starting to think you might be as useless as your mother."

Anger flared inside me again.

"No — don't lose your temper," Baba Yaga warned. "Don't waste your energy like that, not so soon after a meal. You'll need it if you're going to do me a kindness."

"It won't be a kindness, Granny," I said. "It will be a payment."

"Well, there's no need to be so nasty about it," she snapped. "If you're going to do something, you might as well be nice about it. Really, I *am* sorry I couldn't keep you out of that orphanage, if these are the manners they taught you, but you don't have to take it out on me quite that much."

My jaw dropped. I couldn't believe it! Ten minutes ago she was talking about all the ways she was going to cook Lauraleigh, five minutes ago she was holding my wrists so hard they still hurt, and now she was trying her grumpy grandmother act again?

"Oh, don't look at me like that," she said. "Pick up your pet and take it inside, and we'll talk. There might be something you could do for me after all."

"Her," I said.

"What?"

"'Her,' not 'it,' Granny. And she's not my pet; she's my *friend*."

Baba Yaga sighed. "Orphanages!" she said to no one in particular, rolling her eyes. And then she went inside.

I managed to get Lauraleigh inside and lay her down on my bed, but I couldn't untie the knots binding her or undo the gag. At least she was unconscious now. I touched her on the forehead and whispered "Sleep" to her, which I hoped would help.

When I went into the kitchen, my grandmother was seated in her usual chair, waiting for the hands to finish making us tea.

"Sit," she said.

I sat.

"Is your temper under control?"

"Yes," I said.

"Good. I don't care to listen to sulky children."

The hands brought us our tea, and for a while, we said nothing.

Finally, I'd had enough. "So," I said. "What can I do?"

"Well," she said reflectively, "there is a certain task you could perform for me."

"What is it?"

"I need you to find an island for me. A specific one."

"What? Why?"

"Because in the middle of that island, there's a tree."

"So?"

"In the branches of that tree, there's a chest."

"You want me to find you a chest? Couldn't you just make one?"

"No, no. You see, inside that chest, there's a hare."

"How do you know this?"

"I just do. Inside that hare, there's a duck."

"What?" Now I was utterly confused. Leaving aside the matter of how there could be a duck inside a hare, how was any of this important?

"And inside that duck, there's an egg. And inside that egg, there's something I want."

"So why don't you go get it yourself?"

"Because I can't find the island. And if I could, I wouldn't be able to find the chest."

"Why not?"

"Because of the enchantment on it. And because of what's in the egg."

"I don't understand. How is there an enchantment you can't break?"

"Because it was made specifically against me. And because of who made it."

"Who was that?"

Baba Yaga looked at me appraisingly.

"Why, my daughter, of course," she said quietly. "Your mother."

I froze. Immediately, I knew what was inside that egg. I knew what my grandmother was asking me for.

"Yes, exactly," said Baba Yaga. She didn't need magic to know I'd worked it out; it must have been written all over my face. "I need your father's heart."

Chapter 18

Dear Diary,

There's no way I can trust my grandmother. She's cruel and wicked and I can't believe how calmly she was going to butcher a person. Lauraleigh. My friend.

But getting my father's heart and giving it to her may be the only way to save Lauraleigh.

Can I risk that? My mother died to make sure Baba Yaga didn't get Koschey's heart. Would I be betraying her memory?

My only hope is that my father's right that she can be tricked...

"Why?" I asked.

"Only for the noblest of intentions," answered Baba Yaga. "I need your father's heart to save the world."

I almost choked. Now she wanted me to believe she was acting for the public good? After she'd just lectured me about how I shouldn't care about people?

I struggled to keep control. I couldn't do anything that might cause her to change her mind, not when it was my only chance of saving Lauraleigh.

"Really," I said. "And how will that work?"

"Well, with your father's heart, I can control the ghosts, which will let me set things right. It has to be done, after all."

"What ghosts?" I asked.

"Oh, don't try to be clever; it doesn't suit you. The ghosts who were surrounding that castle where my Horsemen found you. And others like them."

"What are they? Why are they suddenly appearing?"

"You don't need to know those details. All you need to know is that I need your father's heart." She sighed. "It would all have gone much more smoothly if your mother had just handed it over in the first place."

I felt a burst of pain and sorrow at the thought of my mother. Though I managed to control it, I couldn't help asking, "If she had, would she have died?"

Baba Yaga considered that for a moment. "No," she said calmly. "I don't believe she would have."

I bit back the urge to scream at her. Instead, I asked, "If you just freed my father, couldn't he take care of the ghosts for you?"

"Ha!" Baba Yaga snorted. "That old bag of bones actually doing something useful to help people? No, Anna Sophia, he wouldn't. He's too full of himself. You see, when I control the ghosts, I'll be able to save the world. Save humans from themselves. It will make people much happier. All the materialism will disappear and a new era will dawn. People will finally value love and life and friendship. They're going to find that respect for one another and for the natural world is far more important than the latest model of an overpriced cell phone."

"And what will happen to my father?" I asked.

"Oh, he'll be fine," she said with a wave of her hand. "After all, he's lasted this long without his heart. How much can he need it?"

She was lying, I was sure. But I couldn't let her know I thought that.

"So why me?"

"Because you're the only person in the world who can find it. I can't, because I don't have any connection with Koschey. But you... You're his daughter. You'll be able to feel it. And you're your mother's child. You'll be able to trace Sereda's magic."

"How?"

"By following your intuition, girl," she said. "That's how your mother's magic always worked." Her expression grew dreamy and maybe even a little sad. "Intuition and emotion... She never had time to learn how to use magic properly. And yet somehow she never failed at what she set out to do. She could have been so much..."

For a moment, every thought of my task was banished. She'd never really talked about my mother before.

"What was she like?" I asked.

Granny smiled sadly. "She was a silly little ninny," she said, but there was no harshness in her voice. "A sweet, silly creature who spent so much of her time tending the flowers in the woods. I don't think I ever quite understood her. But she was kind and knew how to care for the world. And cheerful, always so cheerful, even when things were wrong..."

Her voice drifted off, and we sat there in silence, both of us thinking of Sereda. But I wasn't seeing my mother's face as I'd seen it in Koschey's mind. I was seeing Lauraleigh's. They sounded so similar...

My mother had already died because Baba Yaga wanted Koschey's heart. I couldn't let Lauraleigh die too.

But I also wanted to just sit there and keep on talking with my granny and hearing more about my mother...

I shook the thought away. It wasn't helping.

"So," I said in a sharp tone, "I find this island. I get a trunk out of a tree, open it, get a duck out of a hare, an egg out of a duck, and then I bring you the egg?"

"No, you break open the egg to make sure you've found Koschey's heart," she said. "Though you'll have to be careful; you can't touch another person's heart without dying. I'll give you a box you can put it in."

"How will I know it's his heart?" I asked.

"You'll know," she said simply.

I hesitated.

"I need you to swear you'll keep Lauraleigh safe while I'm gone."

"Of course," she said.

"And I need to speak to my father before I go. In case he can tell me anything useful."

She snorted. "You can do that on your own time," she said. "Pretty useless you'll be in finding his heart if you can't even work out how to talk to him."

Good, I thought. *That means she doesn't know that I already found him.*

I spoke again. "And when I get back, you'll have to set him free before I give you the heart."

Her face darkened. "You're getting greedy, girl," she said. "Why would I do that?"

"Because otherwise I won't give you the heart."

"Then I'll eat your pet."

"What good will that do you, if you can't get Koschey's heart?"

She stared at me, her eyes hard. "Find the heart first," she said, "and then we'll talk about it."

"All right," I said. I was sure she didn't mean it, but it was good to get the concession anyway.

"Anything else, *princess*?" Baba Yaga said in a nasty tone. "Or do you think you can manage?"

"Yes," I said. "I'll need to borrow a mop and a bucket."

That actually managed to shock her. "Why?"

"To fly, of course," I answered scornfully. "You don't think I'm going to waste time walking, do you?"

Baba Yaga looked rather impressed. Apparently, she hadn't known I could do that. Perhaps I should not have revealed how much more advanced I was than she had thought; it might have been useful to conceal some of what I was capable of. But there were limits to how much I could hide.

"Fine," said Granny, "a mop and bucket there will be. You can leave in the morning. You might as well make sure you're well rested first."

I hadn't realized how late it already was. Had we really spent almost the whole day arguing?

"There's one more thing," I said, trying to hide my nervousness.

"More?" she said, exasperated. "What a spoiled child you are, demanding all these things from your poor old grandmother. They never gave you anything at the orphanage, so you became so greedy?" She sighed. "Well, what is it?"

"I need you to give me back the energy you've taken from me," I said.

That did it. She was shocked into silence.

"I can't do this if I'm weak," I argued. "I don't know what dangers I'll come across. I have to be able to defend myself. And who knows how much power it will take to get to the island and open the chest? You don't even know where it is, Granny. I need to be as strong as I can."

She stared at me warily. But it was obvious that I was right.

"Fine," she said. "Starve me out of my home, why don't you… What a way to treat a poor old woman. I'll strengthen you up before you go."

"Why not now?"

She chuckled. "Do you think me a fool, girl? Why would I risk you trying to steal your pet away in the night?"

She stood up, her joints creaking. "Well, that's settled then," she said. "With all this talk, we've wasted most of the day." She sighed again. "And now I'll have to go and find a new main course, since you won't let me eat your pet. *Tsk*, the trouble you put me to…"

Muttering along those lines, she went out onto the porch. "I'll be back when I've found my dinner," she said. "Use the hours well, Anna Sophia."

I didn't need to ask what she meant. Even before she settled into her mortar, I'd already started to run toward the wall that hid Koschey's cage.

"Open, open, magic door!" I yelled. But nothing happened.

Why not? Had Baba Yaga changed the spell? Or moved the cage? Or was I just too weak?

No — I was in too much turmoil. I couldn't concentrate. I kept thinking about the conversation and what I had to do, and my rage at my grandmother was starting to spark again as I recalled her poking at Lauraleigh and deciding how to chop her up.

I needed to calm down.

I went to look at Lauraleigh. She was still sleeping peacefully even though she was tied up. *Good.*

"I'll save you, Lauraleigh," I whispered. I sat down by her

bedside and stroked her hair. It was a meaningless thing to do, but it was calming.

When I had regained my composure, I went to talk to Dad. It was time to decide whether it was safe to bring Baba Yaga his heart, or if there was any way to trick her, or if there was some other way to save both him and Lauraleigh.

I reached the end of the corridor, made a foolish twirl and quietly said, "Open, open, magic door!" I danced the hula.

The wall opened, and there was Dad, sitting in his cage. His eyes lit up when he saw it was me. But then his expression started to look worried.

"Anna, what's happened to you?" he said. "The shadow inside you; it's grown. Why are you letting darkness into your heart?"

"It doesn't matter," I said. "There's no time for that."

"Anna, this is important. You can't risk letting the darkness take you over! What have you done?"

"Done?" I snapped. "I haven't *done* anything. All I've *done* is to stop my grandmother from eating my best friend. I don't see what's so dark about that."

Koschey looked shocked. "What's going on?" he asked.

Quietly, I told him everything that had happened. I tried to stay calm, but from time to time, my voice trembled with rage.

Koschey listened carefully, sometimes shaking his head. "This isn't good, *malyshka*," he said once or twice. "Not good at all."

When I finished the story, I asked, "So what do I do?"

"Clearly, you have to save your friend," said my father.

"So I have to bring back your heart?"

"That may be the only way, yes," he said. "I need to think."

"There isn't time to think," I retorted. "I don't know how long Baba Yaga will be gone, and I don't want her to see us talking."

"Anna … be careful. This anger in you, it's dangerous."

I looked at him. "The anger is helping me focus," I said, realizing it was true. "The anger's the only way I'll get this done."

"Anna, that will only make the shadow grow."

"I'm not doing it for me; I'm doing it to save Lauraleigh. And you!" I shouted. "Why does it matter how I do it so long as I do it?" I took a deep breath. "Where do I find your heart?"

He laughed mirthlessly. "Do you really think I know? There have been years during which I could have gone and picked it up, if I knew. I didn't. The only person who knew was your mother."

"And she's dead," I snarled. "Because of her. And because of you."

That hurt him, I could tell. Maybe it would make him snap out of it and tell me something useful.

"So *how* do I find your heart? Or is there some way I can trick her?"

"I don't know if we can trick her. But … it might be possible. You'd just have to give her something else."

"What is there that looks like a heart? This isn't *Snow White*. I can't just give her an animal heart and hope she won't notice."

He smiled. "No, you can't," he agreed. "Our hearts don't look like that when we take them out. But…" He paused, thinking. "There's somebody you need to talk to," he said. "His name's Vodyanoy. He's a water spirit who lives in a marsh nearby, and he may be able to help."

"How? And why?"

"I don't know how, exactly. My thoughts are muddled in here, Anna Sophia. But he was a friend of your mother's; he might know something. Maybe about how to find my heart. Maybe some way to trick your grandmother. Your mother may have left him some clue, I don't know. As to why — because you'll tell him I sent you and you'll remind him that he owes me."

Despite myself, I was interested. "What does he owe you for?"

"Hmm? Oh, nothing major. He lost the last time we played cards, and he hasn't paid up yet."

I stared at him.

"Immortality gets boring sometimes, *Malyshka*," he said with a slight grin. "You have to do something to pass the time."

"So I go see him, and he'll help?"

"I hope so, Anna, I hope so. I hope he can. Certainly, you won't be worse off."

"All right. I'll go see him then." I prepared to close the door.

"Anna…" said Koschey. "Please, I need to tell you something important."

"What?"

"Be careful. I don't just mean of the creatures in the forest, though many of them are not friends of Baba Yaga or me and may want to hurt you if they find out you're related.

And I don't just mean of your grandmother. Be careful of *yourself.*"

"What do you mean?"

"Be careful of how you act. Try not to be angry. Try not to hate. Don't dwell on these things. Try to think of *why* you're doing them. For your friend. For her goodness. For the love of your mother."

"Mother's dead," I said in a dull voice. "And it's Granny's fault."

"Yes. But don't think about those things, Anna. Because then you'll act in rage and spite and the shadow will grow."

"I'm not just going to forget what she's done, Dad. I'm not going to forget that I never had a mother because of her. I'm not going to forget that she wanted to eat Lauraleigh."

"Anna ... you hurt yourself when you think like that."

"But it lets me do magic," I whispered. "And I'll need that to find your heart."

"Yes, of course," he replied. "You understand how that works now, don't you. When you're filled with hate and anger, you can turn that into magic. But it works the other way too, Anna, and that's the important thing to remember. When your soul is filled with love and caring for others, you can create magic too. Concentrate on that. When you need to use magic on this quest, think of Lauraleigh, not your grandmother. Or else the darkness may take you."

I didn't want to hear that.

"Does it matter where the magic comes from, so long as it works?" I said.

"It does, *Malyshka*. It does to me. Because I don't want to see your soul growing dark like your grandmother's. It should be light, the way your mother's was…" He hesitated. "Maybe you shouldn't go."

"I have to," I said. "I'm not letting her get away with it."

"I already lost your mother to death," Koschey said sadly. "I do not want to lose you as well… to the darkness, to Baba Yaga."

"Well, I'm sorry I don't want to let her eat my friend!" I shouted. "I'm very sorry that I don't like that you're locked up in a cage. What does it matter if my magic's angry or not if I'm using it to help other people, Dad? What's so terrible about being angry if it helps me get you out of here? Or would you rather I just left you chained up and helped Granny roast my friend? It's not going to happen, Dad!"

I had my hand on the door to the room. I recalled something Sister Constance used to say, something I'd always hated to hear but which I understood now.

"I'm doing this for your own good," I said, staring directly at him. And before he had a chance to reply, I slammed the door in his face.

Chapter 19

Dear Diary,

It's so strange, being out of Baba Yaga's hut. I'm not even sure how many days I spent there, especially with my mind and memories being so fogged up by her all the time. Sometimes when I was there, it really felt like I had lived there my entire life. And then suddenly I got to leave. It's amazing the things I'd forgotten existed beyond the fence of skulls.

Everything seemed so bright once I'd left. It was as if I could see clearly again, notice things again. After I'd walked under the trees for a while, Dad and Baba Yaga began to seem unreal. How could a man be locked in a cage behind a magic door? That's not how the world works!

If I hadn't been flying in a bucket with a mop as a tiller, for a meeting with a water spirit, everything that had happened since I'd returned to Siberia would have seemed a dream.

I spent most of the evening in the kitchen, making sandwiches for my trip with the help of Granny's hands. Once she came back, she didn't help. She just sat around look-

ing at me. I wasn't sure why she did that or why I had expected anything different.

In the morning, I packed everything that I might need
into my bag, including the box Baba Yaga had left out for
me. I took the mop and bucket out of the closet and went
out onto the porch. Granny followed, looking depressed. She
seemed old and drawn again as when I'd first arrived, as if she
were tired of life and all it involved.

"You're leaving me all alone," she suddenly said, "just
like your mother did."

That was beyond absurd, and she knew it. "I'll be back,"
I said. "With what you asked for. And things will be all right
then, won't they?"

She grunted. Then unexpectedly, she pulled me into a
hug. "I'll miss you, *vnuchechka*," she said, sounding like she
was on the verge of tears.

"I'll miss you too, Granny," I said. It wasn't a complete
lie. A small part of me *would* miss her, miss those moments
when we had just sat around drinking tea or talking about
random things and pretending to be a normal family. I'd
never had that before. There had been moments in Baba
Yaga's hut when, even though she was stealing my energy, I'd
found out what it must be like for people who aren't orphans.

But I still couldn't forget what she'd done and what she'd
threatened to do.

"Remember," I said, "you promised to keep Lauraleigh
safe—"

"I will, I will," she said. "You don't need to worry. And
when you come back with what I've sent you for, we'll set her
free and let her go back to Geneva and its boys and its clothes

and its mobile phones and all the other vain stuff she fills her pampered little head with."

She sounded so much the crotchety old woman that I smiled a little.

"She's not like that, Granny," I said. "She's kind, and she's not pampered. She lived in the orphanage with me. And she doesn't need material things to be happy. Why, she followed me here just because she wanted to backpack around the world. She was quite happy to sleep on the ground."

Baba Yaga chuckled. "That just proves my point," she said. I must have looked confused, because she went on, "If she wasn't pampered, she wouldn't do that. No one chooses to be uncomfortable unless they know they can go back to being comfortable whenever they choose.

"Do you think anybody who has really been home-less would give up the chance of a soft bed to go wandering through Siberia? It's only the privileged who decide to do things like that, Anna Sophia. Just like it's only the well-fed who can decide to starve. All those supermodels on the tel-evision, nothing but bones; they choose not to eat because they could eat if they wanted to. They torture themselves and decide to be hungry.

"Do you think anyone who's actually starving cares about how much cholesterol is in an egg if they're given a chance to eat one? Do you think they care about how great their food tastes, so long as it's there?"

I'd never thought about that, and I couldn't find an answer. Even though I was sure that none of it applied to Lauraleigh.

"I'd better go now, Granny," I said. "I don't want to waste any sunlight."

"Yes, that's likely for the best," she said. "Come, kneel down for your old granny's blessing before you go."

I felt I could trust her at that moment, and I knelt. Baba Yaga put two fingers on my forehead, and then she breathed toward me as if she were whispering the single long syllable, "Shooo…"

I felt warmth trickling through me as if I'd just drunk a whole pot of hot tea at one sitting. I could feel magic tingling as it spread all the way from my stomach to the ends of my fingers and toes and the roots of my hair. I was soon feeling as good as I ever had, and I prepared to stand up and thank my grandmother, but she went on breathing out. It was like an endless sigh, and I felt my energy growing, becoming stronger than ever, far more powerful than the burst I'd almost used against the Montmorencys. But it was completely under my control. It felt wonderful.

At last, Granny stopped.

"There," she said roughly, "a little bit extra. Just a little gift from Granny…" She sounded sad and old, and as I looked at her, I realized she seemed weaker and more ancient than I'd ever seen her. "And the ghosts won't bother you for a few days."

I jumped up and hugged her.

"Let's sit on the road, as the old Russian tradition tells us," she said with an undertone of sadness.

We sat down on the porch and held hands. I went through a quick mental checklist, making sure I hadn't forgotten anything.

After about a minute, Baba Yaga sighed. "Now go," she said.

"Thank you, *babulya*," I whispered, and I meant it. Then I slung my backpack over my shoulders and stepped into my bucket. I grabbed hold of the mop.

Whatever happens, bucket, I thought, *take off properly. I can't fail in front of Granny.*

I needn't have worried. The magic was so strong in me that I had hardly thought of the word *Fly* before I rose into the air and started moving toward the forest.

I looked behind me. Baba Yaga's hut was already growing smaller, and she was just a small, shrunken, hunched-over figure holding a cat in her arms. Then she was just a speck. Then even the hut disappeared behind the trees — and I was free.

I didn't actually fly for that long. It was too tempting to set down among the tall trees and walk. I hadn't realized how much I'd enjoy doing that, seeing what flowers there were, what grew in the shade. Or maybe it was just the fact that I *could* walk wherever I wanted without a skull looking at me, a cat turning into a hare, or my having to pretend to Granny that I'd lost my memory. And with my memory truly restored, it was also comforting, like being a little kid again. I remembered walking like this with Uncle Misha and him telling me about the flowers and the animals and the birds. Sometimes I'd go and play with my foster siblings, the bear cubs, and Mama Bear would look after me. Sometimes she would catch me with a paw and give me a rough tongue bath when my face had gotten too dirty from stuffing berries in my mouth and getting them smeared all over me.

I wondered how Uncle Misha was. He still had to be in Blackwood Castle with Egor. But were they worried about Lauraleigh? They had to be. Where had the Horsemen captured her, anyway? I thought I had asked Granny to pull them back from the castle although now I wasn't sure that she actually had. Had Lauraleigh been foolish and wandered off? The more I thought about it, the more worried I became. Uncle Misha would be going wild, having promised me he'd keep Lauraleigh safe.

If he and Egor were still alive, of course.

I have to finish my mission before he and Egor do anything silly, I decided. For a moment, I toyed with the idea of going to find them. After all, I had my bucket, didn't I? Surely they'd have some advice. Especially Uncle Misha. He could tell me how to find a marsh in a forest.

As I was considering whether this would take too long — the Horsemen or the ghosts might still be around the castle —I was suddenly distracted by some desperate bird chirpings. Confused, I looked around and saw a small bluebird flying frantically in circles over the same spot in the grass. She was staying dangerously low. I hadn't seen any other birds flying that low; they all seemed to be staying up in the tree canopy.

Carefully, I set down my things and walked toward the spot, trying not to startle the bird. The bird's chatter increased; it seemed quite panicked as I got close, and it even tried to dive-bomb me a couple of times. When I was able to peer at the spot it was circling over, I understood why. There was a helpless little chick in a nest on the ground. It must have been blown off a tree by the wind or knocked off by a predator or something. The bluebird had to be its mother. No wonder she was panicking!

I had to help. Kneeling down, I extended my hands to pick up the nest, but the mother started screaming even more and flew down to try to peck at my fingers.

"Ow!" I shouted. "Ow! I just want to help, honest! Please don't hurt me. I'm just trying to help."

As I was thinking how ridiculous it was to try to speak with a bird, I noticed that she'd stopped pecking at me. She hovered in front of me and chirped quizzically.

Could she understand me?

"What can I do to help?" I asked, focusing my mind on my words, willing the bird to understand. I felt the familiar warm tingle of magic as I spoke.

The bird gave a delighted burble and fluttered her way

over to a nearby tree, looking back at me as she did so. Then she settled in the crook of two branches and looked at me pleadingly.

"You'd like me to put the nest there?" I asked. "Is that it?"

She called out, giving me her approval.

"All right," I said, and cradled the nest in my hands. "There you are, little fellow," I said, thinking waves of reassurance at the squawking, flightless chick in the nest. "No need to worry; I'm just going to take you to your mother." After a moment or two, it calmed down.

Reaching the tree, I secured the nest where the mother bird tapped with her beak. She cheeped happily.

"There," I said. "Well, I'd better be on my way." I turned and started walking back to where I'd left my things.

To my surprise, the bird followed me, chirping insistently. It was like she was thanking me. I felt warmth and lightness fill my whole being.

"It was nothing, birdie," I said. I extended my hand and smiled, not really expecting anything. To my surprise, the bluebird hopped onto my index finger. I laughed. "We have to help each other out, don't we?"

She titled her head in an inquisitive attitude.

"Oh! No, no, you don't have to do anything!" I said. "Unless… You don't happen to know the way to Vodyanoy's marsh, do you?"

The bird let out a piercing call and flew off my finger. She flew a few steps ahead of me; then she set down on a branch and looked back. She flew another few meters and did the same thing.

"I should follow you?" I said.

She trilled at me.

"Wait, wait a moment," I said, laughing. "Let me get my bucket! Then I can fly along with you. It will go faster!"

I ran to my things, slung my backpack on again, and hopped into the bucket. A moment or two later, I was flying just behind the bird. It was all so utterly unreal that I couldn't stop giggling.

After about fifteen minutes, I was sure I was totally lost in the woods and would never find my way back again, but I didn't care. There would always be ways to find Baba Yaga, no doubt!

Finally, the bird let out a long call and began to circle down toward the ground. I followed her and soon saw the reeds and rushes of a marsh. I settled my bucket down by its side.

The bird flew back to my finger.

"Thank you so much, birdie," I said, and very daringly stroked the soft top of her head. She chirruped. "I'd never have found this on my own."

She made a pleased sound and fluttered her wings as though about to take off.

"Oh," I said, "if you happen to meet the Great Trapper, could you tell him you saw me? Let him know I'm all right, and I know where Lauraleigh is, and I'm taking care of things."

It seemed a long message for a bird, but I figured she'd be able to get the gist across. She must have thought so too because she gave me a burble of agreement before flying off.

"Thank you again!" I called after her. "I hope your chick grows up safe and strong!"

The bird let out one last chirp and vanished among the trees. The forest became utterly silent. I let out a long breath and lay down in the grass. It had been a long time since I'd felt so at peace with the world. I could take a moment before trying to find Vodyanoy.

The marsh stretched a long way. There were lots of long grasses poking out of the mud, puddles covered with green scum and moss, and bits of ground that looked solid but which I wouldn't trust for a moment. There were broken tree trunks leaning over the water as if they were trying to look at themselves in a mirror, and dragonflies skimming over the top, dipping in and out between the water lilies. A lovely butterfly landed on my shoulder. I smiled; it was a beautiful place. No wonder Vodyanoy chose to live here. Or was it so beautiful because he lived here?

I decided that the best way to find him would just be to call him. If that didn't work, I could always try something else.

"Vodyanoy? Are you there?"

My voice seemed to echo, and there was a rustle over the marsh water.

Then without any warning, the water parted. A strange creature with a tangled beard full of shells and water flowers and long grubby hair streaming with reeds rose up out of it. He looked like some middle-aged hippie whose skin just happened to be a muddy green.

"Who chooses to disturb me?" he demanded in a loud, deep voice. Before I could say a word, he raised a hand, and the waters rose in a huge wave behind him that came crashing down on me. As I sputtered and choked, he leaped out of the water and grabbed me by the hair, dragging me back with him as he plunged headfirst into the marsh.

I was so shocked I couldn't even think. I couldn't scream because I was deep in thick, soupy waters, and my magic didn't seem to be helping me. My panicked mind wasn't able to control it, and Vodyanoy's marsh appeared to have some magic power of its own that blocked mine from working. One of Vodyanoy's hands remained tangled in my hair and the other reached for my throat. *No doubt about it*, I thought, *I'm going to drown here.* Vodyanoy was too strong for me to fight.

I was starting to lose consciousness. There were small dots of color swimming in my eyes. This was hopeless. I had barely even started on my mission and I'd already failed.

Lauraleigh, Dad … I'm sorry, I thought.

And then Baba Yaga's face floated into my mind, wearing that nasty expression I disliked so much. I could tell what she was thinking even before she spoke the word.

"Weak!" she spat.

Hardly even thinking, I grabbed Vodyanoy's arm and sank my teeth into it. He yelled in pain and let go, and I kicked my way to the surface, rolling onto solid ground as he came after me. But before he could form another wave, I flung my arm out toward him and a wall of flames erupted from my fingertips. He fell back howling as drops of water evaporated in front of him, but my flames were between him and the marsh. He crouched on the ground like some strange frog, looking at me suspiciously. I could tell he was trying to work out a new way to attack me.

I let the wall of fire die down but kept flickers of it sparking.

"I am Anna Sophia," I said, magic making my voice powerful and echoing. "Child to the Iron Queen, daughter of Sereda and Koschey the Deathless, Keeper of the Kingdom of the Dead, who sends me to speak with you, Vodyanoy, that you should help me."

I don't even know how I knew to say that, how I knew I should phrase it that way, but it worked. Vodyanoy fell back and suddenly became ingratiating, a hint of fear in his eyes.

"The Iron Queen? Koschey?" he said. "Oh dear, I am sorry... Certainly, I never meant to offend..."

He was clearly worried.

"Yes," I said. To take the high ground and show some manners, I added, "It's lovely to meet you, Vodyanoy."

"And you, and you," he muttered. "Um, I'm sorry, no wish to be a bother, but do you think you could put out the flames?"

I looked at him uncertainly.

"Please?" he said.

I let the flames die. With a great gasp, he dove back toward the marsh and plunged his feet in.

"Aah, that's better," he said. "Thank you. I have to be in contact with the water, you see. If I dry off completely ... well..." He looked at me sharply. "You realize that my telling you this is a secret, yes? And proof that I trust you?"

I smiled but did not lower my hand.

He looked me over.

"Anna Sophia," he said. "Yes, yes, of course. I'm so sorry, I should have known. You look so much like your mother at that age... Ah, it's sad that she's gone. But such is life when your mother's the Iron Queen." Worry suddenly erupted in his eyes again. "*She's* not around, is she?"

"No," I said. "I'm here on my own. On a mission for her, but on my own. It was my father who sent me to you, not her."

"Your father. He really is Koschey? I'd heard he had a daughter, but I couldn't really believe it... He's always been such a gloomy fellow; I couldn't really see him getting anywhere with a woman, especially not a lovely girl like your mother... But there you are. And here you are. How is he?"

"In need of assistance," I answered.

He nodded eagerly. "Of course. Anything, anything! Always glad to do a favor for the Keeper..."

"Well, you could start by not drowning me," I said a bit waspishly.

Vodyanoy raised his eyebrows.

"It was an honest mistake," he said. "Your father might have told you to be careful if you come to my marsh. I don't like visitors. They mess the place up. Those dreadful metal cans humans drink out of, all the trash they leave behind... Much simpler not to give them a chance to ruin the place than to fix things afterward. After all, I'm not a janitor. Why should it be my job to clean up after them?"

"You sound like my grandmother," I said. It's not that I disagreed about people leaving junk in the forest, but drowning them seemed a bit much. Especially when he'd just tried to drown me even though I hadn't intended to do anything to his marsh. He could at least have checked first.

Vodyanoy looked unsure whether being compared to Baba Yaga was a compliment.

"I had heard … I hope this isn't speaking out of turn … but there's been this rumor going around the forest that … well, that Koschey had been captured by your grandmother."

"Yes, that's true," I said.

"Ah, well. I see. And you say you're on a mission for her?"

"Yes, I am."

"Hmm. If I may ask … if it's not too impertinent… This mission … is something you're undertaking, um, of your own free will?"

"What?" I said, confused. Then I understood. Vodyanoy wasn't sure whose side I was on and was afraid of getting caught in the middle.

"I chose to do it," I said, "but only so I can save the life of a friend of mine. She was captured by Baba Yaga's Horsemen."

"Oh, the poor thing!" Vodyanoy exclaimed. "She'll be for the oven, then!" He shuddered. "Nasty things, ovens. All that fire."

"Unless I complete this mission, yes she will. I might even be able to free Koschey as well."

Now Vodyanoy definitely looked interested. "Really?" he said.

"Yes. That's why my father sent me to you for help."

"Well, that's very flattering," said the water spirit. "Of course, I'm glad to assist you in any way I can. After all…" he lowered his voice and spoke out of the corner of his mouth, "confidentially, I consider myself one of his best friends."

"He mentioned that," I lied. I had to keep from laughing at how Vodyanoy preened like he was intensely flattered.

"Hmm, yes, well…" he said. "So, what can I, um, do for you?"

"My father thought my mother might have told you something that could help me."

"Your mother? Sereda? Oh, I've not seen her in years. Well, obviously I haven't. But you know what I mean. And I can't recall her telling me anything I was supposed to say to her child."

"Koschey said you were her friend."

"Yes," he said quietly, "I was. When she was a child, younger than you, she liked to play here. I taught her to swim, you know. She liked the water lilies…" He drifted off. "It's a shame that she is dead," he said. "I miss her."

"You know why she died, don't you?"

"Yes, I do. It's a well-known story in the forest. Everyone's been just a little bit more scared of your grandmother ever since, just a little more horrified. She finds it harder to get help from the forest folk now. She has to threaten more. Not that she didn't always use threats…"

"Have you known her long?" I asked. I realized I was curious about what others thought and knew about Baba Yaga. Maybe that would give me some idea of how to trick her if I needed to.

"Oh, yes," said Vodyanoy. "I have been here a long time. Why, I saw her arrive."

"How long ago was that?" I asked. I couldn't even imagine.

"Look around you," he said.

I did. Nothing but forest as far as I could see. New shoots peeping through the grass, giant old trees towering above us, and dead ones still standing, with young ones starting to grow out of their roots.

"Before there were trees, there was water," Vodyanoy said, "and I was there. I have watched the forest grow."

I could hardly catch my breath, realizing just how old he had to be. And my grandmother and all those other magical beings that I had once thought were just fairy tales.

Suddenly I felt very small and very young.

"What do you need, child?" Vodyanoy asked, his voice kind. There was nothing silly about him now.

I swallowed and looked him right in the green eye. "I need the heart of Koschey the Deathless," I said.

There was utter silence. Vodyanoy's face grew closed.

"My grandmother told me how it's hidden. I just need to find the island where my mother hid it."

"And what will you do with it?" Vodyanoy's voice was expressionless.

"It's the price of my friend's life," I said.

"So you'll give it to the Iron Queen?"

"If I must. Yes."

"And what does she say will happen then?"

"She'll let my friend live. And I've made her promise to discuss freeing my father."

His eyes widened. "Anna Sophia," he said in a severe tone. "Koschey's daughter, Sereda's child… You cannot do this."

"She said she'd be able to use the heart to fix the world.

Make people respect existence again. Just like you want them to stop dumping garbage by your marsh."

He snorted. "Is that what she said? And you believed her?"

"I don't know. But I talked to my father, and he said you might be able to help. My mother might have told you something useful when she was hiding his heart. Or you might have some idea of how to trick Baba Yaga."

"Trick the Iron Queen? I don't think I'm that clever, Anna Sophia. You don't get to my age by trying to trick that sort of witch."

I could feel myself getting angry with him and with Koschey for sending me here. Of what use was this?

"But let's think," Vodyanoy went on. "If Koschey sent you to me, there must be a good reason."

"Do you know where his heart is?"

"No," he said. "But I do know this, and I must tell you: You must not, absolutely must not, let Baba Yaga get Koschey's heart."

"I don't want to," I admitted. "But if it's the only way to save Lauraleigh, then I will."

"No," he said, and his voice was firm. "No matter how much you care about her, your friend's life is not worth what will happen if the Iron Queen gets the heart of the Keeper of the Kingdom of the Dead. I don't know what lies she told you, Anna Sophia, but if she gets his heart, Baba Yaga will not free your father. She will not have to. She will eat his heart, child, and she will absorb all his powers. She will gain sovereignty over the Kingdom of the Dead, and she will rule it just as she now rules the bridge between the living and the dead.

She will take control of all of existence, Anna Sophia. She will become more powerful than any being has ever been before, and she will do with the world whatever she wants.

"And that must not happen. No matter how much you love your friend, you cannot give Baba Yaga Koschey's heart."

Chapter 20

 ear Diary,

I hate my grandmother. I hate her more than I've ever hated anyone or anything in the world. She lies and she cheats and she's cruel and she makes everything she touches dirty. She's evil, and the worst thing is that now I know she chose to be evil. It's her fault my mother's dead, and now she's trying to make me be like her. And she's trying to trick me into helping her rule all the existence.

I'm not going to let her do that. I'm not going to turn all the children in the world over to her for her to feed on.

And if that means I have to kill her, I will.

❖

I spent a long time staring helplessly at Vodyanoy.

"Then what should I do?" I said in a pathetic little voice. "There must be some catch, right? Some way of … well, doing something? Please, Vodyanoy, help me!"

"Let's think, let's think," he said. "Your father sent you to me; therefore, your father believes I can help."

"He didn't sound sure," I admitted. "His thoughts are getting muddled."

"That's not important," said Vodyanoy. "My thoughts get muddled too sometimes, but the basic message always gets through. Koschey may not have known *how* I can help, but clearly he knows that I *can*. I'm not going to suggest I know better than him … even if I'm not sure myself how I can assist."

"This is hopeless," I muttered.

"No, no it isn't yet," said Vodyanoy, "we just aren't thinking clearly. Let's see; let's go through this in order. What *exactly* are you to do? Not what Koschey said; what your grandmother said."

"Well," I told him, "I'm to find Koschey's heart in the egg where it's hidden."

"Hmm, all right. And you take the egg to Baba Yaga?"

"No," I said. "I have to check that it is his heart first."

"All right, all right, I see. That will be dangerous, though. You can't touch another person's heart, you know. You'll die."

"She gave me a box to put it in."

"Ah, that makes sense. Now how will you know that it's Koschey's heart?"

"She says I just will, because I'm his daughter."

"Hmm, true enough. But that means…" Suddenly he looked at me sharply.

"What is it?"

"Just a thought, a very brief thought," he said. "I'm on the verge of working something out, but I'm not sure what. Keep talking. Any details you have, any questions."

"What I don't get is if you die by touching someone's heart, how will Baba Yaga use Koschey's?"

"Well, you have to remember she's a very powerful witch

and she'll be using it to acquire all his strength. She must have a plan for that. But it is very dangerous even for a witch to touch a heart. Why, even if Koschey wanted to take his back, it would be dangerous. Certainly, it's very painful to put your heart back where it's supposed to be. Almost as painful as taking it out in the first place. It might even kill you. In fact…"

Suddenly his jaw dropped and his face lit up as if he'd just realized something.

"Oh," he said. "*Oh!* But that would mean…" He stared at me. "That means…"

And suddenly he plunged directly into the water.

"Vodyanoy!" I cried. "Come back!"

I couldn't see any trace of him. Not even a ripple in the water to mark where he'd been. I looked around, feeling helpless. What was going on?

Suddenly his head popped out of the water, newly draped with weeds.

"Just a moment!" he said. "I'll be back in a jiffy!" And he vanished under the water again.

Now I was utterly confused. What on earth was this weird spirit up to?

After what seemed much longer than a jiffy to me, Vodyanoy jumped out and sat on the bank again, his feet back in the water.

"Aah, that's better," he said, sounding most relieved. "Sorry, dear, but the longer I'm out of the water, the less well I think, and I want to be certain that my mind is absolutely clear for this." He smiled. "Now, let's think this through."

I nodded eagerly.

"You'll hand this box over to your grandmother, and inside it, she thinks, will be Koschey's heart. That's right, isn't it? That's what you're to do?" He seemed intensely hopeful that my answer would be yes.

"That's what she said," I answered.

A big grin spread over his face. "But do you see what that means? That means she's trusting you not only to identify Koschey's heart but to take it to her. She fully expects that when you hand her that box and she opens it, what's inside *will be* the heart of Koschey the Deathless."

"So?" I didn't see where he was going.

"Well, don't you understand? Anything could be in that box. Anything at all." He grabbed a water lily from the surface of the marsh without breaking off its stem. "Look," he said, "you could put *this* in the box, and until she opens it, Baba Yaga will think it's Koschey's heart."

"But if it's not his heart, there's no point in going back," I said. "She'll know. Even if I could enchant a lily to look like his heart ... and I don't even know what that looks like ... she'd know that it's not."

"I know," Vodyanoy said. "But that's not what I'm proposing." He looked absolutely delighted with himself. "Who would have thought," he said, "the Iron Queen would trust someone! Who would have thought that would be her downfall?"

"Vodyanoy," I said, "this isn't helping! What could I put in the box that would trick her or bring about her downfall? It doesn't make any sense."

"Ah," said Vodyanoy, "but that's because you don't have one key piece of information. It's been so long, I'd almost forgotten it. I can't believe that, but I've grown so used to the fact, oh-oh-oh-oh-oh..." He slapped the side of his head a few times. "Growing old, you know, the memory starts to stutter a bit... But this is so perfect, so amazing..."

"Vodyanoy," I said in my firmest voice, sounding more like Baba Yaga than I cared to admit, "will you stop babbling and *tell me what you're thinking?*"

He settled down.

"Yes, yes, of course," he said. "I suppose part of me thought you'd already know or that Koschey might have told you..." He looked at me. *"Baba Yaga doesn't have her own heart either."*

There was dead silence.

"What!" I exclaimed. Why did I not know this?

"It's been so long," Vodyanoy whispered, "I'd almost completely forgotten it, but there was a time when it was well known. That was how this whole thing began."

"I don't understand. What are you telling me? And ... and how does it help?"

"You don't see it yet? Well, I suppose this is all new to you."

"Why doesn't she have her heart? Was it to protect herself like Dad?"

"No," said Vodyanoy. "It's very different. Actually, it may be where the difference between the two of them lies: the reasons they removed their own hearts. Your father did it to protect himself and, he hoped, to protect your mother. Baba Yaga did it so she could stop ... feeling."

I looked at him, shocked. "Is that why she's so evil?" I asked. "Because she can't feel? But why would anyone want to stop feeling? Did she *want* to be evil? Want to … I don't know … stop feeling remorse when she killed someone or something?"

Vodyanoy shook his head. "No," he said, "it's not like that. It's quite sad, actually." He sighed and looked at me. "Anna Sophia," he said, "have you ever been in love?"

"What?" I said. I had no idea what this had to do with anything. "No … I mean there are people I love, like Lauraleigh and Dad and Uncle Misha and Mama Bear. And people I enjoy being with, like Jean-Sébastien. But I don't think I've ever *been* in love."

Vodyanoy nodded.

"I suspected as much," he said. "You are young. So maybe you won't understand. But a long time ago, when we were all young … even me, even Baba Yaga, even Koschey … your grandmother fell in love.

"We were all very different then. Why, I was quite a handsome fellow, would you believe, and your grandmother … well, she was the most beautiful witch in the world."

"Koschey told me she'd been beautiful," I said, "but he also said she had always been totally evil."

"I have known your grandmother for longer than Koschey has," said Vodyanoy. "This was a very long time ago, when things were just beginning, when she had only just arrived. This forest had not yet even begun to think about starting to grow. There was only the water, and some lichens, and me. And Baba Yaga was young. Not much older than you, really. Incredibly powerful already, of course, but still, in many things, a child. We all were. The world was a child then.

"And she fell in love. Well, you've met your grandmother — she's not one to do things by halves. She was completely besotted as only a teenager can be. But he spurned her. He rejected her. Even though she was beautiful, even though she offered him so much power, despite everything, he wasn't interested. And he told her so in the cruelest way imaginable."

"Who was he?" I asked.

"Nobody," said Vodyanoy. "No one really remembers. It wasn't important. I can hardly even remember whether he was mortal or one of us. But Yaga was almost destroyed by grief. It wasn't even that he had wounded her pride; she was truly, desperately unhappy. She had really loved him, you see. When he rejected her, she almost ceased to function. She couldn't take care of her duties anymore. She was hardly able to move. It was as if she wanted to die. She wept so much, some lakes grew salty from her tears, they say."

I tried to imagine my grandmother in tears, tried to imagine even that beautiful girl I'd seen in my father's memories grieving, and I couldn't.

Vodyanoy seemed to know what I was thinking.

"It broke her heart, Anna Sophia," he said gently. "It truly broke her heart. And so eventually, when she couldn't take it anymore, she tore her heart out of herself. So that she could stop feeling the pain."

Vodyanoy picked up the water lily from the grass where he had left it, and carefully put it back into the marsh. He seemed lost in memories.

"It worked, too," he said, looking at the lily rather than at me. "She stopped feeling the hurt. She stopped feeling anything. That's when she started to become the Iron Queen."

"That's … horrible," I said. "I can't imagine anyone doing that."

"No," said Vodyanoy sadly. "But then you've never been in love."

He sighed.

"After that…" he continued. "Well, we all know what she became. Sometimes I wonder if she even remembers what she did to her heart, or if she's grown so used to not having it that she's forgotten. She could have taken it back, you know. I remember suggesting it to her once, not that long after she'd taken it out. I thought she'd have had time to heal. She just laughed."

"So she decided to just keep on not feeling?"

"Maybe she liked the power it gave her. I don't know. I've never cut out my own heart; never wanted to or had to, so I don't know exactly what it's like, but obviously it's still possible to enjoy things. The everyday pleasures and annoyances of life, it seems you still feel those. But the real emotions, the deep ones, the ones that feed magic — those get taken away. I think that's why Baba Yaga's so eager to feast on strong emotions to replenish her powers. They're feelings she doesn't have anymore. Even if she doesn't realize it, I think she may be hungry for them. Which is probably why she has to eat children sometimes. Cutting out your own heart... You must sense there's something missing, certainly..."

He was drifting off again.

"Vodyanoy," I said, "do you feel sorry for my grandmother?"

He shook his head. "Not exactly," he said. "I feel sorry for the girl I knew. I feel sorry she turned into what she did, and I like to think she would have been horrified if she had looked into the future and seen what she would become. I feel sorry that girl wasn't able to live until today as she was, more like your mother. But I don't feel sorry for the Iron Queen or forgive what she's done. Do you see what I mean?"

"I think so," I said, though I'd have to think about it.

"What I wish is that there was a way to undo it all," he said. "There isn't, of course. But it might be possible to undo some of it."

"What do you mean?"

"As I said ... it seems to me, even if consciously she's almost forgotten about her heart, somewhere inside her she must be aware that something's missing. The way she seeks out strong emotions, I don't think it can just be a taste. I don't think she can stop herself from taking them if they're nearby.

Do you see? Somewhere inside her, she may want her heart back."

"But Vodyanoy," I said, "how does this help us?"

"Just imagine," he said quietly. "What do you think would happen if, when she opened that box, instead of Koschey's heart inside, it was hers?"

I gaped at him.

"I don't think she could resist it," he carried on. "I think she'd have to touch it. And then ... well, who knows what would happen? If she took back her heart, if she started feeling again, she would change. Become the girl I knew again, or something like her."

"You said it was dangerous to even touch your own heart," I remembered.

"Yes," he said. "It might even kill her."

"But what if she realized the plot? What if she didn't touch it?"

"She's an eager person. She'll want to see Koschey's heart as soon as possible. You'll be there. It doesn't matter whether she chooses to touch it or not, as long as she does so. Worse comes to worst, you can always throw it at her."

My voice was shaking, torn between hope and fear. "Do you really think it can work?"

"I don't know," he said, "I don't know... But it's definitely worth the risk. There's never been a better opportunity to bring the Iron Queen down. *She trusts you*, Anna Sophia. She's so convinced you'll do exactly what she says to save your friend that she hasn't considered what else could happen. She's sure there's nothing you know that could harm her, or anything you're powerful enough to do to stop her."

"So she underestimates me?" I said. I was starting to feel angry at her again. *She thinks I'm just a silly little girl as helpless as Lauraleigh*, I thought.

"Yes, she probably does," he said. "And that's her mistake." He looked at me. "You can do this, Anna Sophia. You're the only person who can. The only person who ever could."

"Do you know where Baba Yaga's heart is?" I asked.

"There were rumors, a long time ago," he said. "But the world has changed so much since then, forests growing, rivers moving…"

"So what good is this plan?" I burst out.

"I'm thinking, I'm thinking. Clearly, there must be a way to find it. Nothing is ever completely lost. Hmm…" He was becoming the dotty figure I'd first met again.

"How were you supposed to find Koschey's heart?" he suddenly asked.

"Baba Yaga said I'd find my way by trusting my instincts," I answered. I'd be able to follow my mother's magic and feel his heart because I'm related to both of them. That's what Baba Yaga can't do. But then Koschey sent me to you, so I'm not even sure where I'd start."

"Hmm. Well, obviously that won't work in this case. It's been so long, and the magic link would be weaker because you're only her granddaughter… Let's think; let's think. I wonder if… Do I still have…"

And once again, he dove into the water.

I sighed, but at least I was certain he'd be back.

While I waited, I thought about our plan. Would it work? If I found Baba Yaga's heart, would I really be able to stop her plans? Just getting her heart back wouldn't turn her good, would it? She hadn't done anything evil when she'd had her heart, but that didn't erase everything she had done since. It didn't change whom she'd turned into.

But Vodyanoy had said it would hurt her to take her heart back. Giving Baba Yaga back her own heart would cause her pain.

The shadow inside me smiled.

Chapter 21

*D*ear Diary,

It's been so long since I've been among normal people. Other than Lauraleigh, the last one I talked to was Gavril, and that feels like it was months ago. Maybe it was; time got so strange in Baba Yaga's hut, I'm not really sure how long it's been since I left Geneva. And being among a crowd of people — that feels intensely weird. Which is weird in itself; I never had any trouble with it back in Switzerland.

I definitely didn't expect to end up in a four-star hotel when I set out to find Koschey's heart — or Baba Yaga's. Looking around, I can only imagine what Granny would say: The materialism of people who pay for a room here, the fact that a little piece of plastic can buy a room for the night. I don't even want to think about what she'd say if she knew I'd given in to the temptation to stay here.

I don't really care, though. I don't think it's evil to rest for one night in genuine comfort. Selfish, maybe. But since I can't do anything until the morning anyway, it's not as if I'm betraying Lauraleigh. I have to spend the night somewhere. And since I can, why not choose a bed instead of crawling under some bush in the forest and hoping the moss is soft?

Tomorrow I'll find Baba Yaga's heart. And then I'll bring all of this to an end.

When Vodyanoy popped out of the water again, he was holding something in one hand: a golden apple.

He handed it to me.

"Here," he said. "I almost forgot I still had it… This is very old, Anna Sophia, very precious. There aren't many like it left in the world."

"What does it do?" I asked, rolling it around in my hands and looking at it. It felt almost like an actual plump round apple, but it shone like the purest gold, almost as if its skin had somehow been turned into metal.

"It's a guide," he explained. "You ask it to take you where you want to go, and it will roll that way. Then you only need to follow it."

"Really?" That sounded unbelievable. "But … does it work on everything? I mean, surely Baba Yaga used some major enchantments to protect her heart. Are you sure the apple will be able to find it?"

"Yes," he said. "I am certain."

"Why?"

"Because Baba Yaga made this apple," he said quietly. "She gave it to me ages ago. Back before she cut out her heart."

I gasped. How could this apple be that old? I held it more carefully in my hands, amazed that I was touching something that had been made by my grandmother when she had been young and beautiful and not entirely evil.

"The magic in this apple, the magic in her heart ... they'll call out to each other. There's not much left in the world that still holds a trace of your grandmother's good magic. It doesn't matter what enchantments are on the heart's hiding place; the apple will be drawn to it as the roots of a plant are drawn to water. All you have to do is ask it to take you where you want to go."

I stared at him. He looked weary and sad as if the weight of all his years was upon him again.

I realized it was time for me to go, to leave this strange, frightening, oddly kind creature.

Biting my lip, I asked, "Afterward ... shall I take the apple back to you?"

"That would be nice, Koschey's daughter, Sereda's child." He smiled. "After all, it is very rare!" He seemed to be cheering up. Maybe he'd had that gloomy expression just because he had spent too much time out of the water. Now he was looking forward to plunging back in, this time for good.

Then a worried look crept into his eyes again. "Oh, and, um... I hate to ask, but, um ... afterward, when this is all over..." He hesitated. "Would you very much mind *not* telling your grandmother who you heard all this from?"

I realized he wasn't as sure of our plan as he had seemed. Or maybe even when she'd had her heart, Baba Yaga had been intimidating.

"If I ever catch you drowning someone who hasn't even done anything yet," I said, "I will tell Baba Yaga absolutely everything you told me today. I'll let her know it was all your idea. And I'll tell her you gave me the apple too."

A panicked expression took over his features. "Anna Sophia … I promise, I won't do anything… If humans show up here, I'll just… I'll only frighten them into cleaning up after themselves, I promise. I…"

I laughed. "And I'll also keep the apple if they come to any harm." I grinned. "Call it a repayment for what you owe my father from your card games."

He groaned. "I was hoping he'd forgotten about that," he said. "He has the most inconvenient recall sometimes. Of all the memories to get muddled, he couldn't forget that one?"

I laughed. "Goodbye, Vodyanoy," I said. "And thank you."

"Farewell, Anna Sophia," he replied, "and may birds of good fortune lay feathers upon you." And with that last odd saying, he plunged and disappeared into the depths of the marsh.

Alone, I considered the apple. Could this actually lead me to Baba Yaga's heart? I suppose I'd just have to trust it and find out. But how far would I need to go? It would be so much more convenient if I could use my bucket.

That idea would never stop being weird.

I put the apple down in the grass, hesitating. What exactly should I do?

After a long while, I said, "Hello." *This is ridiculous*, I thought. "Could you show me the way to Baba Yaga's heart, please?"

The response was immediate. The apple started to spin, dipping this way and that as though it were orienting itself. Then it took off.

Grabbing my things, I began to jog after it. Luckily, the apple shone brightly even in the parts of the forest where the canopy was so thick there was almost no sunlight. But trying to jog with a mop, bucket, and backpack was tough.

"Wait a minute," I called out, and thankfully, the apple paused, though it kept spinning as if it were impatient. I opened my backpack, took out Squire and Knight, and woke them up. They danced about happily around me.

"Hello," I smiled. "I missed you! We're on an adventure. Do you think you two could carry the mop and bucket for me?"

They nodded eagerly; then each hand grabbed one of the items.

"Righty-ho, apple," I called. "We're ready to go!"

Instantly it shot off again, and I jogged after it. I tried not to giggle as I imagined how I looked: a thirteen-year-old girl running through a forest after a golden apple, trailed by a mop and bucket carried through the air by a pair of stone hands.

Then another thought came to me. *Take that, Granny! You keep going on about materialism and useless gadgets, yet not only did you invent the first GPS navigator but you made it out of gold. Hypocrite!*

At that, I actually did laugh aloud. It was like when she made fun of supermodels for being nothing but bones while she had a bone leg herself.

Luckily, since the apple had to be able to roll, it was taking a rather smooth path, so I didn't have to worry about tripping over things very much. Still, after a while, it did get tiring. I had no idea how far we were going.

"Apple," I asked, "is it much farther?"

It stopped, whirled around as if it were looking back at me and paused as if it were considering matters. Then it made a movement that could only be described as a nod.

"Oh... Would you mind very much if I got into my bucket, then? Will this still work if I'm flying behind you?"

I could have sworn the apple sighed, but it nodded again.

"Thanks!" I said. Knight and Squire handed me the bucket and mop, and I lifted myself into the air. This was much better.

The apple took off again, and this time it speeded up. "All right, mop," I muttered, "just follow that apple." Instantly my bucket began to zoom along.

If I hadn't needed to concentrate on flying, I probably would have laughed so hard I'd have fallen out of the bucket.

I'm not sure how long I was flying, but the sun was going down when I realized we were reaching the edge of the woods. I could see a sunset ahead of us. Not knowing if there might be people there, I landed the bucket and crept forward on foot. The apple was waiting just at the end of the trees as if it knew what I was doing.

It was actually harder walking here than flying had been. In the bucket, I'd flown above most of the bushes but below the branches. Now I had to keep pushing branches out of my face. Squire and Knight helped, but I told them not to go beyond the edge.

So I was completely taken aback when I was finally able to see what lay beyond the wood. We had reached a lake — a vast lake whose edges I could just about make out, shining purple and orange and pink and gold in the sunset.

And at its edge, a big white building, a dock with lots of little boats, and a sign that I could read even from where I was: Hotel.

I started trembling without even knowing why. If there was a hotel, there had to be people. And I wasn't used to people anymore. To their noise, to their presence. Why did we have to go where there were people? Even from behind the branches, I could see some people milling about on the deck by the swimming pool, which I could just barely see. (Why have a swimming pool when there was that huge lake right there?) I heard a car engine for the first time in forever, if you didn't count Granny's TV programs.

I almost wanted to turn and run.

"Apple," I said, "why are we here? Surely the heart can't be in that hotel?"

I must have sounded as weird as I felt because Squire came up and squeezed my shoulder reassuringly.

The apple shook a little from side to side like it was saying no. Then it rolled a little bit to one side. Looking in that direction, I saw that there was an island in the lake, straight ahead.

"Is it on the island?" I asked.

The apple made its nodding movement.

"Well," I said, "I suppose we'd better fly out." But when I said that, two things happened.

First, the apple began desperately shaking from side to side in its "no" pattern.

Second, I almost fell over.

I probably would have, if Squire hadn't held me up. That was when I realized I was starving. Well, not *starving*; Granny wouldn't have liked to hear me say that. But really, really hungry. I hadn't had a bite to eat since morning, I'd been running through the woods, talking with Vodyanoy, and flying, which took up a lot of energy. I was completely exhausted. There was no way I could risk flying to the island — especially not with the apple's panicked motion, which seemed to suggest there might be some danger there.

"All right," I said to the apple, "all right, I won't go tonight. Is that what you're worried about?"

It nodded.

"Okay. That's fine. I'll go tomorrow. That way I can eat and get some sleep..."

I sat down. The apple rolled to my side and became quite inanimate.

I wouldn't need it till the following morning. I opened

up my backpack, put the apple inside, and started looking inside for some food. Of course, there wasn't much. I pulled out a pack of the sandwiches I'd made back in Baba Yaga's hut, but they didn't seem very appetizing. And did I even know what was in them? I'd just used the supplies I'd found in her kitchen, and given her habit of eating people…

I rummaged around. I knew I'd put some dried fruit in there too. But where had it gotten to?

My hands closed on something that definitely wasn't dried fruit. What was it? It was thin and hard, and its edges were quite sharp. Curious, I pulled it out.

I almost gasped.

The emergency credit card Monsieur Nolan had given me all that time ago! I'd completely forgotten about it.

My eyes found the hotel, and without even thinking about it, I knew something: I was going to spend the night there. I was going to sleep in a comfy bed and have a real, hot meal that I knew didn't have any human flesh in it and…

And just remember for a while what it felt like to be human.

I threw the sandwiches into the forest. *Let the animals eat them if they want.*

As I did so, I noticed just how grimy my hands were. I'd almost forgotten about being dragged into that slimy marsh. And then I'd been flying for hours. *I must look an absolute mess*, I thought. I looked down. My clothes were all muddy and still damp in parts. I couldn't walk into a hotel, looking like that.

The lake was quite far and there wasn't any water nearby, so I couldn't do much more than rub my face and hope it didn't look too awful. Luckily, I'd packed all my clothes into my backpack when I'd left my grandmother's, not knowing how long I'd be gone.

"All right, boys," I said to the hands as I got some clothes out, "into the bag with you. I need to change."

Both of them flew straight into the bag, and I made sure it was tightly shut. They might be just hands, but they *were* male, and I wasn't going to have them hanging around for this. I could have sent them to sleep, but I still had some work for them, and I was afraid I was too exhausted to wake them up again.

When I had finished changing and had wiped my face some more with the cleanest part of my old shirt, I let them out of the bag.

"Okay," I said, "I'm going to the hotel. I'm going to spend the night there. I need you to hide the mop and bucket somewhere in the forest. Then I need one of you to guard them all night, and the other one to come with me in case I need help or I need to send a message. Okay?"

They both nodded, and Squire proprietarily settled on my shoulder.

I laughed. "Okay," I said. "You can be the one to come with me, Squire. Knight, thank you. Hide them and guard them well, won't you?"

Knight straightened up and, as far as it's possible for a stone hand to do, saluted me.

"Thank you! I'll see you tomorrow," I said. "And as for you," I said to Squire, "back into the bag with you. We can't have people seeing you."

Squire hopped back into the bag. I closed it again, slung

it over my shoulders, made sure I had the credit card in my pocket, and set off toward the hotel.

I was still feeling nervous, but I mastered that with the thought of a comfy bed. After all, I wouldn't have to interact with too many people if I didn't want to. Besides, it had to be around dinnertime; most people would be in the dining room, not milling about.

Luckily, that was true. There were only a few people outside as I walked inside, and though I noticed a couple of odd looks, most of them ignored me. They were just the sort of people Granny hated: men with open shirts and gold chains, wearing sunglasses and talking loudly on cell phones, and women with too much jewelry, talking to each other about fashions and prices. I tried not to listen to them too closely; I kept expecting to hear Baba Yaga yelling at them from over my shoulder.

I walked up to the reception desk, where a young woman with glasses and hair pulled into a very tight bun stood up to greet me.

"Yes?" she asked. "Can I help you?"

"Yes," I said. "I'd like a room, please."

She was clearly taken aback. "A room? You mean you're not already a guest? Where are your parents?"

"It's just me," I said, pulling out the credit card. "I've been camping in the woods with a friend. She wanted to stay another night and I didn't, so we agreed I could come here."

The woman took the credit card and peered at it suspiciously.

"I can't really let you pay with a credit card that isn't yours..." she began.

I interrupted her. "Oh, don't worry, it's mine."

She looked shocked again. She put her hand over the card so I couldn't see it. "What's your name?" she asked.

"Anna Sophia Medvedeva," I said.

She checked the name on the card. "And you happen to have this credit card? At your age?"

"My guardian gave it to me for my friend and me to use," I said. "It's linked to my trust account in Switzerland." I wasn't even lying.

The woman — her name tag said she was called Natalia — still looked quite suspicious.

"I'll need to see your passport," she said. She did not add "please."

"Oh. Yes. Of course," I said, opening my bag and rummaging around. I hadn't even thought of that! *Please, please*

let my passport be in there; I couldn't have forgotten it any-where… But then I felt it pressed into my hand. Clever Squire had been listening! Thank heavens I hadn't put him to sleep.

I handed my passport over, and Natalia scrutinized it for a long time. But it and my credit card definitely matched.

She huffed. "I'm afraid we're almost fully booked," she said. "There aren't many one-person rooms left."

"What's available?" I asked.

"Well, it's likely to be a bit beyond your range, and much bigger than you need…"

"Please, Natasha," I said, ignoring her displeased look at my use of the friendly version of her name. "It's a very big trust fund. And I'm very tired, and I'd like a shower. Can you please just find me a room?"

She frowned. "I can give you one of our suites," she said, "but they are rather big…"

"I'll take a suite, then."

Her frown grew even deeper. Clearly she didn't like being treated like this by me, but I was past caring. I even wondered if I might have enough energy left to use some magic to hurry things along.

Still, she started clicking away at her computer keyboard and eventually swiped my credit card. I had a moment's worry that it might be declined, but much to Natalia's annoyance, it worked perfectly.

She handed me the keycard. "Here you are," she said. "It's on the eighth floor. Lovely view of the lake."

"Thank you," I said. "Is there room service?"

"Of course," she responded in a clipped tone. "You'll find a menu on the desk, and you can use the phone to order.

Breakfast is available from six to nine in the dining room, or you can order room service as well."

"Thank you," I said, almost sickeningly sweetly.

She looked keen to snap at me, but she didn't dare. I tried not to laugh as I watched her force herself to stay in control. Then I walked to the elevators and went up to the suite.

It *was* huge. Not only did it have two beds, each bigger than Granny's, but there were a full kitchen, a living room, and a wide balcony overlooking the lake. The sun was almost completely below the horizon. I could still just make out the little island I needed to get to. I wondered why I wasn't supposed to go in the evening.

Then I was struck by three conflicting wishes: for sleep, for food, and for a shower. I couldn't choose between them. In the end, I decided food was the most important. I looked through the menu, picked up the phone, placed my order, and asked them how long it would take. They said twenty minutes, so I went into the massive marble bathroom with taps that shone almost as brightly as the golden apple and took a quick shower, enough to get clean. *I'll take a longer one in the morning*, I told myself.

When my food arrived, I ate it out on the balcony, looking at Lake Baikal as it grew dark and then as the moon began to be reflected in it. I knew that the locals called this lake a sea because it was so vast. Now that I had looked at it for the first time in my life, I understood why they did so.

As I looked, I couldn't help but think about the story Vodyanoy had told me about my grandmother. Had she really been so deeply in love? It seemed impossible to imagine. It was such a sad story. Surely somebody who'd been hurt that much should have tried not to hurt other people? How bad the pain must have been for her to prefer to cut out her own heart than to continue feeling it!

Still reflecting on this, I chose one of the beds and climbed into it. It was the most comfortable thing I had ever lain on.

I don't care if it's materialistic of me, Granny, I thought drowsily. *This is wonderful...*

I collapsed into a deep, dreamless sleep.

Chapter 22

Dear Diary,

That does it. I am never going to let myself feel sorry for my grandmother again. I don't care if she suffered thousands of years ago. I refuse to forget all the suffering she has caused now. I've just been reminded, and it's enough. This madness ends now. I'm going to end it.

She abuses everything she's been given, all her power, and for nothing. I don't even know if it counts as selfishness or if she just does it out of habit. And who knows what she actually means to do if she gets her hands on Koschey's heart? Save the world? What does that even mean? She's so deranged it could be anything.

She is not going to get that heart. I am going to give her back her own. And if it destroys her — well, I'll look at her as she's dying and I'll laugh at her, for the sake of everyone she's ever hurt.

I was awakened by a loud banging on the door at a time that felt way too early.

"Wha... Jus' a moment, Granny, I'll be up soon..." I muttered sleepily. Then I jolted awake. I wasn't at Baba Yaga's; I was in a hotel, surrounded by normal people, and someone was hammering at the door.

"Just a moment!" I shouted. Who on earth could be here? Nobody knew where I was. Unless... What if Monsieur Nolan had been getting worried about not hearing from me and had decided to track the credit card? They could do that, couldn't they? Then he'd know I was here, and he could send people to get ahold of me.

I couldn't let that happen. I couldn't risk the delay.

I threw on one of the dressing gowns the hotel had provided and went to the door. Standing on tiptoe, I peered out the peephole. Three police officers were standing there.

I gulped. *I was right,* I thought. *Monsieur Nolan was worried, and now I'm about to be put on a plane back to Switzerland. Somehow, I have to get out of this. But how?*

One of the officers knocked again. There was no way out of it. If I didn't at least talk to them, they'd knock the door down.

Taking a deep breath, I unlocked and opened the door.

Two of the officers walked right in, looking around the room to see if there was anyone else there. The third put a hand on my shoulder to keep me from going anywhere. Behind him, I could see Natalia. She had a weird look on her face, almost as if she were hoping I was in trouble.

The police officer holding me closed the door while the other two came back.

"No one," one of them said.

"And that's not her," said the other.

The cop holding me cursed. "You sure?"

"Absolutely. Hair's all wrong. You could cut someone's hair off, but growing it like that? Nah."

The cop let me go.

"I'm sorry," I said, "but can I ask what's going on?"

"What's your name?" asked one of the cops, a blond with a round face.

I told him.

"All right, Anna Sophia," he said. "Now, we'd just like to have a chat. We'll explain what it's about, but it's important that we hear what you have to say before you know, okay?"

I was feeling very *not* okay at this point, but it sounded

like they weren't looking for me. What was happening?

I nodded.

The second cop looked at me with narrowed eyes. "Have you ever met a girl named Olya Sumarokova?"

"No," I answered, quite honestly.

"Or heard the name?"

"No." Now I was even more confused.

"Okay. So you say you've been camping?"

What? Oh, right, the story I told Natalia yesterday evening. "That's right," I said. "That's not illegal, is it?"

"No, it isn't. But we were wondering if you might have seen anyone in the woods. Or anything that seemed … unusual."

I stared at him and struggled not to burst out laughing. I knew I couldn't laugh because that would just make them more suspicious that I had something to do with whatever they were investigating.

But honestly, what *hadn't* seemed unusual in the woods yesterday? Starting with me flying in a bucket!

"No," I said, hoping my magic energy would make the lie convincing. "I mean it all just seemed like forest to me. My friend and I didn't see anything out of the ordinary."

"Ah, yes, this friend of yours," said the third cop. "Any chance we could talk to her?"

"I doubt it," I said. "It's not that she wouldn't talk to you; it's just that she said she was going to move around a bit in the woods before coming here. I'm not actually sure where she is now." Looking at their concerned expressions, I added, "She's eighteen. And my legal guardian has allowed us to come here. It's all under control." Oh, how I wished it was true. "She'll join me later today."

"She's just wandering in the woods on her own? Do you have any idea how risky that is? Even when nothing's going on?" The cop sounded genuinely worried.

"What *is* going on?" I asked. "I'm happy to help, but…"

The blond cop took a breath. "Okay, Anna Sophia," he said. "A girl's gone missing. Olya Sumarokova. We think she's been kidnapped. So you understand, when the clerk at the reception desk told us about this girl showing up here all on her own, naturally we thought — hoped — you might be her. You're not, obviously, but we hoped you might have seen something that would help…"

"We're looking for a man," said the second cop, the one with the suspicious eyes. "He was seen near where Olya was last, and no one can remember seeing him in this area before. His description matches that of a man seen near several other cases of missing children."

I felt my mouth go dry.

The third cop spoke. "He's tall, with long black hair tied in a ponytail and sharp cheekbones. He tends to be dressed entirely in black, and people feel there's something odd about him, but none of them can explain what it is. Does any of this sound familiar?"

"No," I managed to say while trying not to choke. "No, I haven't seen anyone like that anywhere."

The blond cop looked disappointed but patted me on the shoulder. "Thank you, Anna Sophia," he said. "That's helpful. Now look, we'd rather you didn't go into the woods to find your friend, just in case. We'll ask our rangers to keep an eye out for her. If she doesn't join you here just as planned, alert the front desk. But since you're on your own, we'd like you to be extra careful. There seems to be a kidnapper on the loose, and we don't want you to be next."

"Thank you," I said.

"Don't leave the hotel," said the second cop. "Stick around. If you want to take a boat ride, make sure the person you go with is a hotel employee and someone sees you leave together. Okay? It's for your own safety."

"Okay," I said. "And thanks again."

They insisted on taking Lauraleigh's description — and got visibly worried when they learned she was a foreigner and unable to speak Russian. Eventually they left, and I could let myself start quivering with rage.

I knew what had happened. I knew what had happened to Olya Sumarokova, and I knew that these policemen would never find her and her parents would never see her again. Because I knew who'd taken her.

The Black Horseman. He had stolen Olya away and taken her to my grandmother. Because she had to stock her larder, and I made her promise to keep Lauraleigh alive.

That was enough. I couldn't waste another moment, however much I wanted to relax at the hotel some more. It was time to go find Baba Yaga's heart so I could stop her once and for all.

I looked out the window. There was the island. It would be easy enough to get to. I'd just have to take one of the boats as the cop had said.

I got dressed and was packing up my things when I yawned. *That's not good*, I thought; *after all, I slept well…* But maybe not long enough. My energy level did seem a bit low.

Was it safe to go like this?

I'll have breakfast here. That should help.

Taking my backpack with me, I went down to the lobby and looked for the dining room. As I spotted it, I saw that Natalia was at the desk again. She glanced up and saw me, and her face fell. Clearly, she'd hoped the police would take me away.

The front desk was a bit of a detour on my way to the dining room, but I couldn't resist. As I walked in front of her, I turned and gave her a dazzling smile. "Still here," I said as sweetly as I could.

She smiled grimly, but I could feel the rage burning inside her. She *really* didn't like me! I managed not to laugh.

Almost involuntarily, I felt myself taking just a little bit of her energy. It would have been hard not to. Her anger was so strong it was like she'd thrown a bucket of water over me; how could a few drops not get into my mouth?

I felt stronger immediately. That was good; I'd need everything I could get. I suppose I should have felt a little sorry, but Natalia didn't seem to be a very nice person.

The dining room was almost as gorgeous as my suite, with tall ceilings, light wood paneling, and windows over-looking the lake that were so huge there didn't even seem to be a wall. One of the servers took me to a table, and I was able to look out at the island while I ate. I was hungrier than I thought, even after last night's meal, but I wasn't tasting everything I was eating. I kept looking at the island and thinking, *I'm coming for you.*

I was pretty much done when I noticed that the voices

had quieted down and everyone seemed to be glancing at the entrance. I did the same — and gulped. The blond cop had just come in and was heading for a table in the corner, where a couple was sitting. I didn't have to be told who they were. I knew at once they were Olya Sumarokova's parents.

Mrs. Sumarokova didn't look good at all. She looked like she hadn't slept in days, and her hands kept twisting a napkin as if she were trying to tear it into pieces. Her husband's face was drawn, and he seemed in shock. He kept glancing at his wife and looking away, completely unsure of what to do.

The blond cop went up to them and whispered a few words. From the way Mrs. Sumarokova's face crumpled, I guessed he told them that they hadn't found her daughter here after all. Had they driven all the way to the hotel just in case I'd been Olya?

I felt hatred for my grandmother burning in my stomach like an ulcer. It was all I could do not to scream and jump through the window to get to the island. But that would be stupid. I needed to go carefully and get the heart. Then I needed to get back to Baba Yaga's hut as quickly as possible, confront her, and force her to touch her own heart. And if that didn't work, I would need to fight her.

After all, it wasn't as if I could tell the cops who had taken the children, was it? My insane old grandmother who lives in a hut on chicken legs in the woods? They'd lock me up.

No. I had to do this on my own. I'd always known that, and this just made it clearer.

If I didn't find Baba Yaga's heart, there was no way I could take her Koschey's. I would *never* let her take over my father's power. I'd fight her first. She might beat me, but at least she wouldn't be able to manipulate me into working for her again.

To fight Baba Yaga, though, I'd need a lot more energy than I had.

I guess the birds Vodyanoy had talked about had laid their lucky feathers on me after all. Just as that thought occurred to me, Natalia walked into the dining room.

Sorry, I thought, *but this is necessary.* I shot a blast of magic at her feet. One of her heels snapped off, and she stumbled right into a server carrying an enormous platter of full coffee cups. The platter went flying, and the coffee spilled all over the nearest table, most of it landing on a big man dressed all in white, who leaped up with an angry roar.

"What did you do that for, you stupid pig?" he yelled.

As I'd expected, Natalia's temper snapped.

"Who are you calling a pig, you overstuffed, overfed, fat cat?" she yelped. "You think accidents aren't allowed to happen in your sacred presence, *bolvan*?"

"Do you know who I am, you little hick?" he bawled at her.

But before he could go on, Natalia was screaming at him again, and he was yelling back. They were calling each other things that I'd never heard Uncle Misha say, things that would have had Sister Constance reaching for a bar of soap. I couldn't even understand half of what they were saying. The server was trying to get Natalia to calm down, the big man was yelling right back at her, and the people at the table were trying to clean up, some of them shouting as well. It was starting to look like they'd be all be hitting each other soon.

I could feel all their anger, their hatred, everything they were letting loose. They were spinning out of control, even if they didn't know it, and I could feel myself growing stronger as I let their energy flow into me. There were tingles up and down my arms and legs; this was better by far than the breakfast, the showers, or even the bed.

If I get closer, I thought, *I may be able to get more.*

Picking up my backpack, I carefully edged toward them, but I didn't even have to use magic to keep them from noticing me. No one was paying me any attention. Even if they were weakening by what I was draining from them, they hadn't noticed yet because they were still yelling. The closer I got, the stronger the energy I was able to pull from them. Then I felt something different in the mix and looked. The blond cop was coming in to try to restore order. He was angry, too, but also worried, and there was something else in his emotions: maybe sorrow…

It may be time to go, I thought as I crept around, when suddenly I felt a completely different, overpowering emotion. I started sucking energy from it at once without even thinking. There was more power in it than in all the rest. Where was it coming from?

Suddenly I understood and looked up. For a moment, I hesitated. Mrs. Sumarokova was weeping in her corner, silent tears pouring down her cheeks. It was her grief I was feeling, grief being made worse by the stupid, pointless fight that had just erupted near her.

This didn't feel quite right. But there was so much power in her energy, and I'd need it — need it to avenge her.

"I'm sorry," I whispered, "but this is for your own good, I promise. I need it to help you. For Olya." For a moment, I thought she was looking directly at me, but I closed my eyes and drank as deeply as I could from her.

The yelling seemed to grow fainter in my ears. I could feel so much power coursing through me as if I could feel every drop of my blood going through my veins.

When I stopped and opened my eyes, I found that there was still an argument going on, but the blond cop's voice seemed to be in control. Mrs. Sumarokova was bent over the table. I couldn't tell if she'd fainted or was still crying. Neither could her husband. He was leaning over her, shaking her shoulder. I tasted his worry and drew off some of his energy as well. *Every little bit helps, as Granny says.*

Things were calming down, and the blond cop might notice me at any moment. *I'd better leave before anything else happens.* I slipped out of the dining room while everyone was still looking at the fighting and made my way to the doors leading to the docks.

As I reached them, I felt a bit sick. *Did I really have to do that to Mrs. Sumarokova?*

It would help, I reminded myself. It was for everyone's own good: No other mother would ever have to feel like that again. Moreover, I hoped I had taken the edge off her grief, making it easier for her to endure.

I pushed the doors open and walked out into the sunlight toward the docks, feeling more powerful than I ever had before. I was almost surprised that I wasn't sparkling, that there weren't currents of energy visibly flowing up and down my forearms. I was ready for the next step in my quest.

For a minute, I thought about sending Squire to fetch Knight and my mop and bucket, but I decided that would be too risky. If I tried to fly to the island, people might notice. So a boat it would be.

There were a bunch of teenage boys with their shirts off lounging around the boats, a couple of them playing cards, one or two of them cleaning one of the craft or checking its rigging.

"Hello," I called out.

They looked at me. The card players exchanged a couple of lazy comments and returned to their game.

"Are you who I talk to about boat rides?" I asked.

"Sure are," one of those cleaning the boats called back. "You one of the guests at the hotel?"

"Of course," I said. "I wouldn't ask otherwise."

"You'd be surprised how many people try to use the hotel's things when they're not staying there," one of the others said. He had dark greasy hair peeking out from under his cap, which he wore backward.

"Well, I am," I said. "I'd like a ride to the island, please."

For some reason, they all burst out laughing.

"What?" I said, irritated. "What's so funny?"

That just made them laugh harder. This wasn't funny.

"*What?*" I shouted, holding my magic back with difficulty. After a while, they quieted down although they were still grinning.

"Which island is it you want to get to?" said the kid in the cap.

"That one right there, of course," I said, pointing. Then I looked closer.

The island wasn't there.

The look of shock on my face set them off again, while I stood gaping.

"Hey, come on," said the boat cleaner, getting up and coming toward me. "She's just a kid."

I bristled, provoking a fresh burst of laughter.

"Oh, I don't think she likes being called a kid, Lyoha!" one of the card players called out.

"She's still too young for you," said the kid in the cap.

"And even if she weren't, you know we're not supposed to mix with the guests!" said a third.

I was moments away from blasting them all into the water when the guy they called Lyoha — which is a nickname for Alexei — spoke up.

"Hey, shut up, you guys!" he said. "Don't be jerks." Then he looked at me. He seemed kind enough.

"Look," he said, "you've got to understand, this happens pretty often. We keep expecting people to know, but a lot still don't, so it's always funny... I've been telling them they should let all the guests know as soon as they arrive, but for some reason they don't."

"Know what?"

"Well … the thing is, for centuries, people have said they've seen an island there, on and off. But it's not real. There's no island there at all. Just a lake that's hundreds of meters deep."

"What do you mean?" I asked. "I saw it clearly enough yesterday when I got here, and it was still there when I looked from my balcony. And from the dining room just now!"

"Yeah, I know, that's the weird thing about it," Alexei said. "Sometimes people see it from all directions at all times of the day. But it's only from the water that you realize it's not there."

"So why do people see it, then?"

"Well, it's… Do you know what an optical illusion is?"

He really does think I'm just a kid, doesn't he? I thought.

"Don't treat me like I'm stupid," I said coldly. He might look about three years older than me, but I wasn't going to let him think he could impress me.

"Sorry, sorry! It's just … we get all kinds here; you'd be amazed how ignorant some rich people can be. Anyhow, that's all the island is: a weird optical illusion. It has something to do with the magnetic fields around here that are off because we get many earthquakes. We know because we've been sending boats after it for years. Centuries, probably. Every once in a while we try again, just in case, but there's no island there."

The boy in the cap spoke. "This one time, a friend of mine went to look from the hotel roof while I took a boat,

344

and we each had our cell phone, right? So he could definitely see the island, and he directed me, but it wasn't there. He saw me plow right through the island, but from where I was, it was just water. It creeped him out big time."

I swallowed. Surely this couldn't be. Had the apple made a mistake?

No, I thought. *A disappearing island is exactly the sort of place where Baba Yaga would hide something.*

But how could I get to it?

I stared at where I knew the island had been, and I thought.

"Look, I'm sorry," Alexei said. "We shouldn't have laughed. But if there's anything else we can do for you…"

As the boys lost it again, whooping and laughing at him, I closed my eyes and felt around me with my mind. Was there anything unusual here?

Yes — there it was. A disturbance in the air which felt familiar. It was like some sort of wave or a breeze only I could notice. Almost like a hum, actually. And it felt like…

It hit me hard in the chest, and I almost gasped. It felt like Baba Yaga. And it was tugging at me; I could feel it. Now I knew there was a direct connection between *something* out on the lake and me. Something was calling me. When I opened my eyes, I almost expected to see a long ribbon in the air, tied around my chest and leading out across the water.

Even with my eyes open, I could still feel it. It wasn't rigid; it seemed to pulse as I concentrated on it. Pulse like a heart.

Alexei had just turned back to me.

"Okay, Alexei," I said cheerfully. "Could you just take me out on a boat ride?"

"Call me Alyosha," he said. "And sure. Where to?"

"Oh, just around," I said. "I'll let you know, Alyosha."

He looked a little confused, but he said, "Right," and went to pick a boat for us.

I breathed in deeply. This was it. I was sure of it.

Baba Yaga's heart was nearly mine.

Chapter 23

Dear Diary,

I have to admit Grandmother is clever. Hiding her heart on an island that doesn't seem to exist is smart. But of course, that wouldn't be enough for her, would it? No, there had to be extra guards as well.

I'm very glad the apple didn't let me go on last night. It's now quite clear that if I'd arrived at night, my heart would have been ripped to shreds.

These may be the last words I write you. I just had to take a moment. As soon as I'm done, I'm going to pick up Grandmother's heart.

And I'm really not sure what will happen then.

When I stepped onto the small boat Alyosha had powered up, I felt sure I was on the right track. Being on the water made me feel the island's magic even stronger. It was like a huge stretched-out banner; all I had to do was get ahold of it and pull, and I'd get to where it sprang from.

"Where to, princess?" Alyosha asked with a smile. I wasn't sure if he was making fun of me or not, so I just pointed.

He grinned. "You want to be sure it's not there, don't you? Don't worry, you're not the first. And it's a beautiful day; you'll have a good trip even though it's not there."

I just smiled. I didn't know what was going to happen, but I did know it wouldn't be like anything Alyosha had ever experienced before.

Even though I could imagine what Vodyanoy would have said, I was glad we were using a motorboat. I wouldn't have wanted to wait all the time it would take to row out there. I couldn't see anything, but the magic rope — or whatever it was — was still there, leading me on.

Still, Alyosha set a slow pace to make sure I got the good trip he'd promised. Even though it was slower than flying in my bucket, it wasn't a bad thing; I could make tiny course corrections without him noticing, which he would have if we'd been going faster.

I didn't say anything to Alyosha even though I could tell he wanted to ask me some questions. I could imagine what they were, and I wasn't interested in answering. I just let one of my hands slip into the water, pretending I didn't have a care in the world even as I concentrated on the magic guideline we were following.

I wasn't sure what to expect, but I could feel the guideline growing shorter, and I could sense something powerfully magical in front of us, something becoming stronger with every passing moment. The sun was high and quite hot by now, and there was a bit of mist rising around us.

On the opposite side of the sky was the moon, my eternal companion. Looking at it, I wondered if this island was just like my moon, which only I could always see in the sky.

"There, you see, princess?" Alyosha finally said. "This is about where the island ought to be, and as you can see, there is absolutely nothing… Wait… What the…" His eyes were growing huge and his jaw dropped.

"No," he went on. "No, no, no. That's not possible. This is… This is totally nuts. I'm having a fever dream. Too much sun. I never woke up this morning. You don't exist. This is *not real.*"

Right ahead of us was a small island, the same one I'd seen the evening before, right where it had been when I'd seen it again from the dining room.

Alyosha looked like he was about to have a panic attack. "Okay, this is weird. We are *not* going there. This isn't normal. We've… We've got to get back and…"

He reached for the motor to cut it off or turn around or something, and I zapped his hand. He jerked it back like he'd received an electric shock.

He stared at me. My finger was still pointing at him, and there was no hiding what I'd just done.

"Would you land me on the island, please?" I said quietly. I hoped I didn't sound threatening, but it must have been pretty clear that the only answer I'd take was a yes.

He gulped, nodded, and set a course for a small beach we could see nearby.

"This is *weird,*" he said over and over again. "Really, really, really weird."

He landed us on the sand and, still looking dazed, jumped out of the boat to give me a hand down — and, I think, to check that it was safe first. I hadn't expected that from him. Maybe he really wasn't such a bad guy.

I jumped into the water lapping around the boat and walked onto the island. Alyosha followed, staring.

"I don't believe this," he said. "I really don't believe this. I mean there's no island here. I know there's no island here. The lake is hundreds of meters deep. I mean, they explore with submarines here. So where am I?"

I smiled at him. "Do you think you could get my bag from the boat for me?" I asked. "I forgot to take it." Actually, I hadn't forgotten at all, but it seemed kinder to trick him than to let him know what I was about to do.

"Yeah, okay," he said almost automatically. He climbed back into the boat, picked up my backpack and handed it to me.

Then he looked at me, frowning. "Who are you, anyway?" he asked. Or at least started to ask, because halfway through the last word, I hit him with a soft blast of slow-moving energy that put him right to sleep.

"Sorry," I said, "but it's really better for you if you don't know anything more." I wondered if there was a way to erase this incident from his mind, but I decided that might be too dangerous for him. Besides, I didn't have much time. He'd probably just put it all down to sunstroke.

I gave the boat a gentle magic push and it started to float back toward the hotel. I concentrated on it to make sure it was set on its course and would stay that way; then I let out a long breath.

I tried not to think about what he might be asked if someone remembered he'd set off with me and noticed I hadn't come back with him, especially with the cops around looking for kidnappers. But hopefully, the way he was coming back would keep him from being suspected of anything.

But then again, maybe I'd made a mistake. Everything was so confusing — all the decisions I had to make. Boy, I wasn't ready to be an adult just yet. I've never felt so thirteen than when I stood on that small beach, watching Alyosha's boat drift toward the hotel.

But now it was time to get down to business.

I took Squire out of my bag. He jumped out excitedly, but then he seemed to cringe. I didn't blame him; this whole island was heavy with magic as if there were some invisible fog crowding around us, and it all felt too much like Baba Yaga.

But it felt different from that at her hut. I couldn't quite work it out, but it felt — I don't know — fresher. Lighter. And older.

A shudder went through me. This was even weirder than arriving at a hut on chicken feet. This wasn't some bizarre magical spot in the middle of a normal forest. *Everything* here was magical, every grain of sand under my feet.

I looked around. The beach didn't take up that much of the island. A short distance up, it turned to trees; not a thick forest, more like a park. It wouldn't be too difficult to work through.

Still, I had to be careful. There must have been a reason the apple hadn't wanted me to come here the night before.

"Squire," I said, "I need you to go fetch Knight and bring back my mop and bucket. Is that all right?"

He nodded.

"Fast as you can, please. And thanks!"

He flew up into the air, waved, and rushed off.

It's probably safer to wait for him, I thought, *even though I don't want to*. I sat down on the sand to think.

The island looked peaceful, but I knew I couldn't trust that. I wasn't silly enough to think that invisibility was its only defense. The fact that I could get to it — probably only because I was Baba Yaga's granddaughter — didn't mean I could get past whatever else there was here.

For that matter, how would I know if I did find the heart? What did it look like?

I took the apple out of my bag and looked at it. *I'll just have to put it on the ground and hope it can still guide me*, I thought.

As I wondered how long it would take the hands to come back, I heard someone singing.

At first, it was just a thin thread of sound that I thought might be the breeze. But then I realized it was more than that. It was a tune, and there were words.

"*Slavnoye Mor-r-r-re, Sviyashchenny Baikal…*" Someone was singing the words from an old song, "Glorious Sea, Sacred Baikal."

It was such a strange voice. It was high like a child's, but there was something else about it. It didn't sound young, and it didn't sound quite human — but it was also an incredibly familiar sound.

I stood up and looked around. No sign of the singer. But the song continued:

> "*Shol ya i v notsh, i sr-r-r-red' byelovo dnya*
> *Vkr-r-r-ug gar-r-r-adov ozir-r-r-rayasya zor-r-r-rko…*"

I was walking at night and during a bright day, watching for danger around cities… someone sang, studiously articulating every sound, rolling long, thunderous *r*'s off his tongue.

I yawned. Why was I suddenly feeling so sleepy? I had so much energy that I shouldn't have needed to sleep for days. But the sand was so warm in the sun, and it was so tempting to just lie down and take a nap… I felt my eyelids getting heavy.

I slapped myself. This wasn't helpful. I didn't have time for a nap. I had to find Baba Yaga's heart.

The voice was still singing. Was that what had almost put me to sleep?

I had to be careful. I was on an island that disappeared whenever it felt like it. I couldn't trust anything I heard or saw here.

Deciding not to wait for the hands to return, I put the apple on the ground. "Take me to Baba Yaga's heart," I whispered.

It spun to life and began to roll up the slope toward the trees. I noticed it was going slower than it had at any time the day before.

The singing had been getting slower too. It eventually faded out as if the singer had grown tired and dropped off to sleep. But I stayed on my guard as I followed the apple.

The sand turned to grass and we were soon beneath the trees, with the sunlight dappling the ground. It was a beautiful day. At any other time, I would have sat down and just enjoyed the place. It was too bad. *Maybe I'll be able to come back someday*, I thought. *It might be nice to spend some time here…*

That was when a huge cat lying just under a bush to the side of our path whipped out a paw and trapped the apple under it.

I stared. It was the biggest cat I had ever seen, a massive fluffy beast with long gray-and-gold-and-black-and-white fur that his face almost vanished into. His tail was nearly as long as my forearm and so bushy it was probably thicker than my wrist. Stretched out, he would probably be at least as long as I was tall.

Part of me wanted to run forward and snuggle him, but I sensed that would be a bad idea.

He purred and looked up at me out of his mismatched eyes, one a piercing blue, the other just as bright but yellow.

"*Mrrr*. What have we here?" he asked.

You'd think that by now, I would have ceased being shocked by things. But I hadn't. Even after the hut on chicken legs and a cat changing into a hare, a giant talking cat was able to surprise me. Especially since I recognized the voice. The cat was the one who had been singing.

He stretched out, rolling off his side onto his feet, still keeping the apple trapped.

"Little human, *mrrr*," he said, and yawned. "Wasn't expecting you." He batted the apple to one side and grabbed at it with his other paw. The apple spun around wildly but couldn't get away.

I wasn't quite sure what to do. I had to speak, though. What was it I had said to Vodyanoy? "Hello," I said. "I am Anna Sophia, daughter of Koschey the Deathless and—"

"Oh, do I really look like I care who you are, little mouse?" the cat interrupted as he continued to bat the apple from paw to paw. "It's still no reason for you to disturb my nap."

"I'm sorry," I said. "I don't mind if you go back to sleep, honestly. I'm just here to—"

"But you *did* disturb my nap. And even if you hadn't..."

He let the apple go, and it rolled wildly away from his grip. He pounced, light and fast, and caught it again. He looked back at me.

"I wouldn't have been too pleased if you'd come by when I was awake either." He yawned again. "Oh dear, I *am* weary. In fact, I'm not sure I can be bothered to rip your soul out. So very tiring..." He lay down again, the apple still trapped under one paw while the other poked at it. His huge bushy tail flicked a little as his eyes started to close.

I stared. "Well," I said, trying to laugh, "I won't object much if you don't."

"*Mrrr?*" He raised the eyelid of his yellow eye at me. "Oh, dear. You think you're being clever." Without warning, he gave the apple a hard push that sent it rushing toward my feet; then he jumped and caught it. He stared up at me, his head as high as my knees, grinning. His teeth looked sharp. "I still might, you know," he said. "After all, you're trespassing."

"I'm here for a reason," I said. "I need to—"

"Again, I really don't care. Even if it's a good reason, you're still trespassing."

"It *is* a good reason! I have to find Baba Yaga's heart."

He blinked. "*Mrrr.* What a strange thing to *have* to do." He walked away a little, his tail swishing from side to side. "Koschey's daughter," he said. "With that Sereda child, I suppose. *Mrrr.* What did you say your name was, again?"

"Anna Sophia," I answered. Maybe we were getting somewhere. "May I ask yours?"

"*Mrrr?* Oh, I'm Kot Bayun," he said. "But that's not important." He rolled onto the grass, displaying an incredibly soft-looking belly that I really wanted to nuzzle. His eyes were still fixed on me.

"I am *awfully* tired," he said, yawning. "Not at my best during the day. If you'd only come at night, I would have really just torn your soul away and been done with it, but it's such a bother in the daytime … all that blood… *Mrrr.* Still, it's not like I can just let you pass. Dreadful example to set…"

I narrowed my eyes at him as he rolled over again, pawing at the air. *Maybe I should just blast him out of the way*, I thought. *If I set his fur on fire, say, I can probably get past him…*

He looked directly at me.

"I wouldn't try that," he said quietly. "Your little magics won't work here. But it would still make me rather irritated if you tried."

I gulped.

"Still … let's play a game," he said. "Since you're here, you might as well amuse me."

"What sort of game?"

"Oh, the easiest kind. You just have to answer my questions. But, *mrrr*, you have to answer them correctly."

"What happens if I don't?"

He looked at me. And purred. It was not a reassuring sound. "Sophia," he said, rolling the name over in his mouth. "Tell me, do you know what your name means?"

What sort of question was that? "What?"

"Do you?"

"It's just a name," I said. "My name."

"You're not answering my question," said Kot Bayun. He started to lick one of his paws.

"No," I said, "I don't."

"*Mrrr.* It means 'wisdom,' little human. A fine name, though I'm not entirely sure you deserve it. Tell me, what is wisdom?"

I was confused. What was this cat talking about? Why did any of this matter? Was this one of my grandmother's tricks? I had to remember why I was here.

And anyway, what *was* wisdom?

"I don't know," I said, as steadily as I could. I had no idea how Kot Bayun would take this.

"*Mrrr.* Well, that's an honest answer, so I suppose a correct one. But if your answer keeps being that you're ignorant, I might start getting bored, and we don't want that, do we?" He rolled over onto his side and continued giving himself a bath.

I didn't know if I was supposed to say anything, so I stayed quiet. However docile he seemed, I sensed that this cat was dangerous, and not just because of his talk about tearing out souls.

After a while, he looked at me again. "So tell me, Anna Wisdom, do you know anyone wise?"

I thought. "Well … there's Uncle Misha," I said. "He seems pretty wise to me."

"What makes you say that?"

"Well … he knows so much! He taught me all about the animals and the trees and the other plants, and he just seems to be able to answer any question I have."

"Do you think he could answer my question?"

I tried to imagine Uncle Misha faced with this cat. "I think he'd just laugh and give you a saucer of cream," I said.

Kot Bayun hissed, showing his sharp teeth. "He has knowledge," he said, "but is that wisdom?"

"I don't know!" I said. "How can I know if someone is wise, when I'm not even sure what wisdom is?"

Kot Bayun purred. "Correct," he said. "You're not quite as dim as you seem, then."

He was the second person today to call me stupid, and I didn't like it any more than when Alyosha had done it. But I couldn't risk reacting the same way. I was just going to have to play the cat's game, whatever it was.

"Do you think it would be wise for someone to give me a saucer of cream?"

I thought about it. "Wiser than not doing so," I said eventually.

"So where's my cream, little mouse?"

"I don't have any. But I'd give you some if I had."

"And that would be wise?"

"If you liked cream, yes. And even if you didn't … it would show I meant no harm, wouldn't it?"

"Or that you were trying to trick me or bribe me," Kot Bayun said lazily. "But no matter. You think it would be a wise action, yes?"

"Yes."

"Does that mean that the person giving me the cream would be a wise one?"

"I…" I was about to say "yes," but then I started to doubt. "I know you don't want me to say 'I don't know,'" I said cautiously, "but … I'm not sure. Would it depend on the intent? I mean, if it was wise to give you cream because you like it, I'd be wise to know that, wouldn't I? But if I was actually trying to bribe you and you didn't like being bribed, then it would probably not be a wise thing to do. So even if you did like cream, I'd be unwise to try. But what if I didn't know that? I'd think I was wise, but I wouldn't actually be… So…"

I was starting to feel very confused. "So giving you cream might be either wise or not wise, depending on everything else. And … I guess the wise person would be the one who knew which was wiser? But then, how would you…" I stopped babbling. This was not helping.

Kot Bayun delicately rolled the apple between his paws. "So wisdom *is* knowledge, then?" he said.

"Well … I guess so. I mean, that's why Uncle Misha's wise, I think. Except that he taught me all those things about the forest, and, well, I'm not sure that made *me* wise. Except I know he never managed to teach me everything he knew, so of course it wouldn't. But…"

My head was starting to hurt.

"Do you think *you're* wise?" the cat asked.

"Not at this very moment!"

"*Mrrr.* You said an action could be both wise and unwise. Do you think there's such a thing as an action that's only one or the other?"

I thought about it. "I'm pretty sure it would always be unwise to stick your hands in a fire."

"What if there was a baby in the fire and that was the only way to get it out?"

"I… It would be brave, but that's not the same thing as wise. Is it?"

"How should I know? You're the one who bears the name of Wisdom," he mocked. He rolled over on his side again, still looking at me. And then, unexpectedly, he started singing again.

> "*Rastsvetali yabloni i grushi,*
> *Poplyli tumany nad rekoy;*
> *Vykhodila na bereg Katyusha,*

Na vysokiy bereg, na krutoy..."

I knew the tune; I'd even heard it recently. Some blonde woman on Granny's TV had been singing it, wearing a pretend military uniform with an especially short skirt. It had set Granny off on a fine rant. But I'd never heard that energetic song — about saying farewell before going off to war — sung so sleepily before.

"Kot Bayun?" I said, wondering if his singing meant the game was over. Was he hinting it was time for me to go?

"Yes, little mouse?" he replied.

That epithet answered my question before I could ask it. Quickly I found something else to say. "I've never met a singing cat before."

"*Mrrr.* Many creatures sing, Anna Wisdom. Even mice sing. Even moths. Apparently, wise Uncle Misha didn't teach you everything after all." He yawned. "Do you know anyone else who's wise?" he asked.

"Well, my father, of course," I said.

Evidently, that was a wrong answer. Kot Bayun leaped to his feet, his back legs crouched, ready to spring at me. My heart pounded with fear. I knew if he decided to attack me, I couldn't do anything about it. He was right; there was something about this place that completely blocked my magic. I couldn't feel its energy at all.

Kot Bayun's eyes narrowed as he looked at me, and I knew that I had to answer his next question very carefully.

"You think Koschey is wise, little mouse?" he hissed. "How wise do you have to be to get yourself locked up in a cage, forced to send your helpless daughter to do your dirty work for you?"

"I'm not helpless!" I protested before I could think.

He hissed again. "Oh yes, you are, little mouse. Right at this moment, you are. And do you think it was wise of you to agree to do his will?"

"I chose to myself," I said. "If I succeed, that will prove he was wise to ask me, won't it?"

"So you can only judge the wisdom of an action afterward? You can't predict? Are you trying to tell me that whoever succeeds is wise, and whoever fails isn't? That wisdom equals pragmatism?"

"Well … no, that can't be right. Because then … well, then Granny would be wise right now, but if suddenly Koschey beats her, she will no longer be, and he'll suddenly be wise again and…"

Kot Bayun purred but did not relax. "Are actions wise?" he asked.

"No," I said, suddenly certain. "People are. But you can tell if people are wise by their actions."

"*Mrrr.*" He settled on his haunches, slightly less threatening. "So let's see if you merit your name, Anna Wisdom. On this little quest of yours, have you done anything wise?"

"I… I don't know. Some things turned out well. I helped a bluebird, and that was a good thing to do. She helped me afterward."

"*Mrrr.* Delicious things, bluebirds. So that was a wise action, was it? Was that how you thought of it?"

"No. I just wanted to help. It was … well, being kind, I guess. I wasn't expecting anything in return."

"So it was wise of you to be kind?"

"As it turned out, yes."

"Would it still have been wise if the bird hadn't helped?"

"I don't know, but it would still have been kind."

"*Mrrr.* So you didn't know if what you were doing would help you. Does that mean you can be wise without knowing it?"

"If … if helping her counts as wisdom, then I guess so, yes."

He purred and lay down on the grass. There was a daisy near him, and he began to slowly stretch a paw toward it. Finally, he spoke again, his eyes fixed on the flower. "Do you think it's wise of you to be on this mission?" He extended his claws and started poking at the daisy with one of them.

"No," I said. "But it's right."

"Oh, I'm much too tired to debate the nature of right and wrong right now," he said, looking over his shoulder at me. "All those twists and turns..." He yawned, his teeth glinting in the sunlight. "So why are you doing it?"

"To save a friend," I said. I didn't trust this cat enough to tell him that I wanted to bring down Baba Yaga, though he'd probably guessed that already by now.

"Why?" He sounded bored and continued to prod the flower.

"Because she's my friend," I said.

"So? Those are only your feelings. Bit selfish, aren't you?"

"Because I'm *her* friend. And because she should be saved."

"Do you think it's wise to save her?"

I flared up. "I don't care if it's wise or not." I was starting to get sick of this cat. "I'm going to do it."

"Not if I don't let you pass," he said casually. He snipped the daisy off its stem. Then he rolled over and picked up his song again:

> "*Vykhodila, pesnyu zavodila*
> *Pro stepnogo, sizogo orla,*
> *Pro togo, kotorogo lyubila,*
> *Pro togo, ch'i pis'ma beregla.*"

It was a sad song about a woman waiting for her beloved to return from war... I wondered if the cat was hinting that Lauraleigh would be waiting for me in vain.

"Kot Bayun," I said, trying to keep my impatience and

growing anger out of my voice, "what would it take for you to let me pass?"

"Are you trying to bribe me, little mouse?"

"No," I said, thinking fast. "I am trying to grow wise."

He snickered. "Do you think you can be taught to be wise?" he asked.

"I don't know if knowledge is wisdom," I said, "but it can't do any harm."

"Is it wise to be knowledgeable?"

"Yes. But I'm not going to say it's the only way to be wise."

"You're growing subtle, Anna Wisdom."

"It must be your influence, Kot Bayun."

He stretched out in a pleased sort of way. "Do you think it is wise to flatter?" he said.

"Wiser than not to do so."

"*Mrrr*. This friend of yours. Why is she so worth saving?"

"Because of who she is. Because of how kind she is."

"Kindness again, *mrrr*. We seem to be coming back to that. So she's kind, then. Is she wise?"

"I don't know. If kindness is wisdom, then yes."

"But *is* kindness wisdom, or wisdom kindness?"

"I don't *know*, Kot Bayun!" I shouted, half in desperation and half in anger. "She would have helped the bluebird too; that's why she's worth saving."

"Why, because she's as kind as you?"

"No," I said, "because she's kinder."

"You humans and your kindness," said Kot Bayun in a bored tone. "It's really quite remarkable your race has lasted this long."

"Maybe we're wiser than you think."

He made a curious little noise and started batting the apple around again.

I couldn't take it any longer. "Are *you* wise, Kot Bayun?" I asked.

"You're getting the hang of this game, little mouse. *Mrrr.* Certainly I seem to be wiser than you."

"Do you think it wise to anger me, knowing who my parents are? What's to stop me from bringing Koschey or Baba Yaga down on you?"

He laughed sharply. "For starters, you can't leave the island unless I let you. Second, Koschey's in a cage. Third, the dear old hag will never attack me. I know too many of her secrets."

"If I freed Koschey—"

"If you freed him, what?" Kot Bayun spat, suddenly on his feet again, his fur bristling and his eyes on fire as he snarled at me. "Have you really fallen for the idea that Koschey is some sort of untouchable, omnipotent being? Oh, he has a fine self-image, I'll grant you that. He thinks he's so powerful with what he does when the lot of you die and you run around like a mouse between a cat's paws, yowling 'Oh no, I'm dead!'"

Kot Bayun moved a step closer to me. "He helps you find where you should fit in the choir of existence — if you should be crushed in the depths and growling with the basses, or become some crystalline treble half-vanishing into nothingness! He likes to think he has some say in the matter, that he's not merely a guide leading you to where your own actions have already marked you as belonging. Ha!"

366

The force of his anger sent me scurrying away from him until my back hit a tree and I couldn't get any farther from the screaming beast in front of me.

He growled like a small lion, sending shivers of terror down my spine. "But when I rip your soul from you, Anna Wisdom," he said with a cold, threatening undertone in his voice, "I'll drag it to whatever layer of the afterlife I choose. And even if he were free, he could do nothing about it, daughter or not. Don't try to frighten me with Koschey the Blusterer, little mouse. It won't end well for you!"

There was nothing lethargic or cuddly about Kot Bayun now. He was nothing but an incarnation of fury, his every hair on end, his claws out and sharp as nails, the daggers of his teeth flashing as he raged at me.

I had never been so frightened of any being in my life. Not the Montmorencys, not the Black Horseman, not Vodyanoy as he tried to drown me, not even Granny. I realized I had absolutely no idea what this cat might do next, no way to tell if he was about to come and curl around my ankles or tear out my throat. Not only was he clearly afraid of nothing but he was also unpredictable — and that was the scariest thing of all, even scarier than the fact that I had no magic to use against him.

My terror must have been evident as I clutched at the tree behind me to stay upright.

He smiled. "Now then, little mouse, do you think that was *wise* of you?"

"N-no," I managed to stutter, "no, Kot Bayun, it wasn't."

He paced closer to me, his tail swishing from side to side, his claws still extended, his fangs all too visible. "Do you think you'll do it again?"

"No, Kot Bayun."

"Well then... Can wisdom be taught?" He had sat down on his haunches, looking up at me, and he was starting to look like just an oversized house cat again. But I was not reassured.

"Sometimes, Kot Bayun," I said. "It looks like sometimes it can be."

He purred. And then he rubbed the top of his head against my knees.

I would have scratched behind the ears of any other cat who did that, but not Kot Bayun. Never.

He was sauntering away from me again now. I didn't move, trying to get my breathing back under control.

He started singing again:

"Ne odna, ah ne odna,
Ne odna vo pole dorozhka,
Ne odna dorozhen'ka..."

I wondered if there was any significance to the things he was singing, if the songs could be hints to the game. What was this one? "There is not one path through the field, not one, not one little path..."

I had no idea if that meant anything at all.

Then something he had said during his fit sank into my mind. "Kot Bayun..." I said. "Did you say that my father leads the dead to ... well, guides them after they're dead?"

"*Mrrr.* Didn't you know? They have left you ignorant, haven't they? To put it in terms your feeble little brain might understand, he helps them settle down in heaven or hell, wherever might be suitable for them."

"But … is that for everyone who dies? I mean, does he meet … everyone?"

Kot Bayun looked at me and yawned with disdain. "Why yes, little Anna Wisdom. I daresay that *was* where he saw your mother for the last time, and I daresay that *was* how he found out she was dead. And yes, before you ask, he treated her just the same as everyone else. Not that he'd have done any differently even if he had the chance. Cold as a witch's kiss, your father."

"But that's … horrible," I whispered.

Kot Bayun gave me a look I knew only too well from Sister Constance. "Really, Anna Wisdom, have you not yet worked out that *everything* about your extended family is horrible? *Mrrr?*"

"Lauraleigh isn't," I said quietly. "She's not family, but she might as well be. And she makes it better."

He grinned. "What a pity she's going to be dinner, then. Chomp-chomp-chomp."

I wanted to scream at him, but I didn't dare. "What must I do for you to let me pass?" I asked.

"Finish the game, little mouse," he said. "You only have to finish the game."

I swallowed. "Then keep playing," I said. "Ask me again."

"What?"

"Anything."

"*Mrrr.* No. No, I think it's your turn to ask."

"What should I ask you?"

"Telling you would be cheating," he said with a lazy smile.

I slumped to the ground. I was exhausted. I had no idea what to ask him. All I wanted to do was lie down and sleep forever. I almost didn't care about what I had to do anymore. Realizing how Dad had found out my mother was dead and what he must have felt guiding her soul to its final destination, was just too awful.

Mom … oh, Mom.

"Kot Bayun," I said. "Did my grandmother kill my mother?"

His tail swished from side to side, but the rest of him was completely immobile. "Does it matter?" he said.

I bit back what I wanted to yell at him for being so callous. "You're not supposed to ask questions," I said as steadily as I could, "you're supposed to answer them."

"What makes you think I'd know?"

"Because you know so much. I never told you Koschey was in a cage. I never told you my friend had been captured by Baba Yaga, and yet you knew she's in danger of being eaten."

"*Mrrr.* Perhaps you're not completely un-clever, then. But my question remains: Does it matter? How do you assign blame? Baba Yaga did not *technically* kill Sereda. She did not murder her directly. Oh, when Sereda died and released all that lovely energy the old hag finds so tasty, I don't doubt she feasted on it, but that's profiting, not causing."

"What?"

"You really are stunningly ignorant, aren't you? That's what Baba Yaga likes most of all. When people die, they let off so much more energy than at any other time in their life. *Mrrr.* The old hag is responsible for the transition itself before Old Bones shows up, so I imagine that's where she acquired such a taste for it."

"And you think she'd have done that even with her own daughter?" I didn't even know what to feel: revolted, angry, sad, stunned. Every time I thought I'd found out the worst thing about my grandmother, something came along to top it.

That wasn't about to change.

Kot Bayun looked at me with some pity in his colorful eyes. "You are a naïve child, aren't you, little mouse?" he said. He yawned. "Oh, dear, it really is much past my bedtime."

"The game's not over yet," I said sharply. "What did you mean, Baba Yaga didn't kill Sereda 'directly?'"

"*Mrrr.* Well, think about it, Anna Wisdom," he yawned again, stretching out on the grass. "Do you really think Granny Dearest couldn't have kept Sereda alive if she'd wanted to? Cured her or whatnot? Really, now. All the Iron Queen had to do was raise a finger, and her child would have remained safe, whether Sereda wanted to be kept healthy by her or not."

He closed his eyes and hummed as I tried to deal with my horror.

I stumbled toward him. "You mean she *wanted* Sereda to die?"

"Mmm?" Kot Bayun lazily opened one eye. "How should I know? I'm just a cat. She may have thought of it as letting nature take its course. But then again, how often have you seen the old hag do that, with her hut on chicken legs, her flying mortar, her guard-skulls…"

He seemed to be drifting off to sleep. I couldn't stop myself from shaking.

"But Kot Bayun," I whispered, "how *could* she…"

He rolled over. "Maybe," he said, "people aren't kind."

"Does that mean people aren't wise?"

"Did we ever decide if one was necessary for the other?"

I sighed. "I don't know, Kot Bayun. I don't remember."

He seemed amused. "You know, I met your mother once or twice," he said.

"Really?" Why was I surprised?

"Yes, *mrrr*. She had this dreadful habit of—" he shuddered — "*cuddling* me." He extended all his claws and opened his mouth wide to show his teeth. "Do you think that was a *wise* habit to have, little mouse?"

"It depends, Kot Bayun. Did you greet her cuddling with your claws like that?"

He purred noncommittally.

"I've heard my mother was kind, Kot Bayun," I said. "Was she wise?"

"Was it wise to refuse your grandmother?"

"Was it kind of Baba Yaga to do that to her daughter?" I snapped.

He gave a gentle snort. "Of course not. All her kindness is hidden on this island."

I felt a lurch in my chest. "So her heart *is* here!" I burst out.

Kot Bayun rolled his eyes. "You are slow for a child of your parentage," he muttered with disgust. "As well as ignorant."

I ignored his rudeness. He wasn't answering my questions. Did that mean he was giving up on the game?

Now I knew that Baba Yaga's heart was here. I had even more reasons to want to get it now. And yet … some of the things Kot Bayun had made me think about were still running through my mind.

"Do you think my grandmother's wise?" I asked. *Let him deal with that one for a change.*

"Well," he said, yawning, "she must think so. Who am I to say she's wrong?"

I was dumbfounded. What sort of answer was that? "You said you were wise, Kot Bayun; you must be able to judge!"

"*Mrrr?* No, no, if you recall, I said I was wiser than *you*, which seems an undeniable fact. I never actually claimed to be wise, little mouse."

"So if she thinks she's wise, she is? Is that what you're saying?" That was the stupidest thing I'd heard since … I didn't know when.

"Tell me, loud, not-conducive-to-napping child," he said in a sleepy tone, "I assume your granny's in the throes of another of her grand schemes at present?"

"Yes," I said.

"Saving the world again or something like that?"

Granny tried that before? "Something like that," I said.

"Do you think it's a wise plan?"

"No," I said.

"Do you think she does?"

"I… Well, she must, right? Otherwise, why would she try?"

"So which of you is right?"

I wanted to yell "Me!" but didn't dare. "Is this another of your trick questions? Will the answer depend on whether one of us is wise?"

Before I knew what was happening, Kot Bayun had leaped off the ground and thrown himself directly at my chest, knocking me off my feet to land flat on my back. He pressed down on top of me with all of his weight, his face just in front of mine.

"Little mouse," he said, "what am I?"

"A cat," I managed to gasp with the little air I could get into my lungs.

"So you're not completely ignorant. Good," he purred. "Now tell me, what do they say about cats, *mrrr*?"

I scrambled to think what he could mean. Then I got it. "That you have nine lives," I said.

"Yeeesssss… It's quite true, you know," he murmured. "But people have some strange misconceptions about this. They think it means that we cats can fall from the top of a tree eight times and won't die until the ninth, or that we're resurrected or reborn eight times before we die for real. But that isn't actually true. We live our nine lives *concurrently*, Anna Wisdom. At the same time. And so we see and feel and know and experience the world nine different ways at once. And they're all real, and they're all true. So who am I to say that your granny and you aren't both right?"

"That's not possible," I said in my constricted voice. "What I think and what she thinks are complete opposites. Enemies. We can't both be right; we can't both be true…"

"Little mouse, little mouse," he said. He raised a paw and

trailed it down my cheek, his claws unsheathed, almost but not quite breaking the skin. "Look into my eyes."

I didn't have much choice; he was staring directly into mine from barely a centimeter away. The yellow and the blue bore into me.

"Do you think my eyes each see the same thing?"

"Of course they do…"

"Close one of your eyes," he said. I did. Only his blue eye remained in my sight.

"Now the other," he instructed. Again I obeyed. His yellow eye was all I could see.

"Did they see the same thing?" he asked.

"No," I answered, "but—"

"But together they do. Only together. One of your eyes sees colors a little brighter than the other, doesn't it? They don't see the same angle. Yet they both see the truth, and together they see more of it than they can on their own. So do mine, Anna Wisdom. So do my nine lives, always experiencing nine ways of looking at a thing, all of them true. Together they let me see its greater truth and how to weave my path between the lesser nine."

"I don't understand," I said. "And I can't breathe."

"Of course you can't, child," he said in a kindly tone, though which of the two he was referring to, he didn't say. Still, he lifted some of his weight so that I could get more air into my lungs.

"The world is a hall of mirrors," he continued. "Of mirrors and perspective glasses. And until you see how the mirrors hold their equal truths and how to balance them, you'll never find your way out."

"You're speaking in riddles, Kot Bayun."

"Of course I am. But you'll remember my words, I'm sure. One day they may mean something to you. One day."

He rolled off me and yawned. "Nine lives..." he mused. "It's not unlike how your uncle sees the world, I imagine, though of course he does it on a much more pedestrian level."

"Uncle Misha?" I asked as I got up, confused. Uncle Misha had never given me any sense of seeing the world more than one way at a time.

"*Mrrr*? No, of course not him. Your actual uncle. Sereda's brother. Well, half-brother, I suppose." He caught my look. "Oh dear," he mocked. "Am I telling family secrets? Have I, as they say, let the cat out of the bag? *Mrrr*? They really ought to keep you better informed, little mouse."

"I have a real uncle?" I managed to say.

"A little extra knowledge for you," he said, still in that sarcastic tone. "Does it make you feel wiser?"

I didn't even know what to think. Why was I only finding this out now? And why was I only finding it out from this mean-spirited cat?

"You're not answering my question," Kot Bayun said.

"No!" I yelled, my patience snapping. "No, it doesn't! All it's doing is making me more confused. Is that what you're playing at? Is that what you're trying to do, muddle my mind so much that I can't remember what I'm here for? Are you just trying to keep me thinking until it's night again and you wake up properly so you can rip my soul away? If you're so desperate, just do it and get it over with!"

376

I expected him to jump on me. I didn't know what I would do, and I didn't know why I'd let myself yell, but for an instant I was certain I was about to die.

Instead, he just hissed. There was nothing sleepy about him now.

"So if it's not knowledge," he said, "what about this kindness you find so precious? What about this precious kind friend of yours? Does caring for her make you feel wise? Does it make you feel kind? Does being able to care about her make you feel better about yourself? Does being kind make her feel better about herself?"

"No," I said, "it's not like that; she's not like that…"

"How can you know?" His voice was taunting, cutting across my speech, goading me.

My temper flared again in some weird form of grief, and suddenly I was shouting again, almost in tears. "*No!* Lauraleigh didn't have to learn to be kind! And I've never, never met anyone else like that. She *would* put her hands in the fire to save the baby. She *would* have helped that bluebird, and it would never have crossed her mind to ask it for anything. If she met you, she wouldn't just give you cream, she'd try to find some if she didn't have any. And she wouldn't want anything in return. She doesn't do it to feel good about herself; she just does it!"

I was crying, but he didn't seem to care, pressing on with his questions, not giving me time to think.

"What's more important to you to find in others," he asked, "wisdom or kindness?"

"I still think it's wise to be kind." I sobbed. "But if I have to choose, I'll take kindness."

"And is that a wise choice on your part?"

"It doesn't matter," I said.

"Why not?"

For some reason, that was too much. I sank to the ground, tears still trickling down my cheeks, feeling completely empty. "Because..." I choked back another sob. "Because I don't get to choose if I'm wise or not," I said. "I don't get to decide. Maybe I am, maybe I'm not. I don't know. Maybe I can learn to be. Maybe that's impossible. But it's only someone else who can tell. I can't judge. If I try to, it's just proof that I'm not."

I looked up at him. He was nearby. The expression on his face was odd, one I hadn't seen there before. It was almost kind.

"That's why you never claimed you were wise, isn't it, Kot Bayun? We don't get to say that we are. If we do, we're lying. Lying to ourselves. Even if I found you wise. The things you say might sound wise and be wise for me and guide me, but for someone else, they might just be useless nonsense. For anyone who believed what Baba Yaga said, what she's doing would be wise too..."

Kot Bayun purred. It was a comforting sound.

I didn't know why I was crying, but I hid my head behind one arm on my knees. Kot Bayun came closer and nuzzled the palm of my other hand. I stroked the top of his head and started to scratch his neck, my fingers completely lost in his fur.

Finally, my tears stopped, and I took my hand away. Kot Bayun turned away and started to walk toward a sunny spot nearby.

"Kot Bayun?" I called.

He glanced back at me as he settled in the warmth. "Yes?"

"The game's over," I said.

He smiled gently. "The game's been over for some time, Anna Wisdom," he said. "It's just that you didn't notice when it ended."

I stared at him. He yawned widely, his mouth like some weird pink flower with sharp white petals. Then he rolled over onto his back.

"Oh, joy," he muttered. "More intruders." He was looking up at the sky. "Are they with you?"

I looked up. Squire and Knight were flying toward us, mop and bucket well in hand. Had it really taken them this long to get here? Or had my conversation with Kot Bayun not actually taken that long?

The cat batted vaguely in their direction with one paw. He didn't seem hugely invested in tackling them.

"They're with me, Kot Bayun," I said. I looked around, found the apple and picked it up.

"Oh, don't bother with that," Kot Bayun murmured drowsily. "What you're looking for is that way." Again he batted a paw, this time vaguely toward the north. He sounded extremely sleepy.

"Thank you, Kot Bayun," I said.

As Squire and Knight came down to join me, I picked up my backpack and started to walk in the direction he had indicated.

I had only gone a few steps when the cat spoke again. "Anna Wisdom," he said.

I turned back. His blue eye was half-open and looking at me.

"Yes?"

"Your parents chose your name poorly," he said. That mocking tone was back in his voice. "I said it was that way. And I'm not going to stop you or hurt you. You can go ahead." He grinned. "But I never said it was safe." He closed his eye.

I didn't have any choice, though. I had to go on, dangerous or not. I wondered if I should ask him another question or if that would be pushing my luck.

And then he started to sing again, utter mockery in his tone:

> *"Proschay, radost', zhizn' moya!*
> *Znayu, yedesh' bez menya.*
> *Znat' odin dolzhon ostat'sya*
> *Tebya mne bol'she ne vidat'..."*

I couldn't believe it. I couldn't believe it for a moment. I had thought he had a kind streak in him. Here he was, watching me go into what he said was danger, and he was mocking me: *Farewell, my joy, my life! I know you will leave me. It seems I have to live alone, without ever seeing you again.*

How could he turn that whole song into a sneer?

Lying bathed in sunlight, he continued to sing. *The night is dark*, the words went. *Oh, I cannot sleep.*

Kot Bayun began to snore.

Chapter 24

Dear Diary,

I am not going to feel sorry for Granny. Even though I know what she felt when she cut out her heart, I also know what she's done since then. I will not forget that. I refuse to forget that.

I'm glad I have you. Rereading some of my entries helps me remember why I hate her and why I have to do what I'm going to do.

She chose to cut out her heart and stop feeling. She chose to be evil. I am going to get my revenge on her — for me, for Lauraleigh, for everyone she's ever hurt.

Including herself.

It wasn't until I was out of hearing range of Kot Bayun's snores that I noticed my magic energy coming back. It's not that it suddenly flooded me or anything. I just became aware that its tingles were back up and down my arms, that I could feel it spreading its web from beneath my ribs. I still had just as much power inside me as when I'd arrived. Kot Bayun hadn't taken it away from me; he'd just blocked it for a while.

A spasm of anger clenched my gut, the magic welling up as I thought of that nasty, sarcastic cat and how he'd played with me. He was sleeping now, and I was tempted to turn back and set the whole clearing where he was on fire.

But I didn't. I was surprised to feel that violent urge. I also had to be wise, as he'd have said. I didn't know if my magic was back just because I was out of his presence or because he was sleeping. And I didn't trust him to be sleeping deeply. He was quite capable of pretending to be taking a catnap.

Besides, he wasn't my real target.

How could I not have heard that I had another uncle? Why had no one ever told me that my mother had a brother? That Baba Yaga had another child? Unless he wasn't Baba Yaga's child but my grandfather's? Who *was* my grandfather, anyway? Who was Sereda's dad?

Granny, Dad, Uncle Misha — they must all have known. Probably even Vodyanoy. Any of them could have told me. Didn't I have a right to know? Why did they leave me to find these things out from an oversized housecat who wanted to rip my soul out and wouldn't stop playing with me until I was in tears?

In my anger, I rubbed my face with my sleeve. I still had no idea why I'd started crying, but I didn't like it. I didn't like that Kot Bayun had made me cry, that he'd been able to, that he'd seen me cry, and that my family had put me in this position. Why did they treat me like that? All of them — not just Granny — all of them seemed to think I wasn't important, just some useful puppet or something.

"I'm allowed to know things!" I shouted. The hands flew back from me, fluttering worriedly. "You don't get to keep them from me!"

I'd already had to spend thirteen years not knowing I was a witch, who my parents were, how my mother had died. Did Uncle Misha really think that teaching me about the birds made up for all the other things he could have told me? At least Mama Bear had the excuse that she couldn't talk.

My magic was curling up inside me as if gathering itself to strike out. *When I get back*, I thought, *I'll have some things to say to them. All of them.*

Then I started wondering why I should even bother going back. Why should I want to have anything to do with their stupid wars and quarrels? Granny couldn't fulfill her plan without me, so if I just vanished, I wouldn't be condemning the world to be destroyed or anything. And Kot Bayun was right. Dad probably deserved to be in that cage, if he was stupid enough to get caught.

If it hadn't been for Lauraleigh, I would have just gotten into my bucket, flown back to Switzerland, and told Monsieur Nolan to find me a nice quiet place to live far from my nasty relatives.

Still, I'd promised Lauraleigh I'd save her. And I'd told the cat too, and I wasn't about to give Kot Bayun another opportunity to make fun of me. I had to find that heart.

Kot Bayun had indicated the north, so we went that way. The hands flew a little in front of me, scouting. I wondered if I should let them set the mop and bucket down, but I didn't want to risk losing those items.

Kot Bayun had said this area wasn't safe, and I was going to believe him.

North was up a bit of a hill, and soon the trees started to thin out. Rocks began to emerge from the grass, spotted with lichen. Stunted berry bushes dotted the landscape. The air was even thicker with magic here than it had been on the beach. I felt as if I were walking through layers and layers of sheer curtains swaying in the breeze.

I still wasn't sure how to find the heart, though. I wondered if I should ask the apple again. But Kot Bayun hadn't seemed to think I'd need it.

It occurred to me that this might be another of his tests. He'd said it wasn't safe. He wouldn't stop me or hurt me, but that didn't mean I was safe from his tricks. If I used the apple after he had said I didn't have to, would I be cheating?

I closed my eyes. Now I could almost hear the vibrations of magic, like some huge hum swirling around us. Surely there would be some sign?

Almost all the island's magic had felt like Baba Yaga's ever since I had sensed it on the shore. That had to be due to the heart, didn't it? If Granny wanted Koschey's heart so she could absorb its magic, then hearts were powerful. Could I trace the heart that way?

With my eyes still closed, I started to examine the magic. I concentrated on its texture, how the hum seemed to span from a deep bass to the merest high whisper. It was like a swirl of sound and color melting together, but the more I focused, the more I could distinguish its shades. The magic didn't all originate with Baba Yaga, but she was present in all of it. As if her magic were the varnish on the paint. *Or,*

I thought, remembering one of her stews, *as if she were the garlic*. Everything was flavored with it, but I had to find the actual clove.

Where was it strongest? What felt most like her?

It was like plunging into the depths of the sea and trying to find a current. I traced the layers of magic with my mind, like sweeping my hands over the strings of a harp, hearing each string's note, matching the colors, seeking out the one tone that would resonate with my memories of my grandmother.

At first, it seemed impossible. But the more I focused, the more I could see the gradations in color, the faint differences between the notes, like looking at a piece of woven cloth and slowly becoming aware of each individual thread. One of which was—

There.

In my mind, it seemed a deep violet, and I let my own magic find it, a thin thread of blue that went to touch the violet to make sure I wouldn't lose it. Then I'd be able to trace the thread all the way back to its beginning, and surely that would lead me to Granny's heart.

My magic made contact with hers, and suddenly my eyes were open again and I was gasping for air as if the wind had just been knocked out of me. All the energy in the atmosphere felt dimmer, more distant. I was all too aware of the wave of Baba Yaga's power, which seemed to be clamped around my own pounding heart, a long rope lassoed around me and pulling me toward its source.

I wasn't even sure that I'd ordered my feet to move. They just did. And I had no doubt whatsoever that we were going in the right direction.

As we went on, the island grew greener again, as if making up for the stunted place we'd just been through. That didn't make much sense. But this island spent most of its time being invisible, so I didn't think much of it, even as the vegetation grew downright lush. There were apple trees and cherry trees, and despite the season, they were in bloom. There were huge rosebushes with bees buzzing around the flowers, and blackberry and blackcurrant shrubs heavy with ripe berries.

Uncle Misha had taught me well enough for me to know this wasn't right. The berries shouldn't have come until months after the trees had stopped flowering.

I stopped, managing to resist the pull of the magic, and thought. My conversation with Kot Bayun came to mind again. The fact that the plants were wrong for the season was knowledge. What would wisdom be?

Kot Bayun had said there was danger. He'd said the world was a hall of mirrors and that I had to balance different truths to find my way through it. Here were two truths colliding. First, the flowers were right there and blooming. Second, they shouldn't be.

Wisdom would be wariness.

But I still had to find Baba Yaga's heart. All I had to do was follow the trace of the magic. I just had to be more careful as I did so.

That was when I heard the laughter, soft and light, chiming like bells. It was a sound I'd heard before. But where? And what was it doing here?

It was coming from the same direction in which the magic was pulling me.

"Squire? Knight?" I said. "Could one of you fly ahead and see if it's safe, please?" I wasn't exactly afraid, but I was definitely feeling cautious.

Squire flew down, set the mop on the ground beside me, and went on ahead. He came back soon, waving excitedly. I didn't understand what he meant, and I wondered if I should get him a pen and paper, but he beckoned me on. What had gotten him so agitated?

I moved forward with great care. Squire grabbed the mop and followed me.

The silvery, tinkling laughter grew louder as I advanced, still tracing that flow of Grandmother's magic. *I wish I could remember where I heard it before*, I thought. But then we crested the hill, and I knew.

Over the hill, there was a hollow, covered with soft grass and flowers and more blossoming fruit trees. In its very center sat a large, shining gemstone, sparkling with violet light as the sun played on it.

A charoite. Of course — like the one I'd seen with Lauraleigh on my way to Uncle Misha's all that time ago. And the laughter — that was the Mountain Mistress.

I walked cautiously into the hollow. I knew I had to be careful not to disturb the stone. Otherwise, the Mistress might think I wanted to steal it, and I didn't want to find out what she did to thieves she caught. I'd already gotten on the bad side of one magical creature today, and I didn't want to push my luck. For all I knew, she'd be able to neutralize my magic too, and then where would I be? It would be silly to fail now when I was so close to my goal.

Which I was — wasn't I? I felt around. The band around my heart seemed to have loosened. It wasn't pulling me anymore. Strangely, even though there was still a lot of magic in the air, it didn't feel as heavy — or as much like Baba Yaga's.

This was weird. I hadn't walked past where the heart was hidden, had I? That wouldn't make any sense. But then again, a lot of things here didn't make sense.

I laughed. Trying to make sense of a magical island! Most things in my life hadn't made sense for the last few months.

Well, I can't wait here forever, I thought. *Something is going on.*

I took the apple out of my backpack and placed it on the ground. "Take me to Baba Yaga's heart," I commanded.

But the apple didn't move. It didn't even spin.

The laughter was back, close to my ear, mocking. I flushed. It sounded too much like Kot Bayun.

"Look, don't worry," I snapped. "I'm not going to steal your silly stone. What would I do with it, anyway?" I was not in the mood to deal with any more sarcasm. "I'm just looking for one thing, and then I'll go and leave you to do whatever it is you do."

That just made the Mistress laugh again.

I tried to ignore her and focus. Kot Bayun had confirmed that Baba Yaga's heart was on the island; the magic had definitely led me here. So why couldn't I find it? Why was I standing here, being mocked by an invisible voice I hadn't heard since—

Wait.

What was it Gavril had told us about charoites? That they were rare? Yes, but there was something else.

They were so rare that they could be found in only one place on the planet. In an area of just a few square kilometers.

I looked around.

A gemstone that was hundreds, if not thousands, of kilometers from where it should have been. Fruit trees that were blossoming at the wrong time of the year. Roses when there shouldn't have been any. The Mountain Mistress far from her own mountains. An island that shouldn't have been here, but was.

"The world is a hall of mirrors," Kot Bayun had said.

"None of this is real," I realized with a gasp.

I didn't notice I'd spoken aloud. But the effect was immediate. I experienced a terrifying crash and a burst of light so bright, I closed my eyes. And when I opened them again, all the green was gone: the trees, the grass, the flowers, the bees, everything. Nothing was growing here. The hollow was just a crater of blackened rock, surrounded by the ghostly remnants of fallen trees. It was as if some huge bomb had exploded, knocking down everything that grew and poisoning the land so that nothing could ever sprout here again.

And in its very center, bright among the tarry blackness of the rock, just where the charoite had been, was a pulsing white-and-violet glow.

I had no doubts at all. I had found Baba Yaga's heart. It was just lying there, right where she had thrown it all those centuries ago when she had torn it from herself. An act of magic so powerful and desperate that it had marked the land around it, leaving it desolate and barren.

And coming from the hollow was a soft sound I couldn't quite make out. It wasn't laughter.

Very, very slowly, I began to move toward it. I didn't know if there were other defenses around it, though I didn't think so. The thick fog of magic seemed to be gone.

As I stepped onto the black stone, it was as if I'd stepped into the land of the dead. There were no insect sounds, no birdsong, no breath of wind; even the sky had somehow become overcast without my noticing. In that gray-and-black world, there was nothing; nothing but the beat of the violet light and that soft, inescapable sound that I recognized as I drew closer.

Weeping. Terrible, heartrending, despairing weeping, the sobs and crying of grief beyond imagining. It was worse than anything I'd ever heard, worse even than Mei's crying in the Montmorency dungeons.

It hurt to listen to it, and I felt my own throat growing tight and tears welling in my eyes. The quiet mourning went on and on.

As I listened, it brought back every moment of sadness I'd ever felt. I remembered having to leave Uncle Misha, the first time I'd realized what it meant that my mother was dead, the helplessness I'd felt when I'd discovered what the Montmorencys had been up to. Every unhappy thought I'd ever had seemed to be crowding into my mind, even the ones I'd forgotten long ago, even the silly ones. I felt as if my chest were being flooded, as that steady stream of desperate crying flowed on.

I fell to my knees, trying to hold back my own tears. How could anybody have gone on suffering like that? No wonder Baba Yaga had torn her heart out, if it could keep her from feeling that awful grief.

But she'd left her heart to grieve alone.

It was a strange thought, but it was enough to break through a little of my own sorrow. Even if it didn't make much sense, I was thinking of that heart as some small creature, a living thing in its own right. The idea that it had been crying here for thousands of years gave me just enough anger to be able to move again. It was Granny's fault that it was here, her fault that it was still weeping. Cutting it out had been her first great act of cruelty. I had to get to the heart so I could set things right.

At that point, I didn't even remember what I was meant to do. I just knew that I had to get to the heart no matter what. But I was still so overpowered by my memories, by the sound of that crying, that I couldn't stand up.

So I crawled.

On my hands and knees, I managed to crawl toward the light. I was able to get right to its side, to look down at its source. And I gasped.

The sight of my grandmother's heart was enough to shake off more of the sorrow I was feeling. I couldn't help it. It was a lot to take in.

It looked very much like a charoite, all violet and white, but it was bigger and crystalline. Inside, the light was pulsing to some irregular rhythm, like broken heartbeat or someone's sobs. There were small droplets of moisture on it, like dew — or tears.

It was beautiful. Even though it was splintered, lying in two pieces on the rock.

Vodyanoy hadn't lied.

Baba Yaga's heart was literally broken.

Chapter 25

*ear Diary,*

That's when I had to reread bits of you from the past. Because at that moment, I almost felt sorry for her again.

But I remembered what Vodyanoy had said about feeling sorry for the girl Baba Yaga had been, not for the Iron Queen.

So that's what I'm going to do.

If Baba Yaga touches her heart again, she will feel thousands and thousands of years of grief fall on her. All at once.

And I hope it will hurt.

The shock of seeing Baba Yaga's heart gave me enough strength to stand up. The weeping continued, but it didn't seem to have the same effect on me anymore. I walked back to the edge of the crater.

Now I had to get the heart into the box she'd given me. I got it out of my bag; it was a lovely little thing of carved wood. When I opened it, I saw that it was lined with velvet. It was clearly a magical object; I could feel its power just by holding it. There had to be all sorts of enchantments on it, to make sure it could hold Koschey's heart safely.

That was when I started to worry.

Koschey's heart had to be more powerful than Baba Yaga's, right? Granny's had been here on this island for ages. Koschey's had to be stronger because it hadn't been out that long, right? So if the box was able to hold Koschey's heart, it had to be able to hold Baba Yaga's.

Right?

I could trust Granny to have done the enchantments, couldn't I? I mean, she knew what she was doing when it came to magic, didn't she? This wasn't going to be a *big* risk to me.

Except I had to get the heart into the box, and I didn't know how. Even though I was feeling better now, I had no guarantee that I wouldn't be overcome with grief again if I tried to get close.

And besides, I couldn't touch the heart. I'd die if I did. Everyone had seemed to agree on that: Granny, Dad, Vodyanoy…

Wait a minute.

How was Granny planning to absorb Koschey's heart if she couldn't touch it? She had to have some plan in mind. Was being the most powerful witch in the world enough to reduce the danger?

I began to panic.

Was it safe to take Baba Yaga her own heart? Sure, she had never come back for it in all those years, but that didn't mean anything. My plan was still just something dreamed up by a half-senile old water spirit who had admitted not knowing if it would work. How could I be sure that taking her this heart wouldn't make things worse?

She wanted Koschey's heart because she could get power from it. That meant that hearts held massive amounts of energy. Without his heart, Koschey had been weak enough to be captured.

That meant that the Baba Yaga I knew, the one everyone knew, the Iron Queen, was just a weak version of what she could be.

How powerful would she be once she had reabsorbed her own heart? There was no proof that it would hurt her. And even if it did, wasn't she strong enough to get through it? Just because she hadn't been able to deal with the grief all that time ago, didn't mean she wouldn't be able to now. And then I'd have just made her even more powerful — maybe so much so that she could do without Koschey's heart. But I'd have broken my agreement with her, and she'd have Laura-leigh in her oven before I could do anything.

Could I risk that? Did I have to try?

I wondered what my father's advice would have been. But then … he didn't even know about this plan.

I wondered what Kot Bayun would have said. *Something nasty*, I supposed. Nothing helpful anyway, even though I was fairly sure he'd know. But he'd be too interested in seeing what I'd do and what would happen to tell me.

All I had to go on was what Vodyanoy had said and what seemed likely. But I didn't actually *know* what would happen when I took the heart back.

I could imagine Kot Bayun smirking at me. "Would it be *wise*," he'd say, "to take this heart to Baba Yaga?"

"I don't know," I said aloud. "I really don't."

But then I realized that I'd asked myself the wrong question. It wasn't whether it would be wise to take her the heart; it was whether it would be wise to take the risk.

I looked at the pulsing light. That heart had to contain so much energy; I couldn't even imagine how much. And if Baba Yaga could absorb that heart as she wanted to do with Koschey's, who knew what the most powerful witch in the world would do then? Nobody would be able to fight her. Even right now, filled with more energy than I'd ever had, I didn't want to risk taking her on.

And that's when a thought occurred to me.

People weren't supposed to touch other people's hearts. They'd die. But somehow, being a witch, Baba Yaga was planning to manage to absorb Koschey's.

Baba Yaga was a witch. I was a witch.

My own heart started to beat faster as I looked at the center of the crater. I already knew how to feast on other people's energy. I was overflowing with magical power right now, able to do more than I could ever have dreamed of only a few days ago. Why shouldn't I be able to absorb Baba Yaga's heart?

If I did that, I'd have no more worries at all. I could fly back to her hut and free Lauraleigh in an instant and break Dad out of his cage if I felt like it. I'd be able to make him sit down and listen to me. I could deal with Baba Yaga any way I wanted to.

I was pretty sure I could even take on Kot Bayun. And I would. I'd teach that stupid cat to mock me, to make me cry. Who did he think he was anyway, talking to me like that?

I found myself trembling. I wanted to do it. I wanted that power. I wanted to be able to tell Baba Yaga that I'd taken her heart away from her. I felt tendrils of my magic unfurling inside me, darker than usual, the shadow licking its chops. I could have everything if I did this. I'd be able to do anything I wanted, and no one would dare to tell me otherwise. And *that* was worth the risk of trying.

I smiled. What did I care about some whining teenager from millennia ago who couldn't even get over some boy? How stupid had Baba Yaga been back then? She didn't deserve her power. She didn't deserve her heart. How much risk could there be? Even if she stopped blubbering long enough to notice what I was doing, what could she do to me?

I walked firmly into the crater again. This time I felt nothing.

The two pieces of the heart kept sobbing, sending out their beams of white and violet light in rhythm with the sobs, like a light show at one of those rock concerts that would get Granny so riled when she saw them on TV. *Who are you to complain about reality stars, Granny,* I thought, *considering what you were like as a teenager?*

The mix of violet and white is interesting, I thought as I got nearer. The violet was just the shade I'd seen when I was finding the traces of Baba Yaga's magic earlier; curious that it was just like the purple of a charoite. And the white seemed … familiar. Where had I seen it before, that particular shade of white, glowing like that? It was fairly recently. Was it in a dream? It wasn't in my everyday life, whatever that was. It sure wasn't the kind of light that comes from a crystal; it was like what I'd seen when Koschey was talking about—

I froze.

I realized what I was about to do. I turned and ran from the crater as fast as I could. Because the white light looked just like my mother's soul as I'd seen it in Koschey's mind.

Everybody had talked about how kind Sereda had been and wondered how she could be Baba Yaga's daughter. But Kot Bayun had said all of Granny's kindness was on the island. Of course it was; it was in her heart, and she had passed it on to Sereda all the same.

And I had been about to take that away.

Rage at my grandmother exploded inside me. This was what she was turning me into! She was making me into a clone of herself. I didn't want to absorb her heart, but the shadow inside me, the evil part that was so much like her, did. If I did, I would be acting like her; I'd be doing to her what she wanted to do to Koschey. Just by existing, Baba Yaga was ruining my life.

I am not going to be like you, Granny, I thought. *I'm not going to let you make me into a nasty, miserable old bat like you. You think I'm going to let you make me as evil as you are?*

I'm going to take your heart, all right, but I'm going to use it to destroy you, you cruel, insane witch.

I looked up at the floating hands.

"Squire, Knight," I called. "I can't get that heart myself. But I need it in this box." I put the open box on the ground. "I'm not sure which would be easier: you taking the box in or you bringing the heart out."

They bobbed up and down uncertainly.

"I can't promise it's safe," I admitted. "I've been told that I'll die if I touch it. But I don't know what will happen to you."

Now they looked even more uncertain. They flew close together and consulted each other.

Without warning, still carrying the mop and bucket, they flew into the crater. I was taken aback by their decisiveness; I'd thought I'd have to do some persuading. But I was also confused about why they didn't leave the luggage behind.

That was answered pretty quickly. Arriving at the center of the crater, Knight swooped down first, set the bucket down, and tipped it onto its side, right next to the heart. Then Squire flew down, Knight joined him — and together, they used the mop to push the two pieces of the heart into the bucket.

I just stared with my mouth open. That was … incredible. Baba Yaga's heart mopped up like so much rubbish.

Perhaps even more surprisingly, nothing happened. I hadn't known what to expect — thunderclaps or an earthquake or what — but there was nothing. Only the clink of two pieces of crystal settling in a bucket.

Carefully, the two hands raised the bucket upright so that Knight could grab its handle again. They flew out of the crater, Squire taking the mop with him. When they reached the box, Squire dropped the mop. Knight placed the bucket right at the edge of the box, and Squire cautiously tipped it. The two pieces of the heart slid right inside.

"You clever, clever hands!" I cried. Just for a moment, all my anger seemed to vanish. I couldn't help laughing. Who would have thought they'd be that pragmatic? "Thank you so much!"

They bobbed up and down, clearly proud of themselves.

"Okay, now I've just got to close it," I said.

I didn't want to take any risks. I sent a jet of magic at the lid to make it close, and then another to latch it. Suddenly things seemed much brighter around me. I wasn't sure why, at first, but then I noticed that the sky was clear again. I couldn't hear the weeping anymore. I'd grown so used to it, I'd practically forgotten about it, but now the silence was wonderful.

I picked up the box and put it in my backpack. I couldn't believe it. I'd actually accomplished my mission.

Well — no. Not quite yet. There was still the last part to get through.

I grinned. This part might be fun. *Guess what, Granny? You've been tricked*, I thought. *And now I can make you pay.*

"All right, hands," I said, and they floated expectantly. "You've done really good work, and I know I've asked a lot of you the last couple of days. But now I've got a long trip, and I don't think I'll need you. So you can rest. Sleep, Squire! Sleep, Knight!"

They both froze and fell to the ground. Maybe they hadn't been expecting this.

Well, I didn't want them getting in the way.

I put them into my backpack and slung it over my shoulders. I looked around one last time. It was time to go.

I wondered what would happen to the island now that it wasn't protecting anything. Would Kot Bayun stay here?

I didn't really care — but just as that thought occurred to me, he started singing again, somewhere in the distance.

"Po dikim stepyam Zabaikalya,
Gde zoloto royut v gorakh…"

He was singing about the savage steppes behind Lake Baikal, where people prospected for gold in the mountains.

I still would have liked to have done something to him — "Something *evil*," the shadows in my heart whispered — but I didn't have time, nor did I know that I could. Besides, I had to save my energy for confronting my grandmother. The sun was a lot lower in the sky, and I didn't want to be on the island with Kot Bayun when night came.

I got into the bucket and made myself rise into the air. I could still hear him singing, but as I flew off, there was no sign of that magic guideline that had led me here. I supposed it was because I had the heart now.

I headed for the hotel. From there I'd be able to work out what direction to take. I wondered how long it would take for the island to vanish.

And yet all the time I flew, all the way across the lake, I could still hear Kot Bayun singing his song.

"Otets tvoi davno uzh v mogile
Zemlioyu syroyu lezhit..."

Your father has been in his grave for a long time; he now rests in the damp earth, he sang.

I wondered if he was trying to tell me something. But then I reached the shore, and I stopped caring.

I was staying high up so no one would see me, but I could still see the parking lot clearly. And I saw Olya Sumarokova's mother as she was stumbling toward her car, helped by her husband.

Suddenly all my rage at my grandmother came back. Anger not only for what she'd done to me but for what she'd done to everyone.

Kot Bayun reached the end of his song.

"Plachut detishki gurboi..."

And all the little children are crying...
I felt my face grow hard.

Never again, I said to myself. With that, I began to fly toward the forest. I went higher and faster than I ever had before, retracing my steps as best I could, trusting that I'd be able to find her hut as surely as I had the island. The wind blew freezing cold, but I didn't care. It felt right: powerful and cleansing, just as I wanted to be as I cleansed the world of Baba Yaga for good.

No more missing children. No more stupid wars. No changing the world because it didn't suit you. And payback for what had come before, for the heartbreak she'd caused. The Iron Queen's reign was about to end.

I flew on and on.

At last, in the distance, I spotted a clearing in the forest. And at its center, a small hut that didn't stay as still as a hut should. Granny's.

The trip back had taken me less time than finding her heart had. I smiled grimly. It was time for the reckoning.

I urged my bucket down and landed just within the fence of skulls. There was no noise; apparently Baba Yaga hadn't heard me return. *Good*, I thought. *Maybe I can surprise her.* I grabbed the carved box and looked back toward the gate.

I started. A little girl was kneeling there, her hair disheveled, her eyes wide and staring. She had a gag in her mouth, and her hands were tied behind her. The rope that bound her stretched back to the fence, where it was wrapped around a post.

Wrapped around the post that had no skull.

I didn't have to ask or think. I knew who she was: little Olya. She looked so much like her mother. I felt the rage growing even stronger in me. My whole body was shaking with it. I felt as though there were flames dancing in my eyes.

At least she was still alive. But this — this wasn't right. This is what I had to stop.

"Olya," I said, in what I hoped was a calming voice. "It's all right, I'll help you…" I took a step toward her, but she scuttled back from me, her eyes growing even more terrified than they had been.

You just landed in a bucket in front of her, I thought. *She knows you're a witch. And you're angry. Of course she's scared of you.*

I closed my eyes for half a second.

This was Granny's doing too. Turning me into someone children were afraid of.

As if I didn't have enough reasons to hate her.

I swung around on my heels, ready to charge into the hut, to scream and yell at Granny, to force her to let Olya go — and found three spears pointing directly at me. Spears whose points were like huge, sharpened precious stones: one red ruby, one blazing, yellow-tinged white diamond, and one black obsidian.

The Black Horseman grinned at me, while his brothers kept their spears steady, just centimeters from my skin.

"Such a pleasure to see you again, child," he said, but there was no pleasure in his voice. He prodded at me with the point of his spear. "Your granny and her guests are waiting for you."

He moved aside so I would have a clear path to the hut's door. The other two stepped aside as well, still keeping me at their spears' mercy, surrounding me so I couldn't escape. The White Horseman made sure to stay in front of the bucket. The Red placed himself between Olya and me. She looked up at him, and I could hear her whimpering through her gag.

As I took a step forward, the Black Horseman leaned down so his face was right beside mine.

"And I hope she eats your heart," he whispered.

Chapter 26

Dear Diary,

I managed to take Baba Yaga's heart to her without her realizing what I was doing.

I was hoping it would destroy her.

I don't really want to talk about what I almost became.

Something seemed different about the hut as I walked toward it, but I couldn't figure out what. Maybe it seemed larger somehow. Or the angles were different. But I didn't care enough to wonder. My rage was just growing steadily worse. I didn't like having spears pointed at me. It was all I could do to keep myself from blasting all three Horsemen away from me in a single squall of anger. The White Horseman, who'd set his wolves on Lauraleigh and me. The Red, who had helped Baba Yaga imprison my father. The Black, who'd been haunting me since Switzerland and who had stolen Olya Sumarokova.

Poor little Olya. She was kneeling there, as terrified of me as of the monster who'd brought her here. I wondered if she knew her fairy tales. Had she recognized the chicken-leg hut, the fence of skulls?

But I had to deal with Baba Yaga first.

As I reached the stairs, the hut crouched down on its legs so that I could easily get onto the porch. It must have been waiting for me. I didn't see how I was going to sneak up on my grandmother. I'd just have to trick her.

After all, she'd tricked me often enough. She deserved nothing better. All I had to do was get her to touch what was hidden in the box, and she'd be done for. My father would be free and Lauraleigh would be safe. We'd find a way to get Olya home. And I would have made Baba Yaga pay for everything she'd done.

But when the door swung open in front of me, I got a huge shock.

"*Vnuchechka*, darling!" crowed Baba Yaga as she saw me. "How nice of you to drop in! Come in, come in. See who's come by for a visit!"

Seated at the table were Uncle Misha and Egor. They were frozen, their hands on the tabletop. They didn't even seem able to blink, but their attentive eyes told me they were hearing every word.

"Most impolite, these people," Baba Yaga chuckled. "They won't say a word, even when I ask nicely! But then, it's not nice to try and break into a poor old woman's house when she's there all alone and defenseless, is it? So I think it's only fair they should learn some manners."

My eyes were darting around, but I couldn't see any way to help them. Why had they come here? Why were they messing up my plans? Couldn't they have just trusted me?

Then I saw that Lauraleigh was still tied up in the corner. Of course. They had come for her. Everybody would always come for Lauraleigh, she was so sweet. Not for me. I knew that now. Why would anybody want to rescue a black-hearted witch like me?

At that moment, I almost hated Lauraleigh for what she was, so sickeningly good and kind. I almost wished I *had* let Baba Yaga turn her into soup.

But that made me remember that my grandmother had actually tried to do that. And all my hatred focused on her again. I could feel it bubbling inside me.

Lauraleigh was looking at me with frightened eyes. I never knew she was such a pathetic scaredy-cat.

"Anna," she said, "what's happened to you? You look … different. Your eyes—"

"Shush, child," said Baba Yaga, and Lauraleigh instantly fell silent. My grandmother sighed. "I do hate a chatty dinner."

Then she looked at me. "You're awfully quiet," she said. "Have you nothing to say?"

"I'm home, Granny," I managed to say through gritted teeth. "And I saw your other guest in the yard."

"Oh, yes." She chuckled. "The boys brought it in. Good lads. After all, on the off chance I'm not feasting on that long-legged blonde tonight, I have to have something else for the larder, don't I?" She laughed. "There's rather less of the new one than that one, but every little bit helps."

I managed to control my trembling. I'm not sure how, but I felt it running through me like magic, gathering, ready to lash out if I couldn't keep control of myself.

"I've brought you a gift, Granny," I said.

"What a sweet child you are." Baba Yaga grinned, showing every one of her black iron teeth. "And what have you brought your old granny?" Behind her smile, she was suspicious, testing to see if I was lying.

"I've brought you a heart, Granny," I said.

Baba Yaga burst into delighted peals of laughter. "A heart!" she whooped. "A heart! Oh, Anna, I knew we'd make something of you yet. Do you think we should let your dear old father know? After all, we wouldn't want him to miss all the fun. And what's about to happen is historic; it should have more of an audience than some silly old men and tonight's roast. Come on, Koschey!" she shouted as she began to leap about in the air. "Come and see what your daughter's brought me! *Let my house become my hall!*"

I didn't know what was going to happen, but I could feel waves of power streaming from her, and suddenly the room began to grow.

The table at which Egor and Uncle Misha were sitting slid to the side, and they went with it. The walls seemed to stretch almost to infinity, and torches hanging on brackets burst into flames so that we were suddenly lit only by fire. And one wall crumbled and fell away, revealing the golden cage in which my father was sitting.

Koschey hardly even looked at Baba Yaga. His eyes found me, and a look of great worry came over his features. "Anna," he said, "what are you—"

But before he could finish, Baba Yaga raised a hand. "Oh, be quiet, old bag of bones," she said, and my father stopped speaking at once. My grandmother looked different now: larger, more powerful. Her back wasn't bent anymore, and as the torchlight flickered over her, I could sense her immense strength.

"Your daughter's decided to be very nice to her old granny, *Koscheyushka*," she said, gloating. "Sweet of her, don't you think? Why, she's brought me something very special. She's brought me your heart." She grinned. "And you know what I'm going to do with it, Koschey? I'm going to eat it. And then I'll have all your power. After all these years, I *will* rule your realm, and soon this one, and eventually the whole world!"

Baba Yaga laughed. "Oh, *Koscheyushka*," she said softly, "why didn't you just give me your heart in the first place, all that time ago? We could have avoided so many unpleasant things…"

I stared at her hard. *Go on*, I thought. *Gloat. Laugh. Enjoy yourself, because you don't have much time left to do so.*

"Why are you looking at me like that, *vnuchechka*? Come on, give Granny her present, and then we can have dinner."

"Anna Sophia, don't!" Uncle Misha suddenly croaked.

Evidently, Baba Yaga had been having so much fun laughing at Koschey that her magic bonds had weakened. She turned toward Uncle Misha and waved a hand. A burst of dark energy streamed from her and hit him in the face.

"The Great Trapper!" she sneered. "Do you even know how bad you smell? You should take a bath from time to time, Misha the Bear."

The knot of darkness in my belly churned even more, growing tighter like a fist ready to strike. I pulled the box out of my bag. "Granny," I said.

She turned and looked.

I held the box toward her. "My present for you is in here, Granny."

Her eyes grew hungry. Even as she kept one hand aimed at Uncle Misha and Egor, she moved closer. The air was thrumming as if there were some invisible creature in there with us, humming softly.

Baba Yaga licked her lips. "Open it, Anna Sophia," she whispered. "Show me this heart you've brought me."

Egor tried to move, but she swatted him back in place. I didn't take my eyes off her as I unlatched the box.

The thrumming increased, and now there was a rhythm to it, like a low, heavy pulse.

I could hear Lauraleigh sobbing in her corner.

"Stop making that noise!" Baba Yaga yelled. She spun around on her heels, and suddenly three pairs of hands flew in, each holding a length of rope, which they wrapped around the throats of Lauraleigh, Egor and Uncle Misha.

"Make another sound and those ropes will tighten," Baba Yaga warned.

It took all my willpower not to throw myself at her, not to roar like a bear and attack her with tooth and claw. But I did not. I saw Uncle Misha's look of despair, Egor's look of fear, Lauraleigh's tear-stained cheeks, my father's worried features, and Baba Yaga's warty, ugly old face in the torchlight.

I lifted the box's lid.

The whole world seemed darker. The torches still burned but seemed to give no light. My father's cage looked dull instead of like shining gold. It was as if shadows had fallen on all of us.

But nothing had changed. It was just that the light streaming from the box was so bright that it made everything else look darker.

Beams spilled from the box as if refracted in a crystal, silver and purple and blinding, spreading from the burning kernel of pure whiteness in the center of the box, pulsing to the heartbeat we could all hear. The light danced on the beams of the ceiling and the walls, reflecting off the glass bottles on Baba Yaga's shelves and off the eyes of her prisoners. It glowed nearly as bright as the sun, and yet nobody looked away.

It was almost unbearably beautiful.

Baba Yaga's arms had dropped. She stared, wide-eyed, her mouth open, looking uncertain.

"Anna Sophia?" she said, her voice trembling. "What is this?"

"I've brought you a heart, Grandmother," I said. "I didn't say it was the heart you'd asked for." I kept my gaze steady on her. "I've brought you a broken heart, Granny. One as broken as your mind. Your own. I've brought you back your heart. I… I thought you might have missed it." Even I could hear how harsh my voice was.

Baba Yaga's lower lip trembled. Tears formed in the corners of her eyes. That made no sense.

"You want it, don't you?" I asked, taking a step toward her. "Come on, reach out and touch it, Granny. Take your heart back. You can't be complete without it."

"It's so beautiful," she whispered. "So very beautiful…" Her voice broke.

Then she was crying with great, gasping sobs coming from her chest, and she fell to her knees. Tears streamed down her face, which looked much younger than it had just a moment ago.

I knelt as well, still holding the box toward her, the light spilling out of it. "Go on, Granny," I said. "Take your heart back. Take back all the pain you felt. See if you can remember what it's like to be hurt."

"Anna, no!" I heard my father cry, but I didn't care. I didn't care that Baba Yaga was huddled, curled up, like a child. I didn't care that she was weeping but was still unable to take her eyes off the glowing box. I didn't care about the yowls of pain escaping her lips.

"Go on, Granny…"

She stretched out a hand. A look of longing emerged from her tears. "It's so beautiful," she said again, "and I want it so much, I've missed it so much…" Then she curled herself up again, howling like a soul in pain.

"She'll die, Anna," Koschey warned. "Don't let her touch it. If she touches it now, she'll die!"

"*I want her to die!*" I yelled, unable to keep the thought inside me anymore. "I want her to suffer, and I want her to die like she made my mother die! Like she wants Lauraleigh to die!"

"The darkness will take you, Anna. The darkness will take you if you do this, and we won't ever be able to get you back!"

"*I don't care!*" I roared, angry as a she-bear whose cubs are threatened. "*Let it!*" I felt the darkness unfurling inside me, filling me, and I couldn't keep a grin from forming on my face, because it felt so good.

Let the darkness take me. With it, I can do so much. I can do anything… I felt the ground rumbling behind me, tendrils of power flickering away from me like little tentacles, searching for something to attack. I knew I could throw all my power at the sniveling creature in front of me who had been the great Iron Queen and destroy her. But I wanted her to do it herself. As she had destroyed my mother, I wanted her to be responsible for her own end.

"Come on," I said to her. "All you have to do is stretch out your hand, and you can have your heart back."

"I want it back," she sobbed. "I do, I do. I want it back so much. But it hurts. I cut it out because it hurt so bad…" She threw back her head and howled. "Why didn't anybody tell me love could hurt so much?"

"You can have it back, Granny," I said. "It's still broken. You can have all your pain back." I pushed the box toward her, so close she could hardly avoid touching it if she moved again.

Slowly, her hand reached out toward it, inching along the floor. "My heart…" she whispered, "my heart…"

"Anna," said a quiet voice, "why are you doing this?"

I started. I'd almost forgotten there was anyone else in the room.

Lauraleigh was kneeling beside me. How had she gotten loose? But that didn't matter. What mattered was the look on her face, which was … disapproving. No, worse. Disappointed.

"You can't do this, Anna," she said. "Look at her. You can't."

Lauraleigh turned to look at Baba Yaga, still a sobbing mess, and the expression on her face was one of deep compassion. It was like how she had looked in Geneva every time she'd visited with some of the younger orphans who couldn't sleep because they wanted parents. Lauraleigh had comforted them out of the sheer goodness of her heart.

"You know what she wanted to do," I said, my voice shaking. "You know what she's done…"

"But if she didn't have her heart, Anna," said Lauraleigh, "how could she have done anything else?"

"I don't care," I whispered, "I just want her to die."

Lauraleigh shook her head. "Oh, Anna," she said. "What are you becoming?"

I didn't know what to say.

Lauraleigh stood up. She looked from me to Baba Yaga and then back. She bit her lip.

I knew what that meant. "Don't you dare help her," I said, though my voice wasn't very assured. Why was I talking like this to Lauraleigh, my best friend, the kindest person I'd ever met? The darkness inside me hesitated.

"I'm sorry, Anna," said Lauraleigh. "But I can't let you do this."

She stepped away from me and knelt beside the box. She reached out with her hands.

"Lauraleigh, no!" I cried. "You can't touch someone else's heart. You'll die…"

"I'm sorry, Anna," she said. And she plunged her hands into the silver-and-violet light.

What happened next was almost indescribable. I'm not even sure what I saw.

I saw Lauraleigh's hands cutting through the beams of light, and I heard her gasp as they curved around Baba Yaga's heart. Suddenly it was as if I could see and hear the hearts of everybody in the room; the hum grew louder until all the air around us was vibrating to the beats of our different pulses. I saw the hearts more as colors than as human shapes: Uncle Misha's forest-green soul, Egor's slate-gray soul mixed with flecks of rust and gold, and the sheer purity of Lauraleigh's as she lifted Baba Yaga's heart from the box — and did not die.

The two pieces of Baba Yaga's broken heart lay in Lauraleigh's palms, pulsing with light although they no longer emitted beams of light. Lauraleigh pushed the halves back together and held the whole in a single palm. She traced the scar with a finger that glowed with all the intensity of her compassion, and I saw the scar mend. She kneeled before Baba Yaga and held the heart out to her, and Baba Yaga took her heart into her hands and did not die.

She was still crying, but she didn't look like my grandmother anymore. She didn't look like anyone's grandmother. She barely looked as old as Lauraleigh, and she was beautiful. As she had been long ago when she had cut out her own heart…

The girl who had become Baba Yaga lifted her heart in her hands and pressed it to her chest. She squeezed until the heart began to shrink and all that could be seen was purple light escaping from between her fingers. She opened her mouth and filled it with her heart. She swallowed. And she screamed as if it were burning her inside.

Lauraleigh bent over and kissed her on the forehead, as she'd do to a child going to sleep.

The rest of us didn't move. Inside me, the darkness was howling, infuriated that Baba Yaga should be shown compassion by anyone.

Ripples of purple light were dancing over Baba Yaga, and she was still screaming. Her eyes looked like they had gone blind, no pupils or irises, just a solid wave of black that slowly turned to violet.

There was a noise. I turned and saw the door of my father's cage swinging open. Baba Yaga's magic was failing.

From out of the cage walked Koschey the Deathless, the Eater of Death, Keeper of the Kingdom of the Dead, his head held high and his back straight. No longer a pathetic imprisoned old man but a being beyond all imagining.

My father.

He came toward Baba Yaga. Lauraleigh drew back when the awesome shape of my father reached them. He stretched out a long pale hand and touched Baba Yaga on the forehead, and she ceased to scream. The ripples of purple began to flicker onto his hands like little bolts of lightning, and he threw his head back and drew in a breath. Baba Yaga's body started to shake, and his too. I could see the stream as he feasted, as she let go of all the power she had stolen from him, all the magic, all the *prana*, and he took it back into his being. I saw the power flowing, his body growing and glowing, his hair turning black and the weariness leaving his bones. I felt the ground trembling all around us as if an earthquake were rumbling. And maybe one was, because surely nothing this powerful had happened in the world for centuries.

Koschey drew his hand away from Baba Yaga's forehead. She fell unconscious to the floor, and he turned toward me, his robes flowing around him like water.

He approached me and didn't say a word. I shrank back in terror. This could not be my father. There was nothing human in this embodiment of sheer power who was striding toward me, strong and unavoidable as a thunderstorm, his eyes golden and merciless.

He stretched out a hand to my forehead as he had to Baba Yaga's. I tried to escape but there was nowhere to run. His touch was like a thunderbolt; there was nothing of the peace, nothing of the love I had felt when we had touched before. I gasped. It almost hurt.

I felt Koschey peer into my soul. It was as if his hand weren't just resting on my forehead but had actually plunged into me, searching and groping as if trying to find something. The darkness inside me tried to dissipate, but it was too late; Koschey was inexorably gathering it together. I felt like his hand was clutched around my heart.

Even as I felt all this, once again, I saw the world through his eyes. I saw my own soul and the darkness he was searching for. I saw Egor in the corner of the room, his eyes hidden behind his hands, and I knew that he could not bear to see this much power. I saw Uncle Misha; dear, kind old Uncle Misha, and the terrible worry on his face.

I saw Baba Yaga stretched out on the floor, her soul still black as tar. But at its center, there was a small purple spark, the tiniest of flames, that might, just might, grow and start taking her back to the light.

I saw a small white hand stretch out toward my daughter — I mean toward me — glowing almost as pure as Sereda's, almost as kind. And I felt Lauraleigh's hand rest on my shoulder as Koschey began to drag the darkness out of me. I clutched Lauraleigh's hand, feeling for her compassion, fixing my soul on the whiteness of hers as the screaming darkness fought against my father's relentless grip.

It hurt. It hurt as if he were pulling my heart out of my chest. But I knew that it was for my own good, that it would be worth it to have all that evil taken out of me. I hadn't even known it was possible. But now Koschey was as mighty as he had ever been; who knew what he could do?

My father paused as if there were some obstruction he couldn't get past, and my heart clenched in fear. But he drew a deep breath and suddenly let out a long, powerful cry. It wasn't even a word, just a noise, almost a musical note. I could feel how it pushed aside all the haze of magic and power that filled the room, how it overcame the hum, how it redoubled his own power.

He drew the darkness out of me, raising it over his head, forcing it into the shape of a ball, his every muscle straining to control it — and his cry went on and on. I saw that swirling globe of black smoke, one small trail still attached to me, and Koschey's eyes fixed on it as his voice rose to an overpowering note of command.

The sphere crumpled in his hand. He closed his fist over it and squeezed as I would an orange, and it was no more.

He stood in the middle of the room, a near god, my
father, and little lightning bolts of power played on his arms
and the hem of his robe.

There was utter silence. No longer did I feel that darkness curled inside me, and my heart almost burst from relief.
All the magic that had thrummed around us was gone. I fell
sobbing into Lauraleigh's arms.

Chapter 27

ear Diary,

I'm so grateful that Lauraleigh exists. That she's my friend. That she came with me. That she still likes me.

That she saved me from what I almost turned into.

Whether she knows it or not, Lauraleigh is the wisest person I will ever know.

It's weird that Dad's free now and Granny has become so ... almost normal. The way they talk together, they're just like two old friends. Which I suppose they are. After all, who else knows what they've been through? Even I know only a fraction of what they have experienced over so many millennia.

I don't know if I've forgiven Baba Yaga, but I don't think I have any right to judge her now. I know what it's like to have the darkness take you over. I know what I almost did. I still had my heart, and yet I would have let the darkness take me. The only reason I didn't is Lauraleigh. It's not Baba Yaga's fault that she didn't have a Lauraleigh to stop her all those years ago.

Dad told me confidentially that getting her heart back wouldn't suddenly make Baba Yaga nice. Her soul is still black, but there is that little touch of light in it now, and maybe that can grow. Mostly, she just seems tired. She can't even be bothered to watch TV anymore. Actually, she threw that TV out.

I'd like to think that everything's over now, I'm safe, and I can just go on and live a normal life. But somehow, after everything I've been through, I'm starting to doubt that will ever be an option.

I'm not sure that's a bad thing.

Baba Yaga's hut was just that again: a hut. And there was sunlight peeping in through the windows. We were sitting at the table, all of us exhausted.

Dad wasn't that awesome, terrifying figure anymore; now he just looked like a rather old man, although it was hard to tell his age. His face was lined, but his hair was black, almost as if he'd dyed it. His eyes were brown, not golden. Nothing about him would make anyone suspect who he was.

Baba Yaga was old again. Getting her heart back hadn't changed her age; it couldn't turn back the years. She was still guilty of doing all those things since she'd cut her heart out, for which she would have to face the consequences. But her eyes weren't the same; their blackness had a hint of violet now.

Once I'd stopped crying, I managed to stand up, only to find myself smothered in a huge hug from Uncle Misha. Evidently when he and Egor had realized that Lauraleigh had gone missing, they decided to risk going through the ghosts to find her. That's when they discovered that the Horsemen were no longer around Blackwood Castle. The ghosts had paid no attention to them. Of course, when Egor and Uncle Misha got to Baba Yaga's, she captured them with no trouble. The Horsemen had cut off their retreat, and neither of them had nearly enough power to battle her on her ground.

Olya was sleeping on the bed. Lauraleigh had gone to fetch her — she was the only one I trusted not to scare the child — and found her unconscious by the fence. Uncle Misha carried the little girl inside, and Egor laid his palm on her forehead and sent her to a proper sleep where she could rest and revive. Her memories would be fuzzy; some of them would be lost, and that, we all agreed, was a good thing.

There was no sign of the Horsemen. That seemed less good. They had been bound to Baba Yaga. Did losing her power mean she'd lost them, too? And if so, what would they do next?

There was so much to talk about.

The most powerful witch in the world shuffled around her kitchen, muttering about her aching knees. She took a can down from a shelf. "I think we could all use some tea," she said. She chuckled. "I'm fairly sure this one's not poisoned."

"Let me help," said Lauraleigh.

Baba Yaga waved her back to her seat. "Shush, child, you've done enough. The least I can do is make some tea."

"No," Lauraleigh said, "I'd really like to, I'd—"

"Lauraleigh, rest," I said. "You don't know where things are here. For that matter, do you even know how a samovar works? Besides, I can help easily." I pulled Squire out of my bag, conjured up a little flame, and woke him up.

"Why, you little runaway rascal!" Baba Yaga exclaimed.

"I've been looking for you for years. Has he been with you all this time?"

I nodded. Squire quivered in fear on my shoulder.

"Oh, don't worry, little one," said Baba Yaga. "I won't bite. Come on, help me make some tea. I wasn't going to use magic, but since you're here…" And she puttered around making tea for all of us.

Egor had laid his head down on the table. He had fallen asleep, and small bubbly snores started to come out of his nose.

Uncle Misha gathered Egor gently in his arms and carried him to the couch, where he laid him down. "He's not used to this much excitement," he explained.

Koschey smiled with understanding.

Uncle Misha looked out the window. He seemed worried. "The Horsemen are still gone," he said in an uncertain tone. "There's no trace of them."

"Ah," said Baba Yaga as she came back with our glasses of tea. "I'm not sure that's good news for you."

"What do you mean?"

She sighed. "They have felt my power breaking," she said. "They probably won't obey me any longer. Who knows what they'll be up to now?"

She sat, looking excessively weary. We took our glasses of tea as Squire handed out sugar cubes. Lauraleigh looked surprised when everyone except her popped a sugar cube in their mouth and took a sip of tea. In turn, I was surprised I remembered that typical Russian way of drinking tea, but feeling the cube grow warm and its sharp edges break and crumble was an old pleasure.

Always game, Lauraleigh did the same, and I smiled as I caught the enjoyment in her eyes.

"What's going to happen with the ghosts?" Lauraleigh asked.

Koschey took a breath. "I'm not entirely sure," he said. "I'll have to look over the situation first. Talk about it with my old friend here..." He looked at Baba Yaga.

She chuckled. "I daresay we'll find a solution," she said. "Though who knows what my Horsemen will do, now that they don't have to listen to me."

We drank our tea.

"How is that possible?" Uncle Misha asked. "The Horsemen have been in your service for as long as I've known you. Why did they leave you?"

Baba Yaga's smile was wan. "They were my servants, not my slaves," she said. "They saw me weaken. And power is what they answer to, what they've always answered to, since they're *power* themselves. They're made of it, you see. It's not even that I'm weak, just that I'm weaker. I suppose I've lost face in front of them. That is enough for them to feel free to break the contract..."

"And what will they do?" I asked.

"I don't know." She gave a weary chuckle. "They probably won't be stealing any more children, if that's what you're worried about. But I've never been sure what their own purpose was, why they felt the need to serve me in the first place. It's all been so long..."

Granny looked at Koschey. "I am so very tired, you know," she said to him. "I have been for a long time. Every year, people believe in us less and less, and it gets that much harder to stay alive. First, they stopped understanding how important we are; then they stopped knowing our names... Who knows where it will end?"

"We've been through times like this before," Koschey said gently. "We survived."

"Not this time, old friend," she said. "We've never seen it quite like this before."

They were quiet for a moment.

"It's strange," Baba Yaga said. "It hurt so very much, back then, all that time ago. I loved him so dearly, and when he spurned me... I'd never felt anything like it. I had never understood that you could hurt like that without a physical wound. I had no idea that love could hurt — I'd always believed it was this wonderful, magical thing, more real than the magic we wield... But I never knew it was possible for love to make you unhappy. It was so hard. I didn't know how to make it stop, except to get rid of where the pain lay, to cut out my heart… Such a thing to do. Yet now I can hardly remember his face. I've done so much since — not all good things, as you know — that he doesn't seem to matter. How is that possible? My love was the only thing in the world. And now, it's just … gone. And yet…"

"And yet, the stars still turn," said Uncle Misha. "The seeds still germinate and send up shoots. The animals still come together to create children, and the world still moves. The living are born, they live, they die, and existence runs on, with apple trees growing from the earth of their graves."

"I didn't know you were a poet, Misha," said Baba Yaga. She gave a weak laugh. "But I daresay you're right enough."

They were quiet again for a while, as we sipped our tea.

"We'll need to get Olya back to her parents," I said.

"Of course," said my grandmother. "Though it's best if I don't take care of it. Misha, you've dealt with humans."

"I have," said my uncle, "but I think it will be safer if she's simply found. Her memories will be entangled in any case. I'll leave her in the forest, close to her family, and set beasts to guard her. When she wakes, she'll find her way. Anna," he said, looking at me, "do you know where I should take her?"

"Yes," I said, my voice wavering, "but I don't want to… I don't want to go back there." I never wanted to see that hotel or that lake again, magnificent though they were. "Squire knows," I said. "The hand. And Knight, his brother. They can lead you."

"When Egor wakes," Uncle Misha said, patting my hand with an understanding smile, "he can take us where they show. He will be able to take us much more swiftly."

"Will she remember any of this?" I asked.

"With any luck, no. She will simply come to in the forest, unable to tell the others anything. They will be worried and confused. But they will find that nothing is wrong with her, and in the end, they will accept it."

"There will be policemen in the woods, searching," I said. "Probably for me and Lauraleigh too."

"You may trust Egor that we shall avoid them," said Uncle Misha. "All will be well."

All will be well... How many times had he said that to me when I was a child, when I had come home with a scrape or with tears in my eyes? And it had so often proved true.

Would it now? Could I trust that everything would be fine now?

We were silent again, all lost in our different thoughts.

"And what about you, old friend?" Baba Yaga suddenly said. "Will you go and get back your heart now?"

Koschey smiled. "Is it safe for me to do so?"

Baba Yaga laughed. "Yes," she said, "it is. Besides, you wouldn't want those Horsemen to find it, would you? You haven't got your full power without it. How are you going to deal with the ghosts?"

I shivered. If I hadn't yet seen Koschey at his full power, what would he be like when he was?

"You may well be right," said Koschey, "though I rather doubt they'll present much of a challenge. But there is one small problem."

"What's that?"

"I have no idea where my heart is."

"None?" my grandmother asked, sounding surprised. "I

always thought that had to be a lie. How could you let your heart go without some hint as to where to find it?"

Koschey smiled quietly and cast a glance at me before replying. "I didn't expect that Sereda would die," he said evenly.

Tears filled my grandmother's eyes. "Oh," she said, "yes … of course." She swallowed. "This whole having-a-heart-again business is going to take some getting used to," she said as if she were trying to make a joke. Then she took a great gulp of tea. "Anyway," she went on in a businesslike tone, "clearly we have to find your heart."

"'We?'" Koschey asked. "You'll forgive me, my dear, but I'm not sure I want to send you to find it."

"No," Baba Yaga said. "I wouldn't expect you to trust me. But you can't go yourself, can you?"

Koschey looked troubled. "No," he said, "I can't. I have to stay here and see what I can do to keep the ghosts from overrunning Siberia. Russia. The world." He glanced at Uncle Misha.

"No," said my uncle before Koschey could even speak. "I'm old, Koschey. I haven't the energy, haven't the skills. And I'm needed here as well. Don't even think of asking Egor; he's such a homebody, he'd never go more than a day or two away from his castle. And as I remember Sereda, I very much doubt she hid your heart anywhere near. Most likely it's very, very far away. Maybe even on the other side of the world, where our powers don't run and we can't feel your heart."

"That would be like my daughter, yes," said Baba Yaga. "We have a problem, then. We can't let anybody else know. And yet we do need to find your heart, but we can't do it." She turned and looked straight at me. "But she could," she said.

Uncle Misha grunted. It was not a pleased sound. "I thought you might be leading us to that," he said. "It's not an idea I'm very happy with."

"I hate to lay another burden on her," Koschey said, shaking his head. "Hasn't she already done enough?"

"Has she not earned a rest?" Uncle Misha added.

None of them seemed to be paying any attention to the fact that I could hear them.

"The other girl would have to go as well," Baba Yaga carried on as if the two men hadn't spoken. "We've seen today, I think, how Anna Sophia needs Lauraleigh to keep her in check. Besides, two heads think better than one."

"Still," said Koschey, "she is very young. And if she does need to leave Russia…"

"I haven't lived in Russia for most of my life," I broke in.

They started, as if they'd forgotten I was there.

I don't know where the idea had sprung from. Maybe just hearing them talk about it had given me the idea. Another quest would be difficult and risky, and part of me didn't want that … it just wanted to rest.

But it would be something to do. It would be a way to make up for what I'd done.

I translated their conversation to Lauraleigh and looked at her, a question in my eyes. After a moment, she nodded.

"Do you truly want your heart back?" I asked my father.

"Yes," he said, "I do. Not only for myself but because I cannot fully help the world without it."

"Then I will find your heart for you, Dad," I said. "With Lauraleigh. We'll get it back for you."

"Are you sure?"

"Yes," I said. "No one else can, so I have to, don't I? And anyway..." I looked over at Lauraleigh and switched into French. I could see the same joke sparkling in her eyes. "It's not like we've really had much of an adventure yet," I said. "And I promised Lauraleigh I'd help her have one."

As the three grown-ups stared at us with dropped jaws, Lauraleigh and I burst into laughter.

So now we're off to wander the world and find my father's heart. We have no idea where we'll end up.

But this we do know.

Together, we're ready for anything.

Afterword

Dear Diary,

Most of us returned to Blackwood Castle before moving on, although Baba Yaga and Lauraleigh decided to stay on in Yaga's hut for a couple of days. My Granny said that she wants to return to her energy practice but she's a little afraid to face the powerful energies of Yoga on her own.

I was thinking: If I'd ever seriously wished for a father — a specific one, I mean — would I ever have imagined Koschey? I don't think so. Now that I have him, I wouldn't change him for the world, but even though the world has brought me back my father, he's not exactly what I would have wished for.

The world turns, and what it brings us may not be what we want — I've heard my father say that a few times. But just because it's different doesn't necessarily mean it's bad.

What we want is all so complicated, isn't it?

My father was looking at me. We had finished our discussions and knew what we were going to do next. Knew that I would soon leave to search for his heart.

It hadn't struck me until now what that meant: Just after finding my father, we would part. And not because we had to, but because we chose to.

That was the price of not being human, I guess.

"Anna," he began — and I felt a little warm spot in my stomach just hearing his voice. My father was speaking to me, my real, actual father, whom I loved and who loved me.

"I know it must seem unfair, this parting," he said. "But the way the world turns is not always what we wished for."

"I know, Dad," I said.

"But before you leave, there is one more thing we must do. We must free the ghosts."

"We?" I said, surprised.

He smiled. "Well… I could do it on my own, of course," he said. "But I thought you might like to join me. We have not had much time on our own, after all. And this is something only you and I can see. The others, even your grandmother, if they came with us … they'd see the ghosts, and they would see them as they vanished. But they wouldn't be able to perceive the spheres of light and sound to which I send them. To see them meld into the universe from where they came, watch as they become again as they were, as they join the great choir that is existence and become a part of that chord. As they recognize and take the place they have earned in its harmony. It's not something the others can hear, that sudden addition to the chord that makes it more perfect."

"And I can?" I said, eyes wide. I'd swum in magic, yes; at least, I thought I had. But this… This was beyond anything I'd imagined.

"If you are with me, yes, you can," he said. "You are my daughter. How can you not?"

I couldn't help but grin. It was something I could share with him, only with him. If I understood him right, even my mother couldn't see what he said I could.

"All right," I said. "Let's do it. Just let me check with the others…"

"They have already gone," he said.

That startled me.

"They wished to return that child Olya before the hour grew too late. You will meet again at Misha's cottage when we are done. And then you'll be able to tell them, if you choose, what we'll have accomplished together. Or keep it to yourself. Best to decide afterward, don't you think?"

I was still a bit shocked that Uncle Misha, Egor, and the two floating hands had left without me, but maybe that was intentional. I wouldn't be surprised if they'd wanted some time away from me. And they must have known my father would make sure I didn't do anything stupid.

But this way we were alone together. With a secret to share.

"All right," I said again. "Let's go."

He chuckled. "I don't think we'll have to go far."

He was right. We had hardly left the gates of Blackwood Castle when we saw three ghosts close to its walls, almost as gray as the stones. They stirred in confusion. Then they began to drift toward us.

"Not here, I think," said Koschey. "There are so many of them that doing them one by one would be inefficient. We'll go farther, to the clearing..."

We did, walking side by side. And then there they were.

The ghosts. Hundreds of them. No, thousands. Far too many for me to count. They were like a mist in front of the trees, and still more kept joining them, emerging from behind branches. I couldn't see how they would all fit, but then they were ghosts and insubstantial, they had to be blending into each other somehow... I had learned that the two worlds, the ghosts' and ours, were like different radio frequencies: They and we could coexist in the same place without interfering with each other. Maybe there was a similar arrangement for different kinds of ghosts...

"Stay close," Koschey said. "There's nothing to fear, but remain by my side all the same." He walked toward the sea of ghosts, his robe trailing on the ground so that he seemed to float almost as much as they did.

There was a movement among the apparitions, a shudder like a gust of wind over a field of tall grasses.

So many, I thought. *So many people who have died recently.*

But none of them was Olya. None of them was Lauraleigh or Egor or Uncle Misha. Or even my grandmother. Was it selfish to think that way? Maybe. But there are only so many people we can help, or care about, or even know.

I could sense that power from my father again, like when he broke free from his cage. He seemed larger than usual; his every motion seemed to move even the air around him like the ripples that a swimmer causes in water. And the ghosts could feel it too, sense it, like flowers drawn to the sun even if they don't know why.

They swirled around, a chaotic mass suddenly discovering the center of gravity which was my father, whose eyes by now must once again be golden. I felt no fear, though, for a moment, I was worried that they would fall on him like a wave and possibly drown him. There were just so many ghosts! But I shook my mind clear. He was my father. He was *Koschey*. These were his charges. He was here to make things right, and he would.

One of the ghosts came forward. Just one. Pale and disoriented, he stretched his hands out toward my father. He looked as if he'd had a kind face back when he was alive.

My father put out one hand and glanced back at me with those gilded eyes of his. "Watch, Anna," he said. "It's like receiving a friend, welcoming them home after an illness, where they're still not quite sure where they are. But they know that…"

He stopped.

The ghost had tried to take his hand, but nothing had happened. The pale hand had passed by Koschey's fingers.

A confused look appeared on my father's face. I rushed forward to be next to him. Frowning, he put out his hand again to grasp the ghost's hand. But the two would not connect.

"What?" he said. Again and again, he tried to seize the ghost's hand, but they kept slipping away from each other as if there were some cushion of air between them that would not let them pass.

The ghost uttered a low moan. He too was trying to touch my father — if not his hands, then his face, his chest, his clothes, anything. But they couldn't come into contact.

Worry swept over my father's features. "I can't…" he said. "This isn't possible; this isn't right. I must be able to…"

But he wasn't.

What was going on? There shouldn't have been any trouble at all. This was Koschey; he was free, he was as powerful as he had ever been. I knew that. I'd seen what he was able to do. He'd been able to draw the darkness out of me when I was almost drowning in it, and he wasn't even supposed to be able to do that. Helping these ghosts was his entire purpose; it was why he existed. Even at his weakest, he could do that.

But to do so, he had to be able to touch them and lead them away. And he couldn't.

Something worse than worry was on his face now: fear.

It had never occurred to me that my father could be afraid. Realizing that he could was almost more terrifying than the question of *what* could make him fear.

The ghost fell back, confused, moaning. Koschey looked at me, his eyes large like those of a frightened child, but there was nothing I could do, no way I could help. We both knew I couldn't risk trying to touch the ghost.

Koschey's eyes were flickering between gold and brown. He no longer seemed that awesome embodiment of power but just a thin old man caught up in something beyond his understanding.

I grabbed his arm. It was all I could think to do.

The ghost stared helplessly at us. Then he looked away and began to wail, uttering a long, rhythmic sound like the whimpering of a large dog. It seemed to sound more in our heads than in our ears as it was taken up by the other ghosts. All those others who had been patiently waiting and now realized that what they'd hoped for wouldn't happen, joined the wail with terrifying power. The sound filled me with a sense of gravity vanishing, with a feeling of loss like clouds breaking up before they've rained. The ghosts began to move again, stumbling around like the blind on an uneven field.

Soon, Koschey and I were left alone.

He looked at me with his anxious brown eyes.

"I can't help them, Anna. Why can't I help them?"

All I could do was shake my head. I didn't know. How could I?

"All those trapped souls," he said. "So many of them." He looked toward where they had been. "What can we do?"

TO BE CONTINUED in BOOK 3: FIGHTING WITCH

ALSO BY VIC CONNOR

"MAX!" (AGE 8+)

The year is 1983, and the Cold War between America and the Soviet Union is escalating again. In the small Soviet town of Belsk though, a young Russian teenager has bigger things on his mind, matters much more pressing to a boy in the seventh grade.

TOMMY HOPPS AND THE AZTECS (AGE 9+)

When he takes a family vacation to Mexico City, Tommy Hopps is just a normal, fourteen-year-old kid – but that's all about to change.

Sleeping soundly in his family's hotel room, Tommy is awoken by a ghostly presence: a threadbare, swashbuckling pirate. When the strange intruder attacks his mother and father, Tommy fights back. And that's where the story begins.

IF YOU ENJOYED THIS BOOK...

...I would really, really appreciate if you could help others enjoy it, too. Reviews are like gold dust and they help persuade other readers to give the stories a shot. More readers means more incentive for me to write, and that means there'll be more stories, more quickly.

By leaving a review of this book, you can make a difference. And the good news is that it doesn't take long.

You can do it at the book's page here: http://www.amazon.com/dp/B01AF1HDDA.

About the Author

Vic Connor is a dad of three curious kids. He writes books for children and teenagers together with fourteen-year-old Ivan, ten-year-old Naomi and seven-year-old Maya, who all share their passionate opinions and creative ideas. They even draw in Vic's manuscripts, and they love it when professional illustrators build on their suggestions.

In fact, Vic only publishes those books which his children loved and wanted to share with their friends.

He makes his online home at http://maxedoutkid.com. You can connect with Vic on Facebook at https://www.facebook.com/TheVicConnor, and you can send him an email at vic@vicconnor.com, if you so wish.

Made in the USA
San Bernardino, CA
10 September 2017